Luke

— ♘ CORAL CANYON COWBOYS —

LIZ ISAACSON

ISBN-13: 978-1-63876-257-7

The Young Family

W elcome to Coral Canyon! The Young family is BIG, and sometimes it can be hard to keep track of everyone.

The graphic on the following page might help you with that.

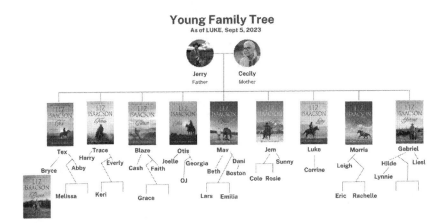

Young Family Tree
As of LUKE, Sept 5, 2023

<u>This is updated through Luke (Sept 5, 2023).</u>

Here's how things are right now:

JERRY AND CECILY YOUNG, 9 SONS, IN AGE-ORDER:

1. TEX
   Wife: Abigail Ingalls
   Son: Bryce (21)
   Children he and Abby share: Melissa (3) / due in May

2. TRACE
   Wife: Everly Avery
   Son: Harry (16)
   Children he and Ev share: Keri (3 mo)

3. BLAZE
   Wife: Faith Cromwell
   Son: Cash (13)
   Children he and Faith share: Grace (2 mo)

4. OTIS
   Wife: Georgia Beck
   Daughter: Joelle (Joey / Roo, 12)
   Children he and Georgia share: OJ (Otis Judson, 2)

5. MAV

Wife: Danielle Simpson
His daughter: Beth (9)
Her son: Boston (11)
Children he and Dani share: Lars (4), Emilia (1 mo)

6. JEM

Engaged to: Sunny Samuelson
Son: Cole (8)
Daughter: Rosie (5)

7. LUKE

Daughter: Corrine (7)

8. MORRIS

Wife: Leighann Drummond
Children he and Leigh share: Eric (6), Rachelle (1)

9. GABRIEL (GABE)

Wife: Hilde
Daughter: Liesl (5)
Hilde's daughter: Lynnie (15)

1

Lucas Young picked up a plastic cup of warm apple cider, though he hated the stuff. He felt like he spent so much of his life doing things he didn't like doing, so what was holding a cup of apple cider? Nothing.

It was nothing.

He lifted his chin and smiled as he approached Morris, and he couldn't take two steps in the farmhouse without running into a brother. This New Year's Eve party had been thrown by Hilde and Gabe—another brother—and they'd decked out the furniture store Hilde owned for the backdrop to the festivities.

Luke had shown up with his daughter, because he'd literally fought with his ex-wife in court over being able to bring Corrine to things like this. Gabe, the only lawyer in the family, had stood right beside Luke, and they'd managed to keep his ex from taking Corrine out of school, out of the home Luke had established for her over the past four years, and out of the country.

So Mandi, his ex, had come to Coral Canyon. At first, she was supposed to arrive at the beginning of November. That had turned into "by Thanksgiving."

Then, "for sure by Christmas."

She'd been in town for two weeks now, and Luke had not seen her. He'd once again fought to have Corrine shielded from the mother who'd abandoned her as a four-year-old, run off to Canada, and then gotten married and pregnant again.

No great surprise, but Mandi was currently divorced again, and Luke honestly lived in fear that she'd leave her three-year-old son on his parents' doorstep for him to raise. There'd be no paternity questions then.

Luke lost his mind for a moment and lifted the apple cider to his lips. When the horrible, clove-infused liquid filled his mouth, he nearly spat it back out. He managed to stop himself in time, because Hilde wouldn't have been happy. She'd dressed up this part of the store, which held about seven couches in a big circle, with tea lights and holiday balls hung from wide ribbons. Music played nearby but not to deafening levels, and everyone could actually move around.

A long row of tables held the food they'd catered, and everyone had been allowed to invite anyone they wanted. So Morris and Leigh usually brought along her brother, and tonight was no exception.

Hilde's siblings and momma were also here, as were Sunny's, Georgia's, and Abby's. Everly's brothers had come, and so had Faith's sister and her family. With all the Youngs, and all their significant others, and all their kids, Luke estimated there were probably sixty people there to ring in the New Year.

He and Corrine were only two, and he hadn't minded his tiny core family until very recently. Until last summer, if he was being honest, and Luke wanted to start this New Year off on the right foot.

He had to be honest about everything, and he had to start talking. It was that last one that either got him in trouble or...got him in trouble. If he said what was on his mind, he got jumped on. If he didn't, everyone told him not to just stand there silent.

He honestly couldn't win.

"It's not about winning or losing," he muttered to himself as he walked over to the drinking fountain and poured out the disgusting apple cider. If he was keeping score, he didn't have very many points. Zero, in fact.

In his bank account, he wanted a lot of zeroes. With women, he didn't want any.

Too bad all he had were zeroes when it came to women. A failed marriage that should've never made it to an I-do. After his paternity had been questioned, he'd dug in deep and sworn off women. In the past couple of years, as brother after brother fell in love and got re-married, Luke had started to emerge from his bunker.

He'd been out with two women, both of whom were completely wrong for him. The woman he'd been crushing hard on for the past eighteen months came forward in his mind, and as he turned back to the party, he swore he saw her standing between Everly and Hilde.

He blinked as Gabe shifted, and he couldn't see if Sterling Boyd stood there or not. He wouldn't be shocked if she did. She was good friends with Hilde and Ev, and all of the wives had been going to her for massages lately.

He'd gone out with her once, a lunch date that had ended as awkwardly as it had begun. She'd refused to break her date with another man for the following week, and Luke's tongue had tied itself into a knot and refused to loosen.

Gabe moved over to talk to Tex about something, and that left the view to the women unobstructed. Sure enough, the tall, gorgeous Sterling Boyd stood there, her curly blonde hair tamed back by clips behind her ears.

Plenty of it spilled over her shoulders, and she wore a silver, glittery dress that sparkled under the low, yellow party lights. Luke's mouth instantly turned dry, because he knew every inch of Sterling's face.

The handful of freckles sprinkled across her nose. The way her eyes could burn blue when she was upset or twinkle sapphire when she wasn't. He knew the shape her mouth took when she laughed, and he knew how her hands felt along every inch of his body.

That right there was the real problem, but when he didn't book his massage therapy with her, she yelled at him. When he did, he couldn't say anything. Both were huge zeroes in his book, and Luke sighed.

The next song kicked the vibe up a notch, and the kids—all ages of them—started yelling and dancing. Luke loved the kids in his family, and he often took Otis's daughter, or Morris's son, or any of Mav's kids. They repaid the favor and took Corrine whenever he needed them to, which wasn't often.

Maybe in the summer when he had appointments or whatever. Whenever he had to go out to the recording studio at Tex's house. Otherwise, he didn't have a normal job he had to work, and he fit in everything he wanted to do around his daughter.

In fact, they did a lot together, and Luke loved the dark-haired girl currently jumping up and down, her dark ponytail bouncing along, with everything inside him. That was why he didn't want to allow Mandi back into their lives, not even a little bit.

He'd agreed to court-supervised visits, and the judge had too. Apparently, a parent couldn't just walk away from a toddler and expect to be welcomed back with open arms. Luke would sacrifice whatever he had to in order to protect and provide for Corrine, and that had unfortunately included asking Sterling on a second date.

She looked away from Everly, her eyes landing on his as if they were polar opposites and couldn't help the fierce attraction between them. Luke had gone for a few more massages since the disastrous date, and Sterling knew about his legal troubles with Corrine's mother.

He did most of the talking during massages, and as he wasn't particularly loquacious, that meant she spoke even less. He didn't know if she was still dating that other guy or not, and he didn't ask. He figured he didn't need to jab a pointed stake into his already bleeding heart.

Sterling said something to Everly, and then she came his way. Luke once again lifted the plastic cup to his mouth, because he needed something to do with his mouth and hands that didn't involve grabbing onto Sterling and kissing her.

At the same time, why couldn't he do that? People kissed when the clock struck midnight, didn't they?

It's not midnight, his mind screamed at him. *And get rid of that blasted cup!*

He mashed it in his fingers and turned to toss it into the garbage can beside the drinking fountain. The lights shone out here, but Luke had definitely removed himself from the party. His heartbeat thumped louder and faster with every step Sterling took in those sexy heels. He wanted to look past her to see if the wives were watching, but he couldn't force himself to look away from her.

She carried one of the bottles of water that had been set out, with silver cord and red ribbon tied around the top of it, and Luke suddenly wanted a drink from it.

"You're not enjoying the party?" she asked.

"I was," he said. "I am." He cleared his throat. "Yeah, I am. It's great." He reminded himself to calm down, that he'd been out with women before. None as pretty as Sterling. None as talented. None he wanted to go out with as badly as her. "Are you enjoying it?" he asked, employing his new motto a few hours early.

New Year = New Luke.

A man who wasn't going to be tongue-tied around Sterling. Who wasn't going to hold back. Who knew who he was and what —and who—he wanted. Heck, he'd just witnessed Jem get out of his own way this year, and it was Luke's turn.

No more excuses. No more distractions.

"Yeah," Sterling said, turning and falling to his side. "Hilde knows how to put on an amazing event."

"Yeah," he said, watching the dark-haired wife of his youngest brother watch him. "She does a great job with that Memorial Day Faire too." He glanced over to Sterling. "Are you doing that again this year?"

"I think so, yeah." She smiled, but her gaze remained on the other party-goers. "I get some good contacts every time I do."

Feeling brave and about as flirty as Luke got, he nudged her with his elbow. "I told you I'd write you a testimonial."

She did train those sparking sapphire eyes on him again. "You did? When did you say that?"

Luke's smile slid from his face. He couldn't remember the exact date Sterling had shown up at Jem's and berated him in front of a few of his brothers. Oh, wait. Yes, he could. The same week Jem had broken his wrist. The second week of March.

March fourteenth, if anyone was keeping track, and apparently Luke was.

His first reaction was to clamp his mouth shut and say nothing ever again. He fought against that and forced himself to say, "Oh, I, uh, I offered to do it in one of the online bookings I did after you yelled at me at Jem's."

Sterling's eyes rounded. "I—I kind of did yell at you, didn't I?"

Luke scoffed, turning the sound into a laugh. "Kind of? Sterling, you do know what a yell is, don't you?"

She laughed too, and Luke relaxed even more. Laughing was good. Talking felt good, and Luke had never thought that before. With his brothers, sure. With women, he didn't seem to have the capability or the ability.

He'd graduated from high school and gone straight into the family band. No college. Not even a single class. His first wife had been someone he'd met here in Coral Canyon before Country Quad had really taken off, and it was a summer fling that never should've been more than that.

He didn't have a lot of experience, and his fantasies and amazing conversations with beautiful blondes rarely matched up with his reality.

"We've gotten along okay since," she said.

"You still seein' someone?" He didn't mean for his voice to come out gruff as rusted nails, but it did.

She sighed and shook her head, sending her curls springing and swinging. "No, sir. That was like going out with my brother." She gave him a smile and looked back to the party. "You?"

"I don't want to go out with anyone," he said.

"You don't?"

Luke swallowed, his throat rough and dry like sandpaper. "Just you, Sterling." He exhaled a bit too long too but refused to call it a sigh. "I've had a lot goin' on with Mandi, but things are calming down now a little. Maybe we could...." He let the invitation sit there, but Sterling didn't pick it up.

"Go to dinner," he finished lamely and almost under his breath.

"Uncle Luke," Bryce said, distracting Luke from Sterling. He turned toward his nephew, who'd brought home a funny, bright woman who loved horses as much as he did. Kassie stood next to him, but they didn't hold hands or otherwise touch.

Bryce had pulled a fast one, telling everyone he was bringing home a woman for the holidays—and then Luke had discovered they were best friends, not dating. Still, he was happy for his nephew, because Bryce had been through a few years of hard times of his own, and Luke was just glad to see him smiling so broadly again.

"I told Harry you have the best dance moves." He tugged on Luke's arm. "He says Miss Everly's been teachin' him a thing or two, and well, I may or may not have started a dance-off with you at the center of it."

"Bryce," Luke warned, resisting the pull on his arm. "No."

"Oh, go on," Sterling said, giving him a little push. "I've seen your dance moves, and he's not wrong. You're good."

Luke glared at her, dissatisfied that he was being bullied into performing when he'd rather hang out in the shadows. Not to mention that Sterling hadn't said yes or no to his dinner invitation.

That churned in his gut as his sister-in-law beckoned him forward. The next thing he knew, the music screeched into silence, and Trace said into a mic that sent his voice echoing through the entire furniture store, "All right, folks. Gather 'round. We've got ourselves a dance-off happening in the Living Room section."

The children erupted into cheers, including Luke's own daughter. He looked helplessly over to Tex, who simply laughed and clapped along with everyone else. Otis and Mav weren't going to save him from this, and Trace was on the mic, for crying out loud.

Everly bounced on the balls of her feet, clearly excited for what the next few minutes might bring. Luke wanted to crawl into a hole and hide. Yes, he could bring out the performer inside him when he toured with the band. For everywhere else?

No. No, thank you.

He'd rather be the dark cloud, the black sheep, the grumpy cowboy in the corner.

Blaze grinned at him, handed Faith their baby girl and tugged his jeans a little higher. "All right, all right." He held up both hands. "The champion has stepped onto the dance floor."

Luke scoffed as the family crowd went wild.

"Come on, now," Trace drawled into the mic. "Everyone come on out who wants to throw their hat into the ring. Anyone from one to one hundred."

Luke's mood lightened as practically everyone joined him in the spotlight, the couches and coffee tables getting pushed back to clear more space.

He managed to toss one look over his shoulder to Sterling, and she gave him a thumbs-up and that gorgeous smile before he had to face the front again.

She thinks you're a good dancer, he thought. *Perform just for her.*

He stretched his arms above his head and bounced on the balls of his feet too.

"Oh, it's on," Everly teased. She leaned in close and said, "Don't worry, Luke. I won't make you look bad."

"Much appreciated, Ev," he murmured. Then the music started.

2

S terling Boyd's tears lingered so close to the surface. One, because she'd just survived one of the hardest years of her life, professionally and personally. She'd been talked about all over town, disappointed, and ignored by people she'd once counted as friends.

She thought she'd lost Luke, only to get him back again for one of the best reasons ever.

Two, she had so much hope for this year ahead of her. She'd taken some business classes and a grant-writing course this fall, and she was finally ready to take her future by the horns and make her dreams into reality.

She just needed backers. Donors. Investors.

She'd told Everly and Hilde about her ideas, and they'd allowed her to practice her pitch on them. Now, she just needed to get up the nerve to call some businesses and see if she could get someone besides her friends to believe in her vision for her health and wellness studio, Deep Purple.

Hilde, as kind and as good as she was, had immediately said

she'd donate to Sterling's business. Everly had said she could talk to Trace. Sterling appreciated the sentiment, but she didn't just want their money. She wanted someone to help advise her. A partner.

In life, love, and business—but they didn't have to be the same person.

Abby had found out about the endeavor, and she'd been the one to bring up Luke as a potential investor. He clearly valued and believed in body work. And he had over a billion dollars to his name.

He was perfect—and as Sterling watched the loud, out-going, celebrity side of him emerge from the cage inside him, she thought so even more. In multiple ways. He didn't rip off his shirt as he'd done years ago during the Independence Day concert, but Sterling had done more body work on the man than almost anyone else in town.

He lifted up two children at the same time, and they shrieked with delight as he swung them around to the music. Someone switched off the music, and Trace yelled, "Freeze!"

It took a couple of seconds, because a child's reaction time wasn't as fast as an adult's. Sterling laughed along with several others as some of the tweens and teens clearly struck poses.

"All right," Trace drawled into the mic. "I'm going to nominate Abby, Momma, Daddy, and Denzel to choose those who'll go on to the next round. Ladies and gents." He gestured to the dance floor, and no one moved a muscle as the four nominated judges strolled around as if seriously considering who they'd pick.

"Three each," Trace said. "We've got to narrow the field just a little."

Luke made it through to the next round, and he lifted both hands high into the air when the final selection was made. Trace didn't waste any time getting the next song queued up. "This is a slow one, folks," he said into the mic in a sultry, slow voice. "Show us your best control."

Everly had made it through to the second round too, and she clearly had better lines than Luke. She could lift her leg higher, and she moved with all the grace and ease of a trained dancer. Sterling found herself in a volley between her, and then a moment later, looking to Luke—who was copying everything she did.

Thirty seconds later, Trace paused the music and said, "Judges, if you would. Two people this time please."

The field got narrowed to eight, and once again Luke and Ev made it through. So did Bryce, who high-fived his friend Kassie, and Otis's daughter, Joey. She twirled with her younger brother, who'd just turned two a couple of days ago. OJ didn't seem to notice or care that he wasn't in the competition anymore, and he stayed on the dance floor with Harry, Everly, Luke, Morris, Bryce, Joey, Beth, and Hilde.

Luke rotated his shoulders and shook out his hands, like he might go into full battle mode in this third round. Leigh came to stand next to Sterling, and they laughed together at how seriously Morris and Luke were taking this.

"Morris played professional football," Leigh said. "His competitive streak is insane."

"Must be a Young trait," Sterling said, unable to look away from Luke. Tex leaned over to Otis and whispered something, and they both laughed.

"Must be," Leigh said just as another song started up for the third time. The worst polka music Sterling had ever heard blared through the store, and Luke was the only one who immediately jumped into action. He pranced around the dance floor, lifting his knees practically to his chest as he swung his arms around.

Trace laughed right into the mic, stopped the music, and said,

"Well, since he's the only one who danced...I declare the winner to be...*Luuuuke!*"

Everly stood there, slack-jawed and open-mouthed, as Luke roared his glee at winning. His brothers, all the kids, and many of the wives swarmed him, while the others clapped and cheered. Sterling could give this family one thing—there was never a dull moment.

When she'd gotten invited to the New Year's Eve party, she'd known that, but she hadn't anticipated a dance-off. Or hot apple cider, because it wasn't Halloween. This party had no alcohol either, because Jem was strictly dry, and his whole family supported him in his endeavor to stay sober.

Sterling managed to switch her gaze to Sunny and Jem, who'd just gotten engaged last week. As far as she knew, they hadn't set a date yet, but Sterling wasn't super-well connected in the inner circles of the family.

The regular music resumed at its normal volume, and Leigh drifted away to get something away from her youngest child. Sterling headed back to the couches, which the cowboys had pushed back into position.

She'd never heard of anyone having a family party at a furniture store, but she'd never met a family quite like the Youngs.

Luke fell back to her side. He said nothing, and Sterling liked that almost as much as she wanted him to speak. He exhaled, and the sound morphed into a laugh. "That was totally rigged, but it's not like I won a trophy or anything."

Sterling nodded slightly to Ev. "Tell that to her."

"Oh, she loves me," Luke said with a grin and a sideways look at her. The song switched to something slow, and Luke stepped in front of Sterling and bowed. "May I have this dance? It's not every New Year's Eve you get to dance with a champion." He grinned at her, and he really should have to check with someone before he unleashed that thing.

Sterling's heart went pitter-patter, and she nodded deeply and put her hand in his. "I would be honored."

He took her effortlessly into his arms, and Sterling got transported right back to Gabe and Hilde's wedding, when he asked her to dance there. She'd stayed in his arms for hours, and yet, he'd never asked her out.

She took a deep breath and edged closer to him. "Luke," she said. "Can I ask you a question?"

"Shoot," he said.

"After Gabe's wedding, after you'd broken up with Hillary, you didn't ask me out."

In front of her, he stiffened, but he kept moving gently back and forth. "I don't hear a question in there."

"Why didn't you?" she asked. "You stop by my house and tell me you can't come get massages anymore, because you want us to be a couple. But you've got this girlfriend. Then you didn't. And yet, you don't ask me out."

Luke bent his head closer to Sterling, his breath washing softly down the side of her neck. She wanted to push her hair all the way out of the way so she could shiver with the nearness of him for the rest of the dance. "I don't know why," he said. "At one point, I thought it might be kind of skeevy to go from dating one woman at eight o'clock to another by nine."

He cleared his throat and to her surprise, continued with, "I'm pretty much exactly what you said—a coward. But I do have a very public image I have to maintain, and small town or not, reporters pick up on the people I date."

Sterling had never even considered that. "I didn't know that."

"You don't search me out on the Internet?" He pulled back and smiled at her. "I'm shocked by that, Sterling."

"Should I?"

He kneaded her closer, the smile vanishing from his face. "Absolutely not." The song ended, and he stepped away from her. "I don't want to monopolize you tonight."

She wanted him to, but she also realized she'd been invited to his family party as a friend, and she didn't need to make a scene in front of so many watchful eyes. He ducked closer to her again, "Well, I do, but I currently have Abby and my momma staring at us, so I think it's best if you dance with someone else for a minute."

He turned and tapped Bryce on the shoulder. "Bryce, would you?"

"Sure, Uncle Luke." He grinned at Sterling and she laughed as he took her into his arms. He spun her away, and when he brought her back against his chest, he asked, "So, what do you do, Miss Sterling?"

"I'm a massage therapist," she said.

"Ah, you're the one Uncle Luke wanted to bring on tour last year."

"That's right," she said, grinning at him. "I wish I'd done it. I heard you guys were awesome on tour."

"It was pretty amazing," Bryce said. He glanced over to his friend, who currently sashayed around the open space with Harry. "Do you think Kassie is pretty?"

Sterling looked over to the blonde woman with the light blue eyes. "I mean, of course." She glanced back to him. "The important thing is if *you* think she's pretty."

"Yeah, sure," Bryce said. "Do you think Luke would like her?"

Sterling's chest felt like she'd drank bleach. "Luke—what?"

"Abby said not to, but I think if it was me setting him up, he might go out with her."

Sterling's pulse knifed through her, and she moved back from Bryce. "I don't think he'll do that," she said.

Bryce kept his gaze trained on Kassie. "Why not?" He swung his attention back to her.

"Because we're dating," she said, pressing one palm to her chest. "Luke and me. Me and Luke." She shook her head, not sure what was coming out of her mouth. "Luke and I." She felt like she'd gone mad for a moment, and this mirrored how she'd felt when she'd stormed Jem's house and demanded to speak to Luke in front of his brothers.

She pointed over to Luke, who perked up. He said something to Lynnie, who stood next to him, and then he came her way. The song ended, and the couples who'd been dancing split up. Sterling marveled that they all danced with one another. She watched as Hilde pushed against Morris's chest and said, "Stop it." They laughed together, and Gabe came over to them, his eyebrows up.

"What's happening here?"

Sterling wanted to know the same thing. Why was Bryce trying to set up his uncle? And with a woman who didn't even live here, no less?

Panic pumped through her body without restraint, and Sterling needed to get over to Luke quickly.

She started in that direction as the next song started to play. Half of the people cheered, and the other half groaned, and Cecily Young, Luke's mother, yelled, "It's halfway to kissing time, time to kiss again!"

Sterling wasn't sure what this was, because she didn't recognize the song, but the Youngs clearly did. On the next stanza, all the Young brothers yelled the same thing their mother had, Luke included.

She arrived in front of him, and before she could get a single word out, he took her hand and pulled her all the way into his embrace. "This is the song my parents used to embarrass us with on New Year's Eve," he said, grinning. "But now everyone has someone to kiss."

His eyes dropped to her mouth. "I know we're not really together, but—"

"It's halfway to kissing time, time to kiss again!" the room chorused, and Luke didn't have to finish his request. Sterling took his face in her hands and pressed her lips to his. He seemed surprised at first, and boy, she sure was.

After only a moment, he growled somewhere between his chest and his throat, wrapped her up in both arms, and kissed her like they really had been dating. Adrenaline shot through her, sending her pulse through her body like bullets, and everything about this man made her vibrate in a way she hadn't before.

She sank into his touch, determined to tell him...something.

She definitely had *something* to tell him after this kiss ended, and she prayed she'd remember what it was as hard as she prayed that this moment would never end.

3

Luke had finally snapped. Driven to the brink of complete insanity by the scent of apple cider and the high of winning a bogus dance-off at a family party.

Oh, and that insane music.

Watching all of his brothers gravitate toward their wives and kiss them. He had to have someone too, didn't he?

His heart pounded hard against the back of his throat, telling him to *stop kissing Sterling*.

But he couldn't do it. He'd been dreaming of having this woman in his arms for months. The kissing in his fantasies had never been as hot as this—nor as public. Around him, the music started up again, and even then, he didn't stop kissing her.

She matched him stroke for stroke too, and the repressed tension between them finally bled away about the time everyone else started kissing for the second time. Maybe the third. Luke had no clue, because time existed outside the space where Sterling's hands brushed along the nape of his neck, sending showers of sparks down his spine.

He took a deep breath, finally putting a centimeter or two between his lips and Sterling's. But the mouth could say so much, even without words. Remember so much, yearn for so much, send so many tingles down to a cowboy's lungs.

"I'm sorry?" he whispered as a question. He opened his eyes to see she still stood in his arms, her eyes closed softly, her lips parted slightly, as they still sort of swayed to some unheard music.

Luke had muscles bound around every bone, and they'd all turned into marshmallow at the nearness of Sterling. That slinky silver dress. The wave in her hair. The scent of her perfume—which he couldn't identify right now. And the taste of her lips.

Oh, the taste of those lips. He couldn't quite identify that right now either, because his mind still short-circuited from the place of madness he'd visited.

"All right," someone said, and he snapped back to reality. To the end of a couch in a furniture store where he stood, his daughter and all of his family nearby.

Tex laughed into the mic that echoed through the space now, and Luke backed up and tucked Sterling against his side. She opened her eyes, but she didn't look at him. They simply stood hip-to-hip—which was pretty hot for Luke, if he was being honest with himself.

"Now that we've got Momma's version of midnight kissing out of the way, she and Daddy want to head home and get to bed at a decent hour."

"What time is it?" Sterling murmured.

"No clue," Luke whispered back. She hadn't responded to his question-apology, nor his invitation to dinner, and he needed to get her alone so they could talk.

"But first," Tex continued. "We've got a few family announcements Momma doesn't want to miss out on." His wife, Abby, joined him, their daughter Melissa on her hip. Abby was obviously carrying another baby, and since Luke went out to the farmhouse where Tex and Abby lived quite often, he knew she was due in May.

The whole family knew that. Didn't they?

He adjusted his hold on Sterling, and she put her arm around him too. Luke had sweated through plenty of country music concerts, but his body had suddenly never been hotter than standing there with his massage therapist.

Abby took the microphone from Tex, which Luke recognized as an old-school public address system mic that would sit on a counter, and smiled out at everyone. "If you didn't know I was pregnant, you're going to need to get your eyes checked."

Several people laughed, and Luke managed to crack a smile.

"Tex and I." Abby looked up to her husband, and they both beamed at one another with the wattage of the sun. And that right there was what Luke wanted with every fiber of his being. He wanted a woman in his life the way Tex had Abby. He wanted to have silent conversations with her that said volumes. He wanted to share his good days and his bad. He wanted to share his bed and his house and his daughter with the person who would love him even when he came home in a bad mood, messed up a set on stage, or spent too much money on her.

"We're going to have a baby boy come May," Abby practically yelled into the mic, which totally undermined the purpose of a mic.

Luke cringed as feedback rang through the speakers.

Tex plucked the mic away from Abby. "Sorry, everyone. We're just really excited to welcome another boy to our family." He looked around the crowd and found Bryce, more unspoken conversations happening.

Luke loved Bryce with his whole heart, as he wasn't even that much older than Bryce. He'd been eight years old when the boy had been born, which was closer in age to Luke than Luke was to Tex.

Cheering and clapping happened then, but Luke didn't want to pull his hand away from Sterling. So he whistled through his teeth to add his congratulations to the mix.

Tex held up both hands, which caused the mic to reverberate again, and Gabe came forward and snatched it from him. "Sorry," Tex said while he laughed. "Sorry."

He and Abby backed out of the spotlight, and Gabe held the mic now. Luke thought he might just pass it off to whoever had another announcement, but he stood there, his throat moving as he swallowed, and swallowed, and swallowed.

Luke tried to find Hilde, but his eyes didn't move from person to person fast enough. At his side, Sterling said, "Oh, my goodness, she's going to have a baby."

Before he could stop her, Sterling moved away from him, and as he watched, he was able to find Hilde. It helped that more than one woman had started moving in her direction. She held up one hand, and they all stopped instantly.

"Hilde and I," Gabe said. "Are excited to announce that we'll also be welcoming another Young to our family." He looked to Luke's right and held out his hand. Hilde wrapped hers around it, her smile warm and wonderful, and again the exact look Luke would like to see on a woman's face while she gazed at him.

"She's due in July, and we don't know if it'll be a boy or a girl yet."

"Let's pray for a boy," Lynnie called, and that elicited some laughter from the family too. Hilde had a teenage girl—Lynnie—and Gabe had a little girl a couple years younger than Luke's daughter—Liesl. Gabe was the only one with any Y-chromosomes in his family, and though Luke had only recently started maintaining his relationship with Gabe, he knew his brother wanted a boy.

"All right," Gabe said. "That's us." He looked around for someone else to hand the mic to, and no one darted forward. "Is there anyone else? Tex?"

Hilde took the mic from him and said, "I've got it, sweetheart. It just has a button right—"

"I have something," Bryce called from the crowd. All of the air seemed to get sucked right out of the furniture store, but as Sterling fell back to Luke's side, he felt fully oxygenated. She took his hand in hers and flashed him a smile as Bryce made his way through the crowd to the mic.

They all parted for him, so it wouldn't take him long. Sterling leaned closer, and Luke ducked his head to hear her. "I have to tell you something," she murmured.

"Okay," he whispered back. "Maybe we can go for a walk after this."

She nodded once and straightened, and Luke looked back to the mic right as Bryce reached it.

"All right," he said, his youthful energy filling Luke with happiness. The young man had just turned twenty-two a few days ago, and he was a completely different person than he'd been two years ago. Than last year. Bryce had inspired Luke to start seeing a therapist, and after he'd seen such amazing changes in his nephew's life that he wanted for himself.

"Kassie, where you at?" He looked around, and while it wasn't as bright as noonday, it certainly wasn't dark. There were a lot of people there, and Kassie raised her hand and then slipped through the bodies to join Bryce.

Maybe they *were* together....

Bryce did take her hand, gaze at her, some of those unspoken conversations happened, and then he faced the family again.

"There's a horse farm up in Dog Valley," he started. "It's been owned and run by a former racehorse trainer out of Kentucky, and Finn Barber is retiring. His ranch has been for sale for a while, and...."

He motioned to someone else to join him, and Tex returned to the spotlight. "My daddy helped me, and Kassie's daddy helped her, and we bought it!"

Luke's mouth dropped open. If Bryce had bought a horse ranch in Dog Valley.... "He's moving home," he said.

"I'm moving back to Coral Canyon!" Bryce said, and he sure looked happy about it.

"Praise the heavens," Momma said, and she rushed toward Bryce, Kassie, and Tex. Luke wanted to hurry forward and hug his nephew too, but he'd have to get in line to do that. Brother after brother, as well as their wives, piled around Bryce and Kassie, and plenty of laughing and congratulating went around.

"Be right back, okay?" Luke asked of Sterling, and she nodded.

"Of course," she said. "Go."

When he reached Bryce, he took the boy into his arms. "Yes," he said. "I can't wait for you to move back here." He clapped Bryce on the back. "When is that happening? Do not tell me I have to help you move in the dead of winter."

Bryce laughed, the sound so full of joy. Luke had never thought Bryce could make a sound like that, and it gave him hope for himself. "Not until May, Uncle Luke," he said. "We're not suicidal."

Luke pulled away, but he didn't back up enough to let someone else take his place. "Talk to me about Kassie," he said under his breath. "You said you were just friends, but...."

"We are," Bryce said, glancing over to her and back to Luke. "And now we'll be business partners too. That's all, I swear."

"He's always wanted a horse rescue ranch," Kassie said,

causing Luke to turn slightly toward her. "We both know plenty about horses, and I've never wanted to be part of the racehorse scene."

"Finn's going to sell off the rest of his horses, or leave them for us." Bryce wore pure sunlight on his face. "And yeah. I'm gonna move over my four horses from my daddy's, and we're gonna...go from there."

"Yeah," Tex said. "He's gonna go from there."

Luke looked at his oldest brother, noting the masked optimism and the falsely bright eyes. But Tex loved his son, and he wanted him closer, and while Bryce might fail at this, Tex was going to be right at his side.

Luke would be too.

"I can't believe you didn't get up here, Uncle Luke," Bryce said.

He focused on his nephew. "What? Why would I do that? I don't have any announcements."

"No?" Bryce looked past him, but his gaze quickly returned to Luke. "So it's common knowledge that you and Sterling are dating?"

Luke's head pounded in time with his accelerating pulse. "What?" He flicked a look at Tex, who seemed rooted in place. "Who told you that?"

Bryce nodded slightly, his cowboy hat barely dipping toward Luke's right shoulder.

He turned and found Sterling standing there. She raised her chin and said, "I did, Luke. I told him that."

4

Sterling put the best smile she could on her face. "Congratulations, Bryce," she said as diplomatically as she could. "Luke, could I speak to you for a moment?" She blinked, a film of white crowding into her vision. "Privately?"

Luke stood there, the darkest look on his face that Sterling had ever seen. His eyebrows drew down into a nasty V, and if they'd been talking about how Sterling liked tomatoes and Luke didn't, his confusion would be cute.

"Excuse us," she said to Bryce, Kassie, and Tex—and the other dozen people standing around—and she linked her arm through Luke's. She got him past his family members and away from the glow of the tea lights hanging above all the couches.

Once the noise of the party had calmed behind them, and Sterling's eyes had adjusted to the new level of darkness further out in the store, she slipped her hand out of his elbow and into his. "Luke, I'm sorry," she said.

"You told him we were dating?"

Sterling nodded, feeling like her next step in these heels would lead her right off a cliff. In the first place, she never wore shoes like this. And secondly, she couldn't lose Luke now that she'd kissed him. That simple gesture had changed her fundamentally, and she would never be kissed like that again.

She'd never been kissed like that before either, and she'd been overlooked and invisible for so long. But Luke *saw* her, and she couldn't lose that. She couldn't lose *him*.

"When I danced with him, he asked me if I thought you'd like Kassie."

"Kassie?" Luke strolled along at her side, and she could only imagine what people could see between the two of them.

"Yeah," Sterling said. "I was—I panicked. I didn't want him to set you up with Kassie, and I—"

"Everyone knows not to set me up with anyone," he growled.

Sterling took a breath and tried to calm her pulse. That didn't work at all, but she'd come this far. She wasn't nearly as irrational and wild as she'd been marching into Jem's and yelling at Luke in front of his brothers.

"Bryce said that if it was him, you might not be upset." She looked at the ground as they neared a curve in the path that led past another staged bedroom area. She didn't want to trip on the flooring—or her own stupidity.

"So I told him we were dating." She swallowed, but her throat felt so sticky. "Me and you. You and me. And then that song came on," she said, rushing ahead now. "And I started to tell you, and then you said—and we—"

Her lips hummed just thinking about touching his again. "Then I ran out of time."

His hand in hers squeezed, and a sigh escaped his lips. "You didn't run out of time."

"I was going to tell you. See if—I don't honestly know what I was going to see about. Maybe that we could go to dinner like you suggested, and we could find a way for it not to be too awkward between us?" She shook her head, her throat raw. "Something."

Luke took a couple of steps and paused, bringing Sterling to a stop with him. He looked at her. "I'd like something," he said.

Nerves and confusion assaulted her too, especially when he looked at her with such softness in his eyes. Or maybe it was just dark, and she couldn't really see.

"So...." Sterling ducked her head and lifted her other hand to their joined ones. "We start with dinner?"

"I mean." He cleared his throat roughly. "I sort of jumped the gun and went all the way to kissing tonight."

Sterling giggled, almost horrified at the sound coming from her. She couldn't ever remember making it before. "I think I kissed you, Luke."

He leaned closer, and she closed her eyes, her heartbeat pumping through her as hard now as it had during that ridiculous song. "Mm, you might be right. We'll have to rectify that, won't we?"

"Yes," she gasped.

But he only pulled away. Her eyes fluttered open to find his dark gaze on her again. "I can't go fast, Sterling," he said, his voice right on the cusp of being spoken out loud. "You know quite a bit about my ex-wife, but there's still more you don't know."

"Okay," she said.

"Dinner then?"

"Yes," she said.

"Do you have any other dates you'll need to break?" He cocked his eyebrows at her, clearly challenging her, and foolishness drove right through Sterling.

"Look," she said, feeling stronger and braver than she ever had. "It's not like you know everything about me either."

He softened again, and Sterling could get whiplashed around

by this gorgeous, grumpy cowboy. "I'm sure that's true," he admitted. "But I don't want you to see anyone else. Can I say that? I'm not the sharing type."

"Well, that's great," she said. "No one else is asking."

"If they do."

"They won't."

Luke studied her again, and Sterling suddenly couldn't handle the strength of his gaze. "I should probably get home too."

"I thought you were a night owl," he said.

"Yeah." She gave no further explanation.

They started walking again, and Luke calmed back to his normal, quiet, broody self. Sterling enjoyed the quietness of the store away from the party, though she could of course still hear snatches of music, laughter, and chatter.

At the next corner, probably about as far from the party as they'd get, he said, "So...do you want to go to dinner soon? What's your schedule like?"

"I only work during the day," she said. "My evenings are for pajamas, romantic comedies, and caramel popcorn." She flashed him a smile he did not return. "You tell me, Luke. I think your schedule is a bit busier than mine."

"Fair enough," he murmured, and he dropped her hand to take out his phone. The bright screen illuminated his sharp, dark features, and Sterling couldn't believe she'd somehow attracted the attention of this handsome man.

"Looks like...breakfast at Morris's in the morning." He swiped once, then again. "Friday?" He looked up, though surely he wouldn't be able to see her going from bright to dark so quickly. "Barring any insanity from my family, which, as you've seen, can't be controlled sometimes."

"Have you heard anything from Mandi?" she asked.

He flinched slightly, quickly turning the motion into the

shaking of his head. "She'll pop up at the worst time, is my guess." He met her eyes, blinking a couple of times. "Are you prepared for that?"

"No," Sterling said. "But I wasn't ready for Bryce to tell you I'd told him we were dating when we weren't, and I think I handled that okay."

Luke chuckled, and that brought such satisfaction to Sterling. Cracking the cowboy had sure proven tough in the past. "That you did." He pocketed his phone and took her hand in his again. He lifted it to his lips, his eyes never leaving hers. Smoke practically rose between them, and he kissed the inside of her wrist.

"You don't really have to go right now, do you?"

"No," she whispered.

"Good." He drew her into his arms and started dancing with her again. Fine, it was a simple, barely-there sway. "I think I can hear the music from the party right here."

Once he stopped whispering, Sterling could, but she still sighed as she let herself sink into the warm strength of Luke's embrace, imagining herself to be the rescued princess dancing in the cowboy prince's arms.

⁓

WHEN STERLING WOKE UP ON NEW YEAR'S DAY, SHE DIDN'T have a family breakfast at her brother's house to prepare for. She could call her mother in Chicago or her brother wherever he was in Europe right now. France, if Sterling's memory served.

Instead, she stayed in bed for twenty or thirty extra minutes, reading through a few things on her phone. She hadn't scheduled anyone for massages that day or the next, and she saw no reason to start the day earlier than normal.

So she could what? Realize how boring and stale her life had become. Even as she thought that, she had plenty to do today. She needed to update her website with her new pricing. Sterling wanted to practice her speech for the director at the community center, where she was hoping to rent a room and do a weekly meditation class.

Before she started looking for more permanent space, she wanted to know if the women in this town had any interest in a group meditation class led by a trained professional. Maybe they didn't, and she saw no reason to take on rent she couldn't afford until she knew.

Eventually, she got out of bed and took a couple of minutes right there at her bedside to stretch her arms above her head. She held the poses, took the deep breaths, and pulled through the movement in her back and legs. Feeling more awake, she padded down the hall to her kitchen, where she put a pot of coffee on to brew.

She stepped over to her sliding glass door and looked outside. The winter hadn't brought much snow yet, but Wyoming still had a few chilly months ahead of it. Sterling had grown up in Wyoming, and she didn't mind the cold, the snow. She actually found she liked doing work where she could see the results of it—like shoveling snow or mowing the grass.

Her life here in Coral Canyon gave her the opportunity to do both, to see real, tangible evidence of her work. In massage therapy, she rarely got to see that. She could feel someone's muscles and mind soften under her touch, but she wasn't sure how long her treatments lasted. They never looked any different, and she enjoyed work where she could see the payoff of her efforts.

The bare branches of her trees in the backyard blew, as did the evergreens. She liked watching them sway in the wind, and the pure silence and peacefulness in her house did make her experience a slip of joy. Along with the scent of coffee, Sterling might

Luke

have catalogued her life as pretty darn amazing—if she hadn't kissed Luke Young last night.

Now, nothing was as amazing as that. "You have a date with him in two days," she whispered to herself. Really three, as she'd have to go all day Friday before seeing him.

When the coffee stopped dripping, Sterling turned away from her morning ritual and went to pour herself a cup. She nursed that while she sat in front of her laptop at the dining room table, clicking around and enjoying the slow pace of her life.

About midday, she collected her phone from the bedroom where she'd left it to text her mother and brother. They likely wouldn't text her first, and Sterling could get past the pinch in her heart because of that. She absolutely could, because she had before.

"If you want to have a relationship with them—even a small one—you have to reach out." It didn't matter to her that they never reached back. Except for when it did, and then Sterling had to find a way past her hurt feelings and figure out how to text or call first.

She swiped on her phone, shock moving through her when she saw she'd missed over two dozen texts. Her breathing quickened, but she quickly realized none of them were from Lex or her mom.

But from the Young wives. Hilde had started the group thread, and Ev had chimed in second. Then Abby Young, Leigh Young, Georgia Young, Faith Young, Dani Young, and lastly, Sunny—and she wasn't even a Young yet.

"This is unbelievable," Sterling said, her face heating as the spotlight shone brightly on her. No one even stood in the room with her, but she felt them coming at her from all sides.

I saw you walk away from the party with Luke last night, Hilde had said. *And you two never came back.*

That's not quite true, Ev said. *Luke came back a while later...alone.*

Too bad, Abby said. *The strike of midnight is such a perfect time for a first kiss.*

Sterling reached up and touched her lips—the lips Luke had kissed last night, but at the strike of ten instead midnight.

Sterling, we want the news! Leigh had said. *What's going on with you and Luke?*

Tex said you told Bryce you two were dating. Abby had sent a double thumbs-up with that text. *I won't believe it until you confirm.*

Same, Georgia said. *Although, I have seen the way Luke looks at you, so I'm inclined to believe anything.*

Sterling scoffed, but at the same time, she couldn't help feeling like she'd just been initiated into their merry band of wives. "How does he look at me?" she wondered aloud.

I can't believe I missed all of this! Faith said. *Grace was so fussy last night, and you can't see anything sitting on the couch.*

Don't worry, Faith, Dani said. *I missed a lot of it too. I've heard some things second-hand from Mav, but there's nothing as good as the real story.*

Maybe she doesn't want to kiss and tell, Hilde said, and Sterling could just hear the teasing quality of her friend's voice in the text.

They continued to speculate, and Sterling finally started typing. Her grin grew wider and wider and wider as she did, and she didn't even take a moment to proofread the message or go over it again to edit it.

She simply sent it and prayed it wouldn't cause a Young wife riot.

5

Abigail Young reached for her phone as it chimed. She'd already eaten half a waffle, but with her five-month baby bump, she wasn't sure she could squeeze in another bite. She'd rather slowly sip the white hot chocolate Leigh had made than try to stuff in more food, and she'd been doing that for the past twenty minutes while everyone else finished up eating.

Her husband, of course, had a hollow leg, and he shoveled in the last bite of his strawberries and whipped cream waffle—his third one—as Blaze said something that made everyone laugh.

Abby had wanted an easy, carefree morning this New Year's Day, and coming to Morris's and Leigh's for a late breakfast she didn't have to make had fit the bill perfectly. Her three-year-old could run around and play with her cousins, with plenty of other adults to watch her.

As relaxed and yes, a little checked out as she was, it took her a moment to realize who'd texted. When she saw Sterling's name, she nearly dropped her cup of hot chocolate as she gasped.

The laughter started to die down, and she held up her phone.

Several people looked at her, but the husbands wouldn't get it. All the wives did, though, and Hilde practically dove onto her phone.

Abby got to her feet as Tex asked, "What is it, babe?"

"Nothing." She moved away from the table as quickly as her pregnant feet would take her, and she huddled with Dani and Faith as they held their phones in front of them. Abby read as fast as her eyes would allow her, and she had to tap the down arrow to see the whole message.

"Wow," Faith whispered.

Hey, thanks so much for inviting me to your family party. What a blast I had! The apple cider—who knew people served that at New Year's—and the little bows on the water bottles...just amazing.

Yes, I danced with Luke. We talked a little bit. I don't really want to have a big discussion about our relationship with everyone, and I'm sure you wouldn't have wanted that as you started dating your husbands either. Not that Luke is going to be my husband. But we are going to dinner this weekend, and if there's anything I feel like I can share that won't upset him or me, then I'll definitely let you know!

"So she's dating him," Abby said, looking up.

"They're going out this weekend." Dani wore wonder on her face. "I sure hope they can make it to the second date this time."

"What's going on over here, ladies?" Mav asked, settling his arm around his wife. Dani looked up at him and then held up her phone. Abby had half a mind to keep the text string a secret from Tex, because he had to deal with Luke a lot through the band.

Luke came out to the farmhouse for dinner too. Just him and Abby's family. She loved him, and she wanted nothing more than for him to be blissfully happy. She knew him better than a lot of people, and she cut a glance over to where he sat at the big dining room table.

He somehow knew when to look up, and he met her eye. Abby

spun away from him again, totally making him suspicious, she was sure.

"Holy drum sets," Mav murmured.

"Right?" Dani asked.

"Did you guys see this text?" Everly asked as she appeared at the end of the hall. She'd taken her baby down to a bedroom to nurse right when she and Trace had arrived, and now she carried the darling girl in her left arm, her phone in her right hand, and pure awe on her face.

"Shush," Abby said at the same time Georgia very nearly yelled, "I can't believe this." from the couch, where she sat with Sunny.

"What's goin' on?" Blaze asked from the direction of the table.

"Abs," Tex said.

She turned toward him, as did Faith, and it quickly became a line of women facing their men at the table. Ev joined her, Faith, and Dani, as did Hilde. With Georgia and Sunny on the couch, only Leigh stood in the kitchen, and the waffle maker she'd been tending for the past half-hour shrilled out a long tone to let her know the waffle inside was done.

She didn't even move, her eyes glued to her phone. When she looked up, she said, "You guys," and then cut off when she realized how silent the house had fallen.

Luke would hate this, and Abby's heartbeat squirreled through her uncomfortably. Her only saving grace would be that she hadn't started this group text, but she'd definitely been interested in it and participated in it.

She slipped her phone into her pocket. "It's nothing," she said loudly when no one else volunteered anything.

Tex got to his feet too, his dark eyes pinning her. "It's something."

"I don't want to make a big deal out of it," she said almost through clenched teeth. She silently begged Tex to let this go, and it took every ounce of her willpower not to look at Luke again.

Unfortunately, someone must've been, because he stood too. "I think I know what it's about."

"No," Abby said quickly. "It's just a fr-friend of ours that texted some news. It's nothing."

Luke quirked his eyebrows at her, a clear challenge she'd lose any day of the week. "Is that so? Do you have friends you see outside of this room?"

A fire blazed to life inside Abby. "Of course I do, you scoundrel." She took the few steps to him and swatted her palm against his chest. "I used to run the whole library, thank you very much."

He grinned at her, though the gesture didn't quite reach his eyes. "Sure, yeah," he said almost in a deadpan. "And this friend happens to know all of you?" His eyes roamed to Hilde, who held his gaze for a good few seconds before she blinked and looked at Gabe for help.

"Hilde, honey," he said as he lifted a napkin to wipe his lips. "What's going on?"

Silence draped the house, and Abby knew this wasn't going away. Maybe if she went into labor, but that would just be cruel.

Denzel's dog barked, and she jumped about a mile. So did everyone in her line of sight, and Denzel said, "Yeah, boy, there's some tension in here." He shushed the dog and said, "I know what's goin' on, but I don't want to say news that's not mine."

His words did get the attention off Luke and Abby though, as Leigh's brother rarely said too much at parties. He came to everything, and Abby loved him like a brother too. Any of them would drop anything to help him, as that was exactly what Leigh had done in her life. She'd left her bakery and her life in California to come here after a terrible racecar accident her brother had been in.

He lived alone, but she and Morris brought him and his German shepherd, Scout, along to everything. He got to his feet too, and it took a few more seconds than it had taken Tex or Luke. "While I've got all of your attention, I might as well make my announcement."

"You have an announcement?" Morris asked. "Why didn't you say it last night?"

"Not all of us like to be behind a microphone," he said without a hint of a smile. Abby almost did, but she now had another piece of juiciness to hang on. A quick glance at Luke told her this wasn't over, but maybe she could spare him for another minute or two.

Maybe long enough for him to tell everyone he was going out with Sterling this weekend. This weekend! She almost bounced on the balls of her feet she was so giddy.

Denzel leaned into the table and cleared his throat. He wore a cowboy hat like a lot of other men in Coral Canyon, and when he leaned his head down, Abby couldn't see his face.

"I don't want this to be a big deal," he said. "I'm not answerin' any questions. I'm a grown adult, regardless of what anyone else thinks." He tossed a look in Leigh's direction, and she made a soft scoff of protest.

Abby started toward her and wrapped one arm around her as they waited for Denzel to keep talking.

"I started seein' someone," Denzel said, clearing his throat again. "She works over at the coffee shop I like to go to and write. Her name's Michelle Hinz, and that's that. I'll not be answering any questions."

He sounded like he'd become a politician with his last statement, and Abby's own heart had started beating hard with his first few words. She couldn't even imagine what Leigh had going on inside her body.

"You will too," she burst out. "How long as this been going on?"

Denzel settled back into his seat and picked up his fork. "I'm not fourteen, Leigh. I'm not sneakin' out of the house to see her."

"Michelle Hinz is a really nice woman," Hilde said, her voice sort of sticking in her throat. "She doesn't just work at the coffee shop." She glanced around at everyone. "The one just off Main? It's called Daily Grind? They grind their own beans and stuff." She too cleared her throat. "She owns it."

"That's right," Denzel drawled. "She does own it."

"You go there to write?" Morris asked. "What are you writing?"

Denzel pierced him with a sharp look. "If you must know."

"I must." Morris settled back in his seat and folded his arms. He faced Denzel too, so Abby couldn't quite see his face.

"You don't have to say anything," Blaze said. "No one has to say anything they don't want to say."

"I think it's great you're seein' someone," Tex said. "Good for you, Denzel." He grinned at Denzel and clapped him on the back.

"Thanks, man."

"Maybe you could sit down," Trace said. "You're hovering over me, Tex."

"Yep." Tex sank back into his seat, the chair sliding backward as he did. He hurried to grab the table like he might topple over, and that caused Otis to chuckle.

"Daddy," someone said, one of the littles under ten, but no one moved to help them.

"Shh," someone said. "He hasn't said how long they've been dating."

"Or what he writes." Leigh folded her arms too.

Denzel sent a glare in her direction, but Abby could see it wasn't full of anything barbed. A quick look to Luke told her his expression had sharp, pointy sticks all around it. Abby glanced away quickly, her throat drying up.

"Leave the man alone," Mav said, coming out of the living room. He stood at the corner of the table and stared down all of the men sitting there, then he turned and looked at Abby and Leigh in the kitchen before turning all the way around, surveying everyone.

"And no one is going to be going over to this place to spy on him."

"Come on," Otis said. "We wouldn't do that."

"Morris?" Mav asked. "Tell Otis here what you were just thinking."

"I plead the Fifth," Morris said, and that made Abby laugh. Right out loud she laughed, and that caused a ripple effect through the house.

"Daddy," a little voice said again, and this time Abby looked over to find Liesl climbing up onto Gabe's lap. "Larsy went outside."

Everyone looked at her, including Mav. He spun back toward the living room, dashing past his wife and Ev and Hilde as he headed for the front door. "Lars!" he called. "If you went outside...."

"He definitely went outside," Georgia said as she reached for OJ. She picked him up and settled him on her lap, her smile so perfect and so genuine. As Abby looked around the family party, her heart expanded more and more for each person there. She could've blamed it on the hormones, and they probably had a huge part to play in the way her eyes filled with tears and she suddenly had a runny nose, but she simply knew that she loved being around these people.

Family.

As she blinked and refocused, she realized that conversations had broken out all over the house. At the dining room table. In the living room. On the couch. Even in the kitchen, where Morris had come over to talk to Leigh.

"He'll tell us when he's ready," Leigh said, and Abby took a moment to turn away from them and wipe her eyes. A warm body sidled up to her a few seconds later, and she tensed.

"Abby," Luke said. "Everyone knows about me and Sterling, don't they?"

Abby knew he didn't really think he could hide anything from his brothers, especially the ones in Country Quad with him. Sniffling, she swiped on her phone, typed in the passkey, and handed it to Luke. "I just want the record to show that Hilde started the group text, not me."

He looked at her for a long moment, and then he took her phone. Abby had no idea how he'd react, because Luke was unpredictable at best.

"We're here," Cecily called, and that provided another distraction big enough to make all the grandkids start clamoring and rushing toward their grandma and grandpa. Abby once again brushed at her eyes as Cecily and Jerry stopped right inside the living room and both got down on their knees to welcome as many children into their arms as possible.

Melissa was one of the younger kids who could walk, and Abby's whole heart melted as Jerry picked her up and held her in one arm while he hugged Rosie, Jem's daughter, with his other one.

Luke sighed, and that brought Abby's attention back to him. He handed her the phone, and she said, "Luke," as she reached up and ran her fingers down the side of his face. "She's the best, isn't she?"

His jaw jumped, and he said nothing.

"Mama," Melissa said, and both she and Luke looked down at the little girl. "I go potty."

Abby dropped her hand, a new kind of urgency running inside her now. She left her phone on the counter as she took her daughter's hand. "Yes," she said. "Let's go potty."

As she walked away from Luke, she twisted to look over her shoulder. "We'll talk later."

He simply lifted one hand in a wave, and with Luke that could mean, *Sure, we'll talk later.* Or it could mean, *Over my dead body will we talk about this later.*

With Luke, Abby was never really sure, but right now, she needed to get her three-year-old into a bathroom before an accident occurred.

6

Luke knelt down in front of his daughter, his smile wide and feeling so good on his face. "Let me fix this, baby." He untucked her shirt and pulled her skirt around so the zipper sat in the front. Then he made quick work of getting her tee back into the waistband. "There you go."

"Thanks, Daddy," she said. "Do I look so pretty?"

Luke pressed his lips to her forehead. "You're always the prettiest girl in the room, baby." He glanced up to her hair, which hadn't been done yet. Her curls sprouted from her head like snakes, and they actually reminded him of Sterling's blonde hair.

He couldn't help thinking about the woman. Their date sat only six hours from now, and a flutter of nerves winged its way through his chest. "Let me get your hair braided."

"No, Daddy." She stepped back. "I don't want it braided."

"No?" Luke watched her. "Why not?" He'd been braiding Corrine's hair for a couple of years now, after he'd gone to a class at a salon to learn how to do so. "A ponytail?"

"I want momma to see it down," she said.

"Honey." Luke reached for the dining room table and used it to help himself stand. "I don't think that's a good idea."

Corrine skipped away from him, and Luke battled with himself about how big of a deal to make this. Number one, he hadn't heard from Mandi that day at all, though the court-appointed agent had confirmed she'd be there at five-forty-five.

Luke planned to pick up Sterling at six, and he had his doubts that he wouldn't be texting Jem last-minute to say he was bringing Corrine up to his house.

Number two, Corrine's hair would be a knotted mess he'd have to deal with if he didn't tame it back at least a little bit. He turned away from her, weighing his options. He could let this go for a few minutes while he made lunch, and then maybe, when she was sitting at the counter, he could at least try to get a couple of half-ponytails into her hair.

"It's lunchtime, jelly bean," he said. "What do you want?" He pulled open the fridge to see what he could whip up in less than twenty minutes.

"Can we have mac and cheese with hot dogs?"

That met his lunchtime requirement of something that took less than twenty minutes to make, so he said, "Yep," and pulled out the package of all-beef hot dogs. "Get me a box from the pantry."

While his daughter skipped off to do that, Luke reached for the butter and milk too. With the hot water running into a pot so he could boil the pasta, Corrine finally returned to him.

"Did you get lost?" he teased as he took the box from her. She hadn't hit a growth spurt yet, and she was one of the shorter kids in her third-grade class.

She grinned up at him. "It was up too high. I had to get out the steps."

"Thank you, baby." He'd told her about her mother when he'd started hearing from Mandi a few months ago. She'd finally texted on New Year's Day to say she could come this weekend, and Luke had been the one to set up the supervision required by the court.

Luke who'd texted all of the details. Luke who kept asking question after question, so he'd know exactly what was going on, and when, and where.

Since he had a date with Sterling, he'd suggested she come to his house and stay with Corrine there until he returned. Mandi hadn't put up a fuss about any of his suggestions, until he'd sent her a copy-paste reminder from the court order of her supervision.

That included that she couldn't bring any other children with her, and she'd balked then. His thumbs still ached from how furiously he'd texted that day. He'd rather do that than hear his ex-wife's voice, so he couldn't complain.

What he did complain about was her bringing along her three-year-old son from another marriage. He absolutely would not allow it, and he'd put his foot down again. Mandi had argued that the boy was Corrine's half-brother, which was true.

But Luke had the court on his side, and he hadn't even had to get Gabe to intervene on his behalf. Mandi had said she'd show up alone, on time, and that she really wanted to be more involved in Corrine's life.

Luke didn't want to deal with constant texts and requests from Mandi, but he couldn't very well keep her out of Corrine's life. He wanted to be a good father, and that included accepting the fact that Mandi had rights too.

"Daddy, what time is it?"

Luke glanced at the clock on the stove as he turned on the fire under the pot of water. "Twelve," he said, though it was quarter past.

"What time is momma comin'?"

Luke's mood worsened. "Close to six, jelly bean."

Her fingers started coming up as she counted. "So six hours."

"That's right," Luke said, having so many more words to say about this. "If she comes at all," he muttered.

"What, Daddy?"

"Nothin'." He flashed her a tight smile. "Baby, go get the water bottle so I can do those cute piggies on the sides, okay?"

Corrine planted her hands on her hips. "Daddy."

"Corrine." He abandoned the lunch prep and bent down to look her right in the eyes. "Do you want me to have to get out that metal comb?"

She scuffed her feet against the floor, and her hands dropped to her sides. "No, sir."

"I can just put it half-up," he said. "Your momma will still be able to see how amazing and curly it is."

"Okay," she chirped, and she went to get the hair supplies he'd asked for. He fed her lunch, and then got her hair secured into two cute little bobbing ponytails that sat right on the back of her head, one on the right and one on the left.

Luke dealt with stress in a couple of ways—he worked out or he cleaned. So it was that he put a movie on for Corrine after lunch and got to work. He'd remodeled the house from the inside out too, and he loved and knew every nook and cranny of it.

And by the time it was time to go pick up Sterling, his house was probably the cleanest one in all of Wyoming. Too bad Mandi hadn't shown up so he could impress her with his amazing parenting skills.

His doorbell rang, and his heartbeat plummeted to the soles of his crisply shined cowboy boots. Corrine cheered, and Luke wished she wouldn't.

"Stay here," he told her, probably in a little bit of a bark. He knew his daughter wouldn't stay in the living room, and it didn't really matter anyway. His front door opened into the living room, but he didn't need her rushing out onto the front porch in early January.

When he opened the door, he found a petite blonde woman standing there—not his ex-wife. "Good evening," he drawled out, because he knew how to charm people. Out of everyone in Country Quad, Luke had taken the most public relations classes. His surly demeanor required it, and he sometimes hated how suppressed he had to be.

The woman smiled. "Good evening, Mister Young."

He stepped back to allow her to enter the house. "You must be Miranda."

"Yes," she said, moving past him. He watched her take in his house, but at least she wasn't carrying a clipboard.

"Mandi's not here yet," Luke said, his nerves starting to shout at him. He'd be late to pick up Sterling if she didn't ring the doorbell in the next ten seconds, which of course, she didn't.

She didn't in the next ten minutes, and he did his best to make small talk with Miranda, who didn't seem uneasy at all. She engaged with Corrine too, and finally Luke got to his feet. "I'm going to call her," he said, hating everything about his life right now.

He stepped into the kitchen and dialed Mandi. The line rang once, twice, three times, and Luke's patience wore down and down and down. He was going to snap at any moment, and he really just needed to take Corrine and head to Jem's.

He could call Sterling along the way, but his anger and anxiety combined into a horrible tornado of emotion that smoked through him.

"Heya," Mandi said as if he was calling to see if she'd gotten the eggs at the grocery store.

"Where are you?" he growled. "You're late, and I'm only waiting five more minutes before I'm taking Corrine to Jem's."

Since Mandi didn't know where anyone lived but him, he didn't worry about her showing up there to try to get her time with Corrine.

"I got lost," Mandi said.

Luke scoffed. "I don't have to listen to you lie to me," he said. "If you're not here in the next sixty seconds, you'll have to figure out if the court will let you see her again."

"Luke," she tried, and his name in her voice used to break him down. Now it only made him stronger.

"I'm not kidding," he said. "You've made me late, and the court-appointed supervisor has been waiting for you for ten minutes."

"You're just going out with some woman."

The life left his lungs. He had no words to fight with Mandi, because it wasn't worth it. How could he ever tell Mandi or anyone else how Sterling was the complete opposite of "some woman"? She was so much more than that, but Luke liked keeping her close to his heart. He didn't have to justify anything to Mandi, that was for sure.

"One minute," he barked, and then he hung up.

He turned back to the living room, trying to get himself to calm down. He couldn't go into this date all riled up, because that never worked well for him. He took a deep breath and said, "I'm sorry. She said she...." He trailed off, because he couldn't lie to Miranda.

He also wouldn't lie to his daughter, and Corrine wore such hope in her eyes. Luke didn't want to say anything bad about Mandi in front of her, and he could see how badly his daughter needed a female role model in her life.

He wished it wasn't Mandi, and he reasoned that his sisters-in-law had been doing a good job filling the role. But she needed a mother.

Luke didn't finish his sentence and looked back at his phone. He tapped out a message to Sterling that he was running late, but he'd call her as soon as he was on the way. She didn't even have time to answer before his doorbell rang again.

Corrine perked her dark-haired head up, and Luke shoved his phone in his back pocket. He strode to the door for the second time that night and yanked open the door. His ex-wife stood there, and Luke hadn't seen her in years now.

Five years.

She'd dyed her dark hair to a lighter brown, and then streaked that with blonde. Enormous hoops hung from her earlobes, and she wore so much makeup, Luke couldn't tell if she was naturally tan or if she'd painted it all on.

She wore a tight pencil skirt and heels—to sit in his house with her daughter—and a bright pink sweater.

He had no words for her, and he could never truly describe her to others. "Come in," he said gruffly.

"Howdy, Luke," she said like nothing was wrong. For her, there probably wasn't. Luke tried to drain all the poisonous thoughts from his mind, because he didn't need the negativity in his life. It also made him a worse person instead of the man he'd been working to become.

So he took another deep breath and hitched a false smile to his face as Corrine came to his side. She suddenly wasn't so skippy and talkative, and she wrapped her arms around his leg, half-hiding behind him.

"Jelly bean," he said. "This is your momma." He smiled down at his daughter and dropped into a crouch again. "Hey, you're gonna be shy now?" He did not want to leave his precious daughter with a complete stranger either, which was why he'd fought for anything he could. Well, Gabe had, and that was why Miranda was here.

Mandi sat on the couch and crossed her legs. "Come here, baby."

Luke gave Corrine a little push, and she walked over to her momma. They hugged, and while it didn't look like a mother-daughter embrace, Luke reasoned they didn't know one another.

He straightened and said, "Am I okay to go?" He didn't want to leave, but he had to legally allow Mandi to see Corrine. "I should be back by eleven for sure." He moved over to Corrine and picked her right up. "Your bedtime is the same as always, jelly bean. Tell me when it is."

"Eight-thirty," she said.

"Eight-thirty," he said loudly, smiling at her and then nodding at Mandi. "You're okay to then wait here until I get back?"

"Yes," she said. "Go, Luke. We're fine here."

He rubbed his beard against Corrine's cheek and neck, causing her to giggle and squirm. He set her on the ground and said, "All right. Call me for anything, okay?" He took one last look at the situation and had to turn his back on it and walk out.

It was the hardest thing he'd ever done. Even harder than opening his paternity test. Harder than the tour last year, when he was so miserable and had humiliated himself in front of Sterling. Then the yelling. The showing up at her doorstep and admitting all of his feelings.

Well, maybe not all of them, but enough.

"Come on, Luke," he muttered to himself as he got behind the wheel of his truck. "There's a supervisor. It's okay." He looked back to the house, something inside him unable to put the vehicle in reverse and leave.

How could he leave his daughter in the house like this?

His phone rang, and Tex's name sat there. Everything calmed inside Luke, and he reached to answer the call. "Hey," he said.

"Am I interrupting?" Tex asked. "Abby's insisting you're going out with Sterling tonight, but I couldn't shake the feeling that I had to call you."

Luke put the truck in reverse and said, "Just talk to me, brother. I just left my baby with Mandi, and I'm freaking out and on the way to Sterling's right now."

7

Sterling looked up when a knock sounded on her door. It wasn't the same loud, insistent knocking that Luke had done when he'd come over last year to tell her why he'd booked a massage somewhere else.

It wasn't the knock he made when he came for his body treatments. But somehow, Sterling still knew she'd find Luke on her doorstep.

She stood and hurried to the door, noting that he was twenty minutes late to pick her up. She didn't care about that, but she knew Luke would. "Please, Lord," she prayed as she reached for the doorknob.

Any version of Luke could be standing a few feet in front of her when she opened the door, and she hoped it was the dark, sexy, caring, devoted cowboy. He indeed stood there, one hand up on the doorframe, his leather jacket unzipped and open as it hung down.

He wore a sexy pair of jeans, a black T-shirt, and a matching hat. He really went for the black theme, Sterling would give him that. His mouth tipped up into a smile. "I'm so sorry I'm late." He didn't tell her why, and she liked that he didn't have an excuse or say anything damaging about his ex-wife.

For she knew he'd been delayed because of Mandi. She probably hadn't shown up on time, but she could've just as easily engaged him in a frustrating conversation, making it hard for him to leave on time.

"You're fine," she said. "I did take off my shoes, so come in and give me a sec?"

"Yes, ma'am." He stepped into her house, and Sterling let him go by her before she closed the door.

"It's freezing tonight," she said.

"Supposed to snow on Monday," he said.

Sterling went to the spot where she'd been sitting behind her computer to retrieve her shoes. "I suppose we've had an easy winter so far, so we can't complain."

"You don't even leave the house, so you certainly can't complain."

She collected her shoes and stood to face him, finding his face full of teasing. "Did I tell you that once?"

"Yes," he said simply.

This date was already off on a better beat than the only one they'd previously been on, and Sterling found herself grinning back at him. "It sounds like something I would say." She sank onto her couch and toed her way into her shoes.

When she stood again, Luke eased into her, his arm going right around her waist. He brought her flush against his body, and as he took a deep breath of...her, Sterling didn't think anything hotter could've happened.

"Mm," was all he said.

Sterling's eyes drifted closed, and she sure enjoyed the fresh, clean scent of his shirt, the heavier smell of leather and aftershave. She put one palm against his chest, and that made him take a half-step back.

"You hungry?" he asked.

"Yes," she said, though she'd eaten a bowl of cereal an hour ago. She'd already been out with Luke, but it had been awful. She saw him all the time in her massage studio. Heck, she'd kissed him only four nights ago.

But for some reason, she didn't want to be starving on this new first date with him. She didn't want to make a fool of herself by eating too fast or too much.

He took her hand and led her out to his truck, where he opened her door for her and waited for her to get into the truck. She'd dressed carefully tonight, and she'd chosen a pair of wide-leg, billowy cotton pants that were dyed to look like jeans. She'd chosen what she called her "confetti sweater," because it was cream colored with stripes of brightly colored bits of yarn.

She loved it, because it looked like a party in a shirt, and she wanted tonight to be carefree and happy. As Luke got behind the wheel and started the truck, the heater began to blow. "I was thinking of going to Homeplate," he said. "Is that okay?"

"I love Homeplate," Sterling said. "But Luke, if you want steak, we can go to The Branding Iron."

"They'll be super busy tonight," he said. "And I eat other things, Sterling."

"Do you?" she teased, and that got him to look over to him.

She reached over and took his hand in hers. "Talk to me about how it was to leave Corrine with Mandi."

Black clouds flew into place around him, and he shook his head. "I don't know," he said. He backed out of her driveway, using only one hand so he didn't have to release hers.

She wasn't sure if she should press him or not, and Sterling didn't want to ruin their date before they got to the end of the block. "I wish you'd tell me," she said. "But I can start with something hard for me to talk about it you want."

"Or we could just talk about the weather and how loud my brothers are."

Sterling smiled and shook her head. "We could, but is that what people do when they start dating?" She looked over to him, pure anxiety streaming through her. When Luke didn't answer, she shifted in her seat. "I really want to know, Luke."

"What do you mean?"

"I don't think it's any secret that I haven't dated in a while."

"I...didn't...you haven't?"

"No," Sterling said, pure misery filling her now. "And I don't know everything, obviously, but I'm pretty sure you're supposed to talk about yourself. Get to know things about each other that you don't already know." She looked out her window, wishing she'd stuffed a big wad of gum in her mouth so she wouldn't be able to talk much.

At the very least, she'd have been able to think through what came out of her mouth before it did.

"All right," Luke said. "You said you've got something?"

More than one something, Sterling thought, but she sat up a little straighter. "Yeah, okay," she said. "I don't think I've ever told you that I have a brother."

"Yeah," Luke said. "You did...once." He glanced over to her, and Sterling sure liked the strength and squareness in his jaw. "He's a guide or something?"

"Yeah," she said, relief pouring through her. "Lex lives in France right now, and he leads backpacking tours."

"Yeah, that sounds right."

"My mom lives in Chicago," she said. "She moved there after my brother graduated."

"Where'd you grow up?"

"Cheyenne," she said. "I've been in Coral Canyon for years now, though."

"How long?"

"Almost seven years," she said. "You?"

"I've been back for about four now," he said. "Me and most of my brothers came back when Tex did. It's been a riot since." He spoke with a dryness in his tone that wasn't lost on Sterling.

She didn't know if she should say the thing streaming through her mind, but she also didn't want a date like the last one she'd had with Luke. She'd been out with a man from her small business group meeting too, and her date with Landon had been stale too.

Maybe it was her. Maybe she didn't inspire any interesting conversation. If anyone asked her mom or brother, that would surely be the message they'd give.

"I like your family," she said. "At least they text back when you message them."

Luke swung his attention fully toward her as he brought his truck to a stop at the end of her street. "Sterling."

"It's fine." She waved her hand. "But if I were you...." She trailed off. "I don't want to lecture you. I texted my mom and brother on New Year's Day, and it took them both all day to get back to me. Your family? They'd sent me thirty messages before noon, and I don't know. It's nice to have people who care."

She took a breath, her throat so dry.

"I'm sorry, Sterling," he said. "I didn't mean to sound ungrateful."

"I know," she said. "Your family is just so different than mine."

"You have friends in town too." He got the truck moving, and Sterling liked that, because then the spotlight on her wasn't quite so bright.

"Yes," she said. "I have a few good friends here in town." She sighed and decided to put a smile on her face. "I mean, not the ones at Red Carpet, but otherwise."

Luke looked at her again. "Well, I sure like you. I feel like I brought a ton of negativity with me."

"Not true," she said. "I've been so nervous about this for some reason." She tried to laugh, but it sounded forced.

He took her hand again. "I'm nervous too, but it's not going to be like last time."

"Why are we so nervous? It's not like I've never talked to you before."

"Well, I'm nervous because you've seen me naked." He laughed lightly, but Sterling heard the true concern behind his voice. "And I'm trying to work past that."

"I'm not thinking about that when I see my clients," she said. "So you know."

"Good to know," he said. "I didn't mean to sound like a jerk about my family."

"I know," she said. "I didn't mean to put a wet blanket on the date by talking about mine." She took a deep breath. "I haven't been busy enough lately, that's all."

"Is that what you do?" he asked. "Bury the unpleasant things behind busyness?"

"Sometimes," she admitted.

He pulled into Homeplate, and while it probably wasn't as busy as the steakhouse, it still took him a loop to find a spot to park. Maybe that was because of his ridiculously huge truck that couldn't just be parked between two SUVs.

"Do you think there's a law in Wyoming that says all men have to have big trucks?" she asked as he put the vehicle in park.

He looked over at her, surprise in those eyes. It melted away as they crinkled with his smile. "I'm sure there is," he said.

Sterling unbuckled and turned toward him. "Why do you have this behemoth?"

"I need it," he said.

She scoffed. "For you and your seven-year-old daughter?"

He turned toward her too, lifting his arm and draping it over the edge of his seat. "If you'd come on tour with me a couple of summers ago, you'd know why I need it."

Sterling's mind raced as Luke said, "Stay there, sweetheart. I'll come help you down out of this *behemoth*." Before she knew it, he opened her door, and Sterling looked down at him.

Her body seemed to know what to do, and she slid from the truck and into his arms. "You guys drive on tour? For some reason, I thought you had a fancy bus or first-class flights or whatever."

"We have some of that," he said. "But in close quarters—especially down south—we hook up trailers to our trucks, and yeah, we drive. Then I can bring Corrine with me. It's how Otis and Tex and Trace brought everyone with them. Then we—they—always have somewhere to stay."

She slid her hands inside his jacket and around to his back, because she hadn't remembered to put on a coat. "So you're roughing it on tour."

He chuckled and kept her close by wrapping her up. "I would never say that," he whispered, his mouth right at her ear. "Especially in the vicinity of Morris."

"Oh? Why's that?"

"He plans the whole tour," Luke said. "Every detail, to when we ride the bus, and when we drive, and what hotels we stay at. He's meticulous too, and I've learned it's best to compliment him if I want to keep getting what I want."

Sterling grinned up at him. "The first-class ticket?"

He shook his head, his smile slipping into something more serious. "You're beautiful," he whispered. "I'm sorry about your momma and brother, but Sterling, I...." He swallowed, showing that vulnerability that she really liked. "I see you."

Tears pricked her eyes, but she would not make this date memorable by crying. "Thank you, Luke," she whispered, and she tipped up onto her toes and pressed her lips to his again.

He didn't suck in through his nose and immediately kiss her back, and Sterling settled back to her feet, breaking their chaste kiss.

"There you go doin' it again," he said huskily. "Kissin' me."

She grinned at him. "I'm sorry, Luke. I promise I won't do it again until you kiss me first."

"You promise?"

"Cross my heart and hope to die," she said.

He stepped back and closed her door. "Well, my momma always tells me today isn't a good day to die, so let's not be doin' that tonight." He took her hand, and they walked toward the restaurant.

"I suppose I owe you something I haven't told you before."

"Only if you want to," she said. "It's not a requirement."

"I feel like I talk a lot at the appointments," he said.

"Luke, honey, you grumble at your appointments."

He reached for the door, swinging his attention to her too. "I *grumble?*"

She grinned at him and slid her hand up to his collar, gripping it tightly. "Yes, sir, cowboy, you do. They're almost like therapy appointments for you. You get all the stuff you're mad about off your mind, and then you finally relax while I work out the tension in your muscles."

He blinked at her, said, "Huh," and ushered her into the restaurant first.

"Huh?" she repeated back to him. "That's what I get?"

"I think it's probably a pretty accurate description of how I am when I come get a massage," he said. He held up two fingers for the hostess, but she simply stood there and stared at him.

A couple of other parties waited in the area, and Sterling glanced around, wondering how long it would take them to get a table. Didn't seem like too long, but when she looked back at the hostess again, she still stared at Luke like one look at him had turned her to stone.

"How long for two?" Sterling asked, and the woman blinked.

"You're Luke Young."

He ducked his head, and Sterling suppressed her internal smile. She hadn't been out with him when he'd been recognized before, but he had said he had to maintain some sort of image around town. No, it was online. His social media. He had a manager and everything.

"Are you two goin' out?" she asked, looking at Sterling and then back to Luke.

"Walter," another woman called, and Sterling looked over to her. Their eyes met, and Sterling must've been able to communicate telepathically, because the woman moved to the hostess station.

"Andrea," she said, and the younger woman there startled. "I'm taking the Walter party. Have you got these two checked in?"

"Yes," she said clearing her throat. She didn't ask for a name, scratched something on her list, and said, "It's only about a five-minute wait."

"Thank you," Luke said as he nudged Sterling to the left. He sank onto a black leather bench and sighed.

"You froze," she said, joining him. "You just duck your head and what? She'll stop asking questions?"

"It usually works." He focused on her. "Or I glare them into silence, but I'm trying to do less of that these days."

Sterling grinned at him. "She asked us if we were dating."

"I heard her." His eyes dropped to her lips, rebounding quickly. "We're out together. She's probably taking a picture." He put his hand on her knee, which sent a blitz of heat down to her ankle. "Sterling, there might be some...public things to our private life."

"Because you're a country music star."

"It's a small circle," he said. "But yeah. Sometimes it feels very big." He looked down at his hand on her leg and yanked it back. "I guess I'm wondering if you're going to be okay with that."

He lifted his eyes back to hers, and Sterling had dreamed about gazing into this man's face for a good long time. She wanted to kiss him again, but she would not break her promise, and she didn't think Luke would kiss her in such a public place.

"Luke," a woman called, and the spell between them broke. He stood, and Sterling joined him, only glancing at the hostess as she went by. She nodded slightly at her, as if saying, *Yes, we're together. We're dating.*

And when they got to the table, Sterling didn't immediately reach for her menu. She looked at Luke and said, "I think I'll be okay with your public persona from time to time."

Luke grinned at her and nodded. "All right, Sterling. It shouldn't be too terribly often. I mean, it'll be a couple of years until we have to tour again."

"Really? That long?"

"We haven't even started recording yet," he said. "And we'll only go in the summer, so yeah. Not this year. Maybe next."

"Will you ask me to be your massage therapist for the tour?" she teased.

Luke dropped his head again, and oh, Sterling realized it for what it was now. A stall tactic. A way for him to hide.

A way for him to stay silent.

A couple of questions ran through her mind. *Are you going to allow him to do that?* And *what does he want to hide?*

8

"Do you think that's going to work on me?" Sterling asked, and Luke looked up.

"I don't want to say what I'm thinking."

"Why not?" She glanced up as a waiter put a glass of water in front of her. Luke reached for his straw the moment it hit the table.

"Hey, Lucas," the woman said, and he wanted to sink into the floor and somehow find an underground tunnel that led him home. Why did he have to run into so many people he knew tonight, of all nights?

He looked up, the presence of their waitress at the end of the table putting a damper on his date. Of course, maybe Julie Thermin had just rescued him. A smile touched his mouth. "Hey, Julie." He looked over to Sterling. "Julie has a son in Corrine's class. We did the Thanksgiving party together."

"This cowboy knows how to plan a good party." She pointed her pen at him, but her eyes stayed on Sterling, her smile perfectly in place. "You make him celebrate every holiday with you, no matter how small."

Luke chuckled and shook his head. "That's not true. I brought some cookies and a game I printed off the Internet." He looked back to the waitress. "How's Corbin?" Luke asked. "On the road again?"

"He's home this week," Julie said, clicking her pen into action. "Driving me crazy, of course, doing everything *except* the honey-do list I have for him." She smiled at Luke and then Sterling. "Do you guys know what you want?"

"I'd love some of the pork dumplings," Sterling said.

"Fried or steamed?" Julie asked.

"Fried," she said. "And do you guys still have that peach lemonade?"

"Sure thing." Julie wrote as she looked at Luke. "For you, cowboy?"

"Mini sliders," he said. "Diet Dr. Pepper. Two of 'em, please."

"One with ice and one without?"

"You got it," he said, grinning at her.

Julie smiled, tapped her pen against the table, and left. Luke had no choice but to look across the table to Sterling, but he told himself he surely wasn't sitting at zero with her. She'd told Bryce the two of them were dating. She'd kissed him at the New Year's Eve party, and she'd texted with all the other wives.

He cleared his throat. "I saw your text to Abby and the others," he said.

Sterling stared at him, her pretty eyes widening even as they blinked. "You did?"

"It came in while we were all at Morris's," he said, smiling. He reached across the table and gathered both of her hands into his. "You should know that the wives...they're not great at keeping secrets. Abby actually held her phone straight up and then ran over to a couple of the others."

Sterling's features hardened. "Good to know."

"I liked what you said," he said. "You don't need to worry about that."

She slipped one of her hands away and reached up to tuck her hair behind her ear. "What did you like?"

"That you're not going to pull your phone out the moment I drop you off and tell them everything."

Sterling's shoulders softened then, and she tucked her hand under his again. "I wouldn't do that, Luke. I know you at least a little bit."

"I appreciate it." He stuck his straw in his water and pulled it closer.

"You get two drinks? You didn't do that at lunch."

"Well, this is dinner." He grinned at her, but he could tell she wanted more information than that. "I order two drinks, one without ice, because then I don't run out before the waitress realizes I need a refill." He indicated the restaurant beyond their table. "Julie's great, so she'll probably keep my drink full all night. That's my number one thing when I go out."

"Keeping your drink full?"

"Yes," he said.

Sterling grinned at him, ducking her own head. "You're a man of many sides, Luke."

"I'm going to take that as a compliment."

"Good," she said. "Because it is."

She had more grit than Luke had realized, and his heart hurt that her family didn't value her. He couldn't imagine why they didn't, and he really wanted her to know how amazing and fantastic and noticeable she was.

"I can't say if I'm going to ask you to come on a tour in a year and a half," he said, cursing his tongue even as he congratulated himself for starting the sentence. He honestly had no idea if he was about to crash and burn or earn major points.

"Because we might not be together then."

Sterling pulled in a breath, but Luke wasn't done yet.

"Or we might be married, and I won't have to ask. You'll just come, because I want to have that truck out in the parking lot so I can tow my trailer and bring my family on tour with me, just like my brothers do."

He reached for his water and bypassed the straw so he could gulp the icy liquid in greater volume.

Sterling didn't say anything before he set his almost-empty glass down and found the bravery needed to look at her. She smiled, her face so beautiful with that gesture. "I suppose that's how relationships go," she said. "You either date until you break-up, or you date until you get married."

"Yeah," Luke said, suddenly wanting to accelerate things between him and Sterling, though he'd said he needed to go slow.

Pull on the reins, cowboy, he told himself. He had a lot going on in his life—from his work with the band, to his daughter, and the re-introduction of his ex-wife into both of their lives—and he couldn't dedicate every waking minute to Sterling, even if he wanted to.

Therefore, he'd have to go slow, at least for a little while.

"You're the marrying type, Luke?" she asked as Julie returned with their drinks.

"I've been married before," he said, not bothering to stall the conversation with her there. He pulled his double glasses of Diet Dr. Pepper closer and picked up the two straws that Julie put down just for him.

"You two are talking about marriage already?" She grinned at him. "Wow, Luke, I didn't realize you'd started dating someone."

She looked over to Sterling. "How long has this been going on? He was the grumpiest I've ever seen him a month ago."

"This is our first date, Julie," he growled. "And you're ruining it."

"You said the word 'married'," she teased. "Not me." She held up her order pad. "Should I come back?"

"No," he said. "I want the cheeseburger, double, but not that fake cheese. I hate that stuff."

Julie laughed. "I know you do. Pepper-jack, then?"

"Do I look like I like spicy cheese?" He shook his head. "No. I want the muenster I see on the Wisconsin burger, and I want some of those onion straws, and bacon." He glanced over to Sterling to see what she thought of his complicated order. "But not if the bacon is pepper bacon. Is it?"

"No, sugar, we have regular bacon." Her pen scratched and scratched, but she still looked up at him. "Tots, fries?"

Luke peered at the menu. "Do you have sweet potato fries?"

"They're waffle," Julie said.

"Uh, no," he said decisively. "Bring me some tots, okay? Can you mix up some ketchup and mayo for me? Or bring me some of each and I'll do it myself."

"Ketchup and mayo." She grinned like a cartoon character and turned to Sterling. "Ready for you, honey."

"I don't even know how to follow that," Sterling said.

Luke couldn't stop his smile, though she was making fun of him. His brothers ribbed him about his pickiness with ordering too, but they irritated him. Sterling didn't.

"I'd like the chicken bacon sandwich, please," she said.

"Crispy or grilled"''

"Crispy." Sterling folded up her menu and handed it back to Julie. "I'll take tots too."

"You got it." She collected Luke's menu from the table and tapped his shoulder with both of them. "Did you see how she just ordered something from the menu? I'm shocked." With that, she walked away, leaving Luke with his embarrassment and Sterling.

"That was quite the thing," she said.

"I like my food a specific way," he said.

"Do you always order like that?"

"About." He folded his arms in front of him on the table, then reached for his drink. "They can make it, you know. Sometimes they just make you pay extra."

"I suppose you tell them that's fine; you're independently wealthy."

He choked on his Dr. Pepper, some of the liquid coming back out of his mouth. He quickly covered it with his napkin. "What?"

She laughed. "You have to tell them something when they say, 'oh, that's two dollars more.'" Her eyes sparkled like those sapphires. "What do you say?"

"I just tell them it's fine," he grumbled, feeling himself sink into the grumpy side of himself. It was where he was most comfortable, he could admit. But he didn't want to exist here for long.

"When I do want to deviate from the menu, I tell them I'm independently wealthy, so any upcharge is fine." Sterling shook her hair over her shoulders, and he wanted to fist his fingers in it right now. She'd braided it back on the sides to keep it out of her face, but plenty of curls spilled over her shoulders, and there was plenty for him to grab as he kissed her.

She grinned at him, pure joy shining in her face. "I'm not independently wealthy, in case you were wondering. I want to expand my studio, but I can't afford it." Some of her shine faded, and she ducked her head. "I've been putting together a proposal to take to investors, and I'm going to do some meditation classes at the community center to gauge interest."

Some of the tension inside Luke went loose. "That's great, Sterling," he said. "I'm not much for meditation, but my therapist is always having me do some breathing exercises."

Her eyebrows went up. "Your therapist?"

"Yeah," he said, realizing tonight was the night where they were laying it all out. "I see a counselor to help me with my—" He cleared his throat. "Issues. Mostly anger issues. Betrayal, and lately, these massive feelings of being left out."

Sterling didn't congratulate him for taking care of his emotional health. She didn't put on a face of pity. Luke didn't want either of those anyway.

Instead, she got up and came to his side of the booth, sliding in right beside him. He couldn't look away from her, and they faced one another, only inches between them. If she kissed him again, he was going to crawl home in humiliation.

She ran her hand down the side of his face, creating a private pocket between the two of them. "You're a beautiful man, Luke."

He didn't know what that meant, but he had been working so hard over the past four years to be the man he was today. The man sitting there with her, even if their road to this point had been one of the most dangerous he'd ever traversed.

"Mini sliders," Julie practically yelled. "Pork dumplings, fried. And all the condiments I know you'll want later."

Both Luke and Sterling looked up at Julie as she slid the dumplings in front of Sterling, right on the same side of the booth as Luke. "I'll leave you to it," she said. "But I'd hate to have to get out the fire extinguisher tonight. Do not tempt me, Luke Young."

"No, ma'am," he murmured, and Sterling got to her feet and resumed her position across the table from him.

"I don't trust her," she said as she pulled her appetizer plate over to her. "I like her, but I don't trust her."

"Wise and beautiful," he said, grinning at her. The miracle was that she smiled back, and Luke basked in such a simple gesture, wondering if the Lord had finally given him the woman he'd been searching for his whole life.

LUKE SAW THE LIGHT CHANGE ACROSS THE WALL TO HIS LEFT, indicating that someone had entered the recording studio that stood behind his brother's farmhouse. He'd come out here today, not expecting a crowd, and he'd left Corrine inside with Abby, Tex, and Melissa. Bryce had gone back to Louisville for the time being, and Luke simply wanted to practice his drumming without worrying about disrupting the quiet neighborhood where his little house sat.

He finished the song, one of the very first ones Country Quad had toured with, years ago, and then looked toward the door. Trace stood there, his son Harry at his side. His brother lifted his eyebrows and his hand, clearly asking if they could come in. If Luke was recording or not.

Luke took off his headset, wondering what he'd missed while he'd allowed himself to disappear out here. He gestured for Trace and Harry to come in, and they did.

"Howdy, Uncle Luke." Harry went straight over to his guitar and picked it up. The boy probably had another one at home, as he could play circles around almost anyone. Maybe not his father, but otherwise? Harry was a phenomenal guitarist.

"Hey, guys." Luke stood and pocketed his drumsticks in his back pocket. "What's goin' on? Did I miss calls and texts?" He'd left his phone a layer away from him, out in the lobby of the recording studio.

"No," Trace said, coming straight toward him. He drew Luke into a hug. "Ev's on a baking kick, and she wanted to bring some pie out to Abby." He pulled back and smiled—well as much as Trace did. He was the sober older brother, who stood back and listened before jumping into the fray the way some of the other Youngs did.

Luke appreciated his steadiness, the way he truly thought through things before he reacted.

Trace flicked a look over to his son. "Harry's got it in his head that he's going to submit a demo during the open call at Cadence." His eyes narrowed as he looked at his son while Harry refused to look back.

Luke let himself cast a look at Harry too. "He's almost seventeen, Trace. I was barely older than that when I joined you guys in the band."

Trace frowned, the action taking over his whole face. "Not what I want to hear, Luke."

He turned his back on Harry, though this place was built specifically to have excellent acoustics. "Why don't you want him to go into country music?"

"It's not the life for everyone," Trace muttered. "And he wants to be a solo artist. That's lonely, Luke. We had each other." He pinned him with one of his own dark looks, and Luke was just glad he wasn't the only one who possessed them. "You know that's the only reason Momma let you come with us, right? Because Tex was right there, fourteen years older. We both promised her up one side and down the other that we wouldn't let anything bad happen to you."

He looked over to his son. "He won't have that."

79

"Of course he will," Luke said. "He'll have you. Us. We're not done yet."

"I've told him to let me send a demo to King Country." His shoulders drooped, and his head dropped. "He doesn't want me to help him get in."

"If I'm good enough," Harry said. "I'll get in myself."

"You can at least send a demo to King Country too," Luke said. "They have way better terms than Cadence." He tried to exchange a glance with Trace, but his brother still faced the ground. Oh, so he was going to let Luke do this lecture.

Honestly, it might land better if he did.

Harry's fingers moved across the strings already, almost unconsciously. "They don't have an open call."

"No," Luke said. "But you can still send in a demo. It goes in their slush pile." He gestured to the boy's father. "That's how Country Quad got in. Cold slush."

"And videos on the Internet, I heard," Harry said, smiling.

"Yeah." And that had been Luke's idea, thank you very much. He shelved the pride, because it didn't do any good. They had been petitioning King Country to listen to their music for a few years before it happened. Everyone in Nashville got demo tracks, and in the meantime, while they'd played small town celebrations across the country, Luke had recorded those concerts and put them online.

That gave the record labels more to see and hear when they listened to the demo and liked it.

"You'll be on the next album," Luke said easily, though Trace growled, "Luke."

He ignored his brother. "Come on, brother. He's good, and I know you and Otis wrote that guitar duet for you and Harry. Otis can't play like that."

"Uncle Otis is amazing," Harry said.

Luke

"But he's not you," Luke said. "So...you want me to record for you this afternoon?" He did meet Trace's eye this time, and they both nodded at one another. Then they left Harry in the studio while they stepped out, and Trace sank into the rolling chair in front of the soundboard.

A few minutes later, Harry was tuned and ready, recording. Trace leaned back in the chair, and Luke could only stare at his nephew.

"How was your date with Sterling?"

"Amazing," Luke whispered.

"Yeah?" Trace chuckled. "You ask her out again?"

"Sure did." He couldn't look away from Harry's flawless fingers, and then he started singing too. Incredible. Simply incredible. "We're goin' out tomorrow, I think."

"Wow, that's soon," Trace said. "You kiss her?"

"Yeah, on New Year's Eve."

"Whoa," Trace said, and that made Luke blink. He looked over to his brother, who blinked at him. Only then did Luke realize what all he'd said.

"Not a word," he said, sliding back into his growl. "You sly fox. Asking me questions after I'm distracted with *your* son, who *I* helped today."

Trace only laughed, but Luke knew he wouldn't say anything to anyone. He might continue to tease Luke, but he wouldn't betray his confidence. And for Luke, loyalty was one of the most important qualities a person could have.

"So, tomorrow," Trace said. "What does the Date Master have planned?"

Luke rolled his eyes. "I'm not the Date Master."

"So you don't have anything planned."

"I didn't say that."

Trace only laughed again, but Luke wouldn't apologize for

81

being prepared when he went out with a woman. Having some control over the whole process was what allowed him to even start dating again in the first place.

"How was that?" Harry asked through the mic, and both Trace and Luke looked back at him.

Luke leaned forward and hit the button before Trace could. "Harry, you're a star." He grinned at his nephew, who beamed back at him. Now, he just needed to be as flawless on his date with Sterling tomorrow as his nephew had just been on this demo.

9

Sterling bustled around her house on Monday, organizing the drinks and snacks for that day's clients. She had four today, which was a pretty good day for her. If she could book five or six, she would, and that put her at full-time work, depending on the massage they'd booked. She needed time for lunch, for cleaning and passing between clients, and for her sanity.

She didn't look ahead to the next day unless she was trying to book someone, so she hadn't known Luke had an appointment that afternoon, a mere two hours before their date, until that morning.

When she'd texted him, he'd said, *Yeah, I thought I'd just get dressed and we'd go. No good? I can wait until you're ready after. Leave and come back to pick you up. Whatever you tell me.*

You're not working out in the recording studio in the afternoon? she'd asked. He almost always booked his massages in the middle of the day, when his daughter would be at school. She'd known him for long enough—and she'd started caring for all of his sisters-in-law, as well as Trace, his brother, in the past eight or nine

83

months—that she knew the schedule the band stuck to for rehearsing.

Primarily in the afternoons, after the kids got out of school. They all convened at the white barn Sterling had actually never seen, because she had no reason to drive out to the northeast side of town to visit Abby and Tex's farmhouse. They rehearsed starting about three and going until they were done. Luke himself had said there was no given end-time, unless one of them needed to set one.

He said he never did, because it was just him and Corrine, but his life had gotten drastically more complicated since his ex-wife had started trying to be more present in their daughter's life.

She finished lining up the drinks she knew her clients would want and closed the fridge. Only Gigi would want a snack after her massage, and she'd only ever taken an apple from Sterling, despite her offering nuts, beef jerky, or granola bars. So she washed and shined the green Granny Smith apple and placed it on the edge of the table, because Gigi was her first client of the day.

The room sat ready and waiting, as Sterling stripped the table and remade it, cleaned up, and got ready for her next client immediately following every massage. Behind her, the windows rattled in the wind, but in front of her, the doorbell chimed.

Ignoring the winter weather that Luke had said was supposed to arrive today, she went to answer the door. From now on, her clients would simply walk in and take a seat on the loveseat immediately beside the door. She'd put up hooks for their jackets and coats, and she had even invested in a cubby system, which she'd then reworked with Hilde and Ev, for their shoes.

"Good morning," she said to Gigi, a rail-thin woman who came every other week for a full-body massage.

"I'm still deciding if there's something good about it," Gigi said, stepping up and into the house. She detoured over to the couch as she shrugged out of her coat. "It's freezing this morning."

"Supposed to snow later," she said, parroting Luke. All at once, she realized the storm might prevent her from going out with the cowboy for a second time. Their date on Friday—though he'd walked her to the door and *hugged* her—had been amazing. Even the hugging, she supposed, though she wasn't sure why Luke hadn't kissed her. He claimed to want to be the one to initiate that physical contact the next time it happened, but she'd already broken the barrier between them.

"Hopefully I'm home by then," Gigi said, her bright blue eyes shining as she finished hanging her coat and faced Sterling. "With a pot of my mother's lentil soup boiling away."

Sterling laughed lightly with her client and friend. "You love lentil soup."

"So do you," Gigi said, her voice knowing. "I'll bring you some next time."

"Perfect." Sterling led the way out of the tiny formal living room. Before she'd quit at Red Carpet, the full-service spa where she'd worked before branching out on her own, she hadn't realized the usefulness of the ten-by-ten room off the front door. She did now.

In front of her, the kitchen spread to the right, the dining room table sat straight in front of her, and her official living room—where she watched TV and sat to crochet sometimes—continued to the left.

Across from the couch sat a bedroom, and Sterling had put her massage studio in there. She indicated it, and Gigi grinned at her as she rounded the corner. "Oh," she said, spinning back to Sterling. "Did my friend Vicky call you? She was asking about a massage, and I said you're the best."

"Vicky...Turnbow?" Sterling guessed, the last name in her head by a sheer miracle. "Yeah, I talked to her late last week."

"She hated the massage at Red Carpet," Gigi said with a glow in her eyes. "I told her they're not good, and she wanted to know where I came."

"Well, thank you," Sterling said as modestly as she could. "I appreciate it. You'll get twenty percent off your massage today for the referral."

"Nope," Gigi said already stepping out of her shoes. "I don't need that." She looked up again, meeting Sterling's eyes. "As long as I can get in when I need to, I'm happy to refer you."

"There's always room for you, Gigi." Sterling reached for the doorknob and started to pull the door closed. "Undress to your comfort level, and lie face-down to start."

She'd often thought she should record those directions, because she said them so often. Gigi would undress all the way, and Sterling went over to her kitchen sink to warm up her hands. She gazed out the window and into her backyard, her thoughts literally on nothing.

Since her days were spent mostly in silence—she only had a couple of chatty clients, and neither of them had appointments today—she had plenty of time to think. She actually liked it when she found a few moments of pure nothingness, and she pulled her hands out of the water when she realized she'd probably been standing there for too long.

She took a fresh tea towel, this one with an embroidered Sebright chicken on it, with her toward the bedroom. Along the way, Sterling dried her hands, and then she hung the towel on the hook outside the door. She used a lot of oils in massage work, and she'd use that towel all day today, taking it with her from the studio and back to the sink.

Outside the door, she paused and then knocked. "I'm ready," came from inside, and Sterling committed to entering the room.

"Anything I need to know today?" she asked Gigi, who was in position and ready.

"No," she said, her voice already growing quieter. "I just want to relax."

"I can help you do that." Sterling took a moment to lower the lights. She'd lit her scented candles already, and she checked her clipboard, which hung beside the door. "You've got aromatherapy today," she murmured, keeping her own voice and energy low. "Did you want citrus, eucalyptus, or lavender?"

"Eucalyptus," Gigi said.

Sterling collected the right oil bottle, adjusted the volume on her Bluetooth speaker, and made sure her phone had the playlist up that would run for the full ninety minutes. She'd plugged it in, and other than the music, everything else had been silenced.

She was ready.

After administering the oils, she began the massage in her usual pattern. She could work across someone's body without much thought at all, taking her cues from her own rhythm, the strength or weakness in her hands, and the music.

It was now that she let her mind wander, and of course, it had been stuck on Luke for a while now. She went right back to him, but she had so much more than mere fantasy now. She knew what his fingers between hers felt like, and as she watched her hands perform their work, she marveled that a man like him even wanted to hold her hand.

Sterling struggled against her self-depreciative thoughts, because there were so many things that she knew she was good at. She was strong and self-assured in other ways. But men and dating? She'd had so little experience with them in the past decade that she'd figured there had to be something seriously wrong with *her*.

She didn't have a mother or a sister harping on her to get married or lose weight. She had great friends in town, but they all seemed like her. None of them ran marathons or never seemed to eat. Well, besides Everly, who did run her own dance studio and had a perfect little body.

They ate out. They sometimes slept late. They struggled to run their own businesses and keep up with each other, their family, and their bills. She didn't feel like anyone had anything more together than she did, but in the past couple of years, as Ev and Hilde had found their forever cowboys and gotten married, Sterling could admit that she'd fallen further down the rabbit hole of thinking there must be something wrong with her.

So to have the attention of a good man like Luke Young...Sterling almost didn't know what to do with it. *He's so intense too*, she thought, moving from Gigi's left side to her right. She continued the long strokes down her back, seeing Luke in her mind's eye.

He wore serious looks when having serious discussions. He could paint the world with joy when he laughed or truly smiled. Everything he did, he did with an intensity that Sterling had never seen or experienced before, and she wondered if it wore him to the bone.

She thought about Luke all day long, until finally, the cowboy ducked into her house as he called, "It's me, Sterling."

She finished up in the bathroom and went down the hall to greet him. She found him standing on the small patch of tile just inside her door, shaking snowflakes from his cowboy hat. "It started snowing." She turned to look out the back window, where it sure seemed like it had started with a vengeance.

"That it did," he said. "About five minutes ago." He hung up his hat and then his leather jacket, and when he turned to look at her, the world stopped spinning. Sterling got lightheaded, though she'd eaten lunch before her last client.

There was that Luke-intensity, and Sterling managed to smile as he drew closer. "I'm thinking about calling an audible," he said, stopping when he got within arm's length of her.

"Yeah?"

"I'm thinking we might need to cancel tonight, or we should at least stay here."

Sterling's eyebrows went up at the same time her stomach dropped down. "Stay here?" She shook her head, a measure of playfulness creeping into her. "I don't cook, Luke."

"I can," he said, quickly following it with, "Small stuff. Easy stuff." He put his hand on her elbow, and Sterling realized she still held the hand towel from the bathroom. "I'll check the weather after my massage, okay?"

She nodded and indicated the room. "It's ready for you."

He brushed his lips along her cheek as he went by, said nothing more, and went into the studio. He closed the door behind him before she could give the spiel about undressing to his comfort level, and she stood there frozen for a moment.

He'd expressed that he didn't know how to have a relationship with her. Didn't know how to deal with the fact that she saw a lot of his body during his massages, and she wondered how he'd been dealing with that.

Since she'd gone to his brother's house to yell at him, Luke had been coming every month. In the beginning, he'd done either upper body or lower body treatments—anything that wouldn't require him to undress fully. But in the past few months, he'd gone back to the full body massages that he loved and that earned her the most money.

"Something must've changed," she mused as she went to heat up her hands.

She knocked; he said, "Yep," the way he usually did; Sterling entered the room. With everything set, she started on his lower left side, the same way she had twice already today with other clients.

"Tell me if the pressure needs to be adjusted," she murmured.

"It's great," he said.

Sterling didn't usually talk a ton during his massages. Luke would, if he had something on his mind, and she almost always let her clients set the stage for conversation. Today, though, she'd been thinking about him so much, she almost felt like she'd been talking to him all day.

"Luke," she said. "Do you mind if I ask you a question?" His lats seemed tight today, and he always always always had knots in his shoulders. Those came from the drumming, she knew, and the man worked out almost to bodybuilder levels.

"Go ahead," he said, and he sounded relaxed. He didn't harbor a ton of tension in his body right now, and Sterling moved her hands down his left arm to his hand. He even sighed as she tried to find the words to ask him what had been on her mind.

"Where's Corrine today?" she asked. She'd asked such a thing before, when the girl wouldn't be in school.

"Mav's got her," he said. "They're already planning the next couple of months' worth of birthday parties, and Corrine loves that stuff."

"Party planning, huh? She's eight."

"She's actually only seven," he said. "But yeah. She loves it, and Dani's great to let her help. I think Georgia was going to be over there this afternoon too." He sounded like he might be carrying a smile on his face. "Corrine loves to boss around the younger kids, so she'll have a blast."

"That's great," Sterling murmured. "Do you...I mean...." She sighed, not sure how to ask. Her voice sounded a little frustrated too, and she didn't want that. "I'm wondering when you've introduced her to your girlfriends in the past."

To her knowledge, he'd been out with two women in the past couple of years, and she'd never dated a single dad before.

"I didn't," he said.

"You didn't introduce her to them?"

Tension filled his bicep, strained through his shoulder. "No."

"Okay, cowboy," she teased, hoping to get him to settle down. "You don't have to get all uptight about it."

"Did I?"

"Yes," she said. "You're twice as tight as you were a minute ago. Remember, your only job here is to melt into the table."

10

"Melt into the table, right," Luke muttered, almost hoping it wasn't loud enough for Sterling to hear. He had no idea where in the room she stood, but she currently ran her hand or arm or elbow up his bicep, so she was pretty close.

He couldn't melt into the table. Not with her question branded in his mind. He supposed it hadn't even been a question, but a suggestion. "Do you want to meet Corrine?"

"I don't know," she said. "Eventually."

"What does that mean?" Why had she asked then?

She sighed, and he felt like she was running a golf ball along his arm—and it didn't feel great. She pulled her hands back, and Luke felt the loss of them instantly. "I've never dated someone with kids," she said.

Luke softened then. She'd admitted over the weekend that she hadn't dated much, and maybe she just wanted to know how this would go. The problem was, Luke didn't know how it would go. He'd been terrible at picking the women he dated, and even worse

93

at breaking up with them. He'd never introduced Corrine to Tea or Hillary, because neither relationship had made it far enough to do that.

"This'll be new ground for both of us," he said. "I've never introduced her to someone I'm dating, because it never got to that point."

"What point is that?" She slicked her hands over his shoulder, really pushing into the tight spot that always seemed to hurt. She'd stay there for a while, he knew, and he tried to do what she'd said: Melt into the table.

"I honestly have no idea." He took a long breath in, held it for a moment, and then exhaled it out slowly, using the pressure of her hands to help him. "I suppose it'll happen when we're both ready."

"But you don't know when you'll be ready."

"No," he murmured. "Are you ready to meet her as my girlfriend? I mean, she'll know you already, of course." He took Corrine to almost everything around town. Surely she'd seen Sterling at the New Year's Eve party too, and she'd been at the Memorial Day Faire in Hilde's furniture store parking lot last year too.

Corrine would recognize her at least, and Luke started thinking about when he would introduce his daughter to a woman. Gabe had had strict rules for that—which he'd broken almost immediately with Hilde.

Jem hadn't seemed to have anything holding him back from introducing Sunny into his children's lives, and Luke hadn't kept track of anyone else. Maybe he should ask his brothers about this, find out what was normal or usual, and then make a plan.

Luke did like having a plan, and satisfied that he could make one with this, he relaxed even further. Sterling worked her magic, and before he knew it, she said, "That's it, Luke," in a whisper.

He exhaled again, and said, "Sterling, you're a goddess."

She giggled lightly. "I'll wait for you outside." He held very still, as he was still uncovered from the waist up, and waited for the door to snick closed again. Then he pushed the washcloth off his eyes and stretched his hands as far above his head as they would go.

He got to his feet and re-dressed before checking his phone. The weather app he'd downloaded when he'd first moved back to Coral Canyon sat on his home screen, and he tapped it.

A frown settled between his eyes and way down in his soul. "Stupid snow," he grumbled. He pulled on his cowboy boots and went to join Sterling. She stood at the end of the couch, her gaze out the wall of windows at the back of her house.

When she heard him, she turned and offered him the bottle of water she usually did. "Here you go. How do you feel?"

"So good." He uncapped the water. "But also terrible, because I don't think it's going to stop snowing." He should leave now, before full darkness fell. Before he couldn't get out to Mav's to collect Corrine. Before he might be snowed in here.

At the same time, his mind whispered at him that Mav could keep Corrine overnight just fine. He'd done it before, and he had to get his kids to school in the morning just like Luke did. It would be easy. No big deal.

"What do you want to do?" Sterling asked. She turned to face the still-falling snow again, and she moved over to the sliding glass door. The one and only time Luke had stood in that spot, he'd kept his back to the outdoors. He'd faced Sterling and he'd admitted that he wanted them to be more than what they were.

He swallowed, because that confession had definitely cost him a lot and also brought him to this point in his life. "I want to stay here with you," he said decisively. "But I'm not sure it's the smartest move."

With slow, calculated steps, he went between the back of the couch and the dining table to join her at the door. He slipped his arm around her easily, and Sterling sighed as she sank into his side. "Yeah," she said quietly. "You should probably go home before it gets too bad."

The snow had started to stick to the surfaces outside. To everything, and it had been snowing for long enough and hard enough that it had already accumulated. "Looks bad already," he said, though neither of them moved.

"I read online that it could dump eight inches overnight," she said, finally turning to look at him. His first instinct was to bend his head down six inches and kiss her. He hadn't made the move on Friday night, and something held him back today too.

What, he wasn't sure. Maybe the fact that he truly wanted to go slowly with her, and kissing when they only had one date between them—one good date—felt fast. So he smiled and he tucked her hair over her shoulder.

"I sure like seeing you, Sterling," he said. "I'll never understand long-distance relationships, which are only texts and videos and calls."

"You are a very in-person type of person," she said, returning her attention outside.

He chuckled and watched the snow fall for a few seconds. "I don't know what that means, but I do like being in-person with someone. It feels...authentic."

"Mm." Sterling moved out of his arms. "We could have coffee or hot chocolate before you go?" She tossed him a questioning look before she turned and started along her peninsula. "Plus, authenticity is very important to you."

"Mm," he echoed her. She wasn't wrong, but he didn't want to get into heavy topics again today. His body felt mushy and soft from the massage, and he threw back a few swallows of the ice cold water to center himself.

He told himself, *You have plenty of time to tell her about the paternity issue and why you don't trust women.*

As he watched her set a kettle of water to boil, he wondered if he trusted her. Surely he couldn't lump Sterling into the group of "all women," could he? He knew her, and she wasn't anything like Mandi.

"You're not like my ex-wife at all," he said, not quite sure why he'd let the thought out of his mouth uncensored.

Sterling met his eyes, plenty of surprise in hers. "Okay," she said.

He took a seat at her bar, hoping that would get some of the tension in the air to dissipate. She kept working in the kitchen, getting out a couple of boxes of tea, then instant coffee, but it sure seemed like she was doing anything she could to not look at him.

Great. He'd introduced something idiotic by mouthing off.

"You've met Corrine, right?" he said.

"I've been in the same room as her before, yes."

"You know what she looks like."

Sterling smiled at him then, and she paused in her busy-work of getting everything out. "All dark, from head to toe." She nodded to him. "Like her daddy."

He felt utterly exposed without his cowboy hat on, but he ducked his head before he realized it wouldn't protect him.

"Oh, that's not working for you without the hat." She set a tin down on the counter. "I have shortbread cookies." She popped off the lid, and Luke looked at the half-full container of cookies.

"You love shortbread."

"Who doesn't?" She plucked a round treat out of the tin. Luke reached over and pulled it a little closer to him, then pulled out a diamond-shaped one.

The crunchy cookie snapped against his teeth, but he didn't mind the flavor. "My grandmother liked shortbread."

"Are you calling me old?" Sterling turned back to the fridge and got out a container of cream. "This is all I have. I don't think you like hazelnut."

He shook his head. "I'm a cream purist."

She laughed, though he hadn't been trying to be funny. He would have to try not to be funny again, just to get her to make that sound. "What else are you a purist on?"

"Uh, let's see." Luke wasn't sure, though he did have some pretty intense food requirements. "My brothers would probably say steak."

"I can just see you ordering your steak a particular way," she said.

"I only want it seasoned with salt and pepper," he said. "The steak should stand on its own."

"Of course," she said.

"No rubs or sauces needed."

"So you don't eat your steak with sauce? That's a little surprising."

"I do," he said. "But I don't want to *have* to, you know?"

Sterling's eyes shone at him, and oh, Luke liked that. "What about you?" he asked so he wouldn't clear his throat. "You have to be able to make something to eat."

"Sure, I can," she said. "Little things. Easy stuff, like you said. Not anything I'd like to feed my boyfriend when he comes over." Her smile slid right onto the ground, and she was the one grinding her voice through her throat. "Not that you're my boyfriend."

"I'm not?" Luke's lips quirked up before he could stop them. "Did you or did you not tell Bryce that we were dating?"

"I mean, I did, but I explained why."

Luke let himself smile fully. "What does it take to become your boyfriend?"

The teakettle sang, and Sterling got busy in the kitchen again, pulling down mugs and setting out spoons. He gave her the distraction, but she'd have to come sit beside him sooner or later.

When she finally did, she started rotating her wrists and stretching out her hands. He took one and rubbed his thumb up the side of her pinky. "Did you have a lot of clients today?"

"Just four," she whispered.

"How many tomorrow?"

"Five."

Luke nodded, his mind blitzing to the billion dollars he had in the bank. If his hands hurt from his job, he wouldn't have to work the next day. Or the next. At the same time, he'd definitely played more than one concert in pain, so that wasn't entirely true.

The silence in her house sure was nice, and Luke sighed mentally into it. He loved his daughter, and he'd do anything for her, but there was never this level of silence at his house. If Corrine wasn't asking him questions, doing homework, or coloring, she had something playing on a tablet or the TV. Sometimes Luke drove around town in silence, just to hear it. Or rather, to hear nothing.

"I think it would take a not-fake kiss," Sterling said, injecting her voice into the stillness of the house.

"You think that kiss on New Year's Eve was fake?"

"I mean, you said it before I lunged at you. That we're not really together, but—"

Luke honestly did not remember saying that, but he wasn't going to argue about it. "I remember asking you out before then."

She nodded and then leaned her head against his bicep. "I like having you here, Luke. You fill my house with a good energy."

A smile came first to his soul, and he let it warm him from the inside out. "No one's ever told me I have good energy before," he murmured. He kept rubbing her hand, hoping to ease some of the ache from it.

"You spend all your time taking care of others," he said. "Who takes care of you?"

Sterling said nothing, and he supposed that could be counted as an answer.

"Who would you go to for a massage?" he asked.

"You," she murmured. "You're doing a great job there, cowboy."

Another smile to tuck away into his pocket.

Sterling straightened and gently pulled her hand out of his. She poured hot water into a mug and set it in front of him, then repeated it for herself. "I take care of me, I suppose," she said. "I have been for a long time, at least."

He nodded. "Do you mind me askin' how old you are, Sterling? I think you're close to my age, but...."

"Thirty-four," she said. "You're thirty-one, so not too different. Not like Gabe and Hilde."

"No," he said. "Pick me a tea, sweetheart. I don't usually drink this stuff, so I'm not sure what to choose."

She looked at the three choices she'd put in front of him, then straight at him. He held her gaze as his smile grew. And then he started to laugh. "What? Do I have something that'll tell you what tea I'll like written on my face?"

A giggle escaped her mouth too. "No," she said. "I'm just trying to decide." She finally plucked a bag out of the box covered with mostly orange flowers. "This is an orange ginger."

"Yeah? Why will I like it?"

"You seem to like spicier things, like horseradish and stuff. Ginger is a little like that." She dunked a tea bag from the blue box into her steaming cup of water and started stirring. "Plus, ginger is good for upset stomachs and low energy."

"Do I look sick and tired to you?"

She grinned at him. "Not even a little bit, but I did just give you a pretty healthy massage. You've said you're always tired after that."

"I am, yeah." He put his tea bag into the mug of water.

"Plus," she said. "Ginger has been known to treat low libido." She lifted her mug to her lips and took a delicate sip.

Luke sucked in a breath and faced her fully. Those eyes sparkled and sparkled with so much teasing that Luke didn't know what to say or do. No matter what it was, it wouldn't be an adequate response.

He went back to stirring his tea, every cell in his body buzzing over the woman at his side. "Noted," he finally said, and Sterling burst out laughing.

His phone chimed, and he pulled it out of his back pocket. Before he could even swing it in front of him, it sounded again, and then again.

Again, and again, and again.

"My word," he grumbled.

The phone rang as Sterling asked, "Is that your brothers?"

"No." He frowned at the device. "I mute the brothers' thread, or I'd go crazy before I even got out of bed." Mandi's name sat on the screen. "This is my ex-wife."

He got to his feet and paced away from Sterling before swiping on the call. "Hey, Mandi," he said as nicely as he could.

"There you are," she said. "Have you seen the news? The snow is supposed to shut down the town."

"I have a weather app," he said coolly, though his pulse did kick at him to stop sipping tea and get on over to Mav's.

"I'm worried," she said. "Can you and Corrine come over here?"

"No," he said with a scoff. "You lived in Calgary for years, Mandi, and I know it snows there, just like here." He turned back to Sterling, who watched him with a thoughtful look on her face.

He had no idea what she was thinking, and she went back to her tea in the next moment anyway.

"Hush, baby," Mandi said, probably to her son on the other end of the line. "Luke, we don't have any food."

"That's not my problem," he said before he could censor himself.

"We're in a hotel," she said. "You'll just leave me here?"

"You're not my wife," Luke said, his voice definitely straying into grizzly-bear-growl territory. "What does the hotel say?" He couldn't even believe he'd asked that. He wasn't going to go personally save everyone who'd booked a hotel room for the night.

"Well...."

"So there's food there," he said. "Nice try, Mandi. I'll talk to you later."

"Wait," she said, but Luke ended the call.

He faced Sterling and said, "I should go. The snow's not going to get better." He moved over to her and swept one arm down to her hip as he leaned over and kissed her temple. "Thanks for the tea, the cookies, and the massage."

"Sure." She got up with him and followed him to the front door, where he shrugged back into his jacket and settled his cowboy hat back on his head.

"I'll call you tomorrow," he said, and nodding, he ducked out her front door and into the storm. Thankfully, his truck was big and black, or he might not have been able to find it in the snow blizzarding around in front of him.

He dashed to get behind the wheel, and once he was safely in his truck, the first thing he did was pray. "Lord," he said. "I need to get to my daughter and get home safely. I'll take any extra blessings you can provide about now."

While Luke hadn't spent a whole ton of time bothering God with his cares and concerns, he'd been taught to pray, and he knew the Lord heard him when he did. Now, whether He did anything about Luke's pleas or not, he wasn't so sure, but he put his truck in reverse and backed out of Sterling's driveway.

He kept the prayers going as he inched down the street, and not just for himself. For his daughter. His brothers, their wives, and their children. Momma and Daddy. Sterling.

And when he said, "And bless Mandi and her son at the hotel," Luke's tongue froze. He hadn't prayed for his ex or anything remotely concerning her since he'd opened that paternity test and found out he was indeed Corrine's father.

A sense of pure love and forgiveness flowed through him, replacing the dried up river beds of anger and resentment, and replacing them with a flourishing oasis of healing.

Healing he hadn't even known he needed to do.

At the stop sign, he said, "Thank you, Lord." His eyes burned, and Luke hadn't felt like crying over anything in ages. He felt more human—and that sure did feel good.

"Now, guide my feet and keep me safe, if Thy will."

11

After Luke left, Sterling put the teacups in the sink and opened her freezer. She had some frozen chicken pot pies, and she put one on a tray, turned on the oven, and slid her soon-to-be dinner inside.

Then she went to shower, because it was hair-washing day, and she could never do that in the morning. She'd just finished getting all the sudsy shampoo out of her curls when she thought she heard the doorbell ring.

She paused, her heartbeat thumping hard. Why did something have to happen while she was home alone, in the shower? Of course, she was always home alone if she didn't have a client, but there was something especially vulnerable about it while she stood with water streaming down her.

"Can't do anything about it," she said to herself. Someone shouldn't be out in this weather anyway. She didn't hear the bell again, nor could she possibly hear anyone knocking. Her stomach wouldn't settle, because what if someone needed help? "They'll go to the next house."

She finished her shower and stepped out to wrap her hair up in a towel. That done, she brushed her teeth and wrapped herself in a fluffy robe. She'd probably wear it for the rest of the night, then go to bed early with something playing on her tablet, and she went back out into her bedroom to grab her phone before she continued to the kitchen to get dinner out of the oven.

She still had four minutes on her pot pie, so she leaned against the counter and checked her phone. Surprise made her swipe faster, because she'd missed calls and messages. Perhaps she had some new clients trying to book something with her.

As soon as she got in, she saw everything was from Luke.

I had to come back. Can I come in?

You're not answering. I'm gonna wait in the truck.

I really don't think it's safe to drive.

She lifted her head and looked toward the front door. Back on her phone, she saw he'd called twice, the last time about twenty minutes ago. She walked around the corner to her front window and peered through the slats in the blinds. She could just make out the hulking black truck in her driveway, and she sucked in a breath.

After tapping to call Luke, she paced back into the kitchen. "Hey, sweetheart," he drawled. "Sorry about this. Can I come in?"

"Of course," she said. "I got in the shower. That's why I didn't answer or see your texts."

"Is the door unlocked?"

"No." She spun back to get that done. "Come in, and I'll put on coffee and find you something to eat."

"Yep." Luke ended the call, and Sterling dashed back into the kitchen. Surely she had something frozen he could eat. "He can't eat a frozen meat burrito." She scoffed at the ridiculousness of the idea. The man only wanted a salted and peppered steak, because the meat should speak for itself.

She had nothing here to feed a man like him.

"Sterling," he called.

"In the kitchen." She slammed the freezer and turned to face him as his boots echoed against her floor.

He appeared next to the dining table, the smile already on his face sort of sad. Maybe rueful. Something.

He scanned her down to her bare toes and his eyes practically shot back to hers. He reached out and grabbed onto the back of the dining chair closest to him. "Uh." Luke reached up and rubbed the back of his neck, dislodging his cowboy hat and pushing it forward over half of his face.

In that moment, Sterling realized that she wasn't dressed. She gasped, horror cascading through her, as she looked down at her robe. Her purple fluffy robe that barely tied closed around her waist.

And her hair still sat wetly piled on top of her head.

She immediately grasped at the two halves of her robe and pulled it tighter around her. Behind her, the oven beeped, signaling that her chicken pot pie was done. Instead of turning to get it out, she strode toward Luke.

"Will you get that for me, cowboy?" she asked, even managing to throw in a bit of a flirtatious vibe to her tone. "I'll get dressed and be right back."

Sterling hurried down the hall to her bedroom, closed and locked the door, and leaned against it. "No wonder he's self-conscious around me." On an intellectual level, she'd understood his hesitation to go out with her though she'd seen "every inch of his body." His words. Not hers.

But she hadn't really understood it. Until now. The embarrassment coursing through her went on and on, and he'd laid on her table probably a hundred times over the past few years. Fine, maybe not that much, but a lot. She had seen ninety-five percent of his body, though she'd assured him and reassured him that bodies were just bodies. She didn't pay that much attention to them as she worked.

It was the muscles she paid more attention to, and she was almost blind to the skin covering them. "Luke has nice muscles," she whispered.

Then she shucked off her robe and got dressed enough to be decent and cute in front of Luke—who certainly seemed like he'd be staying the night. Panic reared up her throat, but with enough swallowing, she managed to get it to stay down while she hung up her towel and used her blow dryer enough to make her hair stop dripping.

When she padded down the hall a half-hour later, she even wore a thick pair of socks with sole-grip on the bottom of them so she wouldn't slip. "Hey," she said, hugging herself. Luke now sat on the couch, his attention on his phone.

He looked up, and his eyes seemed a little bleary. "Hey."

"My hair is a nightmare when I wash it." She touched the ends of it. "Sorry that took so long. Did you get something to eat?" She looked past him to the kitchen, and her pot pie sat on the tray on top of the stove. Nothing else had been touched.

"No." He got to his feet, his smile so real and so handsome. He should probably have to have a license to use that thing, because it made her stomach riot. He stepped into her and put one hand on the small of her back. He breathed in deep and said, "I like your shampoo."

She smiled softly and put one hand on his chest. "Are you going to stay the night?"

"I have to, yeah," he said. "The town has told people to stay home, stay off the streets. I've called Mav and Dani. They're gonna keep Corrine, and I guess we'll see if they cancel school tomorrow."

Sterling nodded, her worry only multiplying. "I converted my second bedroom into a massage studio," she said. "But the couch isn't bad."

"Yeah." He turned back to it. "I've been testing it out. It's not bad at all."

Sterling stepped into the kitchen, her pot pie looking as cold as it had when she'd gotten it out of the freezer. "I can make spaghetti, maybe?" she said. "Or I have some things in the freezer."

"I suppose we will have to eat." He joined her in the kitchen. "Anything is fine; even just cold cereal."

She turned into him, grinning. "Cold cereal I can do." She went around the corner and into the pantry, grabbing every box of cereal she could carry. "I've got Wheat Chex, and Crispix. I really like those. And this looks like, oh, raisin bran, and shredded wheat, and." She plunked the last box of cereal down on the counter. "Oatmeal Crisp. Almond."

He looked at the boxes of cereal, shock flowing across his face, then at her. He started to laugh, which Sterling didn't understand. "What?" She wanted to yank open the silverware drawer and get out spoons, then toss them onto the counter so they'd drown out his laughter.

"You're nervous." He made no move to get closer to her.

"Yes." She swallowed, taking in that sexy leather jacket and how every piece of him spoke of cowboy perfection. "You're a lot of man, Luke Young." And he'd be *sleeping in her house* that night.

"I'm a lot of man?" His eyebrows shot up, and she realized he'd removed his cowboy hat. "An hour ago, you gave me ginger tea to treat my low libido."

Sterling blinked rapidly. "I did not." Then she too burst out laughing, and all the awkwardness between them evaporated when his low chuckles joined hers. Through her giggles, she said, "I said ginger tea *can* treat low libido. Not that you have it."

"It was implied."

She shook her head, glad when he grabbed onto her and pulled her close. He swayed with her like they were back at his brother's wedding, dancing the night away. "Is being a lot of man good, Sterling?"

"Yes," she whispered. "I just don't know if I'm enough for you." She clung to him too, because then he couldn't pull away enough to see her face. She couldn't control her emotions right now, and she'd rather keep them to herself.

Luke didn't say that of course Sterling was enough for him, and he simply danced with her slowly in her kitchen. When he pulled back, his voice hardly sounded like the barky, grumpy cowboy she'd known for a while now. "I made some coffee. You want some?"

"Yes, please."

"Go sit down," he said, but it wasn't a demand. It was him telling her he was going to take care of her. "I'll bring you a bowl of cereal and your coffee."

She moved over to the couch, surprised to see that it was barely six-thirty now. With how dark it had gotten, Sterling felt like it was almost time for bed. She smiled up at Luke as he passed her a cup of coffee. "Thank you."

He'd mixed in some of her hazelnut cream, and she assumed there'd be the exact right number of grains of sugar. She took a deep breath of it while he returned to the kitchen, and when he returned, he carried two bowls of cereal.

"Yours is right here." He gave her a bowl filled with Crispix, and Sterling wanted to toss it aside and kiss his mouth.

"Thank you." She peered over to his bowl, and he'd gotten the same thing. "Have you had those before?"

"First time." He beamed at her and dug his spoon in for a big bite. Sterling found such joy in simply watching him take the first taste, and his eyes widened as he nodded and chewed.

"Mm, yeah." He took another bite, and things between them didn't seem so serious anymore.

Since Sterling didn't like soggy cereal, she got to work on consuming her dinner. When she finished, she put her bowl on the coffee table and curled into the couch to watch Luke some more. He didn't leave their dishes in the living room, but took them back into the kitchen. "Dishwasher?" he asked.

"You can just leave them," she said.

He didn't, but rinsed the bowls and loaded everything into her dishwasher. Then he wrapped up her uneaten chicken pot pie and tucked that into the fridge too.

"You don't have to do any of that," she said.

"I clean when I'm nervous," he said.

That made her eyebrows go up. "You're nervous."

"You betcha." He wiped down her counter and poured out the old coffee before scrubbing the pot. With literally nothing left to do, he was forced to come sit in the living room again.

He sighed as he sat way down on the other end of the couch. He flicked a look at her out of the corner of his eye, but Sterling sat facing him, watching his every move. "You're like a caged tiger."

"Why are you smiling like that?"

"It's kind of cute to see you nervous."

"Ha ha." He sighed and ran both hands through his hair. "You wanna put on a movie or something?"

"Is that what you do at home?" She faced the front and reached for the remote which she kept in a basket on the coffee table. "If you and Corrine had made it home, you'd put a movie on and curl up on the couch with your daughter?"

"Yeah," he said. "On a night like tonight, probably. After I fed her and she finished her homework." A small smile touched his eyes but barely blipped across his mouth. "She reads to me while I make dinner. Twenty minutes or less."

"Glad I'm not the only one who dislikes cooking." She flipped on the TV, wondering if she and Luke could find something they'd both like. She pulled up the guide and then abandoned her quest. "Here." She extended the remote toward him. "I don't want to pick."

"What do you like?"

She'd like sliding over on the couch and cuddling into his side. "I don't care," she said. "Something light and fluffy seems apt for a snowstorm."

"Light." He hit the T. "And fluffy." He flipped through the channels faster than Sterling could even see what was playing. "Here we go." He pressed the button, and her TV screen turned dark for a moment.

Then the movie came to life as he tossed the remote onto the table. It only took Sterling three seconds to recognize the show. "Do you like Valley Girls?"

"I've never seen it."

"Why did you pick this?"

"The description said 'sweet small town'." He glanced over to her as she scoffed. "What?"

"There is no way you read the description on this. You were flipping like crazy."

He grinned at her. "One of my special skills. Trust me, with eight brothers, if you didn't pick quickly, you lost the remote."

"How many other special skills do you have?"

He considered her for a moment, then gestured for her to slide on over there next to him. Sterling did exactly that, and they sighed in tandem as he put his arm around her and she sank into his side. Luke didn't answer her question, and they both looked up at the TV.

Sterling had seen all of Valley Girls in the past, but she still enjoyed it. Or maybe she simply enjoyed laying in Luke's arms without any interruptions. Without any distractions. Without any tension or awkwardness or fear.

She didn't think about what would happen after the movie, or where Luke would sleep, or if she might be able to sneak down the hall and watch him breathe in and out. She simply thanked the Good Lord for a good house that kept her and Luke warm. She thanked Him for giving her someone to spend this storm with. And she pressed her eyes closed and thought, *Thank You for seeing me.*

Luke saw her too, and for Sterling, that was the best gift anyone could give her.

12

Georgia Young grinned at all the people and animals she loved, the big bowl of popcorn in her hand. "Is there a spot for me?"

"Right here by me, baby," Otis said, indicating the small space between him and Ruby, one of their permanent dogs. They had three right now, but Georgia had promised Otis that the little Frenchie named Hector wouldn't be with them forever.

She stepped over Joey's legs and a wadded blanket to take the spot at her husband's side. He lifted his arm around her and swatted their two-year-old's hand back. "Wait for Momma, OJ. She'll give you some popcorn. Roo?"

She held up the paper bag that he'd given her and asked, "Can I have the whole thing, Daddy?"

"We'll see." He held open the bag and let Georgia fill it. OJ hovered right over her shoulder as if there wouldn't be enough left for him to eat. Georgia smiled at him and held out a popped kernel for him. He grinned at it and took it, smashing it into his mouth.

"He's the cutest boy in the whole world." Georgia's stomach

ached, but she told herself it was just the snowstorm. This was the third one this week, and they'd be going to school into June at the rate the district kept canceling.

Georgia didn't mind at all. Joey would be thirteen next month, and she still seemed too young for junior high. She did great in seventh grade, though, and she had plenty of friends. She hadn't gotten into makeup or boys yet, for which Georgia was eternally grateful.

Her emotions swooped up and then down as Otis shook the paper bag and handed it to Joey. "There you go, Roo." He picked up the remote and started the movie they'd chosen for their snow-in flick.

Joey had gone through their DVDs and categorized them from ones she wanted to watch the most to the least, and Otis had promised her they'd watch a new one every time Mother Nature howled and blew and kept them indoors.

Georgia didn't normally get stir-crazy, but they did have a lot of dogs and cats that needed and liked to go outside. OJ was only two, and he had more energy than any of them.

"All right, baby," she said to him. She lifted the bowl, and Otis took it from her as OJ climbed into her lap. She took the bowl back and said, "One piece at a time, bud. No choking."

She normally loved popcorn, but the greasy smell of it tonight made her stomach lurch. She groaned, and Otis looked over to her. "You okay, baby?" He swept her bangs off her forehead. "You're a little hot."

"Is that a pick-up line?" She grinned at him, but no, she didn't feel great.

He smiled back at her and tucked her and OJ into his side. Georgia loved how safe her husband made her feel. He loved her completely, and that was such a gift to Georgia, who'd never had that kind of unconditional love from someone.

She and Otis had found shelter in one another in the past few years, and she could be her worst self with him, and he'd still love her.

He ate popcorn, and OJ went after it too, until his daddy finally took the bowl and said, "Enough, bud. You're gonna be sick all night," and put it on the table in front of them. Georgia let her eyes drift closed while the wind tried to get in through any cracks in the windows or doors.

"Baby," Otis said sometime later. Georgia opened her eyes, realizing she'd fallen asleep.

She sat up, a groan pulling through her. "Sorry." Glancing around, she didn't see OJ or Joey. "Where are the kids?"

"Joey's helping OJ get his pj's on." Otis pressed a kiss to her forehead. "Come on. I'll help you get yours on." He grinned at her, and Georgia pushed herself off the couch.

She stood, but her head spun, and she quickly fell back to the couch. She landed partially on a couple of dog paws, and she said, "Oops. Sorry, Ruby." But she couldn't get up right now.

"Georgia." Otis crouched in front of her, once again pushing her hair off her forehead. "What's goin' on with you?"

"I'm just tired," she said.

He shook his head, his dark eyes filled with concern. "This is more than that, baby. It's eight o'clock, and you didn't get up until almost nine this morning."

"It's just winter." Georgia blinked a couple of times, and the room finally stopped spinning. "I just stood up too fast."

Otis looked like he didn't believe her, but he didn't argue with her. He did keep one hand on her elbow as she stood again, and this time, she didn't fall back to the couch. They went down the hall together, and OJ came out of the bathroom as she approached.

"Mama," he said.

"Hey, my boy." She bent to pick him up, and her stomach

really didn't like that. She clamped her teeth together to keep the groan inside, and she held her breath as she straightened. She and Otis had always put the kids to bed together, and she led the way into their little boy's room.

She laid him in his crib, as he'd just barely turned two about three weeks ago. She tucked his ducky blanket around him and replaced the thumb in his mouth with a pacifier before she leaned down and kissed him. "Momma loves you," she whispered.

OJ smiled behind his pacifier, and then Otis took his turn to kiss their son goodnight. Then they moved into Joey's room, who sat cross-legged on her bed with a book in front of her. Georgia almost burst out crying, because she loved books with her whole heart, and she always wanted Joey to enjoy them too.

She sniffled, which drew another look from Otis, but she ignored him as she went to help Joey mark her place in her book and set it aside. Otis flipped off the overhead light at the same time Georgia snapped on the stringed lights arcing above Joey's bed.

"Will there be school tomorrow?" she asked as she lay back against her pillow.

"They'll let us know in the morning," Otis said.

Georgia pulled the covers up for Joey and gave her a smile. "Let's hope they cancel it again. Then we can make those chocolate chip pancakes and maybe make a snowman if it clears up in the afternoon."

Joey grinned too, and Georgia swept a kiss along her cheek. "Love you, Joey-girl."

"Love you too, Georgia."

She moved out of the way, and Otis sat on Joey's bed. They always talked for a few minutes at night, and Georgia stole out of the bedroom and continued to the master. Her brain hummed at her, putting together several pieces.

She'd never been pregnant before, and she'd been told she

couldn't get pregnant. But she was so tired all the time. She'd been more emotional than ever lately. And as she moved into the bathroom and closed the door, she realized she didn't know when she'd had her last period.

Her cycle had become irregular over the years, and she didn't pay much attention to it. But as she looked at herself in the mirror, she could only think of one person: Abby.

Her best friend blamed so many things on her pregnancy—her exhaustion, her emotional mood swings, and her cravings or her food aversions.

The only thing Georgia had wanted to eat lately was fruit, fruit, and more fruit. And in Wyoming in the winter, fresh fruit wasn't easy to get. So she'd turned to the pantry for something else sweet to satisfy her. And hadn't she just made her own mouth water at the mention of chocolate chip pancakes?

"You're not pregnant," she whispered to her reflection. But a small voice inside her asked, *But what if you are?*

She and Otis had given up trying to have a baby of their own, but when they'd been trying, before OJ had come into their lives, Georgia had taken several home pregnancy tests. In a flash, she dropped to her knees and opened the cabinet.

Did she still have one? Did they expire? What would she do if she saw two pink lines on the test? Panic rose and rose, because if she was pregnant, she needed to get in to the doctor immediately. And with all the storms they'd had in the past week, that wouldn't be possible.

Luke had stayed at Sterling's during the first one, and Abby and Tex had almost driven off the road as they tried to get home in the second one. The town of Coral Canyon had implemented an emergency texting system, and now they all got alerted hours and hours before the storms were supposed to hit.

When she couldn't find a pregnancy test among half-full

bottles of body wash, rolls of toilet paper, and the first-aid kit, she yanked open the drawer where she kept her feminine hygiene products.

There. At the back of the drawer, long forgotten, sat a pregnancy test. Georgia reached in and grabbed it, then closed everything and hurried into the toilet room. "This is insane," she said, panting for no apparent reason other than she couldn't get enough air.

With the deed done, she took the test out into the main part of the bathroom and set it on the vanity like it might turn into a rattler at any moment. Her chest heaved; her stomach did too. She hadn't been sick in the mornings; only at night.

She flipped on the water, cold, and ran her hands under it. With sufficiently wet fingers, she combed them through her hair. Everything was too hot. The room started to spin again.

"Otis," she called, not sure if her husband would be able to hear her or not. She looked down. The pregnancy test bloomed and developed right in front of her.

It showed two pink lines.

"Otis!" she yelled as she sank to her knees. This wasn't right. It couldn't be. Could it be right?

"What?" Otis said.

Georgia's eyesight blurred as tears filled her eyes, but that only made four lines instead of backing off to just one. Otis came into the bathroom, and she looked over to him. She clung to the vanity countertop to stay upright, and she let her tears fall down her face.

"Hey, hey, hey." He rushed at her, skidding on the floor on his knees too to hold her against his chest. "Are you okay? Do I need to call an ambulance?"

She shook her head, then changed it to a nod as she indicated the pregnancy test on the counter.

Otis held her tightly as he looked over her shoulder to the

counter. He pulled in a sharp breath. "No way." He got up and picked up the stick. "This is impossible." His eyes had never been so rounded. His voice never as full of nothing but air. "Georgia."

"I'm pregnant," she whispered.

Otis started to laugh, and while it sounded happy, it definitely had a bit of a manic edge in it. He roared with laughter—which was a pretty typical Otis-reaction—and helped her to her feet. "You're pregnant."

He swooped her into his arms, her crying like a baby and him laughing like Santa Claus. She couldn't help smiling through the tears as she said, "All this twirling is making me sick."

"Right, right." Otis helped her into the bedroom and right into bed, even though she still wore her clothes. He climbed in behind her and held her close, one hand moving to lay right over her belly.

"You're pregnant," he whispered. "It's a miracle."

"I need to go to the doctor." Georgia could think and breathe better out here, away from the bright lights of the bathroom and those two pink lines. Her mind still spun, but in a controlled way. "Maybe they can help me keep this baby."

"We'll call tomorrow," he promised, and she knew Otis never broke his promises. God didn't either, and a fresh round of tears filled Georgia's eyes and wetted her pillow.

A baby. She couldn't believe it. Just couldn't believe it.

"God is good," she whispered. Georgia probably shouldn't get her hopes up. Carrying a baby for nine months might be impossible for her. She might not be able to keep the pregnancy. But she couldn't help gripping the hope tightly in her heart as it grew, and grew, and grew.

Otis murmured against her shoulder, "That He is, my love. That He is."

13

Bryce Young was tired of driving. Maybe not the driving so much, but definitely the travel. He'd been flying and changing planes all day—and he had his dog with him.

Bringing Lucky had complicated his normally easy trip back to Coral Canyon.

"I can't wait to move here," he said to the golden retriever. Maybe not in the winter, but the spring, summer, and fall in Coral Canyon were unmatched. Even better than in Louisville, where Bryce currently lived. He did love it there too, but when the opportunity to buy a ranch here—even if it was in Dog Valley—had come up, Bryce hadn't been able to walk away.

His dad had helped him purchase the racehorse training facility, and Bryce couldn't wait to transform it into his version of heaven—a horse rescue ranch.

"You need a bath, bud," Bryce said, grinning at his dog, who rode shotgun in the truck Bryce had rented at the airport in Boise. He hadn't been able to get a flight that would allow dogs coming into Jackson Hole, and Bryce figured he could drive the distance the rest of the way.

And he was.

He was just sick of it.

Lucky whined next to him, but Bryce kept the gas pedal pressed. "Almost there," he said, though he then had to pass through town and drive up the highway to the farmhouse on the northeast side of town.

From his daddy's farm, the racehorse facility could be accessed along the north highway, which connected to the apple highway, which led to Dog Valley.

He and his parents had driven it before Bryce had put in an offer, and it had taken twenty-five minutes.

So he'd be close, but not right on top of Dad and Abby and their new family.

Bryce pushed against the thought. "Dad doesn't have a *new* family," he muttered, repeating something his therapist had told him. "He just has a family, and you're part of it."

Never mind that there were nineteen years between him and his half-sister.

His thoughts moved to his mother, who lived in Boise. He should've told her he'd be landing there. Maybe asked if she wanted to go to lunch with him before he started this drive.

He couldn't go back in time and do such a thing now, but his guilt pricked at him.

Dad never brought up Bryce's mother, but Bryce thought of her all the time. He knew he had a wound there that needed to be fixed, but he wasn't sure how to do it.

His mother hadn't reached out to him in at least a year either, so it wasn't like he was ignoring her or snubbing her.

A long, deep breath filled his lungs, and he let it out slowly.

Lucky barked, and Bryce looked over to him. "We're almost there. Do you need to go, huh?"

The dog panted, his big tongue hanging out of his mouth, and he shifted on the seat. Bryce decided he could spare a few minutes to stop to make sure his dog didn't do something in the rental that would be hard to clean up.

He slowed and came to a complete stop on the side of the highway. Because it was long and straight, traffic in either direction would see him parked there.

He put on his hazard flashers anyway, then slid from the truck to go help his dog. He opened the passenger door and said, "All right. Take care of your business."

Lucky leapt from the truck and started into the snow. Bryce grinned as the canine didn't go any further, as if the cold, wet snow offended him.

True, he'd had very little experience with snow, as it didn't stick in Louisville very often. Still, his diva-reluctance to go out into the snow to go to the bathroom made Bryce laugh.

"Just go, bud," he said, and the dog trotted down the side of the snowbank, choosing a spot only a moment later and taking care of things.

When they were both back in the truck, Bryce adjusted the heater to blow harder, as it wasn't warm outside in Wyoming.

February was the deep winter, and he held his hands in front of the vents for a moment before he checked his mirror and got back on the road.

An hour later, Bryce and Lucky finally pulled up to the farmhouse. The porch light shone against the night, and Bryce's soul filled with it over and over.

He was home.

The side door that sat at the top of a flight of steps opened, and

Dad came out. He laughed as he flew down the steps, and Bryce caught the end of it as he got out of the truck again.

"Daddy."

"My boy." Dad wrapped him up in his strong arms, and though Bryce had filled out in the chest and shoulder due to his work on the horse farm in Kentucky, he still found his daddy bigger and stronger. He always had been, and he always would be.

Franny, Daddy's German shepherd, barked, and Bryce's dog responded. He hopped the console and jumped from the truck out of Bryce's still-open door.

Sniffing ensued, and Daddy said, "I've been tracking you for the last hour. Abby has dinner ready. You've got a bag?"

"Two," Bryce said, as he'd be in town for a week, and he'd brought his dog. "I can get one."

"I got it," Daddy said. "Go see the girls."

Bryce faced the house and headed that way, because arguing with his father was a fruitless endeavor. At least Bryce didn't feel like a complete failure on this trip. He didn't carry everyone's eyes as they watched him, judged him.

"Bwyce," his sister, Melissa, said from the doorway.

"Don't go outside," Abby said from somewhere inside. "You don't have shoes on."

"Bwyce," Melissa said again, the golden light from the house haloing her.

"Mel." Bryce took the steps two at a time to the house, and he swooped his sister into his arms. "Wow, look at you." He laughed as she wrapped her skinny three-year-old arms around his head.

She'd be four next month, and she was the prettiest little girl. Abby would be having a boy in May, and Bryce couldn't wait to be closer to his family so he could watch them grow and change.

He'd needed the distance these past couple of years, but he was ready to participate more fully in his family now.

"I got a new nightgown." Mel said, looking down at her chest. "It got ponies on it."

"It sure does." Bryce pressed a kiss to her cheek and put her on her feet. Abby came around the corner, and love filled Bryce from head to toe.

She loved his daddy, and along with that, Abby had always, *always* loved Bryce.

"Abs," he said, his voice strained as he moved into her. She stood a good eight inches shorter than him, but she was also strong and larger-than-life, and Bryce felt like nothing bad could happen while he stood with Abby.

"You made it," she whispered, her baby bump pressing between them. He held her tightly for another moment and then released her.

"Comin' in," Dad said, and that got everyone to move out of the doorway and around the corner into the kitchen.

Bryce kept moving, because the long, narrow kitchen couldn't be stood around in while Daddy carried his two bags.

"I'll put these in your room," he said.

"You hungry?" Abby asked.

Bryce noticed no one else had come over, and he smiled gratefully at his step-mother. "Yeah," he said. "Yeah, I'm hungry."

A COUPLE OF DAYS LATER, BRYCE LOOKED UP FROM HIS BOWL of cereal when he heard music. Not the country kind of music he normally listened to. Not anything his dad and uncles would produce in the recording studio that stood behind the house.

This was a pop song...with barking dogs.

"Lucky," he called, realizing who'd arrived. His dog came trotting down the hall, Franny right with him. "Time for your bath."

Both dogs looked toward the front door, and they both barked as the doorbell sang through the house.

"I get it!" Melissa yelled from the front room, and Bryce jumped to his feet to stop that. He couldn't even imagine what chaos would ensure if the front door got opened with two big dogs jockeying for position near it.

"Mel," Bryce said. "I'll get it." He picked her up again, and she smiled at him. "Does Daddy let you get the door?"

Her smile slipped. "No." She played with his collar, her eyes on it.

"Yeah," he said. "We don't even know who it is, right?" He did —or at least he hoped it was the mobile dog groomer he'd booked for this morning.

The birthday party he'd come for was tomorrow, and Bryce would be headed back to Boise and then Louisville again on Tuesday.

Call your mother. The thought entered his mind, and Bryce brushed it off as he opened the door.

A gorgeous blonde woman stood there, a tight blue T-shirt stretching across her chest that said "It's Poochy Keen." She wore a black fleece jacket that didn't obscure the name of her dog grooming business, and she looked at him with clear, blue eyes.

"Howdy," he said falling into the easy-going side of himself. His pulse buzzed and fizzed, the attraction to her strong.

"Bryce?" she asked.

"Yep." He kept the dogs back with his leg, but one of them pressed against it. He looked down at his canine and said, "Sit. Knock it off."

To his great relief, Lucky sat. Pride filled Bryce, and he looked back to the pretty blonde with confidence soaring through him.

"I'm Codi," she said. "I'm here for Lucky." Her eyes dropped to the dogs too, and Bryce twisted and put his little sister down.

"Take Franny, would you, Mel?"

"I got him," Abby said, and she gave a short whistle. Franny trotted away, and Melissa went after her.

Bryce stepped outside as he said, "Come on, Lucky." He let the door crash closed, flinching as the sound filled the quiet sky. "What do you need from me?"

Maybe he could give her his number, and foolishness filled him when he remembered that she already had it.

"Nothing," she said. "I just need the dog." She indicated the long bus parked in the driveway. "Am I okay to park there?"

"You're really going to do the bath and cut there?" The bus had to be a full-length school bus, but it had been painted white. Cartoon dogs of various breeds had been painted on, along with the name of her dog grooming business.

"Do you own this?" he asked.

"Yes," Codi said. "Come on, Lucky." She went down the front steps, and Bryce wanted to follow her. "We'll be a few hours, okay? If I need anything, I'll text you."

"Yeah," he called after her. "Okay."

She paused and turned back to him. "I usually don't need anything, so I shouldn't be bothering you or your daughter." She flashed the briefest of smiles before turning again, and Bryce's brain took too long to comprehend what she'd said.

"My...daughter?"

14

Codi Hudson got Lucky onto the bus without any problems. She loved dogs like him, who'd clearly been to groomers before, who wasn't afraid of his own shadow, and who would listen to her without a fuss.

Of course, she loved all of her dogs, but the ones who were easy to work with were her favorites.

She sealed the cold out, basking in the warmth of the bus. "All right, Mister," she said to the dog. "It's bath time." She looked out the windows, which she uncovered in the winter and kept covered in the summer, to find the tall, dark cowboy still staring at her bus.

He never had said if she could park here, and Codi hesitated before getting the hoses going. She could do three washes before she had to return home and refill her water tanks, and she only had three dogs today.

Big ones like this took a full three hours, and she tried to schedule similar sized dogs on the same day. At this point, she'd take anyone who called, as her mobile dog grooming bus was still gaining traction in Coral Canyon.

Lucky didn't wear a leash, but thankfully, Codi just pointed to the table where she wanted him, and he got on it. "You're a good dog," she said, appreciation for the animal—and the cowboy he belonged to—starting to rise through her.

Most dogs didn't like it when the table lifted, and Codi gripped Lucky's collar and said, "Up we go." She used the foot pedal to get the table to lift, and sure enough Lucky stutter-stepped and hunched down into his haunches. "Just for a few seconds, bud."

He looked at her with the classic golden retriever smile, and Codi couldn't help smiling back. Canines always made her smile. It was people she didn't like.

Lucky barked as she affixed the short chain that would keep his head up, and he put one paw up on the window. "Yeah, you can see out there," she said. She followed the dog's gaze only to find that tall, dark, drink-of-water man walking toward her bus. He didn't wear a jacket, and it had to be ten below zero today. He practically steamed in the winter air—or maybe that was only in Codi's vision, because she could admit how good-looking Bryce was.

He came around the front of her bus, which she'd hand-painted herself, and tried to open the door. When it didn't fold inward—because Codi had locked it—he rapped on the glass.

Codi sighed and said, "Lucky, why'd you have to do that?" She stepped over the handle and pulled the door in. "What?" she barked. "He's fine."

Bryce climbed on up into her bus anyway, but Codi didn't back up much to give him full access to the area. "This thing has no seats."

"Did you think I'd be taking your dog on a field trip?" she asked.

His eyes came to hers, and oh, stars fell from heaven in those things. Codi immediately shoved against her feelings, her traitorous emotions what always got her in trouble. A slow smile curved his beautiful lips, which sat perfectly against his strong jaw. He wore a light beard that looked like he just hadn't had time to shave in the past few days, but that he normally did.

His eyes swam with a dozen things—questions, interest, irritation, attraction, desire. Codi saw it all, because she'd worked with a lot of people over the years. She'd dated several men—and this one was no good for her.

"How old are you?" he asked, and that caused Codi to close right up.

She cocked one hip and folded her arms. "Is this some sort of quiz about my expertise with dog grooming? Everything's on my site—where you booked from."

Bryce smiled even more, the gesture reaching right up into those glorious eyes. He reached up with one hand and took off his cowboy hat, then ran the other handful of fingers through his hair. He had big hands, and they did look like they'd borne some trials of ranching or farming.

"I don't live here yet," he said, his voice downright soothing and swoon-worthy at the same time. Codi kicked against herself, because she wasn't interested in dating right now. She'd left Boise and struck out for greener pastures. A new start after a disastrous year personally, financially, and emotionally. A place to find *herself*—not find a boyfriend.

"But I'm wonderin' when I do move back, if you'd be interested in going to dinner with me."

Codi sighed, because if she acted put out, perhaps Bryce would get the hint. He ducked his head in an adorable way, and Codi would take that thought to the grave with her. "Ah, I see," he said with a nervous chuckle. "You've got a boyfriend."

"No," she said.

He peered up just enough to see her from beneath the brim of that blasted cowboy hat. Codi normally loved a man in blue jeans, boots, and the hat, but she'd had enough of cowboys for a lifetime.

Idaho cowboys, she told herself. *Maybe Wyoming cowboys are different.*

No. She booted that idea out of her head too. "Where do you live right now?"

"Louisville," he said. "Been workin' a horse ranch there for a bit."

"You're moving back here?"

"In May," he said. "This is my daddy's place, but I bought the Barber Training Facility up in Dog Valley."

The words he said came out English, but they didn't mean a lot to Codi. The way he spoke, though, they must mean something.

Yeah, she thought. *That he's as arrogant as he is handsome.*

"I don't know what that means," she said. "I've only been in town for about six months."

"Okay." He reached out, seemed to think better of touching her, and let his hand drop back to his side. "It's just north of here. I'm going to start a horse rescue ranch. I've got four horses livin' here, and...yeah."

Codi considered him. Did she want to close the door on him completely? It took a lot for someone to knock on the door of the bus and come right in to ask her out. This man hadn't had any trouble getting dates in the past, that was for sure.

Still, she found him stunning in every way, and while she wasn't interested right now—he didn't even live here—she didn't have to slam the door in his face. "So you'll be making a pretty substantial move in May," she said. "To start a brand-new horse operation, which you've never done before?"

"That's about right."

Codi dared to give him a smile. Hers did not reach up to her eyes, at least that she could feel. "Tell you what, Mister Young." She paused. "Your last name is Young, right?"

"That's right," he drawled, and oh, he could lay on the Kentucky accent too. So not fair.

"After you move here, if you're not completely drowning, you already have my number."

He blinked a couple of times as he caught up. "So you *don't* have a boyfriend."

"I left a fiancé in Boise," she said, not sure where the words had come from or why she'd let them out of her mouth. "Eight months ago. So no. No boyfriend." She turned back to Lucky, who stood there clipped to the bar, a cute smile on his face and his bushy tail going *swish-swish-swish* as he grinned at his master.

"And no interest in getting a new boyfriend right now," she added.

"Noted," Bryce said. He didn't leave, and his presence in her bus unnerved her. She'd had this vehicle for five years, working to turn it into what she'd dreamed of it being—a mobile dog grooming bus—in her spare time. Every extra ten dollars had been saved and scrimped so she could afford the equipment she needed. A generator to run her dog dryer and her clippers. A tankless hot water heater. All the tables and chains and leashes and paint and gas and just *everything*.

No one had ever been inside it except for her. She played *Who Let the Dogs Out* when she pulled up to a client's house, and *she* went to the front door to collect the pooch. They sometimes came reluctantly, but they always came—usually on a leash—while their owners worried their hands in the doorway.

Codi reached for the water hose. "You're making me late for my day," she said.

"Right." Bryce cleared his throat. "So I'll...I don't have a daughter."

Codi twisted and looked over her shoulder at him. She raised her eyebrows, as Bryce looked like he'd seen a ghost in the past ten seconds.

"That was my half-sister," he said. "I mean, I guess I do have a kid, but...it's complicated." He blew out his breath. "Never mind." He looked up at the ceiling in the bus. "Lord, I've lost my ever-loving mind."

He smashed his hat onto his head, effectively covering his eyes, and nodded at her with a dark look on his face. Then he spun on his heel and marched down the steps. "I'm not sure—I don't know how to close this door."

"I got it," Codi said, and she re-hooked the hose to go close the door. Plenty of cold air had gotten in, and her generator would be working overtime to heat the space again. Her eyes met Bryce's through the window, and she couldn't tell what swam in his gaze before he yanked away from the tether between them and rounded the front of the bus.

Codi gave herself strict instructions not to look at him as she returned to Lucky. "Do you get to sleep in his bed at night, boy?" She picked up the hose and squeezed to get the water to come out. She methodically wetted his fur, only daring to look up when she was sure Bryce had made the trek down the sidewalk and into the house.

Sure enough, he was gone, and Codi sighed in relief. "Maybe you should keep these windows blacked out year-round," she mumbled to herself. Then, she did what she'd vowed to do for the next few years.

She put handsome cowboys out of her mind and focused on her work.

15

Tex Young heard the back door slam closed as his son went out to do the morning chores. It was early still, and he hadn't heard Melissa stir yet. The little girl usually came into the master suite and climbed into bed with him and Abby, a thought that made him smile into the gray light that had started to seep through the blinds.

"There's something up with him," he whispered.

"He might be nervous about moving home," Abby said.

Tex lifted his hands and put them behind his head, his eyes tracing lines on the ceiling. "Do you think he feels like Coral Canyon is home?"

"I think—I don't know." Abby rolled toward him, which was getting harder for her to do now that she only had two months left of her pregnancy. She cuddled into Tex's side, and he put his arm around her. "You're warm."

"Mm." Tex wasn't sure what he could sense in his son, but there was...something. "Do you think it's anything to do with OJ?"

"I don't know," Abby said. "I doubt it. Georgia said dinner the other night was amazing. Perfect. Bryce doesn't act weird about that stuff anymore."

"Maybe his mom," Tex mused next.

"Daddy," Melissa said, and Tex lifted his head as the bedroom door opened. "Bwyce gone?"

"No, baby," he said. "He's just out with the horses."

She carried a pink plastic horse in her hand, and she made it air-gallop as she came toward him. "We go to the party today."

"Yep." He brought her into the circle of his left arm at the side of the bed. "It's all the parties today. That's why Bryce came, remember?"

She grinned and said, "Momma, I get the pwesents."

"No, baby," Abby said, but Melissa had already turned and started running for the door. Abby sighed and snuggled deeper into Tex's side. "We aren't going for hours," she whispered.

Tex chuckled and pressed a kiss to his wife's head. "I'll go make sure she doesn't cause a problem."

"She's obsessed with presents," Abby said.

"Who isn't?" Tex teased. "Stay in bed, love. I've got her." He stood and pulled a T-shirt over his head before padding down the hall. Melissa put one more present in a stack on the couch and beamed at him.

"Done, Daddy."

"That's great, sunshine." He swooped her into his arms, causing her to squeal. "Want some breakfast? Should we make something special for Bryce?"

"I go ask him." She wiggled to get down, and Tex bent to do that before he dropped her.

But he said, "Baby doll, you can't go outside. It's freezing, and you're still in your nightgown." He beamed at her. "I know what he likes." He glanced down the hall. "And Momma likes bacon and eggs too."

Melissa loved bacon and eggs, and her eyes lit up. "I crack the eggs, Daddy?"

"Yeah, sure," he said, though it would be messier than if he did it himself. "Come on, pumpkin. Let's get your cooking stool."

Abby had the little girl help her in the kitchen all the time, and Tex loved nothing more than walking into the farmhouse and finding his wife and his daughter standing together at the counter, measuring, or mixing, or just plain talking about measuring and mixing.

As he got out a carton of eggs, he took a moment to say, "The Lord sure has blessed us, Mel."

"Yeah," she agreed. "The sun be comin' up today."

He chuckled, because in this winter they'd been having, the sun coming up *was* a blessing. She'd clearly heard him or Abby say such a thing, and Tex reached over and smoothed his daughter's hair down.

"Should I text Uncle Wade and Aunt Cheryl and see if they want bacon and eggs?"

Mel pulled the egg carton toward her. "Let me count." She flipped open the carton's lid and started. "One, two, three, four, five, six, seven, eight, nine, ten, eleven, seven, eight...." She touched each egg as she said it, and Tex didn't have the heart to correct her.

"I think there's enough, muffin." He turned and got a big bowl out of the cupboard. "Start crackin'."

He got out a package of bacon and started laying it in the pan. After every strip, he checked out the window above the sink to see if his son had finished and was returning. It didn't take long to feed four horses, and Tex didn't linger in the barn in the dead of winter.

Bryce, however, didn't seem to feel the cold the way Tex did, and he spent way longer in the barn, talking to his equines. Confessing the very things Tex was trying to figure out.

He and Mel had the bacon crisp and the eggs just coming out of the pan by the time Bryce came back inside. "I knew I smelled bacon," he said cheerfully.

Tex had seen this false side of his son before, but he smiled as Bryce hung up his coat and then came around the corner to wash up.

"Bweakfast ready!" Melissa yelled. "I get Momma."

"Yep," Tex said. "Go get Momma." He finished pouring the scrambled eggs into a bowl, and he moved them to the table. "I've already got the plates and forks over here." He twisted and looked at Bryce at the sink.

"Okay."

Tex faced his son, and he didn't hear Abby or Mel behind him. "What's goin' on with you?"

Bryce looked up, his hands still working through a dish towel to get dry. He wore the mask he'd put on after he'd told Tex and Abby about Bailey, after that terrible summer before they'd moved to Montana, after he'd given up his son to Otis and Georgia to raise.

Thankfully, it crumbled away a moment later. "I met someone."

"You—you met someone?" Tex had no idea how to process those words. He blinked, his eyebrows feeling like they'd become part of his hairline if he didn't relax them soon.

Bryce looked absolutely miserable as he hung up the towel. "Yeah, and it's...confusing, you know? I mean, I asked her out and everything. I went out with Kassie too, you know, before, and it was weird then too."

He stood next to the plate of bacon, seemed to realize it, and picked it up. "And then there was nothing romantic between us, but now I'm wondering if that was because of me. Like, because I —I did something? I don't know."

A sigh accompanied him as he came toward Tex and put the bacon on the table next to the eggs. "Can we eat? I hate it when my eggs are cold."

"Yes," Abby said as she came around the corner. "Let's eat."

"Let's eat! Let's eat! Let's eat!" Mel chanted, and Tex once again picked her up to put her in her booster seat. She giggled and wrapped her arms around his neck as he laughed too.

Bryce and Abby sat, and because Tex was helping Mel, he slid into his seat last. Everyone looked at him, and he bowed his head. "Lord, we thank Thee for this day together as a family. Bless us all at the party this afternoon to get along with everyone. Bless us to forgive those who hurt us, intentionally or not."

He paused to take a breath, his eyelids trembling as he squeezed them shut. He better wrap this up quick, because the eggs were cooling by the second. "Bless Bryce to find a solution to his problems, and bless this food. Amen."

"Amen," Bryce said quietly as Mel yelled, "A-Men!" She reached for her fork and clanked it against her plate.

"Too loud, Mel," Abby told her, frowning. She scooped some eggs onto the little girl's plate, and then turned to Bryce. "What problems?"

Bryce stuffed his hat back onto his head. "Female problems, and I'm not talking about it right now." He cut Tex a look that told Tex he better not push things. "I'll talk to my therapist and figure things out, okay?"

"Of course you will," Abby said airily. "You're not talking about Kassie, are you?"

Bryce looked at Tex, his gaze unwavering, and Tex saw all the strength in his son. He smiled and said, "Abs, he's not talking about it. It's not Kassie." He picked up the plate of bacon and tipped several slices onto his plate. "All right. Who's excited to go to *nine* birthday parties today?"

"I count to nine," Mel said, abandoning her breakfast entirely. "One, two, three, four...."

16

"We don't have to go," Luke said as Sterling buckled her seat belt. He'd just stood on her front stoop to pick her up today, and he hadn't been back inside for a massage since spending the night on her sofa either.

In his mind, it hadn't been too awkward. The storm had raged all night long. They hadn't lost power, and she'd gone to bed in her bedroom after making up the couch for him. Literally making it up with a twin fitted sheet around the cushions, and plenty of puffy pillows, and the warmest blanket Luke had ever slept under.

Or maybe he'd been extra-hot that night because Sterling had been slumbering down the hall. He wasn't sure, and he hoped he'd never have to repeat the situation. The storms seemed to have been coming during the daylight hours now, and they came almost every day for a little bit, then moved on, instead of dumping feet of snow in a matter of hours.

"Of course we're going," Sterling said, her voice calm and unhurried beside him. She glanced into the backseat, which was empty. Luke had taken Corrine to his momma's first, and he'd see them all at the indoor trampoline park in only a few minutes.

He shifted in his seat as Sterling asked, "Why don't you want to go?"

"I do want to go." But his voice sounded like he'd start throwing knives at any moment.

"Luke." Sterling reached over and took his hand in hers. "Is your whole name Luke?"

"No," he said. "It's Lucas, but I haven't ever gone by that." He settled with her skin against his, and this dating experience with her over the past six weeks had been radically different than the other two women he'd tried going out with recently.

He took a deep breath and put the truck in reverse. "I'm just —my family is loud. We're celebrating nine birthdays in one party." He frowned out his side window, then got the truck moving away from Sterling's house. She lived right in the middle of a neighborhood, only a few blocks up from Main Street. The trampoline park had been built in a big, industrial-looking building on the southeast side of town, almost to the highway that ran by the big red barn where Tex and Abby had been married.

If he kept going on that highway, he'd leave Coral Canyon in his rearview mirror and be headed toward Colorado. Luke had once had plenty of reason to run. The absolute urge to flee the state, leave everything behind.

He'd done it too, taking a vacation for himself when he needed it. Morris had done the same, but neither of them had felt that urge for a while. At least Luke hadn't, and Morris hadn't brought it up again either.

Of course, Morris now had a pretty wife and two beautiful children. Out of all of them, he didn't have an ex-wife to deal with, because he'd re-married her. Luke wished he didn't dwell on things like this. He knew Morris and Leigh still went to couples' counseling, and he glanced over to Sterling.

"I think it'll be fun," Sterling said. "You've got a basket of gifts, so you obviously don't hate it."

"No," he said. "I don't hate it."

"When's your birthday?" she asked as he finally made it to the stop sign that would leave the winding roads of the neighborhood behind.

"I'm, uh, one of the ones we're celebrating in this group." He muttered the words to the windshield, but Sterling's hand in his still tightened like a vice grip.

When he didn't elaborate, Sterling said, "Luke," with plenty of frustration in her voice. Then she pulled her hand away completely. "Great. Now I'm going to show up to my first major function with your family, where we're supposed to be celebrating your birthday, and I have nothing for you." She folded her arms, her irritation like a scent on the air.

"It's for the kids, really," he said, disliking himself for not telling her this earlier. Of course Sterling would want to get him something. "Adult birthdays are silly."

"Maybe to you," she said. "Is it really you and eight kids?"

When he didn't answer right away, she scoffed. "Luke. Maybe you're right. Maybe I shouldn't go."

He eased up on the accelerator, his stomach turning into a hollow pit. "I...."

"You didn't tell me this birthday celebration included *you*."

"My birthday is so dumb," he said. "It's on Leap Year, and I get teased every time it rolls around about how I'm finally five years old." He shook his head. "My birthday wasn't this great thing for me growing up, and frankly, I'm glad there's a bunch of kids who were born in January, February, or March to overshadow me." He glanced at her, and Sterling had definitely softened a little. "My mother's birthday is on New Year's Day. She used to say that the whole world celebrated with her, and she'd laugh and laugh."

He focused on the road again, not sure why he was so grumpy today. Probably because it was a Leap Year, and that extra day at the end of February would yield dozens of ribbing texts from his brothers who still thought it was funny to tease him about being less than a decade old.

His body definitely felt all of his almost-thirty-two years. Or maybe that was because he'd been working out hard this week, trying to get this party off his mind—and Valentine's Day next week to come into focus for him.

"Then, I noticed her stop saying that," he said. "As time went on. And she told me last year that she just wants a quiet birthday, filled with love from Daddy and us boys." Another quick glance told Luke that this talking was good, and that he should continue. "And all the new wives, of course. The babies. She doesn't need the world anymore."

"You do, Luke," Sterling whispered.

"Nah," he said.

"I've seen you perform," she said. "You love the attention of the world."

"I have," he said. "Sure." He felt like gunning the truck and rushing past the trampoline park, but he made a turn and drove like he was calm and perfectly cool. "But I think I'm kind of getting over that now."

"Interesting."

"I'm sorry," he said, his mind going a few different directions. "I didn't deliberately keep my birthday from you. There's gonna be so much chaos, and so many people, no one is going to notice you don't have a present for me." He wanted to tell her she never needed to get him anything. If Luke wanted something, he bought it.

"Sure, right," Sterling said with another scoff. "I've met Abigail before, Luke. I guarantee that woman will have something for you."

Luke didn't want to lie. "Yeah, probably." A sigh came with the words, and he didn't try to hide it. "And Georgia is an excellent gift-giver. She always has something for me too. But it's quiet, Sterling. It's not a thing, like it is for the kids."

"Okay," she said, her voice straying up in pitch. "But I'd like to celebrate your birthday with you this year. Is that...is that something we can do? Just me and you?"

Luke looked over to her, letting down another wall as he took in the trepidation in her eyes, the way she held very still as he watched her. "Yeah, of course," he said. "I'd like that."

"Leap Year is on a Tuesday this year," she said, pulling her phone from her purse. "Let me see if I have any clients booked already. I'll clear them, and we can have the whole day together while Corrine is at school."

Corrine.

Luke really needed to decide what to do about his daughter. When he'd had to stay at Sterling's a few weeks ago, she'd asked where he'd sheltered. Yes, she'd used that word *sheltered*. She was a smart girl, and she read a lot, so her vocabulary was impressive.

He'd told her he'd stayed with "a friend—the woman who does my massages."

Sterling was that. Luke hadn't lied. But he felt like he'd withheld part of the truth too, and that wasn't a good feeling down inside his gut. Not a good feeling at all.

"I only have one appointment," she said. "I can move it."

"It's mine," Luke said.

She looked over to him, surprise etched in the lines around her eyes. "You booked a massage with me on your birthday?"

"It's my birthday," he said. "You make me feel good. I—" He

cleared his throat, realizing how his words sounded. "I mean—yeah. I like spending time with you, and you make me feel good."

That was all true too, even if it did sound more sexual than he liked.

"It's a morning appointment," she said. "We can go to lunch after, or see a movie, or...or—I will plan something awesome for you."

"You don't have to do that."

"Luke," she said as she tucked her phone back into her purse pocket. "You're the first boyfriend I've had in a decade. Can you please just let me celebrate your birthday with you? Or are we going to argue about it every day between now and then?"

"I don't want to argue with you," he said. "I'm sorry I'm doing that. I'm...my momma makes a fuss over me, and a couple of the wives."

"And your brothers," Sterling said. "I don't believe for a second that they wouldn't be there for you in a heartbeat if you needed it."

Luke thought of the time he'd passed out at the gym. Whenever he needed help with Corrine. When he needed help with his investments. "Yeah," he said. "But sometimes, you don't need it, and then your family feels like they're suffocating you."

Sterling laughed, and Luke could admit that lightened his mood. "Again, I don't mean to speak badly of them. I know your family isn't what you want it to be." He collected her hand and brought her wrist to his lips. "Forgive me, please. I'm saying so much today that is just stupid. I'll stop now."

"Don't stop talking to me, Luke," Sterling said, squeezing her fingers tighter into his. "I like it, and I deal with my family in my own way. Seems like you do too."

"I try," he said. He turned into the trampoline park parking lot. His brothers' trucks took up the front spots, though he and Sterling weren't late. Luke was used to being the stand-out. The brother

148

who got upset and stormed away. The one with the dark hat with an even darker look underneath it. He wasn't normally late, but he didn't care today if he was.

"We rented the whole thing," he said. "Just for us, so at least the food service will be fast, and we can probably have a ball pit to ourselves."

Sterling laughed again, and Luke sure did like the sound of it. He liked her presence in his passenger seat, at his side, in his life. He liked the black-and-white sweater she wore, with the skinny jeans that showed him all of her curves. He liked her kinky hair, and after he'd pulled into a spot and put his truck in park, he brushed his hand along her cheek.

"Sterling, I really am sorry."

"You've apologized enough," she said. "I forgive you." She smiled at him, and Luke's mind split. Now seemed like the perfect time to kiss her, but did he want this to happen in the cab of his truck? While the Wyoming wind wailed beyond the windows and his whole family waited inside for them?

Without sinking too deep into his mind, Luke leaned forward. He hadn't initiated a kiss with Sterling yet, and she'd been true to her word and had not kissed him again. Her eyes drifted closed, a soft sigh coming from her mouth.

Panic built in Luke as he wondered if he could land this right. His truck shouted, "New text message from Ex-Wife," and he jerked back. The moment broke, and Luke stabbed at the enormous touch-screen in his truck to get it to dismiss the message.

Instead, he touched *play now*, and the truck yelled, "Where are you? I'm at your house to get Corrine, and no one is here," in a smooth, cool, male voice.

Luke heard it in Mandi's accusatory tone, and he swore under his breath and hung his head.

"I'll give you a minute," Sterling said, and she escaped from the truck before he could tell her no. It would've been a bark anyway. She couldn't wait outside, not with Mother Nature threatening to shut down the whole state again.

Luke watched her stride away in those sexy jeans, her head held high and that luscious blonde hair flowing down her back. She didn't toss him a look or seem concerned she was committing herself to the Young Family Lion Den—but she was.

When she opened the door to the trampoline park and stepped inside, Luke's insides lurched. He couldn't leave her alone in there for long, and he hurried to pick up his phone and deal with his flaky ex and her terrible, terrible timing.

Then, he was going to march into the trampoline park with a smile on his face. He was going to hug his mother and introduce his girlfriend around to everyone—including his daughter.

"You want this," he said to himself, because Sterling stirred something in him that he absolutely did want. A new life, one with the tender touch of a woman for him and his daughter. A safe haven from the band, from the physical storms of Wyoming and the emotional storms of life, from himself.

He hoped he could be the man she deserved, and now that they were celebrating his birthday together, Luke would have to reschedule his appointment with his therapist that day. "Probably need to make it sooner," he said to himself as Mandi's line rang. Then he could be at his best for his birthday—for Sterling.

17

Sterling hadn't been to a trampoline park in a long time, if ever. They'd sort of come into popularity after her teens, and she saw no reason to bounce around during her massage therapy training. Just inside the door, the scent of rubber and sweat met her nose, and while it wasn't entirely pleasant, there was something quaint about this place.

In the distance, trampolines took up the space, and closer to her sat foam and ball pits. To her left stood at least six bounce houses, and plenty of the littler Youngs had gone that way. On her right stood the arcade, with flashing neon lights and loud music.

As she tried to get her bearings, she found Abby, Everly, and Georgia standing near a large bank of tables. Those had clearly been set up just for the Youngs and their party, and balloons lifted from each end. They drifted in the air currents in the building, and Sterling finally recognized the scent that overlay across the space.

Bubble gum.

She smiled, because this was the perfect place for a lot of kids to celebrate their birthdays.

Presents had been piled on the tables near the women, and Sterling decided that should be her first stop. She had no idea how long Luke would take with his ex-wife, and she wanted to give him the space he needed.

She tamped down the impatience with the god-of-a-cowboy. He hadn't kissed her in weeks, and she wasn't sure what he was waiting for. At the same time, if she hadn't just blurted out to Bryce that they were dating when they weren't, and if his parents didn't have some antiquated song about kissing, Sterling wouldn't have kissed him on New Year's Eve at all.

All told, it had only been five weeks since then, and that wasn't super slow for a relationship. At least for hers.

"Hey," she said as she approached the women at the table. Ev held her baby, and Sterling smiled softly at the infant. "Can I?"

"Sure." Ev slipped baby Keri into Sterling's arms, and while it wasn't the first time she'd held her best friend's baby, it sure felt like it. So many eyes existed here, and Sterling did like the quieter life of showing up at Ev's in the evening and sitting with the newborn while Ev moved around the kitchen or dealt with her dance studio employees.

Keri was almost five months old now, and she looked at Sterling with Ev's bright blue eyes and Trace's shock of dark hair.

"She is so beautiful," she said. "And you can't say that about every baby."

Ev smoothed her daughter's hair down, her smile so maternal and loving. "She's not so beautiful at two-thirty in the morning, when she's screaming for something to eat."

Sterling only smiled, because she didn't know about things like that. These women never seemed to have a shortage of things to talk about, and Sterling didn't think they did now. But a beat of silence passed, and she figured if she didn't ask now, she'd lose her chance—and her nerve.

"Hey, so Luke just told me his birthday is later this month." She cleared her throat and wished baby Keri would start fussing right now. Then she'd have a distraction to keep her occupied while she spoke the thoughts in her head.

"Yeah, Leap Year," Abby said.

"I didn't know he was a Leap Year baby," Georgia said. "No wonder we never celebrate his birthday."

"Where is he?" Ev looked behind Sterling to the doors, and when her gaze came right back to Sterling, she didn't think Luke had entered. So she had another moment.

"Mandi texted," Sterling said. "He's dealing with it."

Abby's jaw hardened, but otherwise, no one said anything.

"Anyway," Sterling said. "We just started dating, and while I've known him for a while, I'd love some...ideas for what to get him for his birthday." She forced a laugh out of her mouth. "I mean, what do you buy for a guy who has everything he wants and the means to get it if he doesn't?"

She first looked at Abby, because Luke had admitted he spent a lot of time out at Tex's, and that he'd confided a few things in Abby. When they'd been text-talking about who he was closest to in his family, he'd listed his brothers, and then Abby and Everly. He was getting closer with Hilde, he claimed, because he'd been spending more and more time with Gabe.

"I'd probably get him something like I try to do for Trace," Ev said. "I call them 'experience gifts.' You know, something the two of you can do together. An experience you get to have together."

Sterling nodded and made room for Leigh and Hilde as they arrived at the table. "Whew," Leigh said, her toddler on her hip too. She pushed her thick hair over her shoulder. "The wind is not playing tricks right now."

Hilde held Liesl's hand, and she pointed to a bare spot on the table. "Put them right there, darling."

Watching her be a step-mom warmed Sterling's heart. Of course, Hilde had a daughter of her own too, so she knew how to parent. Sterling had never had to take care of anyone but herself for longer than a couple of hours, and she suddenly glanced around for Luke's parents and his daughter.

She hadn't even thought to look for them. What did that mean?

"Can I hold her?" Hilde asked.

"When will you know if you're having a boy or a girl?" Georgia asked as Sterling transferred the little girl to Hilde's arms. Out of all of these women, she knew Hilde and Ev the best. They'd been friends for a few years now, in fact, and Sterling told herself she completely belonged here.

"A couple of weeks," Hilde said with a smile at the baby.

"You know, for Luke," Abby said. "He's more sentimental than he seems." She exchanged a glance with Georgia, and they seemed to have a whole conversation in a breath of time. "And he wants to be seen. Recognized."

Sterling nodded, though that assessment of Luke sort of flew in the face of what he'd just told her in the truck. He *used* to want to be seen and recognized.

"Especially in his family," Georgia said.

"Are we talking about Luke?" Leigh looked alarmed. "And I missed it?" She glanced around like someone would start throwing pumpkins to break up their gossip session. "How are things going with him?"

"That's not what she's talking about," Ev hissed back, her smile huge. "It's his birthday soon, and Sterling needs the perfect gift."

"Oh, boy," Hilde said, her eyebrows high. She looked around at all of the women. "Food. Luke *loves* to eat."

"Yeah," Sterling said. "But he's so picky about stuff. Have you *been* out to dinner with him?"

"I'll leave that to you," Hilde said with a smile.

The other ladies laughed a little, and it was Leigh who said, "I do take him my Christmas crack all the time. He loves that."

"He does have a prominent sweet tooth," Abby mused. "Can't go wrong with something chocolatey and fruity at the same time."

Sterling nodded, feeling like she should be taking notes. "Experiences, food, sweets, something that recognizes him." She glanced over to the bounce houses, where most of the Young brothers stood in a group just like this one. They laughed and talked, and Sterling could just see a spot for Luke among them.

"And of course," Ev said, a sparkle in her eye. "Luke likes his massages."

Sterling's face heated, but she refused to clear her throat. "He's already coming in on his birthday."

"Perfect." Ev turned toward the cowboys. "Let me go ask Trace about something musical." She hurried off before Sterling could say she had enough ideas. Her mind had started percolating now, and she checked behind her to see Luke storming her way.

"Oh, and I'm doing a calligraphy class at the bookshop," Georgia said. "Might be fun for you, Sterling. Abby's going to come do it."

Sterling turned back to her, a smile touching her lips. She couldn't remember the last time she'd been invited out to do something with women. When she'd left Red Carpet to start her own massage studio, she'd lost all of her friends. In fact, those same "friends" had spent the better part of a year dragging her name through the mud everywhere they could, and Sterling almost felt like crying.

"Thank you," she said. "I'd love to come." Luke stepped to her side, his hand sliding along the waistband of her jeans. "When is it?"

"When is what?" he asked, and his voice didn't sound one step above midnight.

"A calligraphy class," Georgia said without giving any further details. "I'll text you, Sterling."

To her horror, Sterling sniffled as she nodded, and Luke zeroed in on her at the same time Hilde touched her arm. She didn't know where to look, and she ended up studying the diamond on Hilde's ring finger.

"Sweetheart?" Luke asked, his voice tender and only serving to open the dam inside her even further.

"Come on, Piglet," Hilde said to Liesl. "Let's go see if your daddy has gotten here yet."

"I'm on food table duty," Abby said, one hand resting on her belly. "So I better go see where we are with that."

"There are duties?" Sterling asked.

"No." Abby grinned and then stepped into Luke and swept a kiss across his cheek. "I just like food, and I know I'm going to be happiest there tonight."

"You and me both," Georgia said, and they linked arms, smiling, and left.

Luke stood with Sterling at the present table, and it sure didn't look like another box, bag, or bauble would fit on it. "Are you going to take a calligraphy class?" he asked.

"Yeah," she said slowly. "I think it sounds fun." She smiled at him, though he'd already been alerted to her emotions. "How did things go with Mandi?"

A cloud crossed his features for two seconds, then cleared. "Fine," he said. "She had the day wrong, of course." He carried the disdain right there in his voice, then he sighed. "Sorry I'm mad about her all the time."

"Not all the time," Sterling said. "And you have a right to be frustrated."

"My momma called too," he said, gently turning her and steering her away from the brightly wrapped gifts and wafting balloons by taking her hand and moving in front of her. "She said they're about ten minutes out."

Sterling's heartbeat shot through her body, a hard pulse that nearly left her breathless. "Okay."

"I want to introduce you to Corrine," he said, moving in front of her to face her. "As my girlfriend." He searched her face. "What do you think?"

"I think...that's fine," she said, looking for something in his expression too. But Luke was far better at hiding behind his walls, boxing everything up tight, and keeping it hidden. "I think we're all going to need time to adjust to our relationship."

He frowned. "What does that mean?"

"It means, Luke," she said with a smile. "That I think you're going to have the hardest time with me being in Corrine's life out of the three of us."

His shoulders fell, and he scuffed his sexy cowboy boots against the floor. "You're probably right."

"I don't think it's bad." She leaned closer so Luke would look at her properly again. "You've both been through a lot."

Luke cleared his throat, and oh, Sterling saw he had more to tell her. "I am very protective of her," he said. "Have you ever read anything—like an article or research study—about how it affects kids when they're abandoned by their mothers?"

Sterling shook her head, so out of her league with this man. She'd spoken true when she'd said he was a lot of man, and he came with a beautiful daughter who Sterling didn't know how to interact with on any level. "No."

"It's not pretty." He faced his brothers and the bounce houses again. "Okay, I'm done being surly. This is a party." He took her hand again and led her over to everyone else.

"Heya, Luke," Morris said, giving him a big smile. Then a hug. "Hi, Sterling."

"Hey," she said. She nodded her way through Howdy's, and Hey's, and Hiya's for the next few minutes. No one seemed to think it odd she was there, and they simply talked to her like she'd been one of them forever.

She watched the kids play, realizing they were all over here, not just the younger ones. And some of them wore crowns and tiaras. "Oh, I get it," she said. "The birthday kids have the crowns."

"Yes," a woman said. "So that means Luke needs one."

"Momma," he protested, but his mother had arrived, and she indeed wore a tiara. A bright, shiny, sparkling-with-gems tiara, not one of the paper ones Sterling had seen on Melissa and Joey.

She lifted a gold crown with red rubies inlaid in it and said, "Bend down for me now, Lucas."

He did, and his momma fitted him with a crown only a king would wear. Sterling grinned and grinned, because if he was a king, that would make her a queen. And oh, how she wanted to be a queen. She wanted someone to lavish her with gifts and cater to her every need. She wanted someone to look at her like she mattered, like she meant something, like her opinion would fall on ears that would listen.

She grinned at Luke while he adjusted his headwear, while he looked softly at his mother and then hugged her, while his eyes met hers. In that moment, she realized she didn't want just any king to praise her, talk to her, worship her.

She wanted King Lucas Young.

"Wow," she said with a giggle. She brushed a lock of his hair back off his forehead from where it had been pinned down wrong. "So handsome."

Luke smiled back at her, and his expression turned much more heated. "Momma," he said. "Daddy." He stepped to her side, and she faced his parents. "You've met Sterling Boyd, I'm sure." He looked at her again. "We're dating."

Just like that. Two words.

"That's wonderful," his momma said, and Sterling struggled to remember her name.

"My momma is Cecily," Luke said. "Daddy is Jerry."

"So glad to meet you," his daddy said, sticking out his hand. "Luke's needed someone good in his life for a long time."

"Daddy," Luke grumbled. "You don't even know her."

"I know she's not wearing bright pink fur to a cowboy family party," Jerry said, grinning as she shook his hand. "Plus, she has a good air about her. A father knows."

"Okay, yeah," Luke said with plenty of bite. "Enough from you guys." He pinned his mother with a look. "I mean it, Momma. No commentary about my love life."

His momma scoffed and swatted at his chest. "That would require me to know something about your love life." She faced the row of bounce houses. "Where are my birthday babies?"

Choruses of "Grandma! Grandma!" filled the air, and not only the kids bearing paper crowns came spilling out of the bounce houses, but everyone.

Everyone, including Corrine, though she'd come with them. She fit with the Youngs, what with all their dark hair and bright brown eyes. Of course, Sterling could spot some anomalies too— Joey had blonde hair, for one, and Boston was blond-blue-eyed from head to toe.

He still crowded in around Cecily and Jerry, who both opened their arms and gathered their chicks in close for hello hugs and welcome kisses.

"Jelly bean," Luke said, and Corrine poked her head out of the fray. He gestured for her to come over to him, and she did, skipping all the way. He grinned down at her, his hand searching for and sliding palm-to-palm against Sterling's.

"Baby." He crouched down, which caused him to release her hand. She wasn't sure if she should too, and as he started to speak again, Sterling copied him. He looked at her in surprise, his mouth open but no words coming out.

Sterling smiled at him, then looked at Corrine. She gazed back at her.

"Corrine," he said, finally using her real name. Luke did love using a pet name, and Sterling sure didn't mind when he called her *sweetheart* or *baby*. "This is Sterling. She's my girlfriend."

Another little girl arrived with Corrine, and she put her arm through hers. "Whatcha doin'? Do you wanna jump with me?"

"Rosie," Luke said, probably for Sterling's benefit. "This is Sterling. She's my girlfriend." He grinned, like he gained strength every time he said it out loud.

"Oh, boy, Uncle Luke," Rosie said in her cute little voice. She leaned closer, her eyes lighter than some of the other kids. "Are you kissin' her the way my daddy kisses Sunny?"

Luke burst out laughing, and Sterling joined him. "She's Jem's," Luke said. "In case that wasn't obvious. And yes, Miss Rosie. Sterling and I are like your daddy and Sunny."

"Will you marry her then?" Corrine asked, looking at Sterling again. Fear edged into her eyes, and Sterling hadn't anticipated that. "Uncle Jem is marrying Sunny, right?"

Luke grinned at his daughter. "Yep, he is." He glanced over to Sterling. "And I don't know about us, jelly bean. It's new, and we'll go through all that together, okay?"

160

He stood and picked her up, his smile slipping too. "Don't look so nervous, okay? I'll start bringin' Sterling around, and you'll get to know her just like I will. Okay?" He rubbed his beard against her cheek until she giggled, and then he set her on her feet.

Sterling held up one hand in a partial wave and said, "It's sure great to meet you girls. Rosie and Corrine." She nodded to Corrine's double-braids. "Did your daddy do those?"

"Yes," Corrine said, her voice barely audible above the party noise.

"They're so pretty," she said. "I think you might be the prettiest girl here."

"Mel's wearing a tiara," Corrine said.

"Honey bear," Luke said. "You'll get one when it's the summer birthday celebration, okay?"

"My brother's got a crown," Rosie said. "Let's go see if he'll let us wear it." She looked at Corrine, who looked at Luke.

"Go on then," he said, and the two little girls ran off.

Sterling's knees protested this crouch, and she reached for Luke. "Help me up, cowboy." She started to lose her balance, and she swiped frantically for something or someone to grab onto. She only managed to hit Luke's arm before she toppled, and that brought him stumbling after her.

"Oof." She landed on her hip and rolled, and a cry went up. Embarrassment filled her instantly, and Sterling couldn't see past her Medusa's mess of curls. She had not tamed back very much of her hair the way Luke had done for Corrine, a fact she regretted in this moment.

Luke hovered above her, concern in his eyes. "Hey, you okay?"

"I...." Sterling didn't know what to say.

Tex arrived, and he knelt beside her. "Hey, Sterling." He touched her arm. "You okay? Did you hit your head?"

Trace hovered just a pace away, ready to help, and Sterling wanted the building to be sucked into the sky.

"I'm all right." She reached for Luke's hand. "I just lost my balance for a second." He helped her to her feet, and Tex didn't go far. Neither did Trace.

"I thought you did yoga and meditation and stuff," Luke said.

"Oh, brother," Tex said. "I thought your therapist had been helping you have more tact."

"Tex," Luke growled, but Sterling tucked her arm through his and leaned into his side. He looked at her, the irritation sliding right away. "Sorry, baby." He pressed his lips to her temple. "Should we go see if we can sneak some birthday cake early?"

"I just fell on my face," Sterling said. "If that didn't earn me cake, nothing will." She grinned at him, and he seemed to only have eyes for her as they edged away from Tex and Trace. That couldn't be true, but Sterling wanted to live inside the fantasy of having the undivided attention of the beastly prince for just a little while longer.

Just for tonight would be fine...if he'd kiss her later to break the spell.

18

Everly Young could be the star if she had to be. She'd danced on a lot of stages, the spotlight on her every move. She ran her own dance studio here in Coral Canyon, and she loved it. She'd taken the last quarter of last year off, but starting in January, she'd taken her baby to the studio with her and overseen the classes and teachers as normal.

The only change was that she herself didn't teach. Everly did miss it, but she would give up anything to be a mother, and that had tempered the fact that she didn't get to teach anymore. She couldn't stop looking at Harry, who was the second-oldest grandchild in the Young family.

He had turned seventeen years old a few days ago, and Trace had allowed him to have several friends over to the house. Fifteen had come, and they'd barely fit. Ev had quickly ordered more pizza, and Trace had shot daggers at his son for a full fifteen minutes before she'd stepped in and said, "How many times will your son turn seventeen?"

Trace had calmed after that, and it wasn't like his displeasure could disrupt rooms, the way Luke's could. But Ev could feel, and Harry knew, and once he'd finally let it go, everyone had enjoyed themselves.

Kind of like they were this afternoon at the trampoline park. Harry loved stuff like this, and while he'd been getting a little taller this year, and his shoulders had started to fill out more, he was still quite athletic.

He, Bryce, and Cash had taken to the real trampolines, leaving the bright bounce houses to the younger kids. Joey was close to their age too, but she didn't seem to have any interest in actually jumping on a trampoline, so Ev stood removed from the group a little as she watched the boys yell and flip and laugh with one another.

Otis had said that Joey's speed was more like sitting in a swing and reading a book, not leaping from one trampoline to another. Ev patted her baby's bottom in perfect rhythm, and she turned when footsteps approached.

"Can I jump with them?" Cole asked.

Ev smiled at him and smoothed his hair back. "Of course you can, buddy." He'd just turned nine at the end of January, and Ev was still getting to know him and his sister Rosie. "Harry," she called. "Cole's comin' out." She heard the small-town swagger of her voice, and it didn't bother her at all.

"Okay." Harry jumped and jumped and jumped and then landed lightly on his feet, running toward them for a few steps. "Heya, Cole. Come on. There's room for you." He grinned at the younger boy, and they stepped out onto a closer trampoline.

They were far more springy than a normal trampoline, and that was just another reason Ev wouldn't be stepping on one.

Sunny joined her, and they sat on a bench together to watch the kids. "How's the hospital?" Ev asked, because she didn't know Sunny super well either. She knew she'd taken Jem's wild heart and tamed it, that she worked as a nurse at the hospital and clinic in Coral Canyon, and that she took care of her elderly parents in town too.

"It's good," she said. "I'm glad I'm not in the ER anymore." She smiled, something haunted behind her eyes for only a moment. "So yeah. Good."

"Good."

"Sugar cookies," Abby announced as she arrived. They'd been cut into the shape of hearts and decorated with a pale pink frosting. Georgia hadn't gotten too far from Abby's side all night, and the two of them sat on the bench next to Ev.

"Is this where the party is?" Leigh asked. She'd relinquished her little girl, who would be two next month, to the bounce houses, and Ev suspected she hadn't seen her since.

"I guess so," Ev said, positioning Keri so she could see out. The baby relaxed back into Everly, which was the best feeling in the world.

Leigh gestured to the others, and before Ev knew it, all of the women and wives had congregated over in the quieter part of the trampoline park. Even Sterling had come, and Ev smiled at her so broadly that her face hurt.

They chit-chatted about school, the weather that had caused so many snow days, and the band. Always the band. They were in the middle of writing songs and producing a couple so they could take them to King Country. Once everything got approved, they'd spend long hours in the studio behind Abby's farmhouse recording.

Morris went to Nashville more than anyone, and Leigh said, "He's going right after Rachelle's birthday. Second week of March."

"Maybe Harry should go with him," Ev said, and that drew some attention.

"Why would Harry go with him?" Leigh asked.

"He sent in a demo to King Country and Cadence," Ev said, her throat filling with pride. She tried to swallow it away, because she didn't want to let it infect her for too long.

"Wow," Georgia said. "That's great."

"Leigh," Hilde said, and Ev looked over to her too. She nodded toward the table bearing all the presents—they hadn't gotten to opening them yet—and everyone gasped at the same time.

"He brought her," Leigh said with plenty of awe in the words.

Denzel stood there with his cane in one hand and that of a pretty honey-haired woman's hand in the other. No dog. Ev tried to remember the last time she'd seen Denzel without his German shepherd, and she couldn't.

He went everywhere with that dog—except apparently, the Young Family First Quarter Birthday Party.

"I'm going to go greet them," Leigh said.

"We all should," Abby said.

"Oh, let's not overwhelm her in the first ten seconds," Ev said. "We can be a lot."

"You can say that again," Sterling said, and all the attention got thrown her way now. Her face shone red as she added, "I'm just saying. Let Leigh say hi first. We don't need to mob her."

Abby giggled, which caused several of the others to start laughing too. Thankfully, Sterling's complexion started to go back to normal, and Ev reached over and squeezed her hand. "You're getting along with Luke?"

"Yes," Sterling said. "It's not so awkward anymore."

"Even after he stayed the night at your house?"

"What?" Georgia said.

"Oh, this is why we came over here, Gracie," Faith said, grinning. "We need the goods on Sterling and Luke."

Sterling laughed lightly and shook her head. "It's not what you think. That first storm? He couldn't get home, so he slept on my couch."

All heads swung back to Faith, whose face had started to flush. "Oh, well, that's nothing. Right, ladies?"

"She shared a bed with Blaze," Abby mock whispered.

Sterling's eyebrows went up, but Faith just laughed and shook her head. "Similar situation. Snowstorm, but this one knocked out the power. I have one bed, in one bedroom, which also happened to have a fireplace."

"And because of Blaze's back," Dani said. "He couldn't sleep on the couch. So they shared."

"There were *so* many pillows between us." Faith rocked her baby girl, who'd gone to sleep. Everly envied her that, and while she tried not to compare, she knew Grace slept better than Keri. She ate better. Everything she did seemed to be better, and Ev hated that she sometimes fell into putting their little girls against each other.

Dani didn't have her little one, and if Ev searched hard enough, she'd find either Mav or Cecily with Emma.

Ev really didn't want to have feelings of inferiority over her precious daughter, and she knew better than most that every single human on the planet came with their own set of wiring. Trace had eight brothers, and not a single one of them was exactly the same.

"Scandalous," Sterling said with a grin. "What other stories have you guys got?"

"Trace and Ev snuck around forever," Abby said with a grin.

"Hey," Ev said, though her own smile wouldn't seem to leave her face. "Trace was worried about Harry."

Hilde laced her arm through Ev's. "Good thing you just knew you and Trace were meant to be, right?"

"Right," Ev said. "Besides, I'm not the only one who sort of led on her cowboy. You wouldn't go out with Gabe for ages."

"We all have to get out of our own way sometimes," Hilde said mysteriously. She had such dark eyes, but they were lit with an interior twinkle right now. "Abby practically chased Tex off his land."

"Oh, that man," Abby said, but she didn't deny it. Ev loved her —and Hilde, and Georgia, and Leigh, and Faith, and Dani, and Sunny, and Sterling like sisters.

"I bet Leigh's going to be busy with Michelle for a few minutes," Georgia said. She watched as Leigh went with her brother and his new girlfriend over to the other brothers and Trace's parents. "I have an announcement, and she'll feel bad if she misses it."

Ev's eyebrows went up as she surveyed the group to judge their reactions to Georgia having an announcement. Otis was in the band too, so perhaps it was something with Country Quad.

She dismissed that, because Trace was in Country Quad too, and they'd agreed there would be no secrets between them. He told her everything the band was doing, so they could plan together as a family what they'd do when he had to travel.

Nerves began to gnaw at her gut. "What is it?" she asked Georgia when she realized that Abby didn't look surprised at all. She and Georgia had been very good friends for a long time, so Ev wasn't that shocked or upset that perhaps Abby already knew the announcement.

Georgia couldn't have babies, but perhaps she and Otis had decided to adopt again. Maybe they'd be getting a foster child soon. Maybe she'd be closing her bookshop.

Ev didn't know what she'd do if Georgia did that. She'd always looked to the woman as an example of a working mother, someone who'd had a baby and kept her small business open.

"Let's give her another few minutes," Abby said. "Okay?"

Georgia nodded and said, "Luke seems really happy, Sterling.

Way happier than I saw him when he was dating those other women."

"Oh, totally," Abby said. "I honestly don't know what he saw in Hillary."

Murmurs of assent went around, but Ev kept her eyes on Sterling. She didn't like gossip at all, as she'd been on the wrong side of it plenty in the past couple of years.

"What do you guys like about Luke?" Sterling asked.

That stumped everyone, and she grinned. "Come on. He's likable, right?" She watched him, and Ev caught him throwing her a look or two as well. "I'm thinking of making him something for his birthday, and I'd love to know what *you* guys see in him that maybe I'm missing, because I'm blinded by how hot he is."

"Dear Lord," Hilde said, laughing. "Heaven help us all."

Sterling laughed too, and Ev couldn't keep hers silent either. As they quieted, it was Abby who leaned forward and covered Sterling's hand. "Heaven will help you, Sterling. And Luke. I know he hates being last, but he'll be okay with the wait if it's absolutely right."

"How do you know if it's absolutely right?" Sterling asked.

"When you suspect it is," Dani said quietly. "That's when you get down on your knees and pray."

Ev nodded to that, and she added, "I like how fun Luke can be. He's never hesitated to get out on the dance floor and have a good time."

"He's strong and hardworking," Abby said. "He bought that house he lives in when a stiff wind would've blown it down. He gutted it and remodeled it himself."

Sterling nodded and smiled. "He's good with his hands."

"Oh, girl," Hilde said, laughing. "Stop it."

Sterling probably wouldn't stop, but she didn't say anything else either. Ev loved her too, and she wanted so badly for Sterling and Luke to carve out their own happily-ever-after.

"Luke always says hello to me," Hilde said. "No matter how many people are around. He's thoughtful that way."

"He sends me private texts to say thank you," Dani said. "He's so grateful for any help he gets, and for his family."

"All true," Abby said. "So he's a little grumpy from time to time. So am I." She looked out toward the trampolines. "I see so much of myself in Luke sometimes. He's a good soul."

"A little wounded," Georgia said. "But so are we all, right?"

"Right," Ev said.

"Luke is a loyal brother," Faith said. "He would literally do anything for one of his brothers, and he defends them religiously."

Sunny was the only one who hadn't said anything, and she studied her hands. "Jem and Luke are pretty close," she said. "He brought me things when I wasn't speaking to Jem, and while I could tell he wasn't happy about it, there he was, doing it."

"Thank you," Sterling whispered.

"He'll always be there," Sunny said. "I like that service-oriented part of him. Jem's called him a couple of times when he needs...someone to be with him."

Ev wanted to wrap Sunny in a hug too. Everyone in the family knew about Jem's alcoholism and his incredibly addictive personality. And yes, it had been Luke and Blaze who'd helped the most with that. Mav and Trace had done a lot to help the kids over the past couple of years too. In fact, everyone in the Young family contributed to each other somehow, and Ev decided right then and there that she needed to recognize the simple things her husband, his brothers, and all the wives did for her. For Keri. For Trace. For Harry.

And she needed to do what Luke did—she needed to send

them private messages outlining why she was so grateful for their love, help, and support.

She caught movement out of her peripheral vision. "Oh, guys, Leigh's bringing Michelle over here." She actually sat up straighter as if that would make Michelle like her more or feel more welcome.

"Guys," Leigh said with plenty of pep and a pretty smile on her face. "This is Michelle Hinz. You may have seen her at Daily Grind, the coffee shop she owns."

"Hello, everyone," she said, her smile wide and full of white teeth. Ev liked her instantly, as she seemed calm and friendly on the outside.

"This is Hilde," Leigh said, indicating her. "She's married to Gabe, my husband's twin."

"I know Hilde," Michelle said. "We've been going to small business meetings for a while now." She scanned the group. "And Georgia. And Sterling."

"Oh, sure," Leigh said with a nervous laugh. "What about Ev? She owns a dance studio. Married to Trace."

"Of course," Michelle said, nodding at her.

"I didn't go to too many meetings," Ev said.

"That's because you're so popular on social media," Hilde quipped. "You didn't need marketing lessons."

"I did too," Ev said, though she knew her social media strategy had been flawless. You know, back when she wasn't posting about diaper rash and a pukey baby at three in the morning.

Hilde said, "Yeah, sure," before she scooted over a little. "Sit down, Michelle." She tossed a look at Georgia. "Georgia had an announcement for us."

"Better hurry," Abby murmured. "I see Cecily heading for the gift table."

Georgia looked that way, as did Ev. Yes, Cecily was leading a few kids toward the tables with all the presents on them, like she was the Pied Piper and her grandchildren the rats. Ev wanted to have so many kids in her life, the way Cecily did.

She already wanted another baby, but she hadn't said anything to Trace yet. Maybe she would soon.

"All right." Georgia took a big breath. "I wanted to tell you guys something, because I'd like to request prayers and support."

Ev focused on her, her mind whirring and whirring and whirring. What could this be about?

Georgia's eyes filled with tears, and they spilled down her cheeks. "Otis and I are going to have a baby." Her fingers went round and round each other. "I'm pregnant and due in September."

Ev sat there in complete stunned silence, as did everyone else.

"She's been to the doctor," Abby said. "Everything is okay for now." She put her arm around Georgia, tears in her own eyes, and Ev's eyes burned with them too. "So we'll pray for her, right, ladies?"

"Of course," Ev said, her voice breaking. She scooted forward and hugged Georgia the best she could with a baby on her lap. "Oh, honey, I'm so, so excited for you."

"I'm trying to contain the hope and excitement," Georgia whispered.

"Nonsense," Hilde said as she piled into the group hug too. "You live every moment of it, Georgia."

Leigh leaned in and said, "What a blessing, Georgia."

"Yes," Sterling said as she wrapped her arm around Ev on one side and Georgia on the other. "I'll pray for you."

"Mav and I will too." Dani joined the group, and so did Faith and Sunny.

"To your continued health," Faith said. "I'll do anything I can to help."

"Me too, Georgia," Sunny said, her voice full of tears. Ev couldn't exactly see her, because she was smashed in the middle of the group. Keri began to fuss, and that broke some of the tension.

She laughed to release some of her nervous energy as the group broke up. Sniffles filled the air among the shouts of the boys jumping on the trampolines nearby, and Michelle alone stood back from them all.

"You ladies are something special," she said, pressing one palm against her heart. "I don't know all of you very well yet, but that was beautiful." She swiped at her eyes and tilted her head back. "I promised Denzel nobody here would make me cry, but y'all have done it."

"You're makin' her cry?" Denzel demanded as he thumped closer to them. "Just what is goin' on over here?"

"Nothing," Leigh said in a pinched voice. "Go back to the boys."

"They sent me over here to break up this little female shin-dig," he said. "Because it's time for presents."

Ev drew in a big breath and looked at Denzel as he arrived at Michelle's side. She beamed at him—positively *beamed* at him—which brightened his dark countenance. "You're okay, sweets?"

"Yes," she said. "Nothing troubling happening here."

"Nope." Ev got to her feet. "Thanks for sticking up for us, Michelle." She moved over to the edge of the trampoline. "Boys," she called. "Time for presents."

Cheering erupted, because three of them wore crowns, and that meant they'd get to tear into the gifts that had been brought. Ev moved out of the way as they hopped and leapt closer, and behind her, the ladies broke up.

She remained, because Sterling was slow to leave, and Ev had brought over her diaper bag and needed to collect it. So she lingered with Sterling, Abby, and Georgia when Bryce arrived.

"Hey-o," he said, quickly taking in the women in front of him. "Abs? Georgia? Why are you guys crying?"

Georgia simply grabbed onto him and held him tight. Bryce looked worried for a moment, but Abby smiled at him and nodded. He hugged Georgia in return, and Ev couldn't even imagine the type of tender, close relationship Bryce had with the woman raising his biological child.

"They sure are sweet," Sterling murmured, and Ev moved with her to give Bryce and Georgia a little privacy.

"Yeah," she agreed. "They sure are."

Trace met her at the edge of the last trampoline and took his baby girl into his arms. "Why are all the women crying?" he asked.

"It's not a secret, do you think?" Ev asked Sterling.

"Honestly? She told us, probably hoping we'd tell the cowboys."

Ev nodded and stepped into her husband's arms. She grinned up at him. "Georgia is pregnant. She wants us all to pray for her."

Trace's mouth fished open and shut, and Sterling kept moving. When Ev was sure no one would overhear them, and with Trace already reeling, she added, "And baby, I want another baby too."

Air burst from his mouth, but as he studied her, he said, "You're not kidding."

"Nope." She pressed a kiss to his mouth. "Now, come on. We need to make sure Harry sees that teeny-tiny present Georgia brought for him. She gets the best stuff, and I can't wait to see what it is."

19

L uke knotted his tie at his throat while Corrine played on his tablet on the bed. He turned toward her, a ball of nerves way down deep in his stomach. "How do I look, jelly bean?"

She looked up and took him in, her smile spreading across her face. "Your shirt is pink."

He looked down at it. "Yeah," he said. "It's Valentine's Day." Luke moved over to sit on the bed with his daughter. "I'm goin' out with Sterling tonight." He swallowed, because this was an important holiday for women, he knew.

He had to look his best. He wanted to be on his best behavior. He had the best-laid plans, and he couldn't wait to sweep her off her feet. He hadn't kissed her again—or in his head, for the first time—and he knew he better get the deed done tonight.

Sure, he'd been putting it off, because he had a war going on inside him. One, the kiss wasn't going to be nearly as good as the almost-fake one on New Year's Eve, or two, he was going to fall completely in love with the blonde massage therapist he'd been crushing on for a long time now.

That was another reason—he wanted to get to know Sterling outside the massage studio. He couldn't act on crushes and honeymoon feelings. Not again. *Not ever again*, he thought.

"Is Mommy coming over?" Corrine asked.

Luke's jaw locked. "Not tonight, sweetie." He got to his feet again and reached for the tablet. "You're going over to Grandma's, and she's having a whole party, so go get your shoes."

"Oh, yeah! The party." Corrine slid from the bed, no argument about finishing her dress-a-doll game, and ran from the room. "I'll get the balloons. Remember she said to bring them?"

"I remember," Luke murmured as he powered off the tablet. His parents had said they'd had plenty of Valentine's Days together, and anyone could bring their kids over for a few hours that night. Luke had immediately taken them up on the offer, because he couldn't ask any of his brothers to stay home with his kid on Valentine's Day. They wanted to go out with their wives too, and he was the only single Young left.

"Besides Bryce," he told himself again. He just as quickly dismissed it, because he could not count Bryce as a Young brother. He was a different generation.

Luke got Corrine and her red balloons in the truck, and he made the quick drive from his house to his parents' condo. They'd downsized from the farm years ago, and it had gone to another family, then another, and then into disrepair. Tex had narrowly saved it in an auction he'd originally lost to Abby, who later became his wife.

Abby had texted him earlier that day, telling him to come over for lunch after church on Sunday, and Luke once again reached for his tie. He'd been attending church a lot more lately, but it was the only other time he wore something so constricting around his neck.

"Lord," he whispered once he returned to the truck, having dropped Corrine off to his momma's care. But he didn't know how to continue. He prayed with Corrine over meals. He bowed his head and removed his cowboy hat when others prayed at family events, big luncheons, or at church itself. But he didn't know how to petition the Lord in a way that didn't leave him feeling completely selfish and inadequate.

With his eyes closed, he remembered something he heard the pastor say on Sunday. *What would you do if you had more faith?*

Luke had looked up at that question, just as he did now. "What would I do if I had more faith?"

Pastor Richards had also said, "Do not diminish the faith you already have." Luke had really liked that too. He'd never considered himself overly faithful, but in the past few years, he'd taken one step into the dark, followed by another.

He realized sitting right there in his silent truck, that he'd been acting on faith for a while now. He hadn't known what his daughter liked to eat when he'd become her full-time parent. He knew everything about Corrine now, inside and out.

Luke had taken classes to learn how to cook, how to budget, how to braid hair. He'd shown up at every school meeting; he'd talked to teachers; he'd volunteered in his daughter's classroom.

He'd taken her to church and involved himself and her in family functions. He still had no idea what he was doing most of the time, and just getting up in the morning and getting breakfast on the table was an act of faith.

Filled with new power, he opened his eyes. "If I had more faith, I'd feel more confident about this date," he said. "Because I want it to go *so well*." Desperation clogged his throat, cutting off the rest of his thought.

But if not....

Pastor Richards' words filled in right there.

"But if not, I'll still be okay," Luke said. That was what faith was. He couldn't just boss God around—he had to have faith that what he wanted and what God wanted for him were the same thing.

And if they weren't....

Luke needed the faith to carry on anyway. No anger. No heated words with the Lord. He could be disappointed, but the true meaning of faith came after the thing he wanted that he didn't get.

"So," he said to himself as he started the ignition, his fingertips already getting a touch cold. "Do you believe you'll be okay if you can't land the perfect date tonight?"

He needed to act like he would be. He needed to demonstrate that faith in God, because he also believed that God was acutely aware of each individual's life—including his. He surely didn't want to watch Luke crash and burn on a date on Valentine's Day, but if he did...Luke had enough faith to pick himself up and move forward.

Satisfied now, and with his heartbeat only skipping every third beat instead of every other, he drove over to Sterling's. Her house made him smile from the corner. One, she always had a festive wreath on her bright red door.

This month, it had been heart-shaped and made from what looked like big, puffy white flowers. But when he'd touched them, they'd been hard and stiff, perfect to stand up to the Wyoming weather while still infusing some cheer into the world.

Tonight, she also had pink lights hanging from her rooftop, the way she'd hang Christmas lights around that holiday. It made the snow on the ground seem magical, and Luke's romantic side could just see himself kissing her with the wonder and awe of pink tea lights, the scent of roses, and the warm air blowing out of Sterling's house.

"Whoa, cowboy," he said as he made the turn into her driveway. "You're thinking of kissing her *before* the date?"

It sure would make the rest of it more fun. Or an absolute nightmare. Maybe his kissing would be so bad, she wouldn't even want to go to dinner. Maybe he'd foul it up so much—"Where's your faith now, Luke?"

He'd come to this house under horrible, nerve-racking pretenses before. He'd gotten himself up to the door and his finger against the doorbell, and he could do so again. The walk was easy, even, though the early evening air had already gone back to sub-zero temperatures due to the sun going behind the mountains so early in the winter.

With the doorbell pealing through the quiet neighborhood, Luke tucked his hands into his coat, hunched his shoulders higher to protect his ears more, and waited.

"Coming!" Sterling called from inside the house, and Luke's chest darn near collapsed on itself. Every time they'd gone out, she'd worn something feminine and beautiful, and he couldn't wait to see what she'd chosen for tonight. He'd told her he'd gotten a reservation "somewhere nice," and that he was wearing a tie.

So when she opened the door wearing a gown—a legit ballgown—made of red fabric, sequins, and lace, Luke felt like he'd hit the jackpot. He could only stare as his eyes roamed wherever they wanted to, without direction from his brain.

"Wow," he finally blurted out. "You look incredible." He reached for her, caught her hand, and towed her closer to him.

She giggled as she put both hands around his neck. "I don't have my shoes on," she whispered.

"Is the footwear going to make this outfit?" he teased. "Because I will be seeing this for months. Years." He ran his hand up her back, the fabric silky beneath the lace, until he met bare skin. She'd piled all of her hair on top of her head, and it looked elegant and beautiful.

She was elegance and beauty.

"You are gorgeous," he said, meaning it from the inside to the outside and everywhere in between.

"You know how to start a date off right," Sterling said. "Do you want to come in while I strap on my shoes?"

Strappy shoes. His mouth turned a little drier. "No," he managed to rasp.

Her eyebrows went up. "No? You don't want to come in?"

He shook his head. If he went inside the house, the pink lights wouldn't bathe them as he kissed her. He backed up a step and tugged her with him, causing her to step down out of her house. "I know you don't have shoes on," he said. "But you've chased me outside without them before."

She smiled at him, confusion running through her pretty eyes. "Luke?"

Before he could second-guess himself, before he got lost in his thoughts on faith again, he acted. After all, faith required action, and Luke took that first step into the dark.

He touched his lips to Sterling's, and God illuminated the next part of the path for him—in quiet, pale pink light.

This kiss was the opposite of the one they'd shared at New Year's. It wasn't the frantic, repressed version of two mouths meeting for the first time. It wasn't because everyone else in his family had someone to kiss, or because his parents had a ridiculous kissing song they wanted to play before they went home early.

It wasn't because she'd just told Bryce that they were dating when they weren't. Or because they happened to be at the same party together.

Oh, no. Luke kissed Sterling this time in a slow, controlled way. He let himself fall into her touch, and start another stroke, and bask in the pink light of love and beauty and wonder around him.

He'd lost his mind during their New Year's Eve kiss.

During this one...he lost his heart.

20

Sterling loved the way Luke took his time as he kissed her. She'd been waiting for this for weeks now, and she had to say—the cowboy did not disappoint. Not even a little bit. When he broke their union, he didn't apologize either.

He didn't say anything. Panic didn't fill her at what she'd done and said only moments ago. They simply stood together, out on her stoop, the winter air somewhere beyond her. She couldn't feel it, because the heat of a kiss that tender, that emotional, that raw... it surely sent waves lilting into the air, melting the snow from her roof completely.

"Okay," he said. "You can get your shoes now."

Sterling opened her eyes and looked at him. Again, she didn't feel the need to smile shyly or duck her head. They'd kissed, and it was magnificent. She turned and stepped up into her house, her shoes down at the end of the couch. She almost didn't want to wear them, but both Hilde and Everly had said she better, because they'd knock off Luke's cowboy boots and *then* his socks.

But maybe the dress had already done that. She still collected the shoes and sank onto a dining chair while Luke entered the house and closed the door softly behind him. Her furnace pumped, but it would catch up quickly to the cold air they'd let in.

"Where'd you get that dress?" he asked. "It seems quite...red for Coral Canyon." He smiled at her, his hands tucked back into his jacket pockets.

"Red, right." Sterling slipped her foot into one shoe and bent to fasten it. "A few years ago, there was this bachelor auction," she said. "They do it a lot around Christmastime, actually. I'm surprised you haven't been asked to do it. It's a fundraiser for the community."

"Who says I haven't been asked?" One eyebrow quirked up, which made Sterling giddy inside.

"Oh, excuse me," she teased. "You've never done it." She bent to get her other shoe, wishing she'd gone with something less showy. Everyone would be staring at her tonight, a fact she'd pointed out to herself multiple times in the past hour since donning the dress.

"Do I seem like the type to do a bachelor auction?" He scoffed. "If the community center needs money, I just write a check."

Sterling threaded the strap through the buckle and secured it. She put both of her hands in Luke's, and he steadied her as she stood. "Well, Mister Big Shot," she said. "Some of us can't do that." She turned and picked up the black fur she'd borrowed from Hilde. "Literally. I don't even have a checkbook anymore. Tell me you don't either."

"I have checks," he hedged, and for some reason, that made Sterling giggle. "And I didn't mean to be a big shot. I was just saying, they've asked me. I said no, and I made a donation instead."

"How very charitable of you," she said with a smile. "Anyway, I went to it my first year in town. It was a masquerade ball theme, and this dress came from that." She brushed her hands down the front of it. "It's weathered well in my closet since."

Luke put one arm around her waist and the other hand came up to touch the billowy feathers rising from her stole. "And this?"

"This belongs to Hilde," she said. "Apparently, it was part of Lynnie's Halloween costume a couple of years ago." She held her head high as she added, "She was Maleficent."

Luke grinned as their eyes met. "You are one of my favorite people."

For some reason, such a simple statement caused tears to burn in her eyes. "Luke," she said, and surely he heard the catch in her voice.

He cleared his throat and stepped back, his hand sliding away from her hip and taking hers instead. "I asked Blaze for a nice, quiet, romantic place for dinner, and he suggested this place called Silver. Have you heard of it?"

"No." Sterling shook her head as she moved to his side. "It can't be in Coral Canyon."

"Dog Valley," he said. "So it's a bit of a drive."

Sterling had lived in the Coral Canyon area—and that included the surrounding smaller towns like Dog Valley and Rusk —for a long time. Longer than Luke, that was for sure. She'd never heard of such a place.

"My dress won't be too much?"

"I think you'll fit right in," he said with a smile.

"You're not wearing a tux." She did like the dark pants, as they seemed to flow like midnight water with every step he took.

"No," he said. "But Blaze said this place doesn't even allow khakis. Your dress pants have to be like, slick. Shiny."

She looked back into his face. "Yours qualify."

"Praise the heavens," he said dryly as he opened the door. "I love the lights, by the way. So festive and fun."

"Thanks. I had one of my clients put them up for me."

He held her hand as she stepped down, her heels a bit of a pinpoint but nothing she couldn't handle. They only added two inches to her height, as Sterling already stood at five-foot-seven, and she didn't really want to tower over others.

Of course, with Luke at her side, she still stood far shorter than him. He helped her into the truck, making sure her fancy skirt was all in before he closed the door.

The bite of winter's breeze didn't reach her in the truck, but her hands still shook. Maybe from the perfect reaction he'd given her. Maybe because of that kiss. Maybe because of the cold—but definitely not because of the cold.

He got behind the wheel of the truck and cut her a glance. "Ready, sweetheart?"

"Yep." Sterling sank into the warmth of the seat and let Luke be in charge of the conversation and the truck as he headed north.

"Tell me your favorite thing to do," he said, shooting her a look as he came to a stop at the sign leading out of her neighborhood. His left-hand blinker popped every other second, but there was a lot of traffic tonight.

"Right now, it's planning for this meditation class," she said. "I'm going over and re-over my notes from my training last year, and I'm really excited to do it."

"This next week, right?"

She nodded. "I'm a little nervous," she admitted. "The class is full, though, and I have a waiting list."

"That's great, baby."

She loved his varied use of pet names. As he turned left onto the highway and accelerated, Sterling wondered how much to tell him. Since she wanted a long-term, meaningful relationship, she reasoned she should probably tell him all of it.

"I'm hoping to explore other options for Deep Purple," she said. "Beyond massage."

"Yeah," he said. "You've mentioned that."

"I want a dedicated space," she said. "That's not in my house. But a commercial space is expensive, and what I'd need would have to be big. You need room for yoga mats and mirrors and couples' massage tables."

"Couples massage?" Luke's eyebrows went up. "That sounds...interesting."

"It's fun," she said. "At the higher-end resorts in like Hawaii and whatever, they even have the couple do a few massage moves on each other." She took a breath, telling herself to calm down. Slow down. "And I really want to do an aerial meditation class," she said. "That requires a big room, with hanging silks, so strong ceiling beams and stuff. And those crystal bowls?" She shook her head. "They're expensive."

Since the highway right here was fairly straight and everyone seemed to be flowing into Coral Canyon and not out of it, Luke looked over to her. "You've thought a lot about this."

"I have diagram upon diagram," she said. "I've been prepping a pitch for investors for a couple of months now." Her hands went round and round one another in her lap, and she pulled one away and tucked it under her leg to get it to stop.

"I just don't know. I haven't approached anyone yet, mostly because I don't know who to approach. I mean, I'm just asking them for money, you know? And I'm not sure I want to give away a percentage of my company to get seed money for this. So I started exploring some business loan options, but really, I have to determine if the population in Coral Canyon would support a wellness studio like what I want Deep Purple to be."

Sterling fell silent, her energy for the night all used up. "Sorry," she murmured. "But you asked."

Luke reached over and took the hand still lying in her lap. "Yeah, I did, and don't apologize. I want to know all of this." He glanced at her again, but it wasn't exactly a brightly lit road, and she only caught a hint of light in his eyes before he faced the road again. "I like this passionate side of you."

"Is that your way of saying I've been boring prior to this?"

He scoffed and laughed and shook his head. "You're anything but boring, Sterling."

She sighed, because that sounded an awful lot like a compliment coming from the dark, growly cowboy she'd started steadily falling for. "I'm still okay to have Corrine next weekend?"

"Yes." The word almost sounded like a bark. "I just want the record to show that I never drop my daughter off for an activity when I don't know what it is and when it'll be over." He gave her another side-eye.

But Sterling wasn't going to apologize for this. "When you were growing up, didn't your momma ever tell you not to look in bags and boxes close to Christmas?"

"No," he said flatly. "She made all of our gifts. We had no money."

"She had to hide them somewhere."

"Well, we never went in our parents' bedroom," he said. "I'm sure she kept them in there. I don't know."

"Well," Sterling said. "Try to imagine it, okay? This is like that. I'm putting together something for your birthday, and I need your daughter's help."

"She's seven."

"I'm aware of how old she is," Sterling said as she rolled her eyes. "Come on, Luke." She turned toward him fully and sandwiched his hand between both of hers. "You tell me your favorite things to do. Or to eat. Or whatever."

"I like working out," he said.

"Boo, no," she said, really laying it on thick. "That's a *chore* people have to do. Nope, that doesn't work for this."

"I didn't know there were rules for what a person could like." He sounded growly and cross, but Sterling kept smiling at him. "Fine." He took a deep breath and blew it out. "I like working with my hands. So that feeds into the working out. Or the cleaning. Or remodeling something or fixing it up. Playing the drums. Guitar. Anything that can entertain my mind and my body, I like."

"Is that why you like getting a massage? Wait, no. You just lie there."

"It's relaxing in a different way than scrubbing something until it shines," he said. "And Sterling, I'd love to hear your pitch for investors."

Her chest turned cold. "No." She extracted her hand from his, confused at her own resistance to this.

"No?"

Every muscle in her body stayed tight. "I thought about asking you, because you obviously believe in body work and massage and whatnot, but...I don't know. It feels weird now." And she'd really said the truth earlier—she didn't want someone else, not even Luke, owning part of Deep Purple.

"You can still pitch me," he said. "I love talking about this kind of stuff."

"You do?"

"Oh, yeah," he said. "I guess another thing I like doing in my spare time is managing my investment portfolio. I've turned it mostly over to Gabe to manage, to be honest. But I like looking at what he's done. I like learning about it."

"You are a learner," she said, thoughtful. She was having Corrine next weekend, and they were going to go thrift store shopping and to lunch, then to the calligraphy class at Georgia's bookshop. She really wanted to talk to the girl about her daddy, and plan a private birthday party for him, just the three of them.

Sterling had no idea what to get a man who said things like, "manage my investment portfolio," but she had some ideas brewing in the back of her mind.

"This is it," Luke said, pulling into what looked like a run-down barn. There weren't even any lights on out front. "This can't be right." He came to a stop and reached for his phone. A moment later, he yelped and then a moment after that, he rolled down the window. "I didn't see you there."

"Sorry 'bout that," a cowboy said. "You're here for Silver?"

"Yes, sir," Luke said.

"Our parking is around back, and our lamppost just went out about five minutes ago."

Sterling leaned forward to be able to see the man past Luke's cowboy hat, but she couldn't. She settled back into place and just let Luke handle things.

"So head to your left there; see Jeanie with the flare?"

"Yep," Luke said.

"She'll lead y'all around the back, and there should be a man named Liam there to help you inside."

"Sounds good," Luke said, and Sterling's stomach did a flip and a flop.

Luke rolled up his window, and Sterling asked, "We'll need help inside?"

"This place looks like yeah, we might need help getting inside," he grumbled. "Blaze. I'm going to kill him if this isn't perfect."

Sterling didn't like the tension rolling from him as he went toward the woman with the flare and then turned right to go between the barn and the fence. "Luke, baby," she said carefully. "This is already the perfect date." Her words stuck in her throat, but she pushed past her nerves. She liked this man. They'd been dating for a month and a half. He'd kissed her so completely only a half-hour ago.

"It doesn't really matter what the restaurant is. We're together."

Luke exhaled in a steady, slow stream. "Thanks, Sterling."

Up ahead, the narrow lane opened up to a brightly lit parking area, where plenty of hanging lights illuminated the cars and trucks below, as well as where to enter the barn. On this side, it definitely looked like a party would be raging inside—but the refined, expensive kind of party with waiters wearing tuxes as they held trays of champagne and fancy appetizers.

In fact, the man currently waving them forward to a parking spot wore a tuxedo, a pair of black earmuffs, and a big smile. "This is crazy," Sterling said as she caught sight of the man standing at a podium under an enormous umbrella of red lights. Heart-shaped red lights. "He's wearing a tux too."

"Good thing you've got the sexy dress," Luke said as he parked. "They might not let me in, but with you on my arm?" He grinned at her and turned off the truck. "We're gold." He didn't tell her to wait; it was implied he'd come help her down from the truck.

In the thirty seconds it took him to open her door, Sterling pressed her lips together to refresh her lipstick. Then she pressed her eyes closed and whispered, "Lord, please let this be the perfect date Luke wants it to be."

And when he offered her his hand, Sterling felt like a queen descending from a chariot. She loved this life with Luke, even if it was a bit unreal, and she hoped she could continue dating him until they did settle into a normal routine, a normal life—one tinged with all the magic of being *his* princess.

21

Bryce held Lucky's leash in his hand, the slack showing no tension. That all rode in Bryce's back and shoulders and everywhere in his body. He'd rung the doorbell at his mother's house in Boise, and she hadn't answered.

He'd leaned in and knocked five or six times, big loud booms filling the quiet neighborhood where he'd lived for about twelve years before he'd moved to Coral Canyon with Dad.

Bryce sighed and looked down at his dog. "She said she'd be home." He'd extended his trip to Coral Canyon until he absolutely had to return to the horse farm in Louisville. He'd missed almost two full weeks of work, and he had a plane to be on in less than six hours.

Lucky just looked up at him, and Bryce reached to punch the doorbell. His mom didn't have one of those cameras, and he imagined himself ripping the button from the side of the house and pulling out all the wires. Then he'd leave it all a big, knotted mess —the way she'd done to his whole life—and walk away.

She was good at that too. Or rather, letting him walk away.

He took a deep breath in through his nose as the doorbell echoed quietly behind the door. But at least he now knew some of his emotions surrounding his mother. He was angry with her, and that would have to be addressed at some point. At least if his therapist was right about anything, and Bryce did trust the man. He'd helped him through so many emotions already. He'd given him alternate paths for his thoughts, and different ways to manage his behavior despite his emotions.

Bryce had spent a good chunk of time in Coral Canyon with Georgia, Otis, Joey, and OJ, especially after he'd learned that Georgia was carrying a baby of her own. He hadn't asked a lot of questions about why they couldn't have children before, and he still wasn't sure now.

Georgia and Otis lived every hour on eggshells right now, he knew that, and his heart tore for his aunt and uncle.

"Mom," he called. "It's Bryce."

He finally heard a thump behind the door, and he shifted his feet and pulled Lucky back a little. "Don't lunge at her," he said. "She doesn't like dogs much." Bryce had texted her about stopping by for an hour or so, and he'd been very clear that he had Lucky with him. Since they'd be flying together soon, Bryce hadn't wanted to leave him in the backyard, which was filled with snow, or exile him in a cold rental truck.

His mother had said it would be fine. She'd be home this Sunday morning. Bryce had gotten up and left three hours earlier than he'd needed to, and he'd given no explanation to Dad or Abby as to why.

His departures from Coral Canyon were always highly charged and fairly emotional, and they probably thought he just couldn't stand being in town anymore. The truth was, Bryce had enjoyed himself a lot. He loved taking care of his horses, and he'd even enjoyed the Valentine's Day party at his grandparents' condo, though he was twenty-two years old.

The door in front of him started to open, and his mother clung to it. She stared at him for a beat too long, and Bryce knew this look. It took too long for her to recognize him, though he certainly didn't look that different.

"Bryce," she slurred, and he fell back another step. "What're you doin' here?"

"I told you I was coming," Bryce said evenly, his grip on Lucky's leash intensifying with every passing moment. His mother had drunk a lot his last year of living with her, and she apparently hadn't changed much in the past five years since he'd left. "I'm flying home today, remember?"

"Is that today?" Something crashed behind her, and Lucky inched forward like he'd be able to fix whatever had just broken. Bryce too looked past his mother, but it took her another two beats to twist and look over her shoulder.

"I can see you're busy," he said, though disgust filled him. He didn't want to feel this way about his mother. She was supposed to be the one who protected him. Who loved him no matter what. Who showed him how to be a man of God—trustworthy and responsible and honorable.

As he looked at her, he wished he could find any of those qualities.

"Babe," she yelled, and to Bryce's horror, a man walked toward them.

"What are we doing? Heating the outside?" He arrived a half-pace behind Bryce's mom, and he looked at Bryce with a curl in his lip. "Who are you?"

"No one," Bryce practically yelled. He met his mother's eye, silently begging her to stay quiet. He'd loved her so much, once upon a time. She'd been a good enough mother, though she spat terrible things about Daddy, his rockstar career, and more while Bryce lived with her.

She raised you, he thought, though he knew such a thing had not generated from him. *Treat her with respect.*

"Sorry to bother you," he said in a quiet voice, his heart wailing and cracking as he looked at his mother. He hardly recognized her now. Her dark hair had grayed at the hairline, and she'd done nothing to cover it up. Her clothes seemed too big and baggy, and it was ten-thirty on the Sabbath Day, and she was already drunk.

"Well, let's close the door, shall we, Corrie?" The man did just that, but not before Bryce caught sight of the gold band on his left hand—which matched the one on his mother's left hand.

He blinked at the off-white door now staring him in the face. "She got re-married and didn't tell me?"

Or his dad. Or anyone.

Pinpricks started in his lungs, quickly moving to his heart and chest and throat. He spun away from the door, the house, and marched back to the rental truck. By the time he got there, the pins had turned into forks, then knives.

"Load up, Lucky," he told the dog, his voice that of a robot. He got behind the wheel and yanked his seatbelt into place. He had to get out of here, and he didn't even look before he roared into reverse, jammed the truck into drive, and skidded away from the house.

He'd taken two corners before the sobs descended upon him. The dam he'd been holding back, the perfect illusion he'd kept of his mother, the way he'd been pretending it didn't matter if she was part of his life—it all broke wide open.

The shards of it sliced through him, and Bryce had enough wherewithal left to pull to the side of the road, put the truck in park, and hold onto the steering wheel with both hands while his world came crashing down around him.

He cried and cried and cried, not even sure why. Only that he needed the release, and the only way it would come was through tears. He slammed his hand against the steering wheel again, and again, and again, saying, "Why—am—I—not—good—enough—for—her?"

Lucky whined, and Bryce looked over to him, a semblance of calmness entering his soul. An errant ray of sunshine fell on the golden retriever, literally making him shine like gold, and Bryce reached for the dog as everything shattered apart again.

A COUPLE OF HOURS LATER, BRYCE HAD HIS HOOD UP ON HIS hoodie as he scuffled through the airport. He'd been to the restroom to scrub his face clean, but nothing could quite get his soul as clean as it needed to be. Both Dad and Abby had texted a few times, but Bryce couldn't even look at the messages without his eyes welling with tears.

He just needed to make it home. Once he got back to his cabin in Louisville, everything would be fine. He'd call Kassie, and maybe they'd talk about it. Or maybe they wouldn't. With Kassie, Bryce wouldn't have to. She'd just let him lay his head in her lap, and she'd stroke his hair and feed him popcorn, and he'd wonder why he was such a failure.

Once he got back to his cabin in Louisville, he could paint a smile on his face and pretend to be happy there. He loved the horses, though it wasn't his own operation. Everything would be okay, because no one would expect him to know how to run a horse farm, and he wouldn't have to explain how he thought he could do so in Coral Canyon. He wouldn't have to tell them that the horses had rescued him more than anything, because he was such a terrible son that his mother had to drink herself to death every night just to put up with him.

Once he got back to his cabin in Louisville, he could shut the door on Boise—on his mother—the way he'd been doing for a few years now. He wouldn't have to think about her, see that glazed look in her eye, or hear her complete silence when her new husband asked her who was standing on her doorstep—and it was him, her son.

A son she'd never wanted, had said she'd been held back by, and whom she clearly never thought about, never worried over, and had probably never loved.

He barely made it into the men's room before another round of horrible, soul-racking sobs started again.

22

Luke carried the last of Sterling's yoga mats into the community center through a back door and found her laying out the first batch he'd brought in. Corrine skipped around the room and put a rolled towel on each one, and Luke smiled at the pair of them.

"Right there, baby," she said. "Thank you."

Luke let the mats roll into the bin where the others had been. "You sure I can't stay?"

Sterling straightened and looked at him. She wore a pair of leggings in black camo—very sexy—and a black tank top that showed the matching camouflage sports bra straps. "No," she said with a smile. "If you wanted a spot, you should've signed up. The class is full."

"I thought I'd have an in with the instructor," he said as she approached. She stepped right into his arms, and he'd learned from Jem that he didn't have to try to hide how he felt about Sterling from Corrine. It was probably good for her to see that Luke could be affectionate with a woman. That was what Sunny and Faith had said anyway.

"I don't have a yoga mat for you." She looked over her shoulder to where Corrine skipped from one mat to another. "Unless someone doesn't show."

"Nah." Luke grinned at her. "Corrine and I will go out to Tex's. I can't wait to hear about it." He leaned in and nuzzled her neck. "You're coming out there afterward, right?"

"I don't know," Sterling hedged. "Should I? You think I'll be welcome?"

He pulled back, surprised at her reluctance. "Of course, Sterling." He stepped away completely and whistled for Corrine to come with him. "In fact, Abby's giddy she might get to feed you lunch, and 'talk.'" He rolled his eyes, though he loved his brother's wife and how protective of him she was. "She says she never gets to chat with you."

Sterling blinked those sapphire eyes at him. "Yeah, Abby and I aren't best friends."

"And that's driving her mad." Luke chuckled and looked for Corrine. "Come on, jelly belly."

"I'm not done with the towels, Daddy."

"Oh, fine." Luke got to work too, laying down mats where Sterling wanted them, and when every last towel had been placed, Corrine looked up at Sterling.

"Is there anything else?"

"No, sweet girl. Go with your daddy now. Get your homework done, so we can just relax once I get there." She checked her phone, as Sterling never wore a watch. She said the mechanics and moving pieces messed with her body's natural rhythms. Luke wasn't going to argue with her; he hated having something strapped around his wrist. It felt constraining, like wearing a tie around his neck.

"Can't I stay?" Corrine asked, her voice straying into whining territory. "Daddy? Sterling will bring me home, right?"

"We're not going home," he said, though he sure did like the fact that Corrine wanted to spend time with Sterling. They were going to be together without him for the first time this Saturday too, and Luke had been told not to ask questions about what they did until after his birthday.

He really liked that Sterling seemed to want to surprise him with something, and he wasn't going to ruin that for her. So he'd promised over his heart and hers that he wouldn't press Corrine for details about what she did with Sterling this weekend.

"We're goin' out to Uncle Tex's. So get your coat and let's go." He looked around for her coat, but he couldn't see it.

"Oh, they're coming in already." Sterling turned her back on the doorway, where three women had entered with gym bags slung over their shoulders. All three of them lasered in on him, and Luke's first thought was to run. Far and fast, he needed to leave.

At the same time, he could totally stay. He wasn't fresh meat in Coral Canyon anymore, and he'd be stunned if everyone in the county didn't know he and Sterling were together. He could still picture her in that red dress, could still feel the shape of her in his arms as they danced under the high rafters in that luxury barn, could still smell the scent of her perfume as he dropped her off after the perfect Valentine's Day date and kissed her goodnight.

"I'm so nervous," Sterling whispered.

"Hon," he said, stepping into her side and putting one hand on the small of her back. "You've got this. You trained for this. They're just women."

She worried her thumbnail between her teeth, her eyes flying everywhere. "Yeah," she said. "They're just women." Settling right in front of him, she turned to look at him. "You used to be nervous around women."

"And look at me now." Luke smiled and brushed his lips along Sterling's cheek. "Do you want me to greet them?"

"No," she said. "I can do it. I *want* to do this." She drew her shoulders back and lifted her chin. She pulled in a breath and turned around. "Ladies," she said. "Pick a mat anywhere. We'll be starting on the floor."

Sterling walked away from Luke, and he let all of his big feelings flow through him. She was simply so good. She had the calm energy Luke craved, and she possessed the poise and grace he wished he did.

"Come on, bean." He put his hand on Corrine's back, took one last look at his strong, sexy girlfriend, and left through the back door where he'd been hauling in yoga mats.

"CORRINE!" MELISSA CALLED FROM THE FRONT PORCH. SHE stood on the top step and waved her four-year-old arm as hard as seemingly possible.

"Go on," he told Corrine as he set her on her feet. He turned back and closed the door behind her, so glad he didn't have to carry a bag with her all the time anymore. She ran toward her cousin, and they started chattering and laughing before she even got to the steps.

Up she went, and Luke waited until the girls had gone back inside the house before he took the side stairs up to the back entrance of the house. It wasn't really the back entrance, but when he'd been growing up here, it was. The deck and sliding glass door Tex had put off the back of the house hadn't existed when Luke had grown up in this farmhouse.

He loved this place, because home had always meant something to him. He'd always been able to find his true self when he came home. He'd left home very young, made a life for himself on the road, and in his mind and heart and soul, there was nothing like coming home.

Of course, now the farm and the house belonged to Tex and Abby, but the nostalgia washed over Luke all the same. He looked straight ahead to a closed door, and when he'd gotten home too late and hadn't wanted to face his father, he'd darted straight down those stairs to his bedroom.

He'd never had his own room, but he'd shared with Jem before, and then with both twins too. Daddy never let Luke get away with coming home late and not talking about it, and Luke smiled to the closed door. "Love you, Daddy."

He may not know what he was doing as a father either, but when he'd talked to his father about it, Daddy had always maintained that, "You're doing great, son. Just don't give up. Listen to two things: your gut and God. You won't go wrong with that little girl."

His gut had been telling him not to let Mandi spend too much time with Corrine, so he'd been very strict with her visitation schedule. She'd already gotten all of her hours for February, and when she'd tried to take Corrine shopping this morning, Luke had retreated to his bedroom and tried to listen to the two things his father said he should.

"If you're here," Abby said from around the corner. "That means your daddy is too."

"Maybe he went out to the barn," Corrine said in a very practical voice. She was the perfect example of practicality, and Luke didn't joke around with her much. They had a job to do to get out the door on time for school. She had homework at night, and he expected her to do it.

"I didn't go out to the barn," Luke said as he shrugged out of his coat and rounded the corner. "I'm right here, and it smells like that dark roast I like, so you best not be teasin' me today, Miss Abby." He hung his coat on a hook beside the door and turned to face the galley kitchen.

Abby beamed at him, and he could see her beauty in her auburn hair and dark hazel eyes. She was the perfect complement to Tex, and Luke had bonded with her fairly early on as well. One, the band spent a lot of time out here. Two, they were the same soul stitched into different skin.

She struggled with her pride and her temper, just like he did. Maybe not to the same degree, but she at least understood him. She'd been hurt in the past too, and while it wasn't the same as Luke's wounds, she sported them nonetheless. She let Tex heal them. She let others in, and Luke had learned a lot from Abby over the past few years.

"Come get your coffee," she said as she pulled down a mug for him.

Luke smiled back at her and did just that. As he stirred in sugar, he said, "I don't really want to get grilled about Sterling today."

"Fair enough," she said. "I'm making the best French onion meatballs for lunch. Just wait until you try them."

Luke cut her a look out of the corner of his eye. "I didn't think you got excited about cooking."

"I do when all the mess is next door." She grinned and said, "I have to run over there and check on them, but I'll be right back."

"Where's my brother?" Luke asked. The only reason Momma and Daddy had let Luke leave home at eighteen and join a band was because it was Tex's band. And Trace's. The two of them were the oldest brothers in the family, and Daddy had told Tex to watch over Luke the way Judah watched over Benjamin when the brothers had to go to Egypt to get food.

"Believe it or not, he's just getting out of the shower," Abby said as she waddled past him. "You'd think he was the one growing another human inside his body for how much he naps." She laughed lightly, didn't grab a coat, and left the farmhouse.

He could hear the girls chittering in the living room, and he took his coffee over to the sliding glass door that led out onto the deck. Tex and Abby didn't use it in the winter, and snow had piled up on it.

"She what?" Tex practically bellowed. "Abby!"

Luke turned toward his brother, who strode into the kitchen area shirtless. "She went next door."

Tex looked like he could call down fire from heaven. His dark eyes blazed—positively blazed with anger—but he also looked a little...lost. "Abby went next door," he said into the phone.

Luke didn't want to eavesdrop, but he wanted to know what was going on at the same time.

"No, no, I hear you," Tex said as he spun on his heel and marched back down the hall. "I'm just saying, it's not okay. I know you're *saying* it's okay, son, but that doesn't make it okay." By the time he finished talking, he'd returned to the main part of the house.

He shook his head, his jaw so, so tight. "Bryce," he said, but the boy clearly wasn't hearing him. He finally hung his head, his chin very nearly touching his chest. "Yes, fine."

That didn't sound fine, but Luke turned back to the window. Still, something clamored in his own soul, because Bryce had already been through enough.

Tex looked up again. "Luke's here is all."

Luke tried not to flinch. He wasn't sure if what Tex had said was a good thing or not. Like, was he so unimportant that he could know what had happened? Or he was so important that it was okay for him to know, because it was just him and both Tex and Bryce loved him and knew he wouldn't spread gossip or rumors?

"I will only tell your mother," he said. "Your *real* mother, Bryce." He lowered his voice and hightailed it out of the room again. That was enough for Luke to know this was about Corrie, Tex's ex and Bryce's mother, who lived in Boise.

Luke sighed and watched the sunlight dance across the snow. Winter really was beautiful, if the cold could be survived.

STERLING ARRIVED JUST BEFORE LUNCH, HER ENERGY OFF THE charts. Luke had been on the phone with her for the entire twenty-five-minute drive, so he already knew her guided meditation and light yoga class had been a huge hit at the community center.

Of course it had been. Sterling was trained. Professional. Calm. A natural at leading others, whether she knew any of that or not. Luke knew it; he'd seen it in her. So when she opened the front door without knocking, he stood at the end of the table, just lowering his phone from his ear.

"You did it," he said smiling. He rushed at her, and she hurried toward him, and their embrace could've sent the earth spinning off its axis. She laughed, and oh, Luke wanted to bask in the sound of that every day for the rest of his life.

"It was so great," she said. "I mean, I've already talked your ear off about it, but Sally Grimes. You know her, right?" Sterling tossed her purse in the corner behind the front door. "She said they want me to come teach a permanent class. Once a week!" She faced him, her cheeks full of pink and her eyes full of diamonds.

Luke maybe started to fall in love with her right then, and he couldn't stop smiling at her. "That's amazing, sweetheart. I'm so glad."

The back door opened, and Abby called, "I see her car, so I know she's here."

Sterling moved to Luke's side, and he instantly put his arm around her. He loved claiming her like this, and he loved the way she allowed him to claim her. He liked that it wasn't just him and Corrine for lunch today, because he hadn't felt like cooking. Because he didn't want to be in full parenting mode, and if he came out to Tex and Abby's, he could let Corrine play without having to police her too much.

Abby plunked a heavy crock down in the middle of the table and clapped together the potholders she'd been using. "Sterling," she said with a sigh. She moved right into her and hugged her, stealing her from Luke. "How did it go?"

"*So* good, Abby." Sterling followed her into the kitchen, her mouth moving a mile a minute as she helped Abby put out the crusty rolls, the butter, and then finally, the showstopper—a huge bowl of buttery mashed potatoes.

"Time to eat, girls," Luke said, and Corrine and Melissa looked up from their ponies and dolls. "Come on, now."

"Mel," Abby called.

"Comin', Momma."

Luke entered the fray with Corrine, lifting her up onto a chair. "Right here, little lady. Don't touch that crock. It's hot." He took the seat beside her, leaving one for Sterling. Tex came in from outside, washed his hands, and sat at the head of the table. It had been pushed against the wall, so one whole side of it wasn't being used, but six of them could fit on the two ends and one side.

"Hey," Mel said. "I want to sit by Corrine."

"Yes, ma'am," Luke said, getting to his feet. He caught Sterling's voice, and he realized she wasn't talking about her meditation class anymore. But the Valentine's Day date.

"...most romantic thing ever," she said. "Once you got inside the barn, it opened up like nothing I've ever seen before. It was filled with, oh, just the stars." She sighed. "It was magical, and we ate and danced and...." She caught him watching her, and she smiled. "Yeah, it was the perfect date."

Luke smiled too, glad she felt that way. Abby said something he didn't catch, and Luke left her a spot by Tex. She'd want to sit by Sterling too, so he left that seat for her. Then Mel, then Corrine, and that left him on the end opposite of his brother.

He took the seat, trying not to be too upset that he couldn't sit beside Sterling. He could've moved the girls around, but that felt like too big of a hassle, and he was a big boy. He could sit on the end by himself.

His eyes met Tex's, and the man hadn't cooled off since his phone call with Bryce, though it had been a couple of hours ago. He'd said nothing either, and in fact, Tex had disappeared back into the bedroom and not come out until he had to go feed the horses.

When Luke had offered to help, he'd said, "No, I got it," and stomped out of the house. Now, Tex nodded as if to acknowledge that he'd been preoccupied today and that he felt badly about it.

"Ain't no thing, right?" Luke said, and most of the tension left Tex's broad shoulders.

"All right," Abby chirped, though the moment she'd returned from next door, she'd gone into the bedroom with Tex. Whatever was happening, she'd hidden it away for now. "Cheryl makes these *amazing* French onion soup meatballs, and I wanted to try them." She lifted the lid on the crock. "They're *phenomenal.*"

She started dishing them out for everyone, and then she looked at Tex. "Sweetheart, will you pray?"

He shook his head, and Abby threw a panicked look to Luke. "I will, Miss Abby." He swept his cowboy hat off his head and pressed it to his chest. He wasn't the one to pray in public, that was for dang sure. Tex usually called on someone far better than him—Trace or Blaze or Otis.

He keenly felt the weight of the adults in the room as he struggled to remember how to even start a prayer. Then he said, "Dear Lord in Heaven, we thank Thee for this beautiful winter day, where the sun shone on the snow, making it brighten with diamonds." He wasn't even sure where the words had come from. Otis often said that when he wrote songs, the lyrics just flowed from him.

Perhaps Luke had picked up on some of that. "Please bless Abby in the last couple of months of her pregnancy, that she won't be too uncomfortable and that the baby will continue to grow properly. We ask a blessing on Georgia and her pregnancy too, that she'll be able to keep it and deliver a whole, healthy baby at the end of the nine months."

Luke's voice scratched in his throat, but he forged on. "We're grateful for this farmhouse, Lord. It has such good memories of family and friends and love. We're grateful for this food, which Thou hast inspired and provided. We're grateful Sterling's class went well this morning, and for the blessing of cousins."

He paused again, but the words were there, and he would not deny them. "Please bless Tex, Abby, and Bryce with whatever difficulty they're dealing with, and help the rest of us in the family to be the support they need, should they require it."

With his mind blissfully blank, he said, "Amen," and opened his eyes.

Everyone stared at him, and that only sent Luke closer to the edge. "Napkins, Corrine," he said, putting some between her and Mel. "No yelling during dinner, now, okay?"

"Yes, Daddy." Only the kids seemed to think it was time to eat, and Luke stared back at Tex, then finally Abby.

"What?" he challenged.

"Nothing," Abby said quickly, her eyes glassy but averting

quickly. "Did Sterling tell you the two of you are going on a double date?"

His eyes flew to Sterling's, and she definitely wore gems in her eyes as she smiled at him. "Yeah," she said. "Michelle was in my class today, and we set up a double date. Us, and her and Denzel."

Luke wasn't so sure about that. Morris and Leigh would want a full run-down of literally every single word spoken on that double date, but since the tension in the farmhouse was already fairly high, he simply said, "Sure, okay," and dug into his meatballs and mashed potatoes.

That first bite was like heaven, and he moaned. Abby clapped her hands a couple of times and said, "Right?" before she forked up her first bite too.

Luke knew life wasn't perfect, but sitting down to eat with his family—and Sterling—sure felt like it. He wanted many more experiences like this, most of them with just him, Sterling, and Corrine. A small core family who relied on one another, helped one another, and wept with one another.

He could *almost* see it in his future, and Luke grabbed onto the images so they couldn't wisp away into smoke, and vowed to hold onto them until they became crystal clear.

23

Sterling put the pink lamp on the counter at the thrift store, and then turned back to Corrine. "That," she said. "And these." She nodded to the spot for the art books she'd found. "Put those right there."

Corrine did, and then she slipped her hand into Sterling's. "Daddy is going to love that lamp."

Sterling smiled down at the little girl. Luke had told her that Corrine really was small for her age, but his pediatrician wasn't worried about it, so he didn't. She gazed up at Sterling with joy in her eyes that made Sterling's heart feel like it hadn't been beating properly for a few years now.

Of course, she'd already known that. She just hadn't realized how starved for oxygen she'd been. How starved for a family. For attention. For recognition.

Luke was very good at offering all of the above, and she simply had to provide for him the best birthday she could.

"I think he'll like it because you like it," Sterling said. "Isn't that right?"

"Yes, probably," Corrine said. She could be a sober child, and she didn't just chatter the way Sterling had expected her too. She probably shouldn't have any expectations for the girl, because she had very little experience with children in general.

"What are you gonna do with the books?" Corrine asked as the clerk picked them up.

"I'm going to maybe paint something for your daddy," she said. "Do you think he would like that?"

"Sure," Corrine said. "He puts my drawings on the fridge."

Sterling chuckled, but she was hoping to do more than get her art stuck to the fridge with a magnet. She couldn't really paint, but she'd liked the books, and they were fifty cents each.

"What does your daddy like to do?" she asked as she handed over her debit card.

"He goes to the gym a lot," Corrine said. "And then we go out to the barn."

"Mm." Sterling knew all of this already. "Does he go hiking ever?"

Corrine looked thoughtful. "We go camping every summer."

Sterling took her card back and slipped it into her holder. She picked up the lamp, and the clerk gave the bag to Corrine. "Okay, come on, baby. We'll put this in the car, and then head down to the bookshop."

"Do you think I'll be able to do the cal-calligify?" Corrine asked, and it wasn't the first time. She wore the worry right in her face, and Sterling wished she could erase it.

She'd taken Corrine to lunch too and let her order whatever she wanted. She'd looked at Sterling with big eyes—and then she'd ordered a plate of spaghetti she'd taken two bites of. Sterling had texted Luke to make sure she hadn't done something wrong, or that Corrine wasn't allergic to tomatoes or something, and he'd said, *That's just how she is. Barely eats. It's fine. I'll pay you back for the spaghetti.*

You will not, she'd sent, and then they'd come to the thrift store. As they walked down the blustery sidewalk toward the small parking lot across the street where she'd parked, Sterling mused through gift ideas for Luke.

"What's your daddy's favorite food?" she asked.

"Steak," Corrine said. "What's yours?"

"Uh." Sterling should've been prepared for stuff like this. If she was going to pepper the girl with questions to try to get intel on her daddy, that was. "I think probably fried eggs and bacon."

Corrine's face lit up. "My daddy makes these eggs called Adam and Eve on a Raft. It's *so* good."

A sense of missing, of pure nostalgia, hit Sterling as they came to a pause at the light. She tapped the walk button and waited. "Hold my hand, baby," she murmured as the light started to change.

Corrine slipped her hand back into Sterling's, and she could've been any other mom out with her daughter that day. She'd had very few experiences like this with her own mother, and this sent barbs of happiness through her. They caught on everything, infusing her with more joy than she'd known was possible.

She'd never felt this way before, like people were looking at her because of Corrine and not because she'd dared to quit at Red Carpet when no one ever had before.

At least no one who'd then stayed in town.

"Sterling, are you sad?" Corrine asked.

Surprised, she looked down at the girl. Her first instinct was to cover up the emotions streaming through her. Instead, she said, "Yeah, a little. See, my momma used to make Adam and Eve on a Raft, and I haven't seen her in a long time."

"Is she dead?" Corrine asked outright.

"No."

"Aunt Ev's momma and daddy died," Corrine said soberly. "She gets sad about it sometimes."

Sterling smiled at Corrine softly. "Yeah, she does."

"Where is your mom?"

They reached the other side of the street, and Sterling tipped Corrine to the left so she'd go that way toward her car. "She lives very far away," Sterling said. "And we don't talk very much."

Corrine walked along for a few steps before she said, "My daddy used to live really far away. At least that's what my momma says."

Sterling reached into her pocket and pulled out her keys to unlock the car. "Yeah, but he's been back for a while."

"And my mom left," Corrine said.

Sterling remembered what Luke had asked her about the research and studies on mothers abandoning their children. She hadn't read one, and he hadn't given her anything more, but the story was implied. "Are you sad about your mom sometimes?"

"Yeah," Corrine said. Sterling lifted the trunk, and Corrine tossed in the art books. Sterling put the lamp in more gently and looked at her phone.

"We have a few minutes, baby. Let's get warm in the car before we have to walk back down there." In fact, Sterling would drive them that way and pray a parking space would open up right in front of the bookshop.

With them both in and both seatbelts buckled, Sterling backed out of the spot. "What's your favorite food? Adam and Eve on a Raft? Spaghetti?"

Corrine looked at her with those serious eyes. "No. I don't know."

"You don't know your absolute favorite food?"

The girl fidgeted. "Uh, I like these tacos my daddy makes. He gets the meat from Grandma. It's sweet and spicy."

"Beef?" Sterling asked. "Pork? Chicken?"

"I don't know," Corrine said, and Sterling found her a complete enigma. She knew so much about some things—like her mom and dad and the situation there. Luke had also said she was quite bossy to the younger cousins. At the same time, she seemed to know very little about her own self.

Sterling reasoned she was seven years old, and she likely didn't have to think about anything too taxing. "I know," she said as she turned at the light and inched down the street, her eyes peeled for a spot. "I bet it's chicken nuggets. You almost got those at lunch." She grinned at Corrine, who smiled back.

"I *love* chicken nuggets," Corrine agreed.

"No spots," she murmured as she passed in front of the book-shop and then the post office. She reached the next light and moved into the left-hand turn lane. She'd go back by, and she looked over to Corrine. "Do you pray with your daddy?"

"Yep," she said. "Every night. He stands in the doorway while I kneel at the bed and everything."

Sterling could just see that scenario in her mind's eye. Then, the dark, stormy cowboy would head down the hall to the master suite, and he'd...what? Sterling didn't know. What she didn't know about Luke frustrated her, and as she flipped around and turned back onto Main Street, she said, "Why don't you pray we can find a spot really close to the bookstore?"

"Okay," Corrine chirped. "Dear Lord, it is mighty cold today. We'd like a close spot to the shop, please. Amen."

Sterling worked hard not to laugh. "Amen," she half-giggled, and to her pure surprise and delight, a car started to back out of a spot only ten yards in front of her.

Her laughter dried right up. "Corrine, look."

215

"God hears prayers," Corrine said simply. "That's what my Grandma says anyway, and she said that she's been prayin' mighty hard for Daddy to find me a momma."

Sterling dang near drove into oncoming traffic. "She said that?"

"She sure did." Corrine pointed to something on the sidewalk. "Look. There's Aunt Abby."

Sterling saw her, but she focused on not crashing and getting the parking spot the seven-year-old had prayed into existence for them. "Don't jump out," she said as she pulled in. Thankfully, Corrine obeyed, and she waited for Sterling to cut the engine and collect her purse.

She met the girl at the front of the car, deciding that she wasn't going to question her further that day. She took her hand and hurried after Abby, and they burst into the bookshop, the wind chasing them like it wanted to seek shelter among the shelves too.

The left half of the shop had been draped in beautiful lettering, done on what looked like ancient paper. Maps drifted among all the beauty, and Sterling stared at what she'd surely classify as art. Three long tables had been set up in front of the display, and a woman currently walked down the length of them, putting out jars of ink.

Excitement built inside Sterling, and she nodded and lifted her and Corrine's joined hands. "Look, baby. That's where we're going to get to make something beautiful."

"Come on over," Georgia said as she appeared from the back of the shop. "There are no assigned seats, and everyone will be able to see just fine."

Abby spied them, and she lumbered to her feet. She hugged Sterling and said, "Hey, you," like they knew each other far better than they did. As she pulled away, she added, "Any good ideas for Luke's birthday?"

Sterling had a few things seeding in her mind, but nothing had taken great hold yet. So she shook her head, and as Abby hugged Corrine, the little girl said, "I always get Daddy this popcorn he likes." She looked from Abby to Sterling, obviously trying to make a decision. "Sterling, will you take me to get it this year?"

Abby looked like a cat who'd just caught a canary, but thankfully, she turned back to the table without saying anything.

"Of course, baby," Sterling murmured. She could get Luke a food gift. What she'd really like to do for him was give him an experience. Something the two of them could do together. But in the winter, when neither of them seemed that into the outdoors... Sterling couldn't think of anything birthday-worthy right now.

Maybe just thrift store shopping, she thought. *Like you did today with Corrine.*

She quickly dismissed the idea, because Luke wouldn't like that.

Why wouldn't he? Her brain would not let this go, and she moved to help Corrine into the seat next to Abby. She took the one on the other side of the little girl, and she didn't pay much attention to anyone else arriving.

She'd learned to live inside a tunnel, because then she didn't have to see the glares, the sideways looks of other women, or the wide eyes of those who felt bad for her. A lot of the gossip had died down in recent months, but Sterling still felt like she'd had a bright red A stitched to her chest permanently.

As the class began, the instructor spoke in a calm, soothing voice. "Calligraphy is a visual art," she said. "And an ancient practice. It is life flowing from you and into your strokes."

Sterling liked that, and she felt a connection to the teacher the way she hoped her students did during her meditation class. That had gone so well for her, and she'd already set up the next eight weeks at the community center.

They were paying her pretty well, providing the space and the equipment, and her name as the instructor would go out to every patron in Coral Canyon. She pressed her eyes closed as her blessings piled on top of each other, and before she knew it, they'd gone over the basic strokes and were supposed to choose a letter and create it.

Sterling moved her pen into the first stroke of art, her first lines of life, on the thick paper in front of her.

She loved how it looked, with the thin lines moving fluidly into thicker ones. As she looked at the letter she'd done—a lowercase L. Two strokes had been required—an ascending loop and an upstroke.

Easy.

L for Luke.

L for love.

"Look at my C," Corrine said. She climbed up onto her knees as if Sterling couldn't just look to her right and see the paper. "It's not quite the oval, like she said."

Sterling beamed at the letter. "It's great, Corrine," she said, meaning every syllable.

"You did an L," Corrine said. "Why didn't you do an S for Sterling?"

"It's not about pressure on the up and downstrokes," the instructor said as she moved down the table. "Look over the basic strokes again. See if you can make a word, with consistent height and width in your letters."

"The S seemed a little too complicated," she admitted to Corrine.

"I don't think I can do the Rs in my name." The little girl looked at her sheet and then back up to the front.

"Remember, you have a cheat sheet right there." She pointed with her pen to the long strip the instructor had put in front of her.

It showed each stroke for every letter, and Sterling sought out the U.

"You'd know about cheating," someone said, and her head snapped up. Her heart pounded, because while she hadn't heard that voice in a while, she instinctively knew it didn't belong to anyone kind.

Sure enough, Marilyn Robbcott sat on the other side of the table, only two people down. Sterling stared at her, an internal war starting inside herself.

She should just leave.

You can't leave. You have Corrine here.

She should fight back.

Don't. It's not worth it.

So Sterling did what she'd been doing since she left Red Carpet. She put her head down again, turning into the meek, mild Sterling Boyd. "Hello, Marilyn," she said.

"I can't believe you're here," she said.

"Why?" Sterling asked as she focused on making a lowercase U out of two underturns. Easy.

"It's not a free class."

Beside her, Abby shifted, and the whole mood of the class had too.

"Look at my O," Corrine said, and Sterling smiled as big as she could at the little girl's paper. Everything felt false and too hot now.

Behind her, the door chimed, and a flutter of cold air entered the shop. Abby leaned back and said, "I did my name." She tilted her paper for Sterling to see, and Corrine rose up to look too.

"Aunt Abby, it's so good," she said. "Can you help me with my Rs?"

"Let's look," Sterling said, her throat so dry and stinging like she'd swallowed a whole hive of bees and they weren't happy about it. "It's an upstroke."

The girl made the mark, and Sterling wanted to hug her. "Yes, like that. Now, it's that comma dot. Right on the edge of the upstroke."

"Like this?" Corrine touched her pen to the top of the upstroke and pulled it down and up in a shallow valley.

"Yep, perfect." Sterling beamed at the little girl, thoughts of Marilyn fading away. "Now, the underturn. That's just the U, baby."

A scoff met her ears, but Sterling didn't look up. Bullies usually gave up if they didn't get a reaction. However, Abby got to her feet, and she asked, "Do you have a problem we need to take up together?"

Horror drove through Sterling, because she'd just interrupted the whole class. All the chatter at the table stopped completely, and the instructor herself had paused several chairs down.

"Abby," she said quietly.

"No, this woman is being incredibly rude." She looked up, her eyes dark and throwing fire and lightning and everything in between. "Georgia? Can you get your security over here? We have someone who needs to be escorted out."

Sterling's face burned, and she was sure she'd be bright red. The heat filled her whole body, and her hair suddenly weighed fifty pounds, causing her neck to bend and her face to point straight at the table.

Not only that, but surely Georgia wouldn't actually have a security guard, would she?

"I paid for this class," Marilyn said. "You can't just kick me out."

Georgia arrived on the scene. "What's going on?" Only a few

steps behind her came Otis, and as he carried his two-year-old on his hip, he looked about as menacing as a lump of cheese.

"This woman is threatening another class member." Abby planted her hands on her hips. "I feel unsafe."

All eyes settled on Marilyn then, and even Sterling dared to look up at her. A twinge of vindication sang through her when her face started to redden.

"We paid for this class too," Abby said, indicating herself and Sterling and Corrine. "They all did too." She swept her arm down the table to everyone else there. "And no one wants to sit and listen to you belittle another human being. You don't get to sit here and make us all listen to that."

"Abby," Sterling said again, and the woman's fiery eyes turned on her.

"At the library, we had a behave-yourself policy. You can't behave yourself? It didn't matter if you paid or not. You didn't get to attend."

"Marilyn," Georgia said. "What—Is she right?"

"She better apologize," Abby said as she sat back down. "Then we can all get back to work." She picked up her brush pen, and Sterling could only stare at Marilyn.

She glared icicles back at Sterling, and her mouth barely moved as she said, "I'm sorry, Sterling."

She nodded, clearly saying *Apology accepted*, and Georgia clapped her hands. "Great. Sorry, Wilma. We're ready again."

"Yes, sorry, everyone," Abby said. "I just can't stand it when someone is so rude." She pinned Marilyn with yet another piercing glare, then switched her smile back on and went right back to lettering.

After a couple of beats of silence, Wilma said, "We have lots of paper if you want to try hand-lettering a piece of stationery or a name in much bigger letters. My daughter makes them for gifts, adding butterflies, gems, and pops of color with various brushes and other medium."

A name in much bigger letters...

Through her embarrassment and humiliation, Sterling got an idea for the perfect birthday gift for Luke. That alone was a testament that God had not abandoned her—as did Abby's courageous defense of her.

She looked over to the other woman. "Thank you, Abby," she murmured.

Abby smiled at her and patted her leg. "Anytime, Sterling. Everyone knows she's the one in the wrong, but no one will say anything."

Sterling's eyes pricked with tears, and she nodded. "I learned to ignore them a long time ago."

"You're better than me." Abby went back to her lettering, but Sterling thought the opposite was true. Abby had stood up for her. She'd defended herself politely. She'd done all the things Sterling didn't know how to do.

"Look at my name," Corrine said loudly, and Sterling did just that.

She put her arm around the little girl and hugged her tightly. "It's perfect," she said.

Corrine looked up at her. "Can I show Daddy?"

"Yeah, of course," she said.

"So it's not a secret?"

Sterling frowned. "Why would it be a secret?"

She shrugged. "He told me it was. That I shouldn't tell him anything we did or talked about today."

Sterling's heart expanded tenfold, and she placed a kiss to the top of Corrine's head. "You can show him, jelly bean. It's fine."

Corrine stood on her chair and reached for another piece of paper. The showdown at the table hadn't unnerved her at all, but

Sterling tossed a look toward Marilyn. She had her head bent now, and Sterling didn't have to meet her eye.

"I'm going to do one for Lucky," she said. "Bryce will like it."

Sterling looked back at her own work. She had a lot of practicing to do before she could make something fit for her cowboy boyfriend. So she bought the supplies—including two packages of paper—to do just that.

24

Luke enjoyed the festive mood at Blaze's house. The man always had a hot pot of coffee on and plenty to talk about, and he'd invited Luke for his birthday breakfast. He said he'd cleared it with Sterling and everything.

"Hey, I'm not sure I ever said thanks about Silver," Luke said as Faith put a cup of coffee in front of him. "Thanks, Faith."

She beamed at him. "Happy Birthday, Luke."

"I love Silver," Blaze said with a sigh. "I wish they were open year-round."

"They're not?" That would explain why the barn looked like it could fall down at any moment.

Blaze shook his head. "Only in the summertime, and for special holidays in the winter. They do a good job, don't they?"

"It was by far the ritziest party I've ever attended," Luke said.

His brother chuckled and shook his head. "I doubt that. You've gone to Country Music Awards and stuff."

"Yeah, and half the people there buy their cologne at the

grocery store." He scoffed, but amidst Blaze's belly laughter, the sound got lost.

Baby Grace began to cry, and Blaze quieted down and got up to get her. He patted the baby girl on her back, and Luke's heart simultaneously opened with love and crowed with jealousy. "Sorry, baby," Blaze soothed. "Uncle Luke was just so funny." He grinned at Luke over the baby's shoulder, and then glanced over to Faith.

"So...I heard there was a scuffle last week. At the bookshop."

Luke's eyebrows went up. "Really? Otis didn't say anything. Georgia either."

"It was Abby," Blake said. "Something about someone not being nice to Sterling."

"I can hear you telling him about it," Faith said from across the kitchen.

"Then you come tell it, so it gets done right." Blaze rolled his eyes, but Luke knew Faith walked on water for him.

Faith returned to the table with a pan of cheesy hashbrowns and a plate stacked with fried eggs. "Sterling didn't want it made into a big deal."

"Then she shouldn't have told all the wives," Blaze said.

"*She* didn't." Faith glared at him. "Abby did." She looked over to Luke, and her expression softened. He raised both eyebrows, though he could just cock the one. He usually only did it as a joke, and this didn't feel like anything he'd laugh about.

"There are some women around town who harass her," Faith said simply. "Old co-workers from Red Carpet. There was someone at the calligraphy class causing a problem, and Abby put a stop to it." She turned and went back into the kitchen. "Now, eat those eggs before they get cold."

Luke couldn't even move. Someone had been bothering Sterling? And he didn't know about it?

He met Blaze's eye, his chest storming with the need to find whoever dared to even look at Sterling wrong and...and...blow down their house. "She has never said anything to me about her old co-workers being mean to her."

"Sterling is a strong woman," Blaze said quietly.

"Why wouldn't she tell me?"

"Because she's embarrassed," Faith called. "I'm not bringing over the bacon until this conversation moves to something else."

"She'll bring it over," Blaze said.

"Blaze," Faith barked as she practically flew back to the table. "She does not want the whole town gossiping about her, and here you are—the two of you—doing just that. Why can't we just do what she asks? She deserves that much from the people who care about her, doesn't she?"

She took the baby from him and left the room completely.

"Faith," he called after her. He tossed down his napkin, his brow furrowed completely. "Sorry, Luke. Eat. I'll be right back." He took a few steps, calling, "Faith," again.

Luke actually liked that not everything in his brother's house flowed like clockwork. It showed him that Faith and Blaze could disagree—fight even—and still love each other.

"Uncle Luke," Cash said as he came into the kitchen. "Happy Birthday."

"Thanks, bud." Luke grinned at him and hugged him around the waist. "Sit. Eat." He glanced over to Corrine, who colored in an old art book Sterling had bought her at the thrift store last weekend.

She'd also gotten Corrine a lamp with a bright pink base and a Kirby shade, and Corrine had been switching on the two lamps she had beside her bed the moment she got home from school. She made Luke turn off the Kirby one last, and it had been hard for him not to ask her what she'd done with Sterling.

227

Obviously the thrift store. Sterling had asked him about spaghetti, but they could've gotten that at any number of restaurants. And Corrine hadn't stopped talking about the calligraphy class all week, so he knew they'd gone there.

"Baby," he said to his daughter. "You need to eat. We have to go soon."

Cash brought over the plate of bacon, and Blaze returned only a few seconds later. He carried Grace, and he sat right back down where he'd been. "Sorry, Luke. I thought you might want to know."

"I do," he said, looking up as Faith rejoined them too. "Sorry, Faith. I—she didn't tell me."

"I know she didn't." Faith didn't look happy. "We told her to, but well, we're still getting to know Sterling."

Luke was too, and he wasn't sure why she wouldn't want him to know this. "I've never seen anyone treat her badly."

"Well, they wouldn't in front of you," Blaze said with a smile. "You'd rip them apart limb by limb." He took a couple of eggs and looked over to his boy. "You're up."

Cash grinned and squirted more ketchup on his eggs. "I smelled the bacon."

"It's good for everything," Blaze said with a grin.

Luke settled into the breakfast, but he couldn't help trying to formulate a way to talk to Sterling about whatever had happened last weekend. He didn't want any secrets between them, not even something small.

Once they'd finished, once Luke had Corrine back in the truck, once he'd started back to his house, he asked, "Corrine, do you like Sterling?"

"Yes," she said simply. "She's very nice."

Luke nodded, his gut churning. "Where did you go to lunch last weekend?"

"That noodle place," she said. "The one with the music notes."

"Notable Noodles," he said, not asking.

"Yep."

Luke didn't ask anything else. Sterling had wanted to come over right after breakfast to "start the celebration," and Luke hadn't had the heart to tell her no. She was so excited about his birthday, and as he drove down his street, he almost drove right past his house.

Because it suddenly didn't look like his house anymore. Someone—Sterling—had tied bright blue and white and orange balloons to his mailbox, his garbage can, and his front door. The garage held a banner that screamed, "Happy Birthday, Luke!" to the neighborhood, and he found himself smiling at it.

"No wonder she let Blaze feed me breakfast," he grumbled to himself. He normally parked in the garage, but he didn't want to ruin her sign.

"Look at her calligify," Corrine said. No matter how many times Luke had corrected her on the word, she still couldn't get it. "See it, Daddy? At the bottom?" She pointed to the sign on the garage, and Luke finally saw it.

32 years old today ~ 8 Leap Day years

She'd acknowledged both numbers for him. No joking. No ribbing. He could celebrate his birthday every year, of course. He often lumped himself in with those who'd been born on March first, but there was something special about being able to celebrate on Leap Day. Why, he didn't know, but Luke didn't try to riddle through every emotion he had.

He simply let himself feel it.

He came to a stop in the driveway and said, "Did you tell her blue and orange were my favorite colors?"

"No," Corrine said. "Can I get down?"

"Yes," he said. "Let's go in." Sterling was obviously already there, and Luke found himself anticipating seeing her, smelling her, kissing her in only a few moments. He always wanted that anticipation, that excitement.

"Hey," he called as he entered the house. The scent of pine trees and smoke met his nose, and if he'd been coming home to an empty house, he'd be terrified. As it was, candles of varying heights stood all over the house. On the mantle. On the coffee table in the living room. On the dining room table. On the kitchen counter.

Sterling stood next to that, wearing a pair of black slacks and a long-sleeved tee that said, "Forever Young" above the date of February 29.

She wore the most beautiful smile in the world, and Luke's fingers clenched into fists. He absolutely would defend her on anything, and that protective streak inside him told him how much he liked Sterling.

He liked her so much, it might even be the first inklings of love.

His throat narrowed then, because he and Sterling had so far to go still. "Happy Birthday," she said, those red lips taunting him as they moved. "I know you just ate, but I thought we'd do presents first anyway."

She smiled at Corrine and bent down to hug her. "Go get yours, okay, baby?"

"Okay." Corrine skipped off, and Luke decided he couldn't just stand there and stare at his girlfriend, even if he wanted to.

"Aren't you a sight for sore eyes?" He gathered her close and pressed a kiss to her temple. "Mm, you smell good. The whole place smells amazing."

"You like pines," she said. "And since I didn't have much time, I had to light a lot of candles." She giggled quietly in his arms. "Don't worry. I'll take them with me when I go."

"Take 'em," he said. "Leave 'em. It's all fine." Everything was fine, because he held her. He pulled away and gazed at her. "Sterling, I'm—" His throat closed, but Luke had done hard things before. "This is becoming very real for me," he said. "Very quickly."

She nodded, the sparkle-shine of her eyes only amplifying. "I know what you mean."

He wanted to talk about last weekend, but he wouldn't kill the mood for her. She'd worked very hard to create it for him, he knew, and he simply leaned down and kissed her. Oh, their first kiss had driven him to the brink of sanity. The one on Valentine's Day had told him how very tightly she held his heart.

This one spoke of love, and Luke honestly didn't know what to do with it. "Mm, you taste like apples," he whispered before touching his lips to hers again.

"Do you want to open mine first?" Corrine asked, and Luke pulled out of the kiss. His daughter stood there watching him, and a flush rose through his neck and into his cheeks.

"Sure." He reached for the bright blue bag that someone had stuffed with orange and white paper, but Corrine pulled it back.

"You have to sit down, Daddy," she said. "Like we do at the parties."

"Oh-ho." He chuckled as he moved over to the dining table. "I don't think there's room here. That bag is going to catch on fire."

"Over here, silly." Corrine went into the living room and put the bag on the couch. "You sit here, and I'll bring you the gifts."

"How many are there?" he asked, suddenly concerned.

"Not that many," Sterling assured him in a quiet voice.

He sank onto the couch as she rounded it and put her arm around Corrine. They looked at one another, and Luke pressed pause on time. It froze, with his daughter looking up at his girlfriend like they had a female language only mothers and daughters could comprehend.

231

He'd known Corrine needed a mother, and in that moment, he knew Sterling could fill the role.

Time rushed forward again, and Corrine said, "Open it, Daddy."

He dug into the paper and pulled out the bright yellow bag of kettle corn he loved so much. Due to his years performing with Country Quad, he could put on a good show no matter what kind of mood he was in.

So he grinned and laughed like this popcorn his daughter got for him every year was exactly what he wanted for his birthday. And it was, because she'd given it to him.

"Thank you, bean."

"I have another one," Corrine chirped, and Sterling handed her a plain white envelope. "I wrote your name on it, Daddy. Look." She crowded into his side on the couch, and Luke put his arm around her.

D-a-d-d-y sat on the envelope in clear, beautifully crafted black letters. "Wow," he said. "You wrote that?"

She nodded, her pride practically bursting from her. She relinquished the hold on the envelope, and Luke lifted the flap. He pulled out a single piece of paper and unfolded it. It had been printed on a color printer—which he did not own—and he scanned as quickly as he could.

"A...."

"We're going to go fishing!" Corrine yelled. "Me, you, and Sterling." She looked up at him, and then Sterling. "Right, Sterling?"

"Right," she said. "We just have to make sure it all lines up, okay? Remember we talked about that."

"Yeah, I know," Corrine said. "But Daddy never does anything."

That got Luke to raise his eyebrows. "Daddy never does

anything?"

"You can skip a day at the gym," Corrine said. "Grandma's always telling me that."

Luke wasn't sure what to address first. His daughter's slightly condescending tone about his workout schedule, or the fact that his mother had been talking about it with his daughter.

Sterling laughed, and then said, "Corrine, your daddy does way more than nothing." She sat down tentatively on the edge of the couch. "He takes care of you all day, you know. And he's in the band, and they practice a lot." She looked over to him. "Plus, I have a very busy schedule, and you agreed that if we got him this trip, you'd be patient about when we could do it."

"And we can't fish in the winter anyway," Corrine said.

"Right." Sterling smoothed her hand down the back of Corrine's curls, but they just bounced right back up. Luke hadn't even tried to tame them this morning. Her eyes met Luke's, and he desperately wished they were alone.

He wanted to ask her if she wanted children, and what had happened last weekend, and if she could possibly really ever fall in love with him. True, deep, lasting love. Luke was a selfish man, and he wanted it all.

Sterling took a breath and said, "Okay, my turn." She put both hands on her thighs and stood. She detoured into the kitchen and came back, bearing a slim package in her hands that looked like it might've held a small TV at some point.

She didn't give any qualifiers for the gift. After simply passing it to him, she sat back down and took Corrine onto her lap. Luke paused time again right there, watching the two of them sit so intimately made his father's heart beat and beat and beat until it fluttered like hummingbird wings.

"Okay." He cleared his throat and blinked. With his focus on the box, he noted she'd chosen a simple paper with multi-colored balloons on a white background. It came off easily, and he sliced open the top of the repurposed box.

He'd been right—it had housed a TV in the past.

Now, he pulled out a framed piece of art, noting the weight of the beautiful wood in his hands.

His name sat in the middle of the pale yellow paper. It was beautifully drawn, with perfect thin lines and bulging thick ones that only seemed more elegant for how much ink they held.

Around the eight-inch letters sat more words, and he read out loud. "Luke loves his family." He swallowed, because that was true. "Luke protects his daughter."

He looked over to Sterling, whose blue eyes held hope and fear at the same time. "What is this?"

"All the things you are," she whispered. "As seen by me."

He looked back at the treasure in his hands. "Smart. The best drummer in the state of Wyoming."

That probably wasn't hard to do, but he didn't laugh or scoff or even smile.

A good dad.

Dedicated to his work and his family.

Faithful.

His tears came then, and Luke could not remember the last time he'd gotten this choked up. He defaulted to anger for his strong emotion, and he didn't know what to do with this other stuff.

"Sterling," he whispered.

She set Corrine on her feet and said something to her. His daughter left the room without another word, and Sterling moved closer to Luke. She pressed her leg against his and threaded her arm through his. They both gazed at the beautiful testimony of him that she had created.

She could've said any number of things, but she said the absolute best thing: "I see you, Luke."

He looked at her, and while he didn't know all of her pain and all she'd been through, he saw her too.

"I'm falling for you," she whispered. "Happy Birthday, baby."

Luke wanted to tell her he thought he'd fallen in love with her right there, sitting on his couch, reading things like,

Will hold any baby he can.

Likes to stand in the back at church.

Loves his Momma with his whole heart.

But he couldn't vocalize it. So he kissed her, hoping the same message got construed, just in a different way.

25

ilde Young walked into her house behind her daughter, who carried the gender reveal box like it might hold a bomb instead of either pink or blue confetti, balloons, and streamers.

"I'll put it on the table," Lynnie said, and Hilde simply watched her move that way. The house she and Gabe had bought to merge their lives and continue raising their family felt huge on a good day and cavernous on a bad.

Today, it would be just right for the number of people coming to see if she and Gabe would be adding a little boy or a little girl to their fold. Only Hilde knew, as she'd done the gender reveal part of the ultrasound alone.

Fine, she'd told Ev, the blonde powerhouse who stood in the kitchen with no less than five cowboys twice as big as her, laughing. "You guys get out of here," she said when she spotted Hilde. "The cake is here." She met Hilde's eyes, so much energy and happiness in hers.

Hilde loved Ev's vibe, and she truly enjoyed seeing how happy she was. Hilde had that same buzz of energy and joy flowing through her too, and she'd never dreamed she'd have the life she currently lived.

"Right here," Ev said. "Harry, take your uncles somewhere else. It's starting to smell too manly in here."

"Too manly?" Otis asked with a grin. "What does that smell like, exactly, Ev?"

"Out," she said firmly. She glanced around as Hilde slid the enormous, six-layer cake onto the space on her kitchen island. Since she only had four more months until her baby was due, her belly nudged into the counter before the rest of her.

Otis turned with Luke, and Trace followed with Morris and Mav. Hilde still didn't see her husband, and she frowned as she took in the rest of the space. Nope, Gabe wasn't there. "Where is he?" she grumbled.

He still had to go to Jackson Hole periodically for court cases and meetings with his team there. He operated two offices of a very busy father's rights family law firm, and they'd talked extensively about his schedule and what might need to change once the baby was born.

Hilde still owned and operated her furniture store, but she'd watched Ev pull back on the dance studio. She only did administrative work, and she'd hired people to take over all of the teaching. She had to run payroll for them, and deal with the bills her building and business required. But she did that from home; the quarterly dances in the parking lots surrounding her studio? She'd quit doing them.

Wanting that same freedom, Hilde had been considering a very drastic change in her life—selling the store completely. She loved it with her whole heart, but one look at Lynnie told her that she had two heart-fulls of love to give to her daughter.

"Momma," a tiny voice said, and Hilde looked down at Liesl.

She was not biologically Hilde's, but she loved her like she was. She'd never known her own mother, and Gabe and Hilde had decided to work toward having Hilde legally adopt Liesl. They'd talked with her and Lynnie about what Liesl would call Hilde, and they'd arrived on "Momma."

It was the single best word in the English language.

Hilde bent and picked up the little brunette. "Look at your hair, Liesl." She grinned at her and pressed her lips to her porcelain cheek. "Did Lynnie do it for you?"

"Nope," Liesl said as she hugged Hilde's head. "Uncle Luke did it."

Hilde found the tall, grumpy cowboy, smiling internally at the many facets of the man. He kept looking toward the front door, and that was when Hilde realized Sterling had not arrived yet either.

In fact, besides Ev and Hilde, there were no other women in this big gathering area of the house.

"Where are the rest of the wives?" She looked over to Ev, who wore a tight teal T-shirt and a pair of jeans that looked painted on. She'd had a baby seven months ago, but Hilde would never know it. She knew Ev's outlet for stress was through dance, and she'd texted Hilde many times over the years to say, *I'm at my studio alone tonight. I'll text you when I'm home.*

That way, if Hilde didn't hear from her, she could make sure Ev was okay, that nothing bad had happened.

"They're putting together...something." Ev wouldn't look at her, and Hilde didn't like that at all. She knew better than to push Ev, though, and instead, she inched a little closer to her and switched Liesl over to her other hip.

"Ev," she said. "I'm thinking of selling the furniture store."

That got her best friend's gaze to fly to her. "What? Where will we do our refurbishing?"

Hilde smiled at her fondly. "Where did you used to do it?"

Ev softened too, and she leaned into Hilde. "My driveway."

"Have you seen my house?" Hilde asked. "Or yours?"

"Hey, our house is one of the completely normal ones," Ev said. "We don't all own houses in the woods, behind gates."

Hilde only smiled, because she loved this house. It had two big offices, and plenty of living space. Bedrooms galore, and yes, it backed up to the National Park land. "I have plenty of garage space here for us to sand out our frustrations."

Ev nodded and surveyed the group as more people came down the hall from the foyer and into the back area of the house. Blaze followed his son, Cash, and Faith brought up the rear with baby Grace in her arms.

Hilde brightened, because that baby was the cutest thing on the planet. Maybe not as cute as Liesl, or Ev's baby Keri—who'd definitely picked up some of Ev's fairer features among the darker Young ones. But Grace had auburn hair, and Hilde loved it, loved it, loved it.

Lynnie had auburn hair too, and she swooped down onto the little girl and took her from Faith. Before Faith could move out of the way, Jem and Sunny arrived, his kids making a ruckus as they joined the other cousins in the living room.

"Doing this indoors was a bad idea," Hilde said. Gabe would hate the noise. At the same time, Gabe loved getting his whole family together. And right now, it didn't matter what Gabe liked or didn't like, as the man wasn't even here.

"They'll calm down once we start," Ev said. "Besides, it's a cake and popcorn party. It'll be over in ten seconds."

Faith joined them at the island and she eyed the white cake box. "Is that the cake?"

"Sure is," Hilde said as she smiled at Faith. "Thanks for recommending Jenny. She did a great job and was super fast."

"She's the best," Faith said with a yawn.

"Are you still doing the morning shift on the doughnut truck?" Ev asked.

Faith nodded as she covered her mouth. "And I missed my afternoon nap with Grace today, because we went to watch Blaze do his demo at the high school." She turned and faced the cowboys too. "He and Jem did great."

"Mm hm," Hilde said as Ev did the same. "You went to make sure Blaze didn't actually do the demo," Hilde added.

"Of course," Faith said dryly. "The man thinks he's indestructible, and he's had two surgeries in the past three years." She sighed as she turned back to them, her own softness creeping into her face. "But he's adorable with the baby, and he's *so good* with those kids in the junior rodeo program."

"I'll bet he is," Ev said. "Who are we missing, Hilde?"

"Besides the father?"

Ev looked at her. "Gabe's not here? Yes, he is. I saw him...." She stepped around Hilde and to the end of the island, but Hilde was pregnant, not blind.

She bent to put Liesl back on her feet and she said, "Go find your daddy, okay?" As she straightened, a pain pulled through her side, and Hilde pressed her hand to it and blew out her breath.

"Abby and Tex aren't here either," she said, finally catching up to who still hadn't arrived. "That's kind of weird, right?"

Before either woman could answer, the band of cowboy brothers erupted into loud laughter. Hilde could admit it was good to hear, though the wave of sound threatened to deafen her. According to Gabe, his family had been splintered and fractured only a handful of years ago. No one would think so if they saw these brothers in this moment.

She grinned as Cecily and Jerry came into the house, and that caused another uproar as the boys greeted their parents. Hilde loved watching them all interact, and her emotions swelled again. She really needed to have this baby, so she could be more in control of her hormones.

"I am so sorry," Gabe said as he swept to Hilde's side. He still wore his designer gray suit, his tie knotted just-so at his neck. "Court ran long, of course, and then there was an accident on the highway between here and Jackson." He pressed a kiss to Hilde's cheek and added, "Give me five minutes?"

He rushed off, waving away his family as he did, and Hilde just watched him go. Neither Ev nor Faith said anything about Gabe's tardiness or work schedule, and Hilde buttoned the words behind her lips too. She and Gabe would talk about it privately.

"All right," Ev called into the fray anyway. "Everyone needs to get on over here. We're going to put some candles on this cake, and I believe the girls are going to be the ones to pull the tab on the box." She looked to Hilde for confirmation, and she nodded.

"Tex and Abby aren't here," Trace said into the quieting room. "And I don't see any of the women either."

"We're right here," someone said, and Hilde's eyes flew to the mouth of the hallway. They could've been in the basement, or down the hall toward the master bedroom, or hiding out in the foyer. No matter what, they did all stand where they had not been before.

Georgia, who moved over to Otis and gave him their little boy. She wasn't due for months still, but she wore a loose shirt to hide the baby bump Hilde could feel when she hugged her.

Leigh, who migrated to Morris's side while their kids played in the living room. Her brother hadn't come to this, and Hilde found she missed Denzel. He'd been coming to everything for years, and while of course she wanted him to be happy with Michelle, she still wanted him here. He was part of the family.

Sterling stepped over to Luke, and she held Corrine's hand, so the little girl had obviously been with her and not the other kids. Luke looked at her with warm, shining stars in his eyes, and he kissed her quickly and faced the kitchen expectantly.

Dani had her baby with her, but their other children played in the living room with Cash, Harry, Cole, Rosie, Eric, and Rachelle. She hitched the baby higher and faced the kitchen too.

Jem stood alone, as Sunny wasn't there today. Out of all of them, she had to work, and Hilde understood the busy life of a nurse. So they just needed Abby and Tex to show up.

"All right." Gabe came back into the room wearing a pair of khakis and a polo, of course. He wasn't really a sweats and T-shirt kind of guy, though Hilde had seen him wear such things for certain occasions. Like lawn mowing or working out. But otherwise? He looked one breath away from going golfing or attending lunch at the country club.

"Are we ready? I get a front row seat for this. I don't even know myself." He wore glee on his face, and it took him a moment to realize no one else had moved or was speaking. "What?"

"Tex and Abby aren't here," Hilde said quietly. "Did he text you? They're coming, right?"

Gabe pulled his phone out of his pocket, because no, he never went anywhere without it. "Nothing from him on my phone...the family text...the brothers' one." He looked up, alarm finally ringing in his eyes. "I'll call him." Gabe tapped and lifted the phone to his ear.

"Sorry," someone called from down the hall leading to the front door. "Sorry we're late. We're here." Abby herded her little girl in front of her as she entered the house. "Go get Uncle Jem, then, if he's so fun."

She sounded cross, and Melissa sure didn't radiate sunshine the way she normally did. She did run over to Jem, who scooped her up with a chuckle. Tex brought up the rear, and he said absolutely nothing as he stood on the opposite side of the room from his brothers.

Something was definitely wrong, but Hilde wouldn't be the one to bring it up. Trace wore a concerned look on his face and a frown between his eyebrows, and perhaps he could talk to Tex later. Then Hilde might get the story from Ev.

"Welcome, everyone," Gabe said good-naturedly. "I think there are two people in the world who know if my baby is a boy or a girl, and I would like to find out." He grinned at Hilde, because he'd allowed her to do this.

She wasn't even sure why she'd wanted to. Gabe had attended the ultrasound for most of it—the part where the doctor assured them the baby was developing and growing correctly. Then she'd had him step out so only she knew the gender.

Feeling older than she was, Hilde looked over to the dining room table. "There's actually four or five people who know," she said. "The cake maker. The doctor. Me. Ev." She paused. "Yeah, four people."

"Let's see it," one of the cowboys called, and Hilde nodded to Lynnie and Liesl, and then Ev.

Lynnie helped Liesl get up on one of the dining chairs, and Ev lifted the box from surrounding the cake. She cut into it, but didn't pull the knife out, so no colored crumbs would be revealed before the precise moment.

"Ready?" Lynnie asked, and she shone like the constellations tonight. She was very excited for Hilde to have a baby, which had been a great relief to Hilde.

Faith, Dani, and Georgia held up their phones, the three of them filming three different things. The girls' reaction belonged to Dani. Faith seemed to be inches from Gabe's face. And Georgia stood back and filmed the whole lot of them.

"Three...two...one!" Lynnie and Liesl pulled the strings that would activate the top on the box, causing it to explode open.

Life held very still for a moment, and then the sound of firecrackers filled the house. People screamed. Babies started crying.

Bright blue confetti, streamers, and balloons lifted from the box, shooting up toward the two-story ceilings and showering the crowd in the living room with blue shrapnel.

"It's a boy!" Ev yelled as she lifted the first piece of cake. It had been frosted in white-as-pure-snow frosting, but the cake inside was the bluest of blues.

She handed the plate to Gabe, who laughed and laughed. For a grumpy lawyer, Hilde sure did like hearing that sound come from his mouth.

He put down the cake and grabbed onto Hilde. Amidst the chaos, the congratulations, the yelling and bopping of balloons, he leaned close to her and whispered, "I love you so much." He pulled back, his eyes shiny and glassy. "A boy. A baby boy."

"Congrats, brother," Tex said, and he wore a remnant of his smile. He pulled Gabe into a hug and squeezed his eyes closed. "We need some boys after that string of girls we've had."

They pounded one another on the back, and Hilde wanted to tell Gabe to talk to Tex. Find out what was going on with him, with their family.

Instead, she hugged the oldest Young brother too, and then started handing out slices of blue cake in honor of her baby boy.

26

Maverik Young stepped out onto his front porch and tipped his head back to greet the sun. March had come and gone, leaving behind drifts of snow. April had started with a bang, but she'd quieted into afternoon rain showers that melted a lot of the snow—and mornings full of sunshine, the scent of fresh water, and pure joy.

Mav loved the morning, and he loved the sunshine, and he loved his life in Coral Canyon. Things had gotten a bit hectic with the addition of a fourth child to his and Dani's family, even if Beth —his daughter—didn't live with them full-time.

Boston—Dani's son from her first marriage—did, and they had two kids together. Lars had just turned five years old a couple of weeks ago, and he'd be starting kindergarten in the fall. Their daughter, Emma, had just been born in November.

All in all, Mav enjoyed his morning routine with the kids. He got them up, got them dressed, fed, and backpacked for the day. Right now, it was only Boston every day of the week, and then Lars on Tuesdays and Thursdays.

He still took Emma with him on the school run, and sometimes he had to swing by Jem's and get his kids too. All of his brothers lived here now, and Mav wanted to be a support to any and all of them. They'd certainly helped him and Dani over the years too.

Today, he bent down to get the paper, just like he had on countless days before. Yes, it was antiquated and maybe even a waste of resources, but Mav had his routine, and that included leafing through the paper while the kids ate breakfast.

He tucked it under his arm and returned to the house. "Lars," he called. "It's pre-school today." The boy had been up with the sun, so Mav didn't have to worry about that. The little boy had a seemingly endless supply of energy, and sometimes Mav simply took him and Boston up into the hills surrounding town and let them both run, walk, jump, skip rocks, and wade through the streams until Lars slowed down.

It gave Dani a break, as she'd been dealing with her mom a lot lately. He found her in the kitchen, and he swept a kiss along her neck. She giggled and leaned into him, and Mav growled as he put his hand on her hip and held her close to him. "You goin' over to your momma's today?"

"Yes," she said. "I'm taking her that soup from Sunday." She glanced at him. "That's still okay, right?"

She'd made an enormous pot of hamburger stew, and while Mav liked it—well, he liked it for one meal, and that was it—he wouldn't be sorry to see it go. "Yeah, sure," he said easily. "Then the florist?"

"I'm there for probably only an hour this afternoon," she said. She'd owned her own flower shop in Louisville when Mav had met her, and she'd given it all up, sold it, to move to Wyoming and be with him. She went into the florist's here to help with big orders for weddings or anniversaries or funerals, and to do some floral arranging classes. "It's for the Westwood funeral." She shook her head. "It's so sad."

"He was ninety-eight," Mav said. "I think he lived a good life, and there's nothing sad about that."

"I suppose," Dani said, finishing with the dishes. "Cereal today?"

"I don't think we have enough eggs to satisfy both boys." He smiled at Dani, because the older Boston got—and he was almost twelve now—the more he ate. "And me."

Dani gave him a knowing smile. "You'll just get one of those breakfast sandwiches on the way home from Fancy Nancy."

He laughed and shook his head. "It's not Fancy Nancy." He didn't deny that he'd get the ham and egg sandwich. It came with chipotle aioli, two eggs, a stack of Canadian bacon, all between a delicious, buttery brioche bun.

Yeah, he stopped for breakfast a lot. "You want me to bring something back for you and your mom? Is Don home today?" Her step-dad worked a few days a week from home, and Mav didn't try to keep up with anyone's schedule but his.

Fine, all of his brothers too. He knew the ins and outs of their lives, and he worked dang hard to be involved in every and any way he could.

"No," she said. "I think it's too heavy." She'd been trying to lose her baby weight for the past six or seven months since she'd had Emma, but Mav didn't mind one bit. He liked her just the way she was, and he actually appreciated all the life changes and how they molded and sculpted a person—physically, mentally, emotionally, and spiritually.

"All right," he said. "Your loss." He looked past her and yelled, "Boys! Cereal today. Come and get it!"

"I'm going to go get Emma," Dani said. "You'll be okay with her all day?"

Mav didn't even answer his wife. Yes, he'd be fine with their daughter all day. He'd once been a single dad to his daughter, and he knew how to take care of kids. Dani didn't wait for him to answer, thankfully, and she bustled out of the kitchen as the boys bustled in.

Boston pulled open the fridge while Mav got down bowls, and Lars went into the pantry to get his cereal of choice—Cocoa Crispies. Mav didn't even argue, that was how good of a mood he was in.

"Uncle Luke is picking you guys up this afternoon," he said as they all settled down to breakfast. "So make sure you find Corrine and look for his truck."

"Yes, sir," Boston said at the same time Lars said, "Okay, Daddy."

Mav poured himself a cup of coffee and lifted it to his lips as he flipped over the newspaper he'd brought in. He'd barely looked at it before he spit out the liquid. He spewed and sputtered, his eyes drinking in the huge black and white photo of Luke.

Yes, Luke.

On the front page of the Coral Canyon Chronicles.

Mav didn't remember setting down his mug. He didn't recall reaching into his back pocket and retrieving his phone. His eyes scanned left-right, left-right, trying to read the whole story—a front page story!—about his brother.

His gaze jumped all over, his pulse bouncing through his veins in a similar fashion, until his eyes landed on the headline.

ANOTHER CORAL CANYON RESIDENT IS A BILLIONAIRE

"Oh, boy," Mav muttered as he stared at his phone. Surprisingly, the brothers' text had nothing on it. The family text had a couple of pictures of Keri, as Ev had finally gotten enough of her wispy hair to go into a ponytail.

"They don't read the paper," he said to the article. His daddy did.... Mav dialed him and paced away from the article.

"Howdy, Mav," Daddy said over the phone.

"Daddy, have you seen the Chronicles this morning?"

"Nope." Daddy groaned. "Haven't been out front yet. Something good?"

"I don't know," Mav said slowly. "I don't think Luke's going to like it." He started brainstorming a way to drive around town and get every copy of the Chronicles before his brother saw the article.

A squeal on Daddy's end of the line told Mav he'd just gone out to his front porch. Rustling. A moment of dead air. Then Daddy said, "No. I don't reckon he's going to like this."

"How do they even know stuff like this?" Mav asked, turning to face his boys again.

"Tax records are public," Daddy said. "And it's a big deal to have that much money. He'll probably be in more than the Chronicles."

So Mav couldn't do damage control. "All right." He blew out his breath. "I'm going to go over there as soon as I drop the kids off for school."

"Good luck," Daddy said. "Do you want me to call him first?"

Mav didn't know what to do. With Luke, he couldn't quite predict what the man would do. He'd settled a *ton* since making Coral Canyon his permanent home and becoming his daughter's full-time father. He wasn't as quick to anger. He thought before he spoke.

And since he'd started seeing Sterling, he'd calmed even more.

"I'm going to put it on the family text," Mav said as he decided. "Just rip the bandage off. Maybe a bunch of us will meet at Luke's this morning after school drop-offs." He returned to the article, feeling much less frantic. "Love you, Daddy."

"Good luck," Daddy said again, and he ended the call.

Coral Canyon is the permanent home of at least two billionaires! the first line read. *With the recent tax filings, it has been confirmed that Lucas Young, a current permanent resident and someone who grew up in Coral Canyon, has reached the level of billionaire.*

"Oh, land alive," Mav whispered as he read the quote by Luke. "There is *no way* he said this."

Ain't no thing, right?

Yes, Luke said that a lot. But there was *no way* on this planet that Luke would've talked to a small-town columnist about his financial affairs. He hadn't even talked to anyone about them until a year or so ago when he'd humbled himself, truly and sincerely apologized to Gabe, and asked for his help.

"Gabe." Mav's mind blitzed again. If Luke was a billionaire, it was because of Gabe and his masterful managing of Luke's assets.

He stopped reading and pulled out his phone. He snapped a picture of the front page, and while it wasn't the greatest photo ever taken, the picture of Luke and the headline leapt off the screen.

Mav didn't know how to caption it. He didn't know how to prepare for any fallout that might come from this news.

So he navigated to the family text—the one everyone was on, including Denzel, Bryce, and Wade and Cheryl—Abby's brother and his wife—and attached the photo.

From this morning's paper.

He sent that, and quickly tapped out one more thing.

Love you, Luke.

Because Mav had no doubts now. Luke would not like this being splashed all over town. Oh, no, he would not.

27

Luke pulled up to Jem's and peered through his windshield. Corrine sang along to the country song from the back seat, and Luke didn't normally have to get out and go get Rosie and Cole. Jem had them ready, practically pushing them out the front door, when Luke drove everyone to school.

But today, they weren't standing on the porch. In high school, when Luke had gone to pick up his friends for school, he'd lean on the horn to let them know he'd arrived. But he was an adult now, and Jem was his brother, not some late teenager grabbing a Pop-tart on the way out the door.

So he waited. All the way to the end of the song he waited, and then his impatience started to vibrate behind his eyes. He wasn't sure why. He didn't have anywhere else to be this morning. Jem had an AA meeting in a half-hour, which was why he'd asked Luke to take the kids to school.

"So he has to be leaving soon," Luke said to himself, glancing at the clock on the radio. Jem was definitely late getting his kids out the door.

Luke twisted in his seat and said, "Jelly belly, stay here, okay?" He then got out of the truck and strode up the walk toward the front door. As he reached the porch, the door opened and Rosie spilled outside, Cole right behind her.

"Hurry up now," Jem called after them, but he walked toward Luke with calculated steps. Plenty of sunlight shone on his brother's face, and Luke's blood cooled instantly.

"What's going on?" he asked as the kids ran past him.

Jem's jaw twitched, and his eyes stormed. Luke had seen him like this plenty in the past, usually as he battled an inner demon Luke would never understand. He tried, because he and Jem were so close in age, and Luke had grown up in the man's shadow.

"You haven't seen the family text yet, have you?"

"No." Luke hadn't even turned his sound back on, and he dug in his pocket to get it out.

Jem moved then, and he covered Luke's hand as it emerged from his back pocket. They stood nearly chest-to-chest, and Luke's pulse went haywire. "You're freaking me out," he said in an even voice. "What happened? Is it Momma or Daddy? An accident? Something with Bryce?" His throat felt like fire by the time he finished asking questions, and he didn't know what he'd do if something else had gone wrong for Bryce.

Or if his daddy had died.

Luke's ribcage collapsed, and he sucked in a breath. "Out with it Jem, or let me look at my phone."

"You're in the paper." Jem pulled his hand back. "I mean, it's not color, but it's Coral Canyon. The USA Today report actually *is* in full color."

Luke frowned as he searched his brother's face. "Why in the world would I be in the paper?"

Jem backed up another step, then another, until he was framed safely in his open doorway. "Check it out."

Luke pressed the power button on his phone, instantly seeing the family text message icon. When he tapped on that, he was already sixty-four messages behind. He scrolled up, his eyes trying to read up and out of order, but he refused to stop.

He got to a message that had been sent this morning, by Mav. It indeed was a picture of him, with a screaming headline about him being a billionaire.

Luke's eyes widened, and he looked at Jem, pure panic streaming through him. "Can they just publish this?"

"They just did," Jem said. "Tex found the national report, which is apparently something these places do once the taxes are in for the year."

Luke's blood sputtered through his system, making his feet cold and his head too hot. "I—I—this isn't anyone's business but mine."

Jem smiled—he smiled!—and Luke wanted to throw his phone at him. "Take the kids to school and come back. Mav's bringing breakfast sandwiches." He nodded to the phone. "That's what the rest of the messages are. Everyone's in." He cocked both eyebrows. "Even Tex, so we might finally get him to tell us what's goin' on with him."

Luke swallowed, because he wanted to know about Tex too. He already knew it concerned Bryce, but he'd never seen his happy-go-lucky brother retreat like this. Not even when Bryce and Bailey had gotten pregnant, decided not to get married, and then gave up their baby for adoption.

"Okay," he said. "School drop-off. Back here for breakfast." His mind caught up to his mouth. "What about your meeting?"

"There's another one at two-thirty," he said. "So...can you get the kids too?"

"Yes." Luke didn't know what else to say or do. His brain reminded him that they were late for school, and he turned on his heel and went down the steps. He drove the kids to school and called to them to have a good day, that he loved them. As the three of them ran off and threw their backpacks unceremoniously in a pile near the fence, Luke sighed.

"Sterling," he said, realizing for the first time why he didn't want his financial status—if that was even a thing—splashed all over the front page of the paper. Any paper. He didn't want *her* to know.

He put the truck in gear and got driving back to Jem's. "Of course you want her to know," he grumbled to himself. "You've been seeing her for four months now, and just the other night, you laid in bed and fantasized about marrying her. What? You'd never tell her about your money?"

Shaking his head, he continued to mentally chastise himself until he rounded the corner and saw all the trucks parked in front of Jem's. Someone had left him a spot in the driveway, and it felt deliberate. It reminded Luke of the way Sterling had created the most perfect birthday gift for him—because she saw him. She remembered him. She knew him.

"You want to tell her," he said. "You don't want her finding out from the newspaper along with everyone else." That got him digging for his phone again, this time much more frantically. He dialed Sterling, pressed his eyes closed, and prayed.

"Hey, Luke," she said, her voice still a little on the deep, froggy side. That meant she hadn't had an early client and hadn't gotten out of bed.

"Hey," he said in a rush. "Can you come over to Jem's?"

"Uh, let me look at my schedule."

"Like, right now," he said. "It's kind of important."

"Important? What's going on? Are you okay? Is he okay?" Sterling wore her concern plainly in her voice, and Luke had to admit he liked it. She'd come to all family functions over the past four months. She fit in with the other wives. She talked to all of the kids, and the last time they'd all been together, he'd found Sterling in the kitchen at Blaze's house, helping Lars get a juice box.

Luke had definitely started to fall in love with her, and he couldn't wait to spend the summer with her. The fall. Another winter, with Christmas and a brand new year all over again.

"Luke?" she said, and he blinked his way out of his head.

"I just have something I want to tell you, and I don't want you finding out another way," he said slowly, trying to make all the pieces come together. "It's not bad. Do you get the paper?"

"The—the paper?"

"Yeah."

"No."

"Good," he said. "Just...don't look at anything online, and come on over to Jem's. Mav will have a breakfast sandwich for you." He looked up as he sensed movement on the porch, and sure enough Blaze and Tex had come outside. They clearly knew he'd arrived and hadn't come in, and Blaze lifted his eyebrows though it had to be obvious Luke was on the phone.

He got out of the truck and said, "Okay, Sterling? I'll see you soon?"

"Yes," she said. "I'm getting ready now."

Relief flooded him. "Okay." He hung up and shoved his phone away as he walked toward his brothers. "Just talking to Sterling."

"You told her over the phone?" Blaze's judging look annoyed Luke, but he didn't let the emotion rise through him.

"You make it sound like having money is akin to being a murderer or something." Luke forced a smile to his face. "Is Gabe here, because I'm going to rip him apart if he is."

Tex laughed—actually laughed—and as Luke gained the top of

the porch for the second time that morning, he stepped into his older brother's arms and hugged him. "I've missed you," he whispered to Tex, who stiffened slightly.

"Let's go inside," Tex said. "It might almost be May, but it's windy this morning." The three of them retreated into the house, and as Luke went into the back of the house where the living room, dining room, and kitchen were, he indeed found all of his brothers there, a literal mountain of wrapped breakfast sandwiches, and Abby.

"Hey, you." She gave him a fast smile that wobbled at the corners and immediately grabbed onto him. She was due any day now, and Luke wasn't surprised to see her. Tex would never leave her out on the eastern edge of town, in that farmhouse alone, to come to Jem's house.

She didn't have to say why she gripped him so tightly. She didn't apologize verbally, but everyone in the house knew that Luke hated being in the spotlight when he didn't want to be. Everyone thought that just because he was a public figure, in a popular country music band, that he must just love everyone in the world knowing the intricate details of his life.

Well, he did not.

"It's all over social," Blaze said. "Even my manager says we're blowing up." He didn't have his phone out. "I mean, everyone already knows I'm a billionaire, so." He shrugged, and Luke tried to smile.

He moved over to Blaze, who also took him into a hug. "This isn't bad," he said. "You'll have a few crazy days of public relations stuff, and then it'll be over."

"Sterling," Luke managed to say, and Blaze pounded him on the back.

"She'll be okay." He pulled away. "She likes *you*, brother. Not your money." He smiled at Luke and then looked over to his baby girl as Grace started to babble. He'd put her in a play seat, and she hit the spinning pieces with her fist and squealed.

"Sandwiches," Mav said. "I got bacon and egg, and ham and egg. Eat up."

Only Luke moved over to the table and picked up a sandwich wrapped in shiny, foily paper. "I guess I should be thankful for your morning routine," he said with a wry smile. He'd started to calm down, which was a good thing if Sterling was on her way here.

"All right, guys," he said to Trace and Otis sitting at the table, cups of coffee in front of them. To Mav and Morris and Jem, who'd been hovering on the other side of the island. To Tex and Blaze, who'd settled in the living room. "Where's Gabe?"

"On his way," Morris said.

"He probably wants to make sure you won't kill him," Trace said in a monotone.

Luke actually chuckled. "No, what I need is a plan to tell Sterling. She's on her way too." He looked at Blaze, then Jem, then Morris. They all had money. Heck, Trace and Otis had almost as much as Luke. They'd just spent more of theirs over the years, and Luke hadn't. Then he'd started investing with Gabe.

"I'm here," Gabe called as he walked in, his jacket flapping behind him as he did. "I swear, I'm going to *not* be last to the next thing we do." He glared around at everyone like it was their fault they'd arrived ahead of him. "Are you going to punch me?"

Luke grinned at him and shook his head. "Nah. But I do need an idea for how to tell Sterling. How do you...did you tell Hilde how much money you had?"

"Very carefully," Gabe said with a frown.

"I think she knows," Tex said from the couch. "I mean, we're country music stars. *Everyone* knows we have money."

"Not this much," Blaze said. "I think you severely underestimate how much money a *billion* actually is."

"I'm just saying," Tex said. "She already knows you're rich. It's just a matter of *how* rich."

"I brought my paper," Mav said, holding it up. "Maybe you meet her on the porch and just let her see it." He shrugged and rolled the hideous black and white picture of him into a cylinder. "We'll give you a few minutes, and then you bring her inside to get a sandwich. She'll need the carbs and protein to absorb everything." He grinned like an over-medium egg and a few strips of bacon would set the world right.

Luke walked over to him and said, "Thank you, Mav," in a very quiet voice as he took the paper. "Give me a minute, okay?" He left his brothers in the house, only turning back when his hand touched the front door knob. "And Tex, you better not say a word until I get back."

"You heard 'im, boys," Tex said. "So stop peppering me with questions."

"You're so talking when he gets back," Otis said, and several others agreed as Luke stepped outside.

He wondered how long he'd have to wait for Sterling, and it turned out, she'd dressed quickly and made good time, because she pulled up to Jem's house only five minutes later. Luke had settled into a sit on the top step, and he didn't move as she got out of the car and tossed a look in his direction.

She saw him, and she seemed to simultaneously slow down and speed up. The next thing Luke knew, she walked up the steps toward him. "Luke?"

He held up the paper, using it to shield his face. He didn't want to see her reaction. She neared enough to take the paper from him, and he kept his head ducked low, his cowboy hat hiding her from view.

With a sigh, she sat next to him. "So this is your burden to bear," she said.

Luke whipped his attention to her, finding her face full of a smile and plenty of teasing. "I—I didn't know how to tell you."

"I know you have money, Luke."

"But you didn't know how much. I didn't want you to think I didn't want you to know."

"I think you made this into a bigger deal than it needed to be."

Luke pressed his teeth together and looked away.

"I'm sorry." Sterling linked her arm through his, but he still did not move to hold her hand or bring her closer. "That was the wrong thing to say. This is a big deal to you, and Luke." She reached over and put her hand on his cheek.

He turned and looked at her again, though it was very difficult and his neck felt like he needed to grease it to get it to move.

"I'm sorry. Truly." Her eyes only held soberness, and Luke nodded. "Of course I want you to be the one to tell me things like this."

He wrapped his fingers around hers and slid her hand down onto his thigh. "I want you to have everything you've dreamed of for Deep Purple." Where the words had come from, Luke didn't know. He hadn't given her massage and wellness studio much thought, and certainly not that morning.

"Luke, no," she whispered.

"Yes," he whispered back. "Did you see the headline? Why not? Why can't you have the money to find a location like Ev has, and get your big studio space, and have rooms for couples' massages, and what was that last thing? Meditation bowls or something."

Sterling sniffled and smiled. "Hanging silks," she said. "For guided meditation, and yes, I need some crystal singing bowls to do that."

"Right," he said. "Those. I can buy those."

Sterling leaned into him, making him feel stronger and braver and better than he was. "I can't ask you," she said. "Maybe if we were married or something."

Luke pulled in a breath, but this was another crucial conversation he and Sterling needed to have. "Okay," he said. "Let's go there. You think you want to get married?"

"Yes," she said.

"To me?"

"Yes," she said. "I mean, it's early days still, but I can see it in the future." She lifted her head and looked at him. "I like you, Luke, a whole lot. I like being with you, and I like your little girl, and I like all those cowboys gathered inside, probably eavesdropping on us." She smiled. "They all came here for you." She touched his chest, right in the middle of it, and a zing moved through his whole body. "*You*, baby."

Luke took a deep breath and nodded. "I guess you're right."

"What about you?" she asked. "Could you get married again? I know the first time wasn't very good."

"I could," Luke said slowly. "I just—I want to make sure it's right. I want all the pieces in place, Sterling. I know that's a little crazy, and it'll take more time, but I have to—" He swallowed, not sure what he had to do. "It's just like with drumming. Every beat goes in the exact right place. I can feel them. I know instinctively where they go." He looked at her, stunned that this gorgeous woman liked him. "I have to feel like that about us. I have Corrine...." He left the words there, not sure if he was trying to protect his daughter—or himself.

But Sterling only nodded, her smile soft and absolutely angelic. "I understand, Luke."

He cleared his throat and surveyed the front yard again. "All right, one more thing, and then we better get inside or Mav will bring out all the sandwiches on a tray and force you to eat one while he watches."

Sterling giggled, but Luke wasn't sure how much he was kidding.

"Kids," he said gruffly. "What are you thinking about kids?"

"I'm thinking I want a whole house full of boys, the way your momma had."

Luke's mouth dropped open, and he turned his attention to Sterling again, expecting her to burst out laughing at any moment. She didn't, and in fact, she reached up and shyly tucked her hair behind her ear. "You...don't want more kids?"

"I—I—" Luke honestly hadn't given it a ton of thought. Fleeting things here and there. "Yeah," he said now. "I'd like more kids. Maybe not a house full of *nine boys*. My word. Do you know what a war zone that is?" He shook his head, and this time, Sterling did laugh.

He got to his feet and extended his hand to help her up. She rose to stand right in front of him, and she said, "Luke, that article doesn't see the real you." She leaned closer and closer until Luke had to close his eyes or go cross-eyed. "But I do, and your money can't hide who you are. It also doesn't change who you are."

She kissed him, and Luke didn't realize how much he needed to hear her say that his money didn't define him until she'd said it. He sighed into the kiss, but Sterling didn't let him linger long.

"*Eight* boys?" she asked.

"No," Luke said instantly.

"Seven?" she teased as they faced Jem's front door together.

"Two," he said. "And let's pray now that they're twins, so we don't have to deal with the younger one complaining that the older one is always leaving him behind." He pulled open the door, and called, "We're comin' in. Tex, I hope you're ready, because I am so done talking."

28

Tex stroked Abby's hair and gazed down at her. She rested both hands on her belly, her eyes closed, and she seemed to cherish the life they'd been building together, the life that grew inside her. She adored Melissa, as well as Bryce, and he could not understand why his ex-wife didn't feel the same about her own flesh and blood.

"Tex?" Trace murmured, and Tex looked up from his beautiful wife.

"Yeah." He sighed and realized everyone had gathered in the living room now. Luke pulled over a barstool for Sterling, and then one for himself, and as he settled, he took off his cowboy hat and tossed it onto the dining table.

Tex watched his younger brother run one hand through his hair while Sterling tucked her fingers into his other one, and that made him marvel too. Luke, who'd been so angry for so long. Luke, who'd closed a dozen doors only to be brave enough to step up to them, fit in a key, and reopen them. Luke, who Tex had worried over and prayed about more than any other brother.

To see him so...happy made Tex's heart take courage. It started to beat in a new rhythm, one not burdened by the weight of his ex-wife and the damage Corrie had done to his sweet son.

He took a deep breath, and Abby opened her eyes and looked up at him. He'd been trying to listen to her for the past couple of months. He had to forgive Corrie, but such a thing didn't just come naturally. He'd spoken to his therapist, and he knew he'd been existing on the fringes of his life, the world only flowing by in various shades of gray.

"Bryce hasn't been talking to his mother for a while now," Tex said, finding a tree in Jem's backyard and focusing on the branches that had started to leaf and bud in the past week. Spring represented such a renewal, and Tex's next breath shuddered through his lungs. He desperately needed a renewal too.

"But last time he was here for the birthday parties, he decided to drive to Boise early and see her. Texted her and got it all set up." His throat ached, and Tex had no idea why. He barely spoke anymore, and he tore his eyes from the landscape outside.

His eyes landed first on Trace, and Tex's chest collapsed. He felt his face wrinkle as he fought his emotions. The atmosphere in the room needed to pop, and he knew all of that tension intimately. It lived inside him, and he had to find a way to release it. Abby had been telling him that, as had Dr. Keith.

Tex switched his gaze to Blaze, who wore a hard mask on his face. Tex knew that look better than anyone. It was the protection Blaze put in place so no one would know what he was thinking and feeling—which meant he had something strong flowing through him.

"She didn't remember he was coming," Tex said, his voice pinched and too-high. "She was already drunk—before noon—and because Bryce is *so good*—" His voice broke, and he reached up with one hand and covered his face. Tears wetted the side of his nose, and he had no idea why this particular thing with Corrie had affected him so strongly.

Yes, you do, he thought. And he did. He'd been at his son's side for the past three years, watching him work through incredibly difficult and painful things. More than Tex thought Bryce could bear at times.

He'd learned so much, grown so much, moved closer to family and God. To have his mother—his *mother*—treat him as a throwaway piece of trash...it angered and saddened Tex to no end.

"There was someone else there," Abby said into the silence. Tex looked at her as she rose to a sitting position next to him. She was so good too. She smiled softly at him, obviously giving him a moment to continue.

He simply shook his head and looked over to Jem. He'd been through a lot in the past couple of years too. Getting sober so he wouldn't lose his kids. Moving out of Blaze's house. Almost losing Sunny and having to call his sponsor. Jem still didn't trust himself, and he had checks in place—Blaze and Luke and Tex—to help him when he felt like he might fall again.

Tex admired him so much, and he loved how the whole family had rallied around Jem. None of them drank in front of him. None of them served alcohol at any family parties anymore. All of that was their silent testament that they loved him and stood by him.

"It was a man," Abby said quietly. "He asked who Bryce was, and I think what Tex was going to say is that because Bryce is so good, he didn't say who he was. He didn't want to embarrass his mother. So he said he wasn't anyone, and he left."

Tex swallowed, his gaze moving to the twins. They stood side-by-side, the way they always had, and Tex loved that they had each other. He'd often relied on Trace or Otis the way Gabe and Morris clung to each other. The twins reminded him not to think of himself as an island—he had plenty of people around him to help. To buoy him up when he felt like drowning.

Not only that, but Morris had come back from a devastating football injury to coach the winningest high school team in the country. All that *before* he returned to Coral Canyon to manage Country Quad—and that was no small task.

He'd been Leighann's steady partner through the reuniting of their family, having another baby, and their constant care of Leigh's brother, Denzel. Tex never heard him complain, and his love for Morris doubled in that moment.

Gabe had always considered himself the black sheep of the family, and his attitude had matched his dark mood. But Hilde had lightened him right up, and he'd been Tex's example of how to be a good dad since the day Liesl was born.

"He just left?" Mav asked, his phone out. He'd probably talked to Bryce plenty over the past couple of months, because that was what Mav did. Even when he had his hands full with four kids, their parents, and all eight brothers, he was there for whoever needed him.

Tex nodded. "Went to the airport. But he saw—" Tex cleared his throat. "Wedding rings on Corrie's hand and whoever that guy was."

"She got married?" Otis asked. He didn't have the greatest relationship with his ex, but it was far better than Tex and Corrie. Tex wondered where he'd gone so wrong. As soon as those horrible, self-defeating thoughts came, he pushed them out.

Dr. Keith said they didn't help, and Tex didn't need the spiral. He worked to change his thinking, the way he'd been learning how.

Corrie got to make her own choices. Tex had paid his child support down to the penny, and he had nothing to feel guilty about. No, he wasn't perfect. He'd been gone a lot for the first decade of Bryce's life.

"She got married," Tex said. "I called her after Bryce told me what happened. She has no reasons, no excuses. She's just...." He looked over to Otis, who had shown Tex how to handle difficult and tense situations with grace and kindness.

Out of all of them, Otis had been the best to Bryce, and his own eyes shone with tears. Tex loved him so much—his brother, and his son. Everyone in this room.

"She's not interested in her son," Tex said, his voice strong. "She's moved on from Bryce, and well, that's pretty hurtful."

"I'll say," Blaze said darkly.

"I'm so sorry, Tex," Luke said, his voice softer than Tex had ever heard it. "How's Bryce?"

"He's coping," Tex said. "Barely. He's questioned if he should move here." His gaze wandered over to Abby. "I think we've managed that okay. He takes possession of the ranch in Dog Valley on May first, and he's still planning to move here the third week of May."

Tex and Abby couldn't go help at the beginning of the month —only a week away now—because Abby was going to have their son very soon. Even in a month, Tex might not have her come with him. They had a very busy four-year-old and a two-hundred-acre farm to take care of. Four of Bryce's horses. Her brother and his wife, who was due with their second child in August.

Once again, he corralled his thoughts. He, Luke, Otis, Trace, Harry, Morris, and Mav were planning to go to Louisville to help Bryce get packed. He claimed he didn't have much, but the young man had been living on his own for years. He had plenty of stuff.

Tex had rented a truck to be picked up in Louisville, and Bryce would tow his horse trailer with the two horses belonging to his friend Kassie, and then have the back of his truck for boxes.

The pair of them would then make the drive across the country, where everyone would be there to greet him and welcome him home.

"He doesn't need Corrie," he said, looking around. Light filled him from head to toe as he looked at Luke and Sterling, then Gabe and Morris, then Blaze, who sat with folded arms. His eyes traveled past Trace, Jem, Mav, and Otis.

He met Abby's eyes. "He has all of us."

"He has all of us," Abby said. "All of you good cowboys, and all of your wives."

"He has *you*," Blaze said, nodding to Abby. "To be his mother."

She started to cry, and while Tex knew she loved Bryce and of course wanted to be his mother, it was a lot to ask of her. He cradled her against his chest and held her tight.

"He's got us," Luke repeated, his voice low and gruff and powerful.

"All of us," Trace said.

"Anytime," Otis whispered. "Day or night."

Tex nodded, his emotions rising again. He'd cried in the privacy of his bedroom, with Abby consoling and comforting him, but as the oldest brother, he'd always wanted to be the strongest. He wanted to show the other brothers how to stay strong through adversity, through trials, through hard times.

Now, though, he simply nodded as Mav said, "You have us too, Tex," and then he let his tears fall as his brothers pressed in and enclosed him in their arms, their support, their love.

ABBY BENT TO GET THE PAN OF ROLLS OUT OF THE OVEN. "Okay," she said, a pinch traveling across her stomach from left to right. She could barely move anymore, what with the watermelon-like baby belly she sported. Still, she managed to get the bread out and she slid the tray onto the stovetop.

"We're ready," she called to the house in general. Tex and Wade had gone out onto the deck to assess whether it needed to be re-stained and sealed this summer or not. Abby thought the wood needed to be sealed at the very least, but she let Tex deal with most household repairs and concerns.

Cheryl came into the dining area of the living room, where she'd been entertaining the kids. Abby smiled at her and pushed her hair off her forehead. "It's hot in here with the oven on."

"Wyoming can't decide if it's cold or hot," Cheryl said with a smile. "I've been running the heater at night and the air conditioner during the day." She laughed lightly and started helping the kids into chairs at the table.

Abby moved over to the sliding glass door and opened it. "Tex," she called. "Wade." They both turned toward her, and Abby loved her tall, strong, faithful husband and her hardworking and handsome brother.

The evening light fell at their backs, and Abby couldn't help feeling like they'd been bathed in gold from heaven. "Dinner is ready," she said. They came toward her as a dull pain radiated through her lower back.

She'd been in labor before, but Melissa's hadn't started in her back. She must've worn something on her face, because Wade asked, "Are you okay?"

In her mind, she said yes, but her brother didn't move into the house. "Abigail." He put his hand on her arm and looked over his shoulder.

Tex pushed past him, his eyes worried. "Abby."

"Yeah," she said. "I'm okay."

Both men continued to look at her, and Abby honestly wasn't sure what had happened. "The rolls are hot. Come on." She turned and went back into the house, her brother and Tex following her.

They all sat down to dinner, and Abby catalogued her stiffness and tightness, the way her back hurt, as normal pains associated with being nine months pregnant. She ate very little, because she had no room for much, and she stayed present and enjoyed the conversation with her family members who lived right next door.

She smiled at Cheryl, who said, "I'll get the cake cut."

"I'll help," Abby said as Mel yelled, "Cake! Yay, cake!"

"I want cake, Momma."

"I know, Ben." Cheryl gave him a bright smile and added, "Stay in your seat and you can have some."

Ben had been starting to get up, and he plopped right back down. Abby loved him so much, as she often had the opportunity to babysit him while Wade had farm work he couldn't take the boy out to do, and Cheryl worked as a paralegal for Gabe.

Cheryl picked up her plate and both of the kids' before she moved into the kitchen. Abby started to stand, a sharp kick hitting the top of her belly as everything else seemed to fall out the bottom.

"Oh." Abby froze in a half-up, half-down position, only her eyes moving to Tex. "My water just broke."

"It did?" Tex jumped to his feet, his expression suddenly wild. "Let's go."

Abby couldn't even move, and the energy in the house changed violently. Wade's hand landed on her back, and that allowed her to straighten. She definitely needed to get to the hospital, and she allowed her brother to guide her to the front door. Tex opened it at the same time his truck roared to life.

"Cheryl," Abby said. "Can you—"

"I'll keep Mel with me for as long as you need," she called. "Go. Good luck."

Abby went, her thoughts scattering as the first contraction hit her. Tex and Wade helped her into the truck, and then Tex got them moving toward the hospital. Twenty-five minutes seemed like an impossibly long time to be in labor and not be in the hospital, but Abby told herself she'd done it before.

She made it through two more contractions before she realized neither of them had grabbed their baby bag. "Oh, no," she said as she looked over to Tex. He'd been going through a lot in the past few months, and Abby had done her best to assure him and reassure him.

He drove now with white knuckles, and he glanced over to her as their truck cut through the dusk. "What?"

"The baby bag," she said. "Did you grab it?"

"No."

She sighed, though it wasn't the end of the world. "Cheryl can bring it to me." She and the other wives had put together a baby bag for Hilde the night of her gender reveal party. Since none of them had known the gender yet, they'd chosen yellows and grays and peaches for the bag, the cloths, and the pacifiers. Ev had said she'd provide the take-home outfit, and Abby knew she'd done it.

Hilde had her bag ready, and she wasn't due for another couple of months. Hopefully she wouldn't forget it the way Abby had.

More tightening began, and Abby pressed her hands to her belly, a groan coming out of her mouth.

"Almost there, baby," Tex said. "You okay?"

"I'm okay," she told him.

"Thank you for loving my son," he said.

"He's *our* son," Abby said as the contraction intensified. She pressed her eyes closed and leaned back against the headrest. "What about this baby?" she asked. "What's his name going to be?"

They hadn't told anyone in the family their plans for a name. With so many opinions, things could get complicated and confusing pretty quickly.

"I still think Bryce suggested the best name," Tex said.

"Carver," Abby said. "But baby, I want his name to be your name." She'd been pushing for using Tex's name, but he'd been resistant.

"Then let's name him Tex Carver," he said. "And call him Carver."

"That's really okay?"

"Yes," he said, looking out his passenger window. "I don't deserve to have someone named after me."

"Tex, you're the best man I know."

His jaw worked, and Abby knew he was working on feeling like what she'd said was true. "I love you," he whispered.

"And I love you." She sighed and said, "So we'll name him Tex Carver Young, and we'll call him Carver."

Tex reached over and took her hand, then rested them both on her belly. "I can't wait to meet him."

"I can't wait for Bryce to move home."

Tex nodded, and then he got them to the hospital, where he took good care of Abby every step of the way—just like he'd always done.

29

Sterling walked through the door at Souper Salad, flashing
Luke a smile as she did. Spring had definitely arrived in
Coral Canyon, and Sterling wasn't complaining about that.
Her backyard had started to come back to life, and thankfully, they
hadn't had any late snow showers.

"There they are," she said, though Luke had two working eyes
and could certainly see Michelle Hinz and Denzel Drummond.
Sterling swept her client-smile onto her face as Michelle turned
toward her. "Michelle, hey."

"Sterling." The other woman stood a couple of inches shorter
than Sterling, but she had the same blonde hair. Hers didn't kink
in every direction, and thankfully, Sterling had tamed hers back
into a couple of barrettes and then straightened the rest down her
back.

"Denzel." Sterling nodded to him, noted he was using his cane
tonight, and let Luke move in and man-hug the other cowboy. Sterling had already been over to Leigh's house in anticipation of this
double date.

Leigh was just worried about her brother, that was all. She'd told Sterling and Luke that Denzel had said very, very little about Michelle, and Leigh had tried to push him as far as she dared. Luke didn't like the idea of "spying" on him, and Leigh and Morris had backed off quickly.

"We don't want you to do that," Leigh said. "If you feel comfortable telling us how it goes, great. If not, that's fine too."

"Denzel's excited to go out with you," Morris had said, and Sterling could see the sparkle in his eyes as he stepped back from Luke.

"Luke," Michelle said, and he gave her a quick hug too. "I'll tell them we're here?" She looked at Denzel, squeezed his hand that rested on the top of his cane as she went by, and moved over to the hostess station.

"Real quick," Sterling said, not sure why she had these words foaming in her mouth. "We're not going to be taking notes or anything during this. We're not going to spread gossip around the family."

Denzel's eyes darkened, and he nodded. "Thank you. I'd appreciate that."

"But how are things going?" Luke asked, his eyes glued to the back of Michelle's head. "You guys have been dating as long as me and Sterling." He slipped his hand into hers. "And we've talked about marriage and kids and dogs and winter and just about everything in between." He grinned down at her, but genuine surprise ran through her.

"That is not true," she said, hipping him. "We have not talked about dogs at all. You want a dog?"

"Sure," Luke said easily. "If I can get one like Denzel's." He smiled over to the man, who lightened and smiled back.

"They're ready for us, honey," Michelle said, returning to the group only to turn around again. Luke waited for Denzel to follow her, which he did. His gait was uneven and a bit stilted, but he almost moved fluidly too, the cane going with him on the left to aid in his balance when he stepped on his right.

The hostess led them to a table, and Denzel said, "Thanks, Mich." Why he'd thanked her, Sterling wasn't sure, but they definitely exchanged a look that said more than she knew. Luke pulled out Sterling's chair, and she sat beside Michelle, women on one side; men on the other.

"Will you be having our soup and salad bar tonight?" the hostess asked. "Or should I bring menus?"

Luke looked at Sterling; Sterling looked at Luke. He turned back to the hostess. "We're just gonna have soup and salad." He gestured between him and Sterling.

He looked over to Denzel and Michelle, and Denzel said, "Same."

"And we'll all be on one check?" The hostess looked between Luke and Denzel.

"Yep."

"No," Denzel said, glaring at Luke. Sterling had met him a few times at the Young family parties and get-togethers, and he did seem to have two settings; sunny or rainy.

"Yep," Luke said again as he looked up to the hostess. "You do know who I am, right?"

Her face colored, all the affirmation Luke needed. Sterling stifled her giggles as the hostess nodded. Luke did too, just once, and then he said, "One check." He got to his feet and extended his hand to Sterling. "Should we go get some food?"

Sterling scrambled to her feet too, wondering how Denzel did at a buffet with his cane. She watched as he stood without it and said, "I'd love a Diet Coke with lemon wedges. If this guy's gonna pay, I might as well make you work so he'll tip you well." He grinned at Luke and waited for Michelle to come to his side.

She did, and Sterling couldn't help smiling and sighing as she walked on his left—where he normally used his cane—and supported him. She leaned in close, and he said something to her. Michelle laughed, and to anyone on the outside, Sterling sure thought they looked really good together.

"What do you think people think when they see us together?" she asked Luke.

He looked at her like she'd just told him she had two heads. "What do you mean?"

"I mean, look at them, Luke. Aren't they so...perfect together? She helps him. He reciprocates in the way he knows how. They look good together, and I don't know. Don't you get a vibe from them?"

Luke watched as Michelle handed Denzel a plate and then moved along the salad bar in front of him. Sterling stepped in that direction, but she kept her pace slow so Luke could join her. "Yeah," he said. "I see what you're saying."

"So what do you think people think when they see us?"

He looked lost for a moment. "I don't know."

Sterling didn't either. Luke wasn't exactly a selfie-taker, but Sterling had a couple of pictures with him. She loved looking at the happy way her eyes crinkled as she smiled, and she loved the brightness in Luke's eyes too.

"I hope we give off that vibe," she said.

"The one that tells other women to leave me the heck alone?" Luke ducked his head as he moved by a table. "Oh, boy. That's Lindsey Cassandra."

"Did you go out with her?" Sterling looked at the woman with medium brown hair that curled around her face. "I thought you only went out with Tea and Hillary."

"I did," he grumbled. "But not for a lack of interest in town."

Which had only increased since his picture had been pasted

on the front page of the newspaper. He reached the salad bar and picked up a plate.

"I thought you wanted soup tonight," Sterling said, plucking the plate from his hand. She grinned at him, but her chest pinched as she added, "And you know, some people would love to have another interested in them, even if they weren't ready for the attention."

Luke stared at her. "Sterling."

"It's fine," she said. "I just happen to know what it feels like to be on the other side of that, Luke." She ducked her head and reached for the tongs to put lettuce on her plate. "And it's not very fun either."

She continued down the buffet, Luke right behind her, and as she reached for the ladle to pour ranch dressing over her fresh veggies, cheese, and croutons, he covered her hand. "Sterling, for the official record between us, I have always seen you."

"Have you?" She didn't mean to challenge him, but she also couldn't help herself.

"When have I not?"

She cocked her head, well aware that she was holding up the line. "Luke, did you or did you not want a different masseuse the first time you came to Red Carpet?" She felt sparkly inside and out. "When you found out I was a woman and not a man?"

"Yes," he admitted. "But, that was because you were so beautiful, and I was already nervous."

She burst out laughing, because she did not think for one moment that Luke had thought anything of the sort.

"Laugh if you want," he said as he ladled ranch over her salad for her and then did the same to his. "But it's true."

"You didn't have romantic feelings for me."

"Sterling, I didn't have feelings at all back then." He turned away to go over to the soup bar, and Sterling stared after him. She waited while he dished himself some beef stew, and when he came back to her side, he asked, "What?"

"You didn't have feelings?"

"No," he said. "The only thing I felt was anger. I was *so* angry, Sterling."

And hurt, she thought. His anger stemmed from the pain he'd been in. He'd first come to her for work on his shoulder, and yes, he'd been tight. Bordering on an injury. But his physical pain had been nothing compared to his mental and emotional pain.

"So when did you know you had feelings besides anger?" she asked as they returned to their table. Michelle and Denzel weren't back yet, and Sterling busied herself with spreading a napkin over her lap and mixing up her salad so Luke could have a moment to formulate his answer.

"I don't know," he said slowly. "I can't pinpoint when. I remember when Tex and I ran into you in the grocery store." He smiled at her. "Tex said you had a crush on me, and honestly? You *were* the first woman I started looking at with anything romantic in mind."

Sterling blinked at him then, because she remembered that day in the grocery store so vividly. Tex had seen something? And had said something to Luke about it? Heat rushed into her face, and Sterling quickly turned back to her dinner.

"You came out on stage and ripped off your shirt," she said carefully. "I think every woman in town had a crush on you. I wasn't special."

"You've always been special, Sterling."

"Did you guys see the dessert bar here?" Michelle asked as she returned to the table. Denzel put down one plate of salad and one filled with at least a half-dozen cookies, bars, or slices of cake.

"Wow," Luke said with a chuckle. "Dessert first, huh?"

"We're eating dinner at a salad bar," Denzel said dryly. "I think it's a requirement for the male species to eat dessert first."

"Den," Michelle said with a laugh. "Men eat salads."

"Do they?" Denzel growled, but Sterling catalogued the use of Michelle's nickname for the man. She saw the way she glanced over to him, plenty of knowing and teasing and flirtation in her expression. She thought she saw Denzel soften like butter melting in the microwave—but only for Michelle.

Luke looked down at his plate, over to Sterling, and then to Denzel. "Where was that dessert bar, Michelle?"

"THEY ARE SO STINKING CUTE TOGETHER," STERLING SAID the next day. She had just walked into Leigh's house, and it looked like a flour bomb had gone off. She paused. "What is happening here?"

Leigh looked up from where she knelt on the floor, a soggy-looking washcloth in her hand. "Eric happened here."

Sterling looked down the hall to her left, and she could definitely hear the boy crying. She wanted to rescue him and Leigh simultaneously.

Leigh sighed as she got to her feet. "I hate it when Morris travels." She went back into the kitchen and started rinsing out the washcloth. "I mean, I don't really, but Eric tries to get away with more when his daddy is gone." She offered Sterling a weary smile. "How was your date the other night?"

"Good." Sterling continued into the kitchen and set down the pan of cinnamon rolls she'd picked up on the way through town. Then she took the rag from Leigh. "I'll finish up." She nodded over to Rachelle, who was strapped in her high-chair, flinging syrup-covered pieces of pancake to the floor.

Leigh went in that direction, and Sterling returned to the task of wiping up flour. But it didn't go so well with water, and Sterling hated the feel of it against her skin. Luke had gone with Morris to help pack and move Bryce. Then, because he could, he'd be driving back with them while Morris, Otis, Trace, and Mav flew back to Wyoming.

That way, Luke had said, he could ride with Tex sometimes, or Bryce sometimes, and he could spell them when they got tired of driving. Sterling tried not to worry about him, but she knew things were tense in the Tex Young branch of the family tree right now, and Luke certainly didn't need more tension in his life.

He handled it well, though, and Sterling had given the care of him over to the Lord. She worked his muscles. God would work on his heart and mind. Oh, and he had a therapist for the mind part too.

"I got a little information out of Denzel," Leigh said as she brought her daughter over to the kitchen sink and sat her right in it. She gave Sterling a look out of the corner of her eye. "He said Luke said you guys were talking about marriage."

Sterling's heart suddenly didn't fit in her chest. It expanded and expanded, because she couldn't believe she had even the remotest possibility of getting married. She ducked back down to the floor before she answered. "We've talked about it," she said. "Once. We're not talk-*ing* about it."

"It's still big," Leigh said over the running water and her babbling baby.

"Yeah." Sterling rose up again and waited for Leigh to pull her daughter out of the sink. She wrapped her in a big bath towel right there next to the sink, and Sterling smiled at both of them. They both had the same dark hair and eyes, such kindness and friendship shining in them.

"So do you love Luke?" Leigh asked.

"I thought I was coming here to give you information about Michelle and Denzel." Sterling cocked her eyebrows and rinsed out her washcloth. "Not me and Luke."

"It's both," Leigh said. "Of course."

"Momma," Eric said, interrupting them. Sterling couldn't have been happier, because she didn't know the answer to Leigh's question.

Did she love Luke?

On some level, yes, Sterling loved Luke Young. He'd been loyal and true to her—except for that one time he'd gone to another massage therapist. He'd had an excellent reason for that, and Sterling couldn't hold it against him.

He'd helped her when he didn't even know it. He'd seen her when no one else did. He'd made her life colorful again, after many years of only black and white.

So yes, on some level, she loved him for all of that. For his friendship. His loyalty. His good heart, even if it was hidden behind a grumpy mask and a wave of anger. It wasn't now, anyway. He'd changed in the few years she'd been giving him massages, and Sterling supposed she had too.

"Oh, I was going to tell you," she said when Leigh returned to the kitchen with her seven-year-old.

She took the washcloth from Sterling and gave it to Eric. "Every last dusting of it, son." With him working, Leigh looked at Sterling expectantly.

"I got the small business loan for Deep Purple." Sterling's words practically busted with pride, but she couldn't stop herself. "Luke said he'd help me start looking for commercial spaces when he's back and Bryce is moved in."

"Sterling, that's so amazing." Leigh hugged her, Rachelle still on her hip. "I'm surprised you wanted a loan, though. Luke has plenty of money."

Sterling bristled, but she covered over it quickly. "Yes," she said. "And it's *Luke's* money." She took the little girl from her mother and smiled at her. "Let's go get you dressed, okay?"

She walked away from Leigh, but that didn't silence the hefty sigh that came out of her mouth. Sterling ignored her and went down the hall to Rachelle's room. To everyone but her, the answer to her dream of expanding her studio was Luke.

Just ask Luke for the money.

Let me help you with it, baby.

Have you talked to Luke?

No, Sterling was not going to take his money for this. She wasn't married to him the way Hilde and Gabe were married. Or Abby and Tex. Or even Leigh and Morris.

"I brought turnovers," Sunny called as Sterling pulled on Rachelle's pants. "And Faith is five minutes behind me with leftovers from Hole in One."

"Doughnuts," Sterling said to the baby. "It is a good morning after all." She smiled and went back out into the main part of the house, putting Rachelle in the living room with her toys and going to hug Sunny.

She'd grown closer to the women in this family over the past several months. They'd added her to their text strings, and the meals she'd shared with them weren't at all like the awkward one from over a year ago when Leigh had accidentally let it slip that she and Morris were babysitting Corrine so Luke could get a massage.

"Less than a month," she said to Sunny. "Did your momma like her dress?"

Sunny rolled her eyes, her mouth full of apple pie. She still managed to shake her head, and after she swallowed, she said, "It's a disaster, Sterling. A *disaster*."

Sterling pinched off a corner of the turnover, but she didn't get any fruit filling. "That bad, huh?"

"It's gorgeous," Sunny said with another eyeroll. "Everything my mom sees is a disaster for at least a week. Then, it grows on her, and then, she'll say, 'I've loved this since the moment I saw it.'"

Sterling laughed with Leigh, but Sunny sure didn't think anything was funny. Sterling liked her a lot, because she possessed a calm spirit and a hardworking energy. It was no wonder she was a nurse, though she confessed her patience for her parents wore thin sometimes.

"Hello," Faith called, and her footsteps came down the hall. She entered the living-dining-kitchen combo room, two pink boxes decorated with sprinkles in her arms. "My sister is coming. That's okay, right, Leigh?"

"Yep." Leigh finished wiping the table where her kids had made everything sticky and sweet and tossed the rag into the sink. "All right, Eric. You're all done. Let's get everything you and sissy need for Uncle Denzel."

"Is he taking them this morning?" Faith asked. "I should've sent them with Blaze. He just dropped me off."

"It's okay," Leigh said. "Denzel and Michelle are actually taking them to the children's museum today." She grinned a little devilishly. "I think it will convince them to never have kids, but Denzel says Eric's fine for him."

Sterling smiled at the little boy who handed her his washcloth. He wore innocence in his face, but he'd definitely been the one to spread the flour everywhere. Probably on purpose.

"Oh, your double date with Denzel and Michelle," Faith said as she reached the counter and slid the boxes of doughnuts onto it. "News there?"

"They're so stinking cute together," Sterling said. "It's obvious they like each other a lot, and well, I think Jem and Sunny might not be the only wedding this year. That's all I'm gonna say."

"Yeah," Leigh called as she followed her son down the hall to his room. "Because she and Luke are talking about marriage."

Sterling sighed as the other two women zeroed in on her. "No," she said feebly. "We talked about it once. Talked. Once."

"Sometimes it only takes once," Faith said.

"Yeah." Sterling scoffed and gave Faith what she hoped was a friendly smile. "This from the woman who had to start over with Blaze three times before she really started dating him."

"Hey, I—" Faith looked over to Sunny, her eyes wide. "I did do that, didn't I?"

Sunny laughed as she held up both hands, as if in surrender. "Hey, I can't talk. Jem and I had four chances, I think."

"I yelled at Luke at Jem's," Sterling said. "In front of his brothers." She looked back and forth between Sunny and Faith, and the three of them started to laugh.

"I got the last order of pecan French toast," Georgia announced as she entered the house. "And Abby's right behind me with specialty smoked bacon from Hamblin's."

"It's going to be a breakfast feast today!" Leigh said as she re-entered the open space where everyone else was. She bustled her kids down the hall and out the front door, and when she returned, she had Abby and Ev with her.

Sterling loved the big family parties. She loved her solo time with Luke. And she loved this stolen, simple time with just women. This morning, Leigh was hosting a brunch potluck at her house, and everyone brought something to share.

"Ooh, who got the cinnamon rolls from the bakery?" Abby alone had her baby with her. Otherwise, today was a no-kid zone. With so many of the Young brothers out of town, they were relying on siblings and parents to help out, and they all had someone.

Sterling wouldn't have anyone. When Luke traveled, she'd be here alone. If she had something while he was gone, what would that look like?

A wave of distress rolled through her, and then she blinked her eyes wide open.

Any one of these women would help her, either with Corrine or any children she and Luke had together. Any of them. Anytime.

"Sterling," Leigh said, and that jolted her back to the present. Yes, she was Sterling, and she'd gotten the cinnamon rolls Abby was currently ogling. She was seen and heard and important here, and these women loved her.

She sure loved them too, and she hoped she'd have more time to fall truly, madly, deeply in love with Luke so she could keep them all in her life. Permanently.

The problem was, Sterling had never had anything like this before, and she wasn't sure how she'd gotten here—or how to keep it.

30

Bryce finished attaching his horse trailer to his truck, and he straightened, everything inside him feeling vulnerable and weak today.

Moving day.

He couldn't believe he was as emotional as he was about leaving Louisville and the horse farm where he'd been working for less than two years. But everything from apprehension to excitement to sadness streamed through him, and he didn't have time to reason through any of it.

He'd been encouraged in his therapy to really examine his emotions. Find out what lived beneath them, and address those issues. But today? He couldn't.

"Save it for later," he whispered to himself. "Save it for God." He turned away from his rig to find Kassie Goodman walking toward him.

"You've got it?"

"Yep."

Nerves radiated from her too, as her move was a far bigger deal than his. She'd been born and raised here in Louisville. The Goodmans owned and trained racehorses and had for generations. Lucky for Kassie, she was the youngest in her family, and her three older brothers had taken over the family business.

She worked for them too, but she really didn't want to be in the commercial part of horseracing. When Bryce had gone out with her for the first time, she'd confessed to him that all she'd ever wanted to do was rehabilitation for horses.

In that moment, he'd known she'd be his best friend, and they'd become exactly that. They were so in-sync, they'd bought a big farm in Wyoming together with the sole purpose to rescue and rehabilitate horses.

Bryce had four at his daddy's place on the east side of town, and they'd be towing two of Kassie's in the trailer currently attached to Bryce's truck. She owned a truck too, but no trailer, and their partnership was already beginning.

"I can't believe we're doing this," she said as she stepped into his arms and gripped him tightly. "I'm so scared."

"You've got a few months until winter," he promised her.

She laughed, but he could still hear the tension beneath it. He pulled away and looked at her. "When my daddy and uncles get here, it'll be complete chaos. You're ready at your place?"

"One hundred percent," she said as she reached up and pulled her already-tight ponytail tighter. "My brothers are coming, and it shouldn't take any time at all."

"If we're lucky, we'll be done by lunchtime, and we can grab something to eat and hit the road." He looked down the lane to the cabin he'd lived in for the past couple of years. He'd known he'd be leaving this job for the past several months, which had allowed his boss to hire someone new. According to the rumors, they'd be here by evening.

In his bedroom, which wasn't his bedroom anymore.

On the farm up in Wyoming, there were seventeen buildings that needed to be cared for. Finley Barber had sold all but one of his horses, and Bryce had said he'd take it. Plus his four, and Kassie's two, they'd have seven horses to take care of every day, all year long.

The facility had room and permits for up to fifty horses, and Bryce couldn't even imagine an operation that big.

He had fields and pastures to care for, and machinery and equipment. He'd done a little bit of everything on the farm here, but he didn't plant, cultivate, and harvest alfalfa. He'd been studying horse care, pasture care, and more, but he felt woefully under-prepared for this next adventure in his life.

You've done things like this before, he said as the front door on his cabin opened and one of his friends came outside. He wouldn't really count navigating a pregnancy, a break-up, and an adoption as an "adventure," but he'd definitely done scary, unknown things before, whether by choice or not.

He'd told exactly one person in Kentucky about OJ, and that was Kassie. He couldn't even imagine having to explain the situation to someone he dated, and he shoved that thought out of his head as Sawyer lifted his hand in a wave.

"Let's go start bringing things out onto the porch." Bryce waved to his cabinmate and looked down the lane. His father had flown in last night with Luke, Otis, Trace, Harry, Morris, and Mav. Like it would take seven grown men—most of them who worked out religiously day after day—to load up his belongings.

He'd volunteered their muscles and manpower to help Kassie, and she hadn't said no.

"Oh, there he is," Bryce said as a big moving truck made the wide turn and started coming toward them. "This is it." He took a deep breath and started walking the block or so back to the cabin.

He'd parked out of the way, so they'd have plenty of room to get in and out with boxes.

He did own a recliner, and a beanbag, and they'd have to stop by his storage shed to get the bed he hadn't needed here. Maybe he had more to pack up than he thought....

Dust came with his daddy and the truck—two of them, though the other one was a King Cab pick-up truck someone had rented just to carry all the uncles around in.

The growly engine died; Daddy jumped down; Bryce's world righted. He jogged toward his father and hugged him, his dad curling one big palm around the back of his head, holding his face right against his shoulder, claiming him. Wanting him.

Bryce hadn't realized how strongly he wanted to belong somewhere, to someone, until his last trip to Wyoming. Boise, really, when his mother had completely un-claimed him. He hadn't spoken to her since, and while he knew Daddy had called her, she had not reached out to Bryce.

Not even once.

He wasn't even sure he wanted her to. He didn't know what he'd do if she did. He'd talked about the situation with his therapist at least a half-dozen times since, and he'd suggested a clean break had been established, and it might be good for Bryce.

Feeling his father's arms around him certainly fed his soul. Inhaling the scent of his skin and clothes and knowing he belonged to him made him so happy. "Thank you, Dad."

"Of course." He stepped back. "Abby said I have to video call the moment we get here. She wants to see the first box being carried out." He smiled like this would be great fun, but Bryce just wanted to get this done.

Abby had had a baby boy about two weeks ago now, and Bryce had been getting pictures and videos every single day. He loved

Abby with his whole heart, and he couldn't wait to be closer to her and Dad, and their two little kids.

"All right," Daddy drawled. "Wave to her, Bryce."

"Heya, Abby." Kassie came to his side, and she smiled and waved too. He hadn't told her anything about his mother, though she knew something had happened in February. She'd questioned him relentlessly if it had anything to do with the horse rescue ranch, and when he'd assured her it didn't, she'd dropped it.

"Let's go get moved," he said, and he led the way into the cabin. "My room is back here."

Daddy followed him, and when they entered Bryce's room, he was proud to say he had everything boxed and ready to go too. "The first box, Abs," he said in an overdramatic way as he picked it up. "I think this one has all of the Country Quad albums in it."

"Otis," Daddy called. "This one's for you. It's fragile."

"Fragile?" Uncle Otis asked as he muscled his way to the front of the line of men who'd come in with them. "Bryce owns fragile things?"

"I have two guitars," Bryce said. "And yeah, those are all the albums you guys have made." He handed the box to his uncle, their eyes meeting and catching. "You better be careful with them."

Otis grinned, and Bryce wasn't sure if he got the inside comment or not. Bryce had literally given Uncle Otis his son to raise. To care for, to love, and to be careful with. Country music albums weren't nearly as important as a human life, and of course, Bryce trusted Otis with every fiber of his being.

"They will not leave my sight," Uncle Otis promised, and from there, Bryce stood in his bedroom and picked up box after box, handing it to the next man in line. They went in and out, out and in, until the room was empty.

Kassie plunked down a bucket full of cleaning supplies. "I'll take them to my place, and you'll meet us...where? The storage unit?"

Bryce only had to clean half of the room, but he wanted to do a thorough job. "Yeah," he said. "Are you sure you don't need me at your place?"

"Bryce." She touched his face in this friendly way she had. "They cleaned out your stuff in ten minutes. I'm pretty sure we'll beat you to the storage unit."

"You have a lot more stuff," he said.

"Are you kidding me?" She laughed. "You're a hoarder, Mister Young."

Bryce only smiled and then he pulled out the duster and got to work. Uncle Luke stayed back with him, and as Bryce wiped baseboards and walls, Uncle Luke took out trash and vacuumed.

"How are things with you and Sterling?" he asked as he picked up the cleaning bucket.

"Good." Uncle Luke nodded, the barest hint of a smile on his face. "I'm under strict orders not to ask you about Kassic again." He unleashed his smile then. "But I do have some questions of my own." One of Luke's eyebrows went up, and Bryce had always liked that.

"You do? Like what?"

"Like, you two bought that farm together." The conversation got put on hold as Bryce entered the living room and kitchen area of the cabin and realized his three roommates all stood there. They should be out on the farm working, but they weren't.

He dropped the bucket and moved into them. He didn't normally hug non-family cowboys, but this seemed like a good time to make an exception.

"You let me know when you get there," Sawyer said as he pounded Bryce on the back. They'd shared a room for the past year and a half, and that brought two people close.

"I will," Bryce said as he pulled back and grinned at his friend.

"And I want to know if y'all need help," Gavin said, drawing Bryce into an embrace. "I might relocate too."

"You're from Florida," Reid said. "There's no *way* you'll survive in Wyoming." He grinned at Bryce and hugged him too.

"I'll miss you guys," he said.

"Onto greener pastures," Sawyer said, his smile so genuine that it held real light to it.

"Yeah." Bryce turned toward his uncle, who now held the bucket, and they did indeed leave the cabin together. Luke gave him the space and courtesy not to ask anything as they walked down to his truck, and he put the cleaning bucket in the backseat.

Bryce turned around and drove past the cabin, then right off the farm. He took a deep breath, needing something besides silence now. "What about me and Kassie buying the farm together?"

"Yeah," Luke said. "Are you going to live there together?" He didn't look at Bryce, and that was a classic Young move. Bryce had seen his daddy do it plenty of times. "Do you have protections in place if something goes south between the two of you? You kept ownership of your horses, right?"

Uncle Luke did look over then, and he wore an expression that said Really Serious. "I love you, Bryce, and I'm sure you've been through all of this with your daddy. Maybe even Uncle Gabe. I guess I just want to hear it from you."

I love you, Bryce.

If Uncle Luke—if anyone—knew how much Bryce needed to hear those words, they'd say them over and over and over.

He pressed his teeth together to get a grip on himself before he answered. "I consulted with a lawyer who does real estate law in Wyoming," he said. "Kassie and I have all the proper contracts signed and in place, just in case something does happen to our friendship."

Bryce didn't even want to consider that right now. She'd been a solid rock for him here in Louisville since the day he'd met her, and he didn't want to imagine his life without her in it.

"The farm has two houses on it, actually, so technically, we are going to live there together." Bryce swallowed, because his words sounded rehearsed. They were. He'd given them to Abby and Dad plenty of times over the course of the last several months. "I'm going to live in the main homestead. I bought and paid for seventy percent of the farm, Uncle Luke."

He cast a quick glance over to him. "It's mostly my place. Kassie is almost going to act as an employee."

"Which could have some tricky steps all by itself," Luke mused quietly.

"True," Bryce admitted. He wasn't sure why it was easier to tell Luke he was right when Bryce hadn't been able to do that for his parents. "But we've talked it to death, and we have the contracts. She's going to live in what Finn calls the North Cabin. The nearest neighbors are actually closer to her than the main homestead, and she's got a decent place."

Or it would be decent, once Kassie sunk her money, blood, sweat, and tears into the place. She claimed to be rip roarin' to go do just that, and Bryce had been praying the house he'd live in and all the barns and outbuildings would simply be standing when he arrived in Wyoming.

"Sounds like you've got a plan at least," Luke said.

"We do," Bryce said, "I own my horses and the one Finn is leaving. She owns hers. No transfer there."

"Good."

Bryce squeezed the wheel, because this was good. He needed

this change; he wanted it; he was ready to do something with his life that wasn't working for someone else.

"It's all a little overwhelming," he admitted, once again saying something to his uncle he hadn't been able to vocalize to his daddy.

"I'll say," Luke said with a chuckle. "It would be overwhelming for anyone, Bryce."

"Yeah?" He shifted in his seat. "I feel like Dad and Uncle Trace—Uncle Blaze—all of you guys. You just take what comes your way, and you know exactly what to do with it."

Luke burst out laughing, which Bryce totally wasn't expecting. "Really? That's what you think?" He finished chuckling when Bryce didn't join in or say anything else. "Bryce, my friend, no. Just no." He sighed and looked out the window. "When I graduated from high school, I had the opportunity to join Country Quad right away. I jumped at it, because I've never been one to settle behind a desk or leaf through a book."

"Yeah, I've heard some of Grandma's stories." He shot a grin at Luke, who smiled.

"I was so out of my league," Luke said. "Tex was thirteen years older than me, and he had a ten-year-old son. I could barely find my boots, and I hadn't done my laundry outside of the farmhouse, ever."

Bryce liked listening to his uncle's voice, and he simply waited for him to go on.

"I was learning new songs, expected to keep up with travel schedules, work out, take drumming lessons, enroll in public relations classes—all while my friends were sipping lemonade, living at home, and maybe buying books for their first semester of college. Overwhelming doesn't even begin to cover it."

"I'm sure," Bryce said quietly. "I didn't mean to make it sound like I'm the only one who's ever done something overwhelming."

"Of course not," Luke said. "I'm just saying—you're not alone.

And it's okay to be overwhelmed. And if you think I've handled things well the past few years, I'm going to pretend that's true." He grinned at Bryce, but the gesture fell away quickly. "I've been learning new behaviors and thought patterns, calming meditations and breathing techniques, for years." Luke didn't shift or clear his throat. He wasn't nervous or afraid or embarrassed, and once again, Bryce wanted to be just like him.

"Because I haven't handled things well in the past. Not even a little bit."

"So you must have a good recommendation for a counselor in Coral Canyon," Bryce said coolly.

"I've got the best one," Luke said. "I'll get you in."

"Uncle Blaze said he had someone too."

"For Cash," Luke said. "Sure. Harry goes too. Your daddy. It's good to get the help you need, Bryce. No shame in that—but that was a lesson I had to learn too." He did look away, out his side window. "A painful lesson. I feel like I've learned a lot of them, actually."

"Dad says that's what life is," Bryce said. "That God sent us here to learn those lessons, to grow, and change, and be better everyday."

"I'll tell him you listen to him sometimes." They grinned at one another, and Bryce felt so much better about everything by the time he pulled up to the storage shed that held his bed and a few other things he'd needed in Nashville that he hadn't needed here. He'd want it all in Coral Canyon, and he'd have to go shopping with Dad and Abby for plenty too.

They'd said they'd help however they could, and Bryce knew his father had a lot of money. Heck, Uncle Luke had just been named a billionaire in financial publications around the world. Not that Bryce was going to ask for help if he didn't have to.

He was finally well enough, whole enough, and wise enough

to start making his own way in the world. And that was what he was going to do.

Maybe, he thought. *When you're not so overwhelmed, you can call Codi.*

The thought sat there while he got out and helped load up the last of his items. Then he put Lucky in the backseat again and rode with Uncle Mav this time over to Kassie's family stable so she could get her horses.

With everything finally loaded, he found himself loitering near his truck with Uncle Otis while Uncle Luke had paired up to first ride with Dad. Kassie would be driving herself for this first leg, and he hugged her.

"We're ready," he whispered.

"So ready." She pulled back and smiled at him. "I'll be in front of you, since you guys have the big trucks and trailers." She glanced over to Dad, who nodded. "We've got the radios."

Bryce held up his, and Dad did the same. He took a big breath. "Okay," he said as he blew it out. "Lunch first?"

"I could eat," Uncle Trace said, and that only made Bryce grin and grin and grin.

"Lunch first," Dad confirmed. "Then we'll hit the road."

31

J em Young had never worked a farm, but he could appreciate
a well-run and well-taken care of piece of land. And the
farm Bryce had purchased was immaculate. Well, it was
now that Jem had finished the mowing at the main homestead. The previous owner had vacated the property at the beginning of the month, about three weeks ago now, and Bryce should
be rolling into town any minute.

In true Young fashion, everyone had gathered at the house and
farm that morning to make sure everything was ready for him,
Kassie, and the horses. Blaze had gone to Tex's and picked up
Bryce's horses, and they currently snacked on the long, nearly
untouched grass in the front pasture.

Bryce should see them when he approached, and that made
Jem's heart so happy. Bryce had needed to come home for a long
time, and Jem had been in that position before. It wasn't pretty,
and it wasn't fun, and while Jem had wanted to be in Coral
Canyon, actually showing up had still been terribly difficult.

He didn't want to project his own experiences and feelings onto

Bryce, but he suspected his nephew had plenty of feelings about being in Dog Valley. Yes, there was a bit of separation between him and the rest of the family in Coral Canyon. About a half-hour buffer zone. But Bryce would still be experiencing all of the emotions, and Jem just wanted to take him into a hug and tell him it would all be all right.

Otis, Tex, and Luke had been on the road with him and Kassie for the past four days, and as Jem parked the lawn mower in the barn where Finn had obviously kept his personal items for use around his house and yard, Mav came in the back door.

"Lawn's done," Jem said.

"Fences are all secure," Mav said as he tore off his gloves. "Blaze and Morris have the stables swept and ready."

The sun shone overhead too, a perfectly bright orb in a cloudless blue sky. "It's the perfect day to move in," Jem said.

"They've got to be so tired." Mav wore some exhaustion on his face too, and Jem peered a little closer.

"You okay, Mav?"

"Just—yeah," he said, meeting Jem's eye. "Dani's mom had a flare-up is all. We didn't sleep much last night, and I know Bryce is going to be emotional, and I just want this to all go easy for him."

"Sometimes easy isn't best," Jem said.

Mav's smile took a moment to curve his mouth. "Look at you quoting Daddy."

Jem grinned too. "I feel like someone better start."

"Let's go see if they got the fridge stocked with food."

"Of course they did," Jem said. "Have you met our mother?" They chuckled together as they left the shed and headed for the house. Momma and Daddy had been in charge of making sure it was clean and ready for Bryce to move in, and when Jem entered through the back door, it actually smelled like freshly baked chocolate chip cookies.

"Momma," Mav said, his voice rimmed in surprise. "Have you been baking?"

"Yes," she said without shame. "He's almost here. Tex just texted." She sounded giddy, and Jem supposed if ever there was an occasion for giddiness, it was today. "I messaged everyone to come in."

Blaze, Morris, and Gabe came in through the garage entrance, the three of them talking. "Stables and fields and barns are a go," Gabe said. "The lawn looks great."

Jem nodded at him, his smile refusing to leave his face for some silly reason. The house felt huge as it didn't hold much furniture. Well, besides the table and chairs Trace and Harry had brought over from their place.

Hilde had donated an entire living room set, which included a big sectional, two end tables with lamps, and a rug. She'd had her moving crew load everything into the house a few days ago, and then she and Gabe had come last night to make sure it was set up properly and positioned right.

Bryce was bringing a bed, and as the house came with appliances, he should have everything he needed to at least be able to function in the house. Food, a table to eat it at, somewhere to sleep at night, and even a couch to sit on in the evenings when he was dead-dog tired.

There had been so many texts about what Bryce might need and who could provide it, and the truth was, any of them could buy this farm and fully furnish it without blinking. Bryce had not asked for that, and he'd be embarrassed if any of them had done it. So a second-hand table, his old bed, and a gift from the furniture store would have to do.

Abby entered the house through the front door, and she brought a whole slew of wives and children with her. More and more people continued to flood the house, until what Jem had thought was a big space actually felt very small.

Thankfully, Sunny didn't have to work today, and Jem didn't have to attend this welcome home party alone. He found her in the kitchen with his momma, getting ice out of the fridge for her water bottle.

When he arrived at her side, she looked up at him. "Kassie's place is spic and span and totally ready."

"Thanks for bein' here today," he said as he swept a kiss along her cheek. "We're getting married in eleven days." He grinned at her. "In case you've forgotten."

"How could I forget?" she teased. "You give me a countdown every single day. Sometimes twice." She nudged him with her hip and added, "I can't wait to be your wife."

Those were the best words in the world, and Jem touched his lips to hers tenderly. The kiss only lasted a moment, because a general roar went up as someone arrived outside. Choruses of "He's here," or "They're here," filled the house. Then a whole bunch of shushing, to which Jem just smiled.

His family. They either annoyed him or he adored them, and sometimes both. Right now, nothing could kill his mood, and it wasn't like it was a surprise they were all there. It took some serious vehicles to get nine families out here, plus Momma and Daddy.

"Is he coming up the front walk?" someone asked. "Or through the garage?"

Jem watched both entrances, and it did seem to take a minute or two before Bryce opened the front door and entered. He raised both of his hands above his head and grinned from ear to ear.

"We made it!" he yelled, and that caused complete chaos. Everyone started to cheer, laugh, talk, and applaud, and all of the children swarmed toward their most loved cousin—Bryce himself.

They mobbed him, and he laughed and laughed and laughed.

Jem couldn't stop smiling either, and he let his happiness run over and over and over. As he waited his turn to welcome Bryce to his new home, he whispered, "Thank You for bringing him home, Lord. Thank You for not forgetting about him."

Jem had once felt forgotten too. Overlooked, because of the bad things he'd done. But repentance is a powerful, powerful thing, and Jem still relied on it to this day. He knew God did not forget even a single one of His children. He was living proof of it, and the brilliant young man now holding Rosie in his arms testified of that too.

"Welcome home, Bryce," he yelled, and that got a few others to do the same. Yes, it was always good to come home.

SUNNY SAMUELSON PULLED UP TO HER SISTER'S HOUSE IN the morning on a beautiful June day. Her wedding day. Laura had been at her side for every step of the wedding planning over the course of the past five and a half months, as their mother had some health problems.

Of course, her momma had helped where she could, but Sunny and Laura had really planned the bulk of the wedding— and that started with a sister breakfast, which would be followed by arriving at Luke's house by ten-thirty.

All of the Young wives would be there, as well as Jem's momma, Sunny's mom, and her brother's wife. She'd invited Sterling too, because while Luke hadn't put a diamond on her finger, whenever either of them was asked how things were going, they both got stars in their eyes and said, "Great."

Sunny wasn't sure what Luke needed to propose to Sterling, but Jem had needed time. She'd been frustrated by that at various points in their relationship, but she'd been as patient as she could possibly be.

She'd also invited Denzel's girlfriend, Michelle, but she'd said she couldn't come. Apparently Sunday morning at a coffee shop wasn't a time she could comfortably take off, and since she was a few steps removed from Jem and Sunny, she'd declined.

Sunny just wanted everyone to feel included, be invited, and come share in the joy with her and Jem. They'd chosen to get married in his backyard, because she'd be moving in with him and the kids in his big house that bordered the woods. They were starting their life there together, and they'd keep building it there too.

The ceremony would be simple. A few of her friends from work. Her family. His enormous family. Some of his friends from the rodeo—oh, he hadn't invited any. She'd pressed him and pressed him on this topic, and he'd said he didn't want to specifically invite anyone.

"It's a life I don't live anymore, Sunny," he'd said. "A life I can't go back to, not even for a few hours."

So he'd invited his sponsor, his family, and his ex-wife. Chanel had thankfully said no, though Cecily and Jerry would then be taking Cole and Rosie to their mother in Las Vegas for the next couple of months. They'd spend the summer down there, and Sunny honestly wasn't sure how she felt about it.

Laura came out of the house with a big dress bag folded over her arm. She came down the steps smiling, and Sunny got out of the car to greet her. She helped her put everything in the back, and then she grabbed onto her sister. "Thank you so much for everything. You've made this wedding come to life."

"I am so happy for you."

Sunny squeezed her sister extra hard, because while she had been her shadow every step of the way these past few months,

Sunny knew it hadn't been easy for Laura. She wanted her own cowboy to love and who would love her, and Sunny wished she could find someone for her.

"Come on," Laura said as she wiped her eyes. "I've been told to make sure you're everywhere on time today, and I am not going to fail at that."

Sunny showed up on time to breakfast, at Luke's house, and finally at Jem's. She caravanned over with Laura, Faith, and Georgia, and all of the women waited out on the front sidewalk when she got there. "Is there a problem?" she asked.

"We've gotten reports that Jem may have been peeking out the window," Georgia said. "Abby's on it. We're supposed to stay in the car." She looked back up to the house, so she didn't see Sunny's smile.

She tried to suppress it, but she couldn't. Jem peeking through the window to catch a glimpse of her. That was *so* Jem.

Sunny's stomach rumbled and tumbled with nerves, and she pulled in a tight breath. Her wedding dress almost felt like it choked her, though not a stitch of fabric touched her anywhere near her throat.

"All right," Georgia said. She got out of the van and opened the back door for Sunny. "She says we're ready to move into the house. They got Jem out in the yard."

"Everything's set there?" she asked, though she knew it was. Luke had texted her pictures after the wedding canopy company had as well.

"Yes," Laura said. "Everything's ready. Daddy and Momma are inside. Jasper. Everyone's here."

Sunny slid from the van, and immediately all of the Young wives encircled her, concealing her from any lingering cowboy prying eyes. She felt so loved in that moment, and tears pressed behind her eyes.

She was so lucky to have found Jem again after all these years. So lucky that this group of women were *her* group of women.

"All clear," Abby called from the front porch.

They moved as one, and Sunny held her skirts up as she stepped with them. The house had blessed air conditioning blowing through it, as well as the scent of bacon hanging in the air. She'd hired Everly's brother to cater the wedding, and he and his staff had set up shop in the kitchen.

She wanted to go thank him, but there wasn't time. All of the wives dispersed to their husband—or in Sterling's case, her boyfriend—and they linked arms. The older kids in the family were handling the younger ones, and some of the wives had siblings who could help too.

Faith's sister had her baby, and Denzel was tending to Eric and Rachelle. Dani's mother had their infant, and Abby's sister-in-law would be holding their month-old-son somewhere in the audience.

Bryce, Harry, Cash, and Joey, along with Cecily and Jerry, could handle the others. No matter what, it took a lot of people to take care of the Youngs, and Sunny couldn't wait to be one of them.

32

Luke found Corrine sitting with Joey and Bryce the moment he exited Jem's house. His jaw jumped, but he kept his smile firmly in place. One, it was his brother's wedding, and he wasn't going to ruin it with his dark cloud of a mood.

Two, Mandi had decided—again—that Coral Canyon "didn't feel like home," and she would be leaving soon. Luke had asked her where she was going, and she'd said she was undecided. How she had money to pay her bills, he wasn't sure. He honestly wasn't even sure where she'd been living for the past six months that she'd been in town.

Her folks didn't live here, and she'd literally sold her house and left Corrine on Momma's doorstep before she'd flown off to Calgary.

He wasn't sure if he should be happy or not about her decision. She'd seen Corrine a few times a month, always with supervision, and Corrine had seemed happy enough with the visits. He didn't want his daughter to hurt, not even for a moment, and he was sure she would.

He'd decided to shelve this news for another day, as Mandi had always been terrible with her timing of things.

The real reason Luke had a swarm of wasps moving through his stomach at the speed of light was because in probably twenty minutes or less, he'd be the only single brother left. He hated feeling left out with the heat of ten suns, and he wished power-fully that he'd been able to get himself together enough to start something with Sterling a long time ago.

This is your path.

The thought came into his mind, and Luke couldn't tell where it had come from. Certainly not from within himself.

The words rang with truth, and he couldn't stop them from coming again and then again. He and Sterling reached Jem, who stood in front of an arch dripping with flowers, and he released her arm to take his brother into a hug.

"You did it," he said to Jem, his voice choked all the way up into his nose. "I'm so happy for you."

"It'll be you soon, right?" Jem squeezed him hard and then let go. His eyebrows rode up on his forehead when he looked at Luke, but Luke didn't confirm anything.

Yes, he and Sterling had been dating for a while now, if five months and a week could be considered "a while." Luke felt really good about their relationship, and she was definitely the first woman he hadn't wanted to break up with by this point.

Even with Mandi, he'd known he didn't really want to be with her after five months. Too bad they were already married by then.

Jem had taken a whole year with Sunny. Not before the proposal, but overall. He'd told Luke he wanted every holiday, every birthday, every season. Bad days at work. Good ones. Bad days with him and his addictions. Good days. Everything with his kids.

Sunny had been patient and kind and loving with him, and as Luke took Sterling's hand, he raised it to his lips and murmured, "Thank you for being here with me."

She snuggled right into his side, and Luke sure did like that.

Sunny came down the aisle with her daddy, her face glowing like moonlight shone right on it. Her skirt had been made of white flowers that billowed as she walked, with the top half of the dress done in lace.

"She's so beautiful," Sterling whispered.

Luke wanted to ask her what kind of wedding she'd plan. When she wanted to get married—summer or winter? How big her guest list would be, as she did have a lot of clients in town.

He wondered what he'd have to do. Tex and Trace had both made public announcements on their social media when they'd gotten married, and Blaze had too. Of course, they all had social media managers—and Luke did too. Perhaps he should ask Rand what he thought.

Are you going to marry Sterling?

"You are the most exquisite woman ever," Jem said right out loud as Sunny reached him. "I am so lucky."

Twitters of laughter moved through the crowd, and Sunny tipped up toward him. "You're speaking right out loud."

Jem looked startled for a moment, and that made several more people laugh. Luke certainly smiled, though pure jealousy raged inside him. He looked over to Sterling, and he wasn't going to do what he'd done before—get married simply so he wouldn't be left out.

Still, he knew he wasn't doing that. He'd been learning to trust his feelings more and more. And he leaned down and said, "I'm falling in love with you, Sterling," right before the ceremony began.

Sure enough, twenty minutes later, Jem and Sunny were running hand-in-hand down the aisle while Luke cheered, whistled, and clapped along with everyone else. Then Blaze stepped up to the mic and said, "Lunch will be served in about twenty minutes, right here in the backyard. Let's just give them time to finish setting up."

Luke wasn't sure what to do next. Find Jem and congratulate him again? Help with tables and chairs? He'd been given no instructions, and employees came out to get the backyard turned into a garden fit to serve lunch to a bride and groom.

That left him to face Sterling. She lifted her eyebrows. "You're falling in love with me?"

"Yes."

Her smile could fill the entire sky and still need more room. "Luke, you're the sweetest cowboy ever."

"Shh," he teased as he glanced around. "Don't be sayin' that too loud."

She giggled and buried her face in his chest. "I didn't handle that very well, did I?"

He held her but not as closely as he'd like. He gently moved, and that made her straighten. He glanced over to his mother, who stood with Corrine's hand in hers as she talked with Gabe and Georgia. Daddy held OJ in his arms at her side, and Luke figured he had a few minutes. Corrine wouldn't get lost here in Jem's backyard.

So Luke took Sterling out of the way and back into the house. A quick glance into the kitchen told him not to go that way, and he really had no idea where Jem and Sunny had gone. He took Sterling down the hall toward the front door. Jem had an office here, and Luke ducked into the cool grayness of it.

Pacing away from her, he took a deep breath and then faced her. "I know I said I had to go slow, but I was just...feeling that, and it came out."

Sterling searched his face. "It's fine. Good. I'm—well, I'm falling for you too."

A couple of seconds passed while Luke absorbed what she'd said. "My family isn't too crazy for you?"

"Georgia said that when the Young Family Crazy gets to be too much, she and Otis just stay home." Sterling ran one hand through her hair, almost nonchalantly.

"I'm not too intense for you?"

Her eyes met his again. "Luke, your intensity is what makes you so strong. So protective. So sweet."

"We haven't even been together when I've been working a lot," he said.

"There's time," she said.

"You have an answer for everything, don't you?"

"Would you like me not to?" She tilted her head to the side. "Luke, are you looking for a reason to end this?"

A scoff flew from his mouth as he faced the window and found the blinds closed. "No," he said. "Of course not."

"Seems like it."

"No," he said again, glancing over to her. "I just...I want to make sure I do this right this time. Corrine doesn't deserve to be put through any more."

Sterling watched him again, her eyes taking in more than he wanted them to know. "Mandi...what's going on?"

"She's leaving," he said miserably. "And of course, I want her to leave, but I don't want Corrine to be upset."

Sterling wrapped Luke into a hug and held on tight. "I'm not going anywhere, cowboy," she whispered fiercely. "Okay? If the ladies at Red Carpet couldn't run me out of town, you can't either."

Luke hadn't known he needed to hear those words from her, but they did heal some part of his cracked heart. He gathered her close, close, and then closer, the way he'd wanted to in the backyard. "Thank you, Sterling."

"We'll tell her together," she said next. "Okay? Me and you. We'll sit down and talk to Corrine about her mom, and us, and everything." She stepped back, a fierce look of determination on her face that Luke had seen several times over the years he'd known her. "Together."

He nodded, the sound of that word when it meant him and her absolutely amazing. "Yeah," he said. "Together."

"COME ON, BEAN," LUKE SAID A COUPLE OF DAYS LATER. Summertime had arrived, and that meant he didn't have to get up and get his daughter out the door for third grade every day. She wasn't as indoorsy as Joey, who liked to read and play with dolls, cook with Georgia, or go to the bookshop.

She loved pink, sparkly things, but Luke could put a good pair of shoes on her and she'd get dirty out in the hills and mountains surrounding the valley of Coral Canyon.

"We're getting Sterling, right?" Corrine asked as she picked up her backpack. It had a brown cow pattern on it, and Luke had already tucked a water bottle and her lunch inside it. "When is Momma coming over again?"

Luke's heart started to thrash inside his chest. "Yes, we're getting Sterling," he said. He would not lie to his daughter, but he didn't know how to tell her the truth. He abandoned his two turkey sandwiches, though he hadn't bagged them yet, and dropped into a crouch in front of her.

"Corrine." He looked right into her eyes, which held so much innocence and faith. He'd pulled all of her hair back into a pony-tail today, and then braided that, so it wouldn't get caught on anything. Sterling had told him she'd do her hair the same way, and Luke loved her fiercely for trying to make his daughter feel so normal, so comfortable.

"Sterling and I have some things to talk to you about on the hike today, okay? Stuff about your mom, and us, and everything. All right?"

"Okay," she said. "Will I be disappointed? Are you going to keep dating Sterling?" She fiddled with the collar on Luke's shirt. "I know you broke up with those other girls."

Luke's eyebrows went up. "You do? Which ones?"

"I don't know." Corrine scuffed one shoe along the floor. "Grandma said you were going out with someone, when you used to drop me off, and then you stopped doing that." She flicked her gaze up him. "She said you broke up with them."

"It's not a break like a broken bone, baby." He drew her close to his chest, wondering if what he'd said was true. Few break-ups were actually amenable, and perhaps Tea or Hillary had gone through some pain akin to a broken bone.

"Will she still let me come to her meditation class?"

Luke smiled as he took time to hold his daughter and think. "Honey, I'm not breaking up with Sterling." He pulled away and smiled at her. "We might be more serious than those other women. Maybe I'll marry her."

Corrine's face lit up, but she said nothing. Luke wasn't sure what she'd even say, because it wasn't like either of them knew what it would be like to have a complete family. It had always been him and her, or her and her mother—but she couldn't even remember that.

You have eight brothers to look to as examples, he thought as he straightened. They'd all somehow managed to create complete family units out of their second marriages. Luke didn't live behind each of their closed doors, but there hadn't been any second divorces yet, and they seemed to add a new Young baby to their family every other month.

"We'll talk when we eat lunch. Now, let me finish my lunch, and then we need to go." Luke did just that, and he texted Sterling that Corrine had already started asking questions. They left, and she waited in her front yard for them, her pack resting against a tree trunk while she weeded nearby.

Corrine rolled down her window as Luke pulled into the driveway. "Heya, Sterling!"

She grinned with all the wattage of the world and waved to Corrine. "Heya, Corrine."

Luke got out and collected her bag for her while she rinsed her hands in what had to be freezing cold water from the hose. Sterling didn't seem to mind at all, and Luke realized as he watched her then run those hands along her hair, smoothing it back, that she liked to work with her hands as much as he did.

He didn't mind yard work, and she clearly didn't either. He drummed; she massaged. He needed to stay busy, and she'd gone right along with him for all of these months.

Her hair was still wild and unclaimed as she approached, and Luke leaned in and kissed her right there in plain sight of his daughter and all of her neighbors who might be watching.

"You've got some serious energy this morning," she murmured as she backed up. Their eyes met for only a moment, and then Sterling went around him. He faced the truck as she went over to

Corrine and said, "Oh, I'm so going to do my hair like that too. Then it'll be out of the way, and it's still so cute."

Luke smiled to himself, felt himself slipping further in love with her, and went to join the girls in the truck. Sterling pony-tailed and braided her hair on the way to the trailhead. She and Corrine talked about the upcoming meditation class, and if Sterling had been able to get in the new yoga mats.

Then something with Abby's newest baby, then Bryce's horse farm, and then finally, Hilde and her due date. "I just can't wait to meet that baby," Sterling said with a sigh.

"There's a lot of babies," Corrine said matter-of-factly. "I always ask Daddy to take me to Grandma and Grandpa's early, so I can get there before the babies."

"Corrine," Luke said, not sure if he was chastising her or not. He shared a smile with Sterling and looked in the rear-view mirror. "What does that mean?"

"Babies are so loud," she said. "They cry over everything, and then Grandma doesn't have time to read to me."

"Babies *are* pretty loud," Sterling said. "But they're so soft, and they smell so good."

"I don't want any babies," Corrine said.

Luke started to laugh, which probably wasn't the best move. He silenced it quickly and met Sterling's surprised look. "Maybe you'll change your mind one day," Sterling said, and she looked away without saying more.

The mood between the three of them had shifted, and Luke didn't even know how or why. They got out of the truck and put on their packs. Luke helped Corrine make sure hers was sitting right on her shoulders, and then he told her to "Lead us out, little lady."

Sterling said she didn't do much hiking, and he didn't care if it took them an hour to go the half-mile to the waterfall. Several cars had been parked in the dirt lot, and he prayed with every step that there would be a picnic table waiting for them.

Don't discount the faith you already have.

The thought came to Luke again and again on the walk through nature. He felt so out of his league. He didn't know what to say or do, and every breath held a little bit of fear in it. Finally, when he could just hear the roar of the waterfall, and Corrine turned back to him, pure joy shining on her face, he heard another thought as loud as if a man had been walking next to him.

"This is not new to me."

Luke actually looked to see if someone had come up beside him. But Corrine still stood a handful of steps in front of him, shouting about how she could hear the waterfall now, and Sterling had stopped behind him.

God had spoken to him again, clearly and loudly, and Luke struggled against his emotions. He struggled with what the Lord had meant. *This is not new to me.*

Everything in Luke's life right now felt new to him. The band wasn't practicing this summer. They'd made final tweaks on the songs, and King Country would choose fifteen for an album, and three for singles. Morris had delivered a list of twenty-four to them, and Luke always mourned the ones that didn't make the cut.

Trace still played some of them, and sometimes Otis would resubmit them for another album. So much of the music industry depended on timing, and Luke felt like that in his life too.

After all, it sure had taken he and Sterling a while—and more than one try—to get to this point.

He didn't know how to navigate this slippery slope of falling in love with Sterling. He wasn't even sure he trusted himself to know how he was feeling. His first marriage had been so terrible, and he really didn't want to mess it all up again. That was why he'd decided not to date in the first place.

And now everything with Mandi and Corrine...it was all new to him.

But not to God. He had been in these situations before. He knew how to lead His children along this path, and Luke sniffled as he caught up to his daughter and swept her up and onto his shoulders.

She squealed, but she didn't ask to be put down, and Luke finished the hike carrying her the way he had many times before. Several people milled about in the shade across from the waterfall, and the pounding noise of it made it hard to talk.

Luke put Corrine down and the three of them leaned against the fence and just took it all in. Finally, Sterling put her hand in his, and yelled, "There's a table back there that just opened up."

He nodded and went with her, putting some distance between them and the waterfall, as well as from other people. Back here, he could hear himself think again, and he said, "All right. Sandwiches," and got out his food. He passed Sterling's lunch to her and made sure Corrine had everything she needed before he sat down on the same side of the picnic table as her.

The weight of the world rested on his shoulders, and while Corrine didn't ask, Luke knew he needed to start talking.

"Corrine, baby," he said. "I know this is going to make you sad, and we can talk about it as much as you want." He refrained from tacking on an "okay?" the way he so often did. He drew in a deep breath and met Sterling's eyes from across the table.

She nodded to him, her bright blue eyes giving him the strength he needed.

He looked at his daughter—his sweet, beautiful daughter, who deserved so much more than a flighty mother. Who deserved so much more than a daddy who didn't know how to be a daddy.

"Your momma left town," he said. "She didn't have a job here, and she didn't have a house here, and she...couldn't stay here."

Corrine froze, her sandwich gripped in both hands. She simply looked at Luke with big, wide eyes, and then it was like the sky falling. Her sandwich dropped to the table, and Luke swept her up and pulled her onto his lap.

"Hey, yeah," he said, telling himself not to tell her it was okay. Nothing about what Mandi had done to Corrine was okay. "You cry if you want to, okay, jelly bean? It's okay to cry."

Cry she did, and only two seconds later, Sterling left her spot across the table and sat where Corrine had been. She enveloped both of them in her arms, and Luke leaned into her while his daughter leaned into him.

"It's not because of you," Sterling whispered to Corrine. "Corrine, honey, I just know it's not."

"How do you know?"

Luke hated the tiny, pinched, pained voice of his little girl. He wanted to rage at the universe that life wasn't fair. That kids deserved better. At the same time, he'd made these choices for her. He'd married Mandi. They'd had Corrine together.

"Well," Sterling said, and Luke had never heard her talk in this thick voice before. "I know, because I'm a lot older than you, and I've been able to think a lot about why my momma left me too."

Corrine turned toward her, sniffling as she wiped her face. "Where's your momma?"

Sterling's face wrinkled like it might break at any moment, and Luke wanted to gather both of his girls and take them home. He'd protect them. He'd make sure no one ever made them sad again. But as strong as his muscles were, he couldn't actually do that. He could shut the world out for a while, and he would. But it always crept back in, lurking to teach him something new, test him to see if this new thing would break him or make him stronger.

"Chicago," Sterling said with a false smile. "It's a city that's pretty far away. I don't see her very often. We don't talk very much." She wiped at her eyes too, and then they came right back to Corrine's face. Luke couldn't look away from her, not when that energy blazed in her expression.

"And you know what? It's not my fault. I didn't do anything wrong." She leaned closer to Corrine. "And baby, you didn't do anything wrong to make your momma leave either. This is not your fault. Now. You can be sad."

A beautiful, soft, genuine smile graced Sterling's face. "Sometimes I lay in bed and watch TV shows I've already watched when I'm feeling a little sad about my mom. And that's okay. But you can't blame yourself. Promise me now."

Corrine moved from Luke's lap to Sterling's, and she wrapped her right up in a tight hug. "Oh, you're such a good girl. I love you so much." Sterling pressed her eyes closed, and Luke could feel her love for his daughter penetrate all of his defenses.

Sterling pulled away. "I didn't hear a promise."

"I don't know what I'm promising." Corrine sniffled and hiccuped, and Luke felt like he was watching a masterclass on parenting right before his eyes.

For Sterling leaned down and pressed her forehead to Corrine's, her smile still there. "You were going to promise me and your daddy that you won't blame yourself. It's not your fault your mom left."

"Okay," Corrine said.

Luke put his arm around Sterling and drew her and Corrine closer to his chest. "I love you, Corrine," he said through his thick throat. "I will never leave you."

"What about you, Sterling?" Corrine looked up at her, really putting her on the spot.

"Corrine," Luke started, but Sterling threw him a look that made him stop.

"Your father and I have been dating for months," she said

slowly. "Do you know what men and women do after they've been dating for a while? If they really like each other?"

"No," Luke said gruffly. "You have to be way further along than *really like each other*, Corrine." He met her eye. "You have to be *in love* with someone to get married to them."

"Like Uncle Jem and Aunt Sunny," Corrine said.

"Right," Luke said, unable to meet Sterling's eye. "But when two people love each other, and they think they can build a family together, they get married."

"And if your daddy and I get married," Sterling said. "Then, no, I won't leave you either."

She wore worry in her eyes. "But what if you guys don't get married?"

Luke once again didn't know what to say. And he was once again reminded of why children needed a mother *and* a father when Sterling said, "Honey, we don't worry about what-if's, all right? Right now, your dad and I *are* together, and I think we're both working very hard on falling in love with each other."

"Is it hard work?" Corrine asked.

"Depends," Sterling said with plenty of teasing in her voice. Luke couldn't stop himself from looking at her then. She had those sapphires radiating in her eyes, and oh, he could get lost there for a while. "It's usually not hard, baby. It just takes time."

It seemed like the whole world took a breath, and then Luke said, "Okay, I'm starving. Are we eating or do we need to keep talking?"

"I can eat." She didn't slide from Sterling's lap, though, and Luke reached across the table and brought his girlfriend's sandwich closer.

His eyes met Sterling's, and he leaned over and pressed a kiss to her forehead. He didn't have to say anything else, and being with her sure felt...easy.

33

"I can *not* believe they didn't tell anyone she'd gone into labor early." Sterling paced in her kitchen, her thoughts scattering. She had one more client today, but when Ev had called to tell her Hilde was in the hospital, she'd immediately wanted to cancel.

And now doubly bad as she knew Hilde had already given birth. That morning. She and Gabe had not told anyone in the family until now, and the urgency running through Sterling to rush over to the hospital and meet Hilde's baby boy had turned Sterling into a caged tiger.

"She didn't apologize," Ev said. "And she only told me, and she only authorized me to tell you."

"Authorized?" Sterling practically screeched. "What does that mean?" She needed to look up who her client was, so she could cancel. She dashed over to the clipboard hanging outside her studio door, but her eyes had somehow forgotten to see.

"Apparently, she and Gabe aren't telling anyone else until tomorrow. So it'll just be us at the hospital tonight." Ev exhaled heavily. "I have a class in twenty minutes—which Hilde knows. I swear, she's torturing me. When are you done with clients? Do you want to call Luke and see if he wants to come with?"

"Can I tell Luke?"

"Yeah," Ev said with a smile in her voice. "Hilde said she would allow seven visitors tonight. Me and Trace, Harry and Keri. You, Luke, and Corrine."

Sterling's pulse finally settled back to normal. "Hilde has always known exactly what she wants, hasn't she?"

"She's the queen of it," Ev agreed. They laughed together, and Sterling admitted she had another client in a half-hour.

"I'll be done at six," she said.

"So will I," Ev said. "Let's meet at the hospital at six-thirty."

"I'll be there." The call ended, and Sterling quickly stripped the table and remade it. Then she grabbed her phone again and wildly texted Luke to let him know and ask him if he'd go with her to meet his new nephew.

Sterling wasn't even related to this baby—this Canyon Jerry Young—and she couldn't wait to meet him.

They had the baby? Really?

It's a secret, Sterling tapped out again. *You can't tell anyone. Where are you?* If her memory served, he'd gone out to the farm-house that day. Apparently, Tex missed having horses to take care of, and he'd bought a couple so he could still go riding with his brothers should he want to.

And apparently, Luke had wanted to today.

Her phone rang, and his name sat there. Sterling swiped on the call and said, "I have ten minutes."

"Are you telling me I can't tell *Abby* about this baby?" he hissed. "How am I going to get out of here in oh, the next thirty minutes?"

Sterling giggled, which was a good release of her tension. "Luke, you're a smart man. You'll figure it out."

"She is like a bloodhound," Luke whispered. "She will know I have a secret the moment she sees my face, and we were supposed to eat dinner here. Did you forget?"

Sterling had forgotten her own name when Ev had said, "Guess what? Hilde had the baby *this morning*, and she wants us to come tonight."

"Yes," Sterling admitted. "I forgot."

Luke sighed heavily. "I'll think of something."

"If you have to tell her," Sterling said, because she knew of Luke's extreme distaste of lying. "Tell her she has to keep it a secret until tomorrow. She can go visit the baby and Hilde and everyone tomorrow."

"And I can bring Corrine?"

"Yes."

"This is so dumb," he grumbled. "Six-thirty?"

"At the hospital." Sterling wanted him to come, but if it didn't work, it didn't work. "I can just go myself," she said. "I can text Abby and simply say something came up, and I can't make it to dinner. That wouldn't be a lie."

"No, I want to come too." He sighed again. "I'll see you at the hospital at six-thirty."

Sterling wasn't even sure where the next hour went. Thankfully, it passed, and she washed up, left her studio a mess, and hurried to the hospital. With plenty of summertime light still streaming through the big windows, it wasn't hard to find Trace, Ev, Harry, and Keri. Sterling moved right into the center of them, and all of them hugged her while everyone laughed.

"Is Luke coming?"

"Yep." Sterling turned to see if he was striding powerfully

through the door she'd just entered, but he wasn't. He arrived a couple of minutes later, alone.

"No Corrine?" Sterling rushed to meet him, so anxious for some reason.

"She wanted to stay at Tex's," he said. "It's summer, and I didn't want to argue." He glanced over to Trace and Ev, then moved to hug them too. "I said you had something come up, and I'd like to come meet you, and yeah."

He sounded out of breath, and again, the tension in the waiting area felt too high to Sterling. Thankfully, Trace said, "You guys. It's a baby. Come on." He led the way toward the elevator that would take them up to the fourth-floor maternity wing.

"Yeah, but it's a *secret* baby," Ev said with plenty of animation in her tone. "It has a new excitement to it, don't you think?"

"It's not a *secret* baby," Trace drawled. "We knew Hilde and Gabe were having a baby. A boy, even."

Ev practically danced onto the elevator, and her whole face held wonder. "What if it's a girl, Trace? What if that's the real secret?"

He looked at her with a face made of stone, which slowly cracked as he smiled. "You know, I don't think Gabe could lie right to my face and tell me he's havin' a boy if he was having a girl."

"Doctors make mistakes." Ev tossed her long hair over her shoulder and faced the doors as they slid closed. She looked over to Sterling. "What do you think?"

"I think Hilde had a boy and named him Canyon Jerry Young." She really emphasized the middle name. "After his grandfather."

"There are women named Jeri too," Ev said. "Oh, it could be spelled like our Keri, but with a J!"

"Ev." Trace shook his head as he chuckled, and Harry burst out into a full laugh. Sterling couldn't help herself either, and even her dark, grumpy boyfriend laughed. Ev laughed at herself, and they all got off the elevator in a much better mood than when they'd gotten on.

Ev knew the room number, and she led the six of them to it. She knocked lightly, and Trace whispered, "If these rooms could lock, Gabe would've done it."

"Good thing they can't," Luke said as he pushed down the handle and then leaned into the door. It swung open, and Ev and Sterling peered in first.

"Look, Canyon," Hilde cooed. "Your second visitors have arrived."

"Second?" Ev demanded, and Sterling could admit the word came out of her mouth too.

Hilde laid in the bed as Sterling entered, and she smiled with a radiance Sterling hadn't seen on her face before. Not at her wedding. Not at a successful Memorial Day Faire. Never, ever.

She wasn't holding her baby, and it took her looking over to the recliner for Sterling to find her mother holding the blue bundle. "Oh, I'll take second," Sterling said.

"Go in," Gabe said from out in the hall. "It's a big room, and Hilde wants the door closed."

Sterling moved out of the way, which allowed everyone else to enter too. While she was good friends with Hilde, she knew Ev was closer, and Sterling wouldn't take that baby first. She wanted to, something in her heart growing and growing and growing.

Something she didn't even know had been hiding in her heart —the desire to have a baby and be a mother. Sterling had not dated a lot over the years. She'd honestly never labeled herself as nurturing or maternal. She'd been working and working toward her goal of opening her own spa studio for so long, and then once she'd done that, she'd made another goal.

None of them had ever included marriage and family. She'd

never thought she'd get the opportunity for such things, and even if she did, she wouldn't be very good at them. But massage? Sterling knew she was good at that.

Now, with Luke at her side, his hand heavy on her hip, and Ev carefully taking the newborn from Hilde's mother, Sterling felt like the universe had been ripped open. "Wow," she said as the little boy grunted and snuggled into Ev's chest. She looked up, her eyes wide and bright with tears.

Sterling couldn't help gravitating toward them, and she gazed down at this perfect tiny human, straight from heaven. "He's so beautiful," she said, her eyes and brain putting together pieces of Hilde and pieces of Gabe.

She met Ev's eye again. "He's a boy."

"Right?" Ev half laughed and half cried, and she pressed her eyes closed and touched her lips softly to the boy's dark, wispy hair.

"I'll take you, Lucy," Gabe said. Sterling turned away from the baby then to see Gabe escorting Hilde's mother out of the room. "Baby, I'm gonna get my parents on the way back, okay?"

"Okay." Hilde sighed as she leaned back in the bed and let her own eyes close.

"He's so perfect," Sterling said as she took the recliner next to her friend's bed. "How did everything go?"

"Good," Hilde said with plenty of enthusiasm. "I just didn't get any sleep last night, as I went into labor about one-thirty."

"Congrats, Hilde." Trace leaned down and hugged her, and Harry followed suit. Luke did the same, and Hilde whispered something to him and patted him on the back before he pulled away.

"Your turn," Ev said, and before Sterling could protest, she slipped the baby boy into her arms. Sterling couldn't look away from him, not even for one second. He molded to her, and he was so helpless and so soft. Sterling's heart filled with love over and over again, and this wasn't even her baby.

"Look," Ev said in a quiet voice. "Baby Canyon. You be real soft." She now held Keri, her ten-month old daughter, and crouched down in front of Sterling. She could barely see the little girl through her tears, and she sniffled.

Ev looked at her, but Sterling didn't care. She had no idea what she'd have to sacrifice to become a mother, but she was suddenly more acutely aware of what her friends had already done.

Abby didn't work at the library anymore. She drove the Book-mobile a couple of times each week. Ev didn't teach dance classes anymore, though she still owned the studio. Hilde had been talking of selling her furniture store. Georgia had hired full-time people so she wouldn't be the only person available to run the bookshop she owned.

Leigh hadn't reopened her bakery, which she'd given up before moving here. She and Dani both stayed home and raised their children, their careers somewhere in their past. Faith only worked the morning shift on her doughnut dessert truck.

Georgia was literally walking on dangerous ground to bring a baby into the world. Her pregnancy had kept, but she was tired and sick a lot, even to this day. She had two and a half more months, and then Sterling would get to meet another hopefully healthy, cute Young baby.

What would Sterling give up in order to have a beautiful, dark-haired baby boy of her own?

As Keri stroked her new cousin's head, Sterling thought she'd give up almost anything—and that sent a needle straight into her heart. A pit opened in her stomach, and it felt like the past fifteen years she'd spent working toward her career goals meant nothing.

"Look right here," Luke said in a soft voice. Sterling looked up and saw he had his phone out. She grinned as wide as she ever had and let him snap the photo. "Gorgeous," he whispered, his focus on the phone as he tapped and swiped.

Sterling's attention returned to the newest Young baby, and she closed her eyes and toed herself and Canyon back and forth, the internal war between her career and this new idea of marriage, family, and motherhood already waging inside her.

34

Luke kept his smile in place as he scrawled his name across another album cover. The heat rained down on him, but he told himself he looked sexy while sweating. That was what his manager had suggested for him to think about anyway.

Tex, who stood next to him, laughed, and he was so good at easy conversation. He posed with the girl who'd brought her album to be signed, the two of them grinning like fools as Luke handed back the cover he'd just put his name on.

The teen boy did look a little awed, and that got Luke to switch his gaze to the next in line. "Howdy," he drawled, wondering what time it was. The shadows had started to fall across the park, so it had to be getting close to time to be done.

Morris had arranged for a meet and greet signing at the Independence Day fireworks celebration this year. They didn't have a new album announced. They hadn't had a single in a while. Their tour was two years old now.

So Country Quad had agreed to two hours of meeting, greeting, and signing. In the evening heat.

"You're Luke Young," one of the young women said. She giggled and looked at her friend.

"I sure am," he said, because that was what Rand had coached him to say. He didn't roll his eyes, and he didn't make some sarcastic remark about how he'd forgotten his own name. "Are you two country music fans?"

They both wore really short shorts and really long tees, and while they couldn't be that much younger than Luke, he felt generations older than them. He took the poster that King Country had provided and slashed his name across it.

They didn't move over to Tex on Luke's left, or to Otis and Trace beyond him.

"Sort of," one of them said. "I've never gotten a billionaire's signature before." She pressed the paper to her chest, and Luke had to work really hard to keep his eyerolling internal as he signed the second woman's poster.

Once they left, he rolled his neck and rotated his shoulder before he looked at the next person in line. Each of them had a line, but most people jostled around to get to all four of them.

Luke blinked as he looked into the eyes of Gray Hammond, and then he shoved his permanent marker in his jeans pocket and threw his arms around the man. They both laughed, and Gray pounded Luke on the back. "Welcome to the billionaire club."

"Stop it." Luke stepped back and gave Gray a mock glare. "If there's one more person who uses that word tonight, I'm gonna start flippin' tables."

Gray just laughed as his wife came forward to hug him. They had their children with them—the younger ones at least. Gray had a son from a previous marriage who was much older than the three with him.

"Jane." Luke took her into a light hug too. "You've got to be graduated by now."

"Just this year," she said with a stiff smile. She held out a poster. "I have a friend back in Ivory Peaks who would love it if you signed this."

Luke's eyebrows went up. "A friend, huh?"

That got Jane to smile. "A legit friend, I swear."

Luke signed as quickly as possible, and Jane did move down the line of brothers to get all of the signatures while Luke asked Gray, "Is Wes coming tonight? I heard he had a broken ankle? Something sprained?"

"It's gout," Gray said. "He can barely walk, but I don't think he'll miss the fireworks for anything." He moved over to Tex too, taking Elise with him, and Luke looked at his younger boys.

"Howdy, fellas." He hugged both Tucker and Deacon at the same time, and if Jane had just graduated, that meant they hadn't. "What are you guys into?"

Tucker looked at Deacon, who nodded like they'd had a conversation prior to this. Luke braced himself to be asked something he'd probably want to say no to.

"Do you think I could ask Blaze and Jem about the rodeo?" Tucker asked. "I'm doin' it this year, and I sure do like it. I think I might want a career in rodeo."

"Sure," Luke said, relieved this wasn't something he'd have to deal with. Not really, anyway. "They'll both be here tonight. In fact, Blaze is working in his wife's doughnut truck tonight." Luke nodded toward the wide circle of them. "It's the bright pink one with sprinkles."

Both boys looked down to it. "Great," Tucker said, swinging back to Luke. He shook his hand, and Luke found him quite mature for his age. "Thanks."

"They're also calling the rodeo next week," he said. "Opening night tomorrow. Runs for five or six days. They got me tickets for the last night. Maybe they'll have some extras."

"We've got some for Friday," Deacon said. "Daddy got them somehow."

Luke nodded, and the boys went to join their family. Luke had more female admirers, and in that moment, he realized that while women went by his brothers too, there were definitely less of them than who stood near Luke. They didn't twitter or brush their hair out of their eyes when they looked at Tex. Only Luke.

"All right," Morris called. "Our time is up, ladies and gents. Thank you so much for coming. We've got to get our cowboys back to their families."

Luke stood still as he posed for a picture, and then another, and then another. It took him a few minutes to realize everyone else had gone, except for him. And the women milling about...they weren't going anywhere.

Morris cleaned up by putting the extra posters in a box, and he glanced over to Luke. They could thankfully communicate without words, and his brother turned toward him. "I'm so sorry, guys," he said diplomatically. "Looks like Luke's daughter is here, and—"

"Aw," the women cooed as one. "She's is so cute."

Corrine loved nothing more than being called *cute*, but horror cut through Luke as he turned to find Sterling standing there with Corrine's hand secured in hers. He had told her what time he'd be done, and all of his brothers had left. She'd probably just come to see what the hang-up was.

He looked at her. Then back at his fans. He wasn't sure what to do. Introduce her as his girlfriend? Keep posing? Insist they all leave him alone?

"Hey, jelly bean," he said as Corrine came over to him. He picked her up and grinned at her. "Tell these guys who your favorite band is."

"Country Quad," Corrine said, and Luke laughed along with everyone else.

"All right." He set her back down. "Go on back to Sterling." He reached for her too, gave her hand a quick squeeze, and hoped he could explain later. She wore a smile as she faded a few feet from him, and Luke faced those still loitering nearby.

"All right," he said. "One big group photo, okay? I have to get back to my family." He spread his arms wide and women immediately fell into his sides. They crowded in more and more, and he kept his smile stuck in place until all the cameras had gone off.

"Are you dating her?" one of the women asked, and Luke didn't immediately answer.

He cut her a look from under the brim of his cowboy hat and said, "Yep." He didn't know this woman, and he didn't have to defend himself. He was allowed to date.

But you do need to protect Sterling from the onslaught of social media. He glanced over to where she'd been, and now she and Corrine wandered along a booth a few down from where Country Quad had been signing.

"Thanks," Morris said. "Thanks, everyone. Have a good night." Everyone finally left, and Morris pinned Luke with an apologetic look. "Sorry, Luke."

"Did any of them get a picture of my daughter?" he asked.

"No," Morris said. "I asked them not to, and I told them we'd check their phones." He nodded down to the festival security guard, who was swiping through one woman's device. He handed it back to her; she left; he nodded to Morris.

Relief painted through Luke. He wasn't a big celebrity. Only in certain circles did his name cause any sort of recognition at all. But the articles about his wealth had definitely caused a stir. Blaze had been right. There had been a lot of account management and social media to be done surrounding the articles, and then things had died back to normal.

"Catch you back at our spot," he said to Morris, and he went to find Sterling and Corrine. They were both peering at rings in a jewelry booth when he caught up to them, and he swept his arm around Sterling's waist.

"I didn't mean to bring her over," she said quickly. "I didn't know Morris was going to announce we were there."

"It's just fine," he said easily. "You guys want rings?"

"I do, Daddy." Corrine pointed to a pale yellow one. "That one."

He nodded to the woman behind the table, and she got it out. Sterling didn't get a ring, which was just as well, because a cheap carnival-type ring wasn't what Luke wanted to buy for her, nor slide on her finger.

"Luke," someone called, and he automatically looked. Sterling turned with him, and he got blinded as multiple flashes went off. These weren't phone cameras, but the professional type that reporters used.

Instant irritation flooded him, and he held up one hand and turned his face away. "Come on, guys," he said. "I'm out with my family."

"Your family?" someone called.

"So did you get married?"

"What's her name?"

"Can't we get a picture of the two of you?"

"You're a billionaire now, Luke, you've got to get used to the spotlight."

The questions and statements kept coming at him, and Sterling's tension radiated from her. He kept Corrine pinned in front of him, and he looked at the woman who he'd just bought a ring from. "Can we maybe go through your booth?" he asked as calmly as he could. "Or at least them? I don't want my daughter in pictures."

"Of course," she said kindly.

Luke looked at Sterling, silently begging her to take Corrine and head back to the family circle where they'd all gathered for dinner, the concert, and then the fireworks. They took a big space, and the Hammonds and the Whittakers almost always joined them.

Sterling nodded and squeezed Luke's hand where no one could see. "Be nice," she whispered, and then she said, "Come on, baby. Right with me." She ducked around the table, Corrine in front of her now.

Luke turned back to the men and women who wanted something from him. Perhaps if he just answered a few questions, they'd let him go. A man came up beside him—the security guard from the signing booth.

"You okay, sir?"

Luke didn't want to make a statement about him and Sterling. They'd likely already gotten their pictures, and he couldn't stop them from printing the ones of her.

"My daughter is a minor," he said. "You can't print her picture without my permission." He looked at the security guard. "I just want to go sit with my family."

"You heard 'im, folks." The man stepped in front of Luke and held up both hands. "If you have pictures of his daughter, delete them. Let him get back to his family. Go on, now."

Grumbles echoed through the crowd, but they did it. Luke wasn't even sure how there was that much press in Coral Canyon, and when the security guard turned back to him, he said, "Thank you. Could you walk me back?"

"Sure thing, cowboy." He led the way away from the booths, and Luke glanced at his name tag. Officer Winslow.

"I didn't realize this event got so much press."

Officer Winslow gave him a side-eyed look. "It doesn't," he said. "You country music stars brought them in. Well, really you."

"Me?" That couldn't be true.

"It's all I've heard for days as we've prepped for this. Luke Young. Luke Young. Luke Young." He grinned. "My wife was hoping I'd get assigned to you." He chuckled and shook his head. "I told her she could probably run into you at the gym. I've seen you there."

Luke nodded, his throat too tight and his stomach suddenly boiling. He hadn't eaten dinner yet, despite the day's light fading into twilight. Momma had promised she'd save him something, but now he wasn't sure he'd be able to eat it.

"Yeah," he said. "Or the elementary school."

"That too, and she goes there everyday."

"Yeah? How many kids do you have?"

"She has about twenty-three or twenty-four every year," he said. "She teaches fourth grade."

"Oh, my daughter's going into fourth grade."

"I know. I've heard all about how she might get her in class." He laughed again. "She's here tonight. Do you mind if we get a quick picture?"

"Not even a little," Luke said, and he smiled with Officer Winslow while the man took a selfie. "And that's me right there? See all the cowboys?"

"This town is full of 'em." Officer Winslow tipped his hat and turned back the way they'd come.

Luke quickly crossed the remaining grass and sidewalk and strode right into the crowd of people who belonged to him. "Uncle Luke is back!" Cole yelled, and that got a few other kids looking up at him.

Melissa got up and came over to him. "I can sit by you."

"Let's go then." He picked her up, noting the sour look on Abby's face. So Mel wanted to sit by Luke because she was in trouble with her momma. He didn't mind, and Abby didn't stop him.

He scanned quickly to find Sterling and Corrine, but he only found the blonde woman he was dating. She sat beside Hilde, his empty seat waiting for him on her left. Away from the sidewalk.

His appreciation for her knew no bounds, and as he maneuvered through everyone and took his seat, he praised the Lord for such a good woman in his life. He settled Mel on his lap, and then his stomach growled.

"Baby, go get something for me to eat from Grandma, okay?"

"Okay," she said, and she slid to the ground to go fulfill his request.

He took Sterling's hand in his and dared to look at her. "You okay?"

"Yes," she murmured.

"I'm really sorry." He couldn't see Corrine anywhere. "Where's Corrine?"

"Jem took her and Rosie to get ice cream." Sterling wouldn't look at him, and Luke couldn't help feeling like he'd done something wrong. Or maybe he was just all keyed up from the signing and the photos and everything.

He did love the spotlight—at certain times. But when it was time to be done, he wanted it to be over.

Sterling turned toward him, but her head was ducked, like she had a secret she only wanted him to hear. "Will my picture show up online somewhere? Printed in the paper?"

"Possibly," he said in a whisper. "I'm sorry, Sterling. I didn't know the signing would cause this big of a thing."

Her eyes flicked up to his and held. "But not Corrine's."

"She's a minor," he said. "They have to have my permission to print her picture, and I don't give it."

She nodded, her jaw tight, and Luke just wanted to kiss her until it loosened up. He leaned forward too, letting his eyes close as he drew nearer and nearer to her. He took a deep breath of her, and said, "Forgive me. Things got away from me. I can't control every situation."

"I'm not mad," she finally said. "I'm just trying to figure out what I should've done. Or not done."

"Nothing," he murmured, his lips brushing the soft skin at her neck. "You did everything right. This is just how it is sometimes."

"Uncle Luke," Mel said, and he moved away from Sterling. "Grandma has steak sandwit-itches." She held up Luke's favorite food in the world, and he grinned at her.

"Thank you, Momma," he yelled, hoping his mother would hear him. Then he took the sandwich and the little girl and let Mel perch in his lap. He couldn't really eat with her there, and he said, "Go sit with Sterling while I eat, okay?"

"Okay." Mel once again slipped from his lap and moved right over to Sterling, who picked her up. She took the girl right into her arms and bent over her as Mel started gabbing about something.

Watching her with the little kids made her ten times more attractive to him than she already was. They'd talked about kids, and she said she wanted them. Heck, she'd suggested they have nine boys, and he'd steadfastly told her no.

His blood heated just thinking about being intimate with Sterling and building a family with her. They hadn't talked about it again, and Luke wondered if he could broach the subject one more time. Just to be sure they were on the same page.

He glanced over to her, but Mel kept her occupied. He couldn't really say something was wrong between them, but things had definitely shifted recently. He couldn't exactly pinpoint when, and Sterling was fairly good at just saying what was on her mind.

So you'll ask her, he told himself as he finished his dinner. Not tonight, as the band started playing further back in the park. But he would soon, and then he'd know what was going on inside her mind.

But tonight, he was going to enjoy the music, enjoy the air as it cooled, enjoy the bright sparks of light in the night sky, and enjoy holding Sterling's hand through all of it.

35

S terling's coffee grew cold as she watched the video from the Fourth of July over and over and over. Fine, she wasn't watching the same one. Different ones. They'd all been tagged with #lukeyoung or #picwithabillionaire.

She'd stumbled upon them when she'd somehow been tagged in one of the pictures. The user had blurred out Corrine completely, but Sterling stood there, looking at Luke with Corrine's hand in hers and a semi-horrified look on her face.

Honestly, she experienced the same feeling now as she had only last night. Luke was not the same person in front of a camera as he was behind closed doors. "He told you that," she murmured to herself as she peered closer at a picture of Luke grinning with two girls probably half his age.

In every one, he looked absolutely charming in that cowboy hat. His teeth were straight and white, his dark eyes dazzling with diamonds. He looked like he was having the time of his life, but Sterling knew he wasn't.

343

The way he could flip a switch and become someone else, act a certain way, did not sit right with her.

The fireworks—the whole day actually—had been wonderful. She enjoyed spending time with a family unit, and the Youngs never disappointed in that regard. Cecily had hugged her tightly, fed her, and kept the conversation light and easy.

The other wives asked her how her small business loan was coming. They shared their lives and their kids with her. Jem had entertained her and Corrine for several minutes with stories from his and Sunny's honeymoon. She'd never been scuba diving or snorkeling, and from all the mishaps they'd suffered, she wasn't sure she wanted to.

Sterling hadn't been holding back with Luke. She'd let herself freefall with him, but seeing how fake he could be, she honestly wasn't sure if she'd fallen for a real person or not. She finally slammed closed her laptop, the work she'd needed to do that morning on her website undone.

She had a client in thirty minutes, and Sterling went through the motions of getting the room ready, getting out the refreshments, and getting herself centered. She stood at the back sliding door, staring out into the backyard, wondering what to do about Luke, just as she had six months ago, after their impromptu kiss on New Year's Eve.

"Morning," Desiree said, and Sterling put on her game face too.

"Good morning," she said, leaving the window and all of her cares behind. She realized in that moment that she'd just done the same thing Luke did. She'd stuffed away her own worries and cares, put a smile on her face, and gone to work.

Luke's job was a country music star. He was a public figure, whether she liked it or not. When things between them had been small-town private, Sterling didn't mind his career or job expectations.

But now that she'd been tagged....

She didn't know what to make of her confusing feelings. Thankfully, Desiree had an injury in her right leg that required a lot of Sterling's concentration. She focused there, and at the end of the forty-five minutes, she said, "I think it's getting so much better." She looked at her friend. "What do you think?"

"I always feel better after I come here." Desiree sat up and rolled her neck. "Any weekend plans?"

Sterling shook her head, because for one of the first weekends this year, she didn't actually have plans. Luke was taking Corrine out on a daddy-daughter camping date, and they were leaving tomorrow and would be gone until Saturday afternoon.

"Nothing much," she said. "My boyfriend is going to be out of town, and I'm actually looking forward to some alone-time."

Desiree lit up at the mention of Sterling's boyfriend. "You're seeing Luke Young, right?"

Sterling turned away from her, already regretting what she'd said. "Yes," she said.

"Isn't he so dreamy?" Desiree got to her feet too, and Sterling hoped that would be the end of it. She wasn't sure how she felt about every woman in the state—in the whole blasted country— crushing on *her* boyfriend.

"Did you want to reschedule?" Sterling asked as she turned to face Desiree again.

"Yes, let's do two weeks again," she said.

"Okay." Sterling tapped on her phone, and two weeks from today was actually her birthday. "Oh, I'm not working that Wednesday...." She tapped and looked up. "What about Thursday, July twentieth?"

"Ten?"

"Ten is yours," Sterling said, because she could schedule someone before and another client after and still eat lunch at a normal hour.

Desiree left, and Sterling sat down in front of her computer again, determined to at least go over some of her plans for her expanded offerings at Deep Purple. Her small business loan had come through, but she hadn't touched a dime of it. Her meditation classes at the community center had been a big draw, and she did two classes each week now—one in the morning and one in the evening.

She sighed as she looked at her list of Big Ideas. "Do you even want this, Sterling?" She could feel the weight of baby Canyon in her arms, and tears pricked her eyes. "What if what you have is good enough?"

Her phone buzzed, and Sterling let it distract her. She had another client in thirty minutes, and as she silenced the reminder alarm and got up to get things ready, a flurry of messages came in on the wives-only thread.

Yes, Sterling had been added to it, though she and Luke were not married. They weren't even engaged, and Sterling had no idea what that even looked like or felt like. Her relationship with Luke was the most serious one she'd ever had, and she didn't know if her confusing feelings were normal or not.

In times like these, she wished she had a mother or sisters to ask.

Abby's name brightened her screen again, and Sterling realized she had eight women right in front of her.

Denzel is engaged! Leigh had said. *He and Michelle are going to get married in October. He is so excited, you guys. It's the cutest thing ever!*

Congratulations had started pouring in from there, and Sterling found her smile genuinely sitting on her face as she added her own, *Wow, that's so great! They are so good together.*

Were she and Luke "so good" together? Why could she see it in someone else's relationship and not her own? How could she find out?

Pray and ask.

The words just came into her head, and Sterling's skin buzzed.

Did you ever find out what he was writing? Georgia asked. *The bookshop keeper in me is dying.*

As is the librarian in me, Abby said.

Sterling smiled at their texts, but her stomach lurched. She hurried down the hall to her bedroom, silenced her phone, and dropped to her knees at the side of the bed. She'd prayed here and there over the years. During a particularly nasty ice storm she'd been caught out in. To know what to do about leaving Red Carpet. To give her strength to message her mother and brother.

Nothing where she truly poured her heart out to the Lord, the way the pastor often spoke of. Sterling felt she'd lived a very mundane life. Nothing too good. Nothing too bad, so she didn't need to get down on her knees and beg God for things constantly.

Now, though, she had a surge of words flow from her. "Dear God," she started, trying to tame her thoughts into some semblance of order.

"First, I want to thank You for all the blessings You have given me. I have enjoyed the past six months of my life so much. I really needed a break after the year I had last year." She took a breath. "I know that's because of Luke's family. It might even be because of him. I don't like these feelings inside me—what's right? Why does this bother me? What should I do about it?"

She stopped, because she knew she wasn't making sense. Hadn't Pastor Richards said once that God could see her heart? Maybe she didn't have to put anything into words at all.

"I need help," she said anyway. "Help to sort through the confusion about my business. About Luke. About why we're together. I know I can't just stay with him, because I like his family. But at the same time, if I lost his family...."

Sterling didn't even want to think about what a negative space that would put her in. She hadn't been really living until this year. Until all of her friendships had been planted, cultivated, bloomed, and grown. She hadn't realized how lonely and isolated she was.

"Yes, I did," she said to God. "I knew, and I was suffering. I don't want to go back to that. Please." Tears fell down her face in a mighty rush, and Sterling couldn't stop them.

She let herself weep into her bedspread for a few minutes, and then she found she was all dried up in words too. She whispered, "Amen," and got to her feet.

Fifteen minutes later, she'd washed her face, changed the table, gotten out a package of trail mix, and washed her hands. She had her massage-therapist-game-face on, and her next client would have no idea of the turmoil raging inside her.

Gina was also late, and Sterling pulled out her phone to find the conversation had continued during her mini-crisis.

He's been working on a memoir, Leigh said. *About his life before his accident, and then after. He let Morris and me read a little bit of it, and it's actually really good.*

More congratulations and expressions of surprise. No one would call her on not answering, because they knew she worked and couldn't have her phone with her all the time.

That's great for Denzel, she typed out quickly. If Gina walked in, she'd abandon this text, and Sterling actually paused and lifted her eyes to the door, tempting God.

When He called her bluff, she continued, her thumbs flying across the screen as she finished her message and hit send. The moment she'd done that, the front door opened, and Gina Randall walked in saying, "I'm so sorry I'm late. Did you know there's construction at the end of your street?"

"There is?" Sterling had not known that. "There wasn't this morning."

"It looked like the house on the corner had a geyser shooting out of their lawn." She slid off her shoes and looked at Sterling. "It's so good to see you."

Sterling returned her smile and said, "And you. Are we doing the same thing today, or do you have somewhere that needs my special attention?"

Gina rotated her left shoulder. She was left-handed and she played a lot of tennis in the summertime. "Well, you may have heard, but Rhonda and I won the doubles tournament yesterday, but I'm pretty sure I tweaked something in my shoulder...."

The urge for Sterling to check her phone was so strong, she actually left it face-down on the dining room table next to her computer as she went into the studio with Gina. She peeled back the corner of the blanket and said, "Undress to your comfort level and lie face down to start. I'll be right back."

Then she stood at the sink and let the hottest water she could stand run over her fingers. After all, she couldn't check her phone with wet hands.

I HEARD YOU'RE GOING TO LUNCH WITH ALL THE WIVES? WAS the text that woke Sterling the next morning.

Yes, she tapped out. *You're leaving for your camping trip today, right?*

In about ten minutes, he said. *Are we still okay to stop by with doughnuts and good-bye hugs? Corrine wants to show you something.*

I was planning on it. Sterling would actually have to get out of bed, but if Luke was leaving in ten minutes and then getting doughnuts, she had at least a half-hour. Her first client of the day wasn't for another ninety minutes, and she had plenty of time.

She hadn't told anyone in the wives' text not to tell Luke about their lunch that day, and she wasn't surprised he knew. Abby had probably texted him Sterling's whole message the moment she'd gotten it.

"That's not fair," she said to herself as she got up. "Or true." Abby had texted her off the group to say she wouldn't tell Luke anything. Perhaps he'd been over at Blaze's or Jem's, as he spent a lot of time with them.

"Could've been Mav," Sterling said with an almost bitter note in her voice. "Or Gabe, or Morris. Trace, Otis, Tex—they're all in the band."

She was well-aware that she'd just named *all* of his brothers, but they were an extremely tight-knit family.

As she brushed her teeth absently, she swiped back up in the chat with the wives from yesterday. Her message read, *Hey everyone, I'm wondering who has time for lunch in the next couple of days while Luke is gone? We can do it at my house or someone else's or a restaurant. I just have some things I want to discuss with everyone.*

Questions had flown in then, and of course, Sterling hadn't answered any of them for a full hour due to her massage client.

Things? What kind of things? Abby had asked.

Luke things? Hilde wanted to know.

Are these good things or bad things? Georgia added.

Sterling hadn't given them much, but when she'd finally been brave enough to look at her phone, she'd texted with, *Luke things, yes. Confusing things, so they're kind of hard. I don't know if they're good or bad. It's confusing.*

No one had responded after that for a while, and then Abby had said, *Hilde's house? One o'clock?*

That had worked for Sterling, and to her shock, every other wife on the thread. So they'd all be there, and yes, any of their children they needed to bring would be too.

No cowboys, Dani had said. *Can I bring my mom? I'm taking her to the wound care clinic in the morning, and I might not have time to get her home first.*

Of course, Sterling had said, and a couple of others had affirmed it too.

Then Abby had texted privately, and she'd said she'd invited Cecily and Cheryl to come. All fine with Sterling. She figured if she was going to blurt out the mess of feelings in her head, it didn't matter how many women were there.

Sterling had a feeling Abby had been doing a lot of private texting over the past eighteen hours, but she found she didn't mind. She actually felt a little lost, and she needed someone to guide her down the right path at the moment.

She got dressed and went to make coffee. Luke arrived, and Sterling simply looked at him while he held the door for Corrine with one hand and a big pink box of doughnuts in the other.

When their eyes met, Sterling wasn't sure what she'd been so worried about. Relief punched through her, and she rushed at Luke. "Oh—okay." He grabbed onto her, so they didn't both topple backward, and he held her tightly with just the one arm. "What's goin' on?"

Sterling couldn't word vomit all over him, not when he was on his way out of town and she had a client soon.

"Sterling, look."

She stepped away, swiped quickly at her eyes, and knelt in front of Corrine. She held up a peach-colored square of crochet that looked like a potholder. "Did you make this?"

"Daddy took me to a class up in Dog Valley." She looked so proud of herself. "I can teach you." She looked from the potholder as Sterling took it, such hope in her dark eyes. "Do you want me to teach you?"

"Yes," Sterling said instantly, though she knew how to crochet already. "Yes, I do." She could tell the loops weren't all exactly right, and she'd never pick this color of yarn. She didn't care one whit. She hugged Corrine and whispered, "You are such a clever girl."

"Oh, and it's almost my birthday," Corrine said. "Daddy said it's the year for a family party, and that I can have my own outside of the big one."

"That's right," Sterling said. "End of the month, right?"

"Twenty-ninth." Corrine wore her hair back out of her face again today, and she was such a pretty little girl. "I'll be eight."

"Did you know my birthday is on the nineteenth?" Sterling asked.

"No." Corrine looked up at her father, but Luke had taken the doughnuts into the kitchen. "Did you tell Daddy?"

"No, I—"

"Daddy, Sterling's birthday is in July too!" Corrine skipped around the corner, where Luke practically steamrolled her.

"It is?"

Sterling got to her feet. She wasn't sure why her birthday hadn't come up for them yet, and she didn't know how she felt about it. She'd celebrated alone for a lot of years, and then she'd started arranging lunches and dinners with friends as a replacement for her family.

"The nineteenth," Corrine said, looking up at her daddy. "Can we have a party with her too?"

Luke's gaze never left Sterling's. "Does she want a party?"

She shook her head, and pure understanding moved across

Luke

Luke's face. He bent down and whispered something to his daughter. She nodded and went past him into the kitchen. Luke came toward her, taking her slowly, carefully, into his arms.

"Something's different about you," he said. "Us." He looked at her, all seriousness and concern. "Is it something I did? You have to tell me, and I'll fix it."

"It's unfixable," she whispered as she finally allowed herself to sink into his warmth and strength. "It's stupid, and I'll move past it."

"Were you going to tell me about your birthday?"

"Maybe," she said. "It's...I try not to make a big deal out of it." Then, she wouldn't be hurt when she was the only one who remembered the day.

"So something small?" he whispered. "Me, you, Corrine? Or just me and you?"

"You decide," she said, because she didn't have any brain cells left to make decisions with.

He swayed with her, and she didn't know what he'd told Corrine, but the little girl hadn't made a re-appearance. "Can I guess why you're upset?"

"I'm not upset."

"Distant, then."

She'd give him distant, and she didn't affirm or deny anything.

"My family was too loud during the fireworks," he said. "Totally killed the romantic vibe."

A smile came to her face before she could stop it. "No."

"You didn't get to see me yesterday at all, because I was out at Bryce's all day, and hoo-boy, that boy is in over his head."

She held him so tightly, because she didn't want him to see her face and know everything instantly. "Maybe that."

"Hmm." Luke tried to pull back, but she wouldn't let him. "You're not a good liar, Sterling."

"Thanks," she whispered.

"That just leaves me, then," he said. "*I'm* the problem. I'm guessing all the social media posts and videos. I noticed you were tagged in quite a few of them."

Sterling didn't have to say that he'd hit the nail on the head. They both knew it.

"I'm sorry," he whispered next. "I did say my life was public sometimes, but I did a poor job of preparing you for it."

"I'll adjust," she said. "I just need a couple of days to reset, and then I'll be okay." She finally pulled away from him, though her silly right eye held enough tears to spill over. She brushed them away and smiled as Corrine came around the corner with a plate bearing one-fourth of four different doughnuts.

"All your favorites," she declared, and Sterling half-laughed and half-cried as she gathered the girl into her and Luke's embrace.

"You two are my favorites," she whispered, but she did pick up a bite of the raspberry fritter anyway. She was emotional, not dead.

36

Abby fed her baby and rocked Carver until he was good and asleep. She didn't want the two-month-old to disrupt her for even a moment today. The others should be arriving any minute—or they were already here—and Abby got up and gently laid Carver in the crib with Canyon.

Hilde had a baby monitor in here, and Abby slipped away and hurried down the hall to the kitchen and living room of the enormous house where Hilde and Gabe lived. Sure enough, plenty of her sisters-in-law had arrived—including Sterling. Fine, she wasn't technically a sister-in-law yet. But Abby would do whatever she had to in order to make Sterling a Young.

Everyone in the room except for Sterling could see how perfect she was for Luke. How Luke had settled into the man he'd been trying to be since beginning to date her.

"We've got lunch," Hilde called, and a couple more women came into the kitchen from the living room. Dani had brought all of her kids and her mother, and her mom tended to the kids in the backyard at the moment.

Georgia had left OJ home with Otis, and she currently pushed on her pregnant belly as a look of pain crossed her face. Abby's heart swelled with love for her, because this might be the only biological baby she and Otis got.

Abby had left Mel with Tex. Cheryl had left Bennett with him too, and he'd said he'd let them bake something and then watch a movie. She and Tex had prayed over Luke and Sterling that morning, and Tex would be anxiously awaiting an update on the conversation happening here today.

"It's a pasta bar from that new place by the post office," Hilde said. "Lynnie went there with her new boyfriend, and she said it's good."

"Mom." Lynnie rolled her eyes. "He's not my boyfriend."

Abby only heard that, because the pretty redhead stood close to her. Others shouted their surprise over Lynnie having a new boyfriend at all, and she glared at her mother until Hilde held up one hand.

"Fine. He's not her boyfriend, but he does come here and pick her up. They go out alone; no group. And it's not for a dance. It's like...he's taking her on dates."

"*That's* the shocking part," Leigh said dryly. She'd left her kids home with Morris, and Gabe had gone over there so Hilde could host all the women here.

"I brought coffee," Michelle sang as she entered the house. That got others to turn, and Ev and Faith went to help her, as they stood closest to the garage exit. Neither of them had brought their kids either, and Abby marveled that all of their husbands could stay home in the middle of the day to tend to babies and children. But they could. Blaze didn't even have a job, and Trace, Otis, Luke, Tex, and Morris weren't doing much right now either.

Mav was likewise retired, as was Jem. Gabe was the only one

still actively working, and he'd taken time off following Canyon's birth to be home with Hilde and the kids.

Sunny stood with Cecily, and neither of them had said much. Abby migrated closer to them as the last of the cup carriers with coffees in them got brought in. She didn't have anything to say; she just wanted them to know they both belonged here.

Sterling stood almost on top of Hilde, her nerves apparent to Abby. She wondered if they were as obvious to anyone else. Her question got answered as Ev said, "No coffee for you, Sterling, until you spit everything out." She actually held Sterling's coffee away from her.

Sterling looked at her with shock moving through her eyes. As she surveyed the group, her mouth closed, and she even lifted her chin in a slight move of defiance. Oh, Abby had seen that behavior before.

"I just need help unraveling a few things about Luke," she said.

"He knows you're here, right?" Georgia asked. "Because Otis said I shouldn't say anything if he doesn't know." She threw Abby a nervous look. "I mean, this is *Luke*. He'd *hate* this."

"He knows I'm here," Sterling said. "He knows I'm grappling with a few things between us right now."

"What things?" Hilde asked gently. "And I'm not sure how you think we can help."

Sterling leveled her gaze at Hilde. "Career and family things. You're selling your store."

"That's...not common knowledge." Hilde threw a look around the group, her eyes not landing on any one of them.

"I'll say it's not," Abby said. "I haven't heard that."

"You quit at the library," Sterling said before Hilde could provide more details. "Ev doesn't dance anymore. I just...I've been working for my *whole life* to make Deep Purple what it is. The past couple of years have been the worst years of my life, and I'm supposed to give all of that up for the chance to marry Luke and have babies?"

Silence filled the whole house, and that was saying something, because this place was huge.

"Yes," Cecily finally said. She stepped out of the wings and up to the island where almost everyone else stood. "There is no greater blessing than that of a good man and a big family." She smiled around the room, her eyes finding each woman's there and holding on for a moment. "At least, that's what my momma used to say. Then I had nine boys, and she never said it again."

Abby burst out laughing, along with everyone else there. Still, what Cecily had said was true. She looked at Sterling, so much love for the woman filling her. "A job becomes just a job," she said. "But my family is so much more. It's my life. It's what I want my life to be filled with." She reached for Cheryl and took her hand, and they smiled at one another. Not bonded through blood, but through marriage. Through friendship. Womanhood. Motherhood.

"It's messy, and complicated, and loud sometimes. I'm not as nurturing, maybe, as others, but I love my kids, and I wouldn't trade anything for them." She looked over to Georgia, who wore wide eyes. "Right, Georgia?"

Sterling's attention moved to her, and she said, "I'm so sorry, Georgia. I'm so insensitive."

"No," Georgia said quickly. "It's a struggle I imagine most of us here have gone through." She nodded to Hilde, to Faith, to Ev. "I haven't given up my bookshop. I can't seem to do it. Maybe I'll feel differently after this little girl comes. But we each make our own decision about that, and I happen to go to God first, then Otis second, and then back to God to make sure I'm doing the right thing for me—and for our family."

Sterling nodded, and sniffling, reached up to wipe her eyes. "Okay. Thanks, Georgia."

"There's more, though, right?" Ev asked, finally relinquishing the cup of coffee to Sterling.

"It's personal," she said. "I don't want to betray Luke."

"I'll bet it has to do with those pictures of him with all the women," Ev said, almost like Sterling had confided in her previously. Which, she may have done, as Sterling and Ev were closer than Sterling and Abby.

Sterling glared at her. "I told you. It's personal."

Abby grinned then, and she moved closer to the island too. "Sterling, I think I can say with one-hundred percent certainty that Luke is not interested in anyone else. He's blind to those other women."

"I know that," Sterling said.

"Do you?" Faith challenged. "Because I think we have a way of tuning out how our cowboys look at us."

Sterling simply blinked at her, and nope, she didn't see it. Abby hadn't been able to for a while either.

"He loves you," Dani said simply. "Mav thinks he's known it for a while, and he's scared out of his mind."

"That about sums up Luke," Cecily said in almost a whisper. "The man has been forging ahead in his life for years, covering up all the things he's afraid of, until he's not afraid of them anymore." She smiled at Sterling and reached for her. She couldn't quite make it, and Sterling made up the distance.

"It was so hard for him to even start dating again," Leigh said.

Abby put her hand on top of Cecily's and Sterling's joined ones. "He said he didn't trust women. All women. But Sterling, he trusts you."

Georgia put her hand on top of Abby's. "Don't give up on him yet."

One by one, the rest of the women put their hand on the pile, some of them saying things and some just showing solidarity. Sterling wept, and since her hand was on the bottom, when she dropped it, they all pulled back.

"I love you all," she said. "So much. You have no idea. I have no family here. No family really anywhere who cares about me at all." She sagged into Hilde, who wrapped her up tight and held on.

Abby wanted to be part of that, feel that sisterhood and bonding love. So as they all piled into a group hug, she did too.

"*We* care about you," Cecily said forcefully. "We love you."

Abby let that love wash through her too, and she needed it more than she knew. She'd come here with the goal of supporting Sterling and making sure she knew how much Luke loved her and wanted to be with her. She hadn't expected to need the cleansing power of these women's love in her own life.

But she did, and it was beautiful and made of pure joy.

"Okay," Sterling said. "Okay." She pulled in a deep breath and their little huddle broke up. Abby wasn't the only one brushing at her eyes then, and Sterling's shoulders lifted as she breathed in again. "I think I can eat now."

"Yes," Hilde said with authority. "Let's eat."

Abby stayed beside Georgia this time, and as they waited to go through the pasta bar, she leaned in and said, "Any luck on the name?"

Georgia rolled her whole head and said, "No. Ever since I showed him that list of dog names and his was on it, Otis is convinced we have to come up with something that could never land on a list like that."

Abby grinned. "So Sweetie is out?"

Georgia threw her a death glare, but Abby had gotten plenty of those over the years of their friendship. "And so is Summer, Andi, and Daisy."

"Oh, I like Daisy," Ev said, clearly not having heard the beginning of the conversation. "I'm going to tell Trace if we have a girl— and you don't use Daisy—that I like that."

"Is that an announcement?" Faith asked.

"No," Ev said quickly. "Not at all."

"Okay," Faith said. "Then I'll make mine—Blaze and I are going to have another baby in January."

The oxygen got sucked out of the house, and Abby could only blink. Then she joined her voice to the cheering and congratulations that rose from the women she loved most.

37

Luke kept adding kindling to the fire until a nice flame licked up into the sky. Then he added on a couple of logs, which would be enough to keep him and Corrine happy and fed for the next couple of hours.

He'd brought hot dogs, chips, and fruit for tonight's weenie roast, and then they'd have s'mores just like he used to do with his brothers and parents. He hadn't heard from Sterling, and he wasn't sure he would tonight.

He didn't like that he couldn't talk to her, and after seeing her that morning and hearing some of her concerns about being with him, his confidence had taken a real nosedive. Would she really break up with him because he was famous?

"She might," he muttered to the crackling fire. He couldn't stand the thought of that. He couldn't stand the thought of attending another wedding that wasn't his. Even though he was happy for Denzel and Michelle—he really was—he had a hard time feeling it through all the jealousy.

"Corrine," he said, and his little girl looked back at him from where she'd been collecting kindling. "We have enough, jelly bean. Come on back."

She did, and Luke smiled at her with all of the nurturing love he had. "Come sit with Daddy while the fire burns down."

Corrine put her kindling in the pile and moved to sit on Luke's lap. He leaned back in the camp chair he'd brought and sighed. "It's real pretty up here," he said.

"Sure is," Corrine said, and she spoke with such a cute Wyoming twang.

"Baby, I'm thinkin' real hard about something."

Corrine tilted her head back and looked at him. "Like what?"

"Asking Sterling to marry me." He looked into his daughter's eyes. "How does that make you feel?"

"Would she be my momma?"

"Yes," Luke said. "And she'd probably come live in our house with us. I mean, maybe." They hadn't talked about that at all. Him and Sterling, nor him and Corrine. His house wasn't big by any means, because he'd bought it during his anti-women and anti-marriage phase, when he'd sworn off romance entirely and planned to never marry again.

"Or we could get a new house," Corrine said. "Uncle Gabe got a new house."

"Yeah," Luke said. "But Aunt Sunny moved into Uncle Jem's house."

"Oh, right," Corrine said. "And Auntie Faith did too."

"Yeah, she did." Luke let his mind wander wherever it wanted, and it came back to Sterling over and over again. He would not watch a woman walk down the aisle to meet him and become his wife if he did not love her. And especially if he didn't believe and know without a doubt that she loved him.

And right now, Sterling had doubts.

Luke sighed again, and he heard the lovesick quality of it. That made him sit up straighter, take notice of his own thoughts and feelings.

"I'm in love with her," he said out loud.

"I love her too." Corrine sighed as she leaned back into him. "She's so nice to me, Daddy. Even nicer than Momma was."

Luke cocked his head. "Really?"

"Yeah."

"What did...?" Luke wasn't sure he wanted to know what Mandi had done with Corrine during their visits. She'd had a supervisor, and he'd not heard of anything nefarious happening. He shook his head to dislodge the thoughts. He had to let this go, and while he wasn't super great at that, he'd been working on it.

He couldn't control Mandi. He couldn't even control Corrine, not really. He couldn't make Sterling's decisions for her. Even if he wanted to do all of those things, it wasn't within his power—and it didn't need to be.

Peace filled him as he settled back into his chair. "I don't want you sayin' anything to Sterling, now, okay? When a man asks a woman to marry him, it's a surprise."

"Is it?" Corrine asked. "So when I get married, it'll be a surprise?"

"Not the wedding," he said, chuckling. "When a man asks you to marry him, bean, it's called a proposal. I'll propose to her."

"Maybe Sterling will propose to you."

"I should hope not," he said with a measure of darkness in his voice. "It's usually the man who does it, baby."

"Will I get a new dress for the wedding?"

Luke smiled up into the dusky sky. "Yeah, jelly bean. You'll get a new dress for the wedding."

She'd gotten one for every wedding since Mav and Dani's, over six years ago now. Luke let himself think through the past several years. He couldn't believe how far he'd come, how much he'd grown. When he'd first arrived back in Coral Canyon, he'd been spitting nails. He carried that anger with him for a long, long time, and sometimes, he still felt flashes of it.

That was when he'd been calling on his faith and using it as a shield against the more negative things in his life. His feelings of inadequacy. His loneliness. His doubts that he could even be loved by someone as good and kind and talented as Sterling.

"Okay," he said when he couldn't hold another thought in his head. "Let's roast hot dogs."

Luke got several messages from Sterling when he reached a certain point on the mountain, and he forced himself to wait until he and Corrine had reached pavement to check them.

I hope you're having a good time! I want lots of pictures.

Had a great lunch with all the wives. I love them so much, and they are so kind and smart.

"Smart," he mused, wondering what she'd told them—and even more importantly, what they'd said in return. He could call Abby and demand to know, and a former version of himself might have done just that.

But Luke wanted to trust Sterling. He'd seen her texts to his sisters-in-law before, and she had never told them too much about their relationship. He didn't think she'd start now. He still wasn't sure why she needed to get together with them and go over—"Oh."

"What, Daddy?"

"She has no family," Luke said as he looked up into the rearview mirror. Corrine wore a smudge of dirt on her cheek, but neither she nor Luke cared. He liked seeing her play outside, hike with him, dip her feet in the mountain stream, and beg for him to build a fire so they could have roasted marshmallows together at night.

He'd planned a trip like this for the two of them every year since moving back here, and it had become a daddy-daughter tradition. Maybe, if he ever had more kids, he could take them too.

"Sterling has no sister to brainstorm things with, the way Sunny does," he said. "Or Faith. She talked to Trinity about Blaze all the time. Sterling just has herself." The wives *were* her family; she saw them as sisters, and she'd needed help to go through her thoughts—about him, about his fame, about whatever else she was questioning.

"Yeah, she said her family lived far away and didn't talk to her," Corrine said matter-of-factly. "But it's not her fault."

"It's not," Luke confirmed as he looked back at his phone.

I just booked four new clients! she'd sent. *Thank you for the testimonial. Apparently, having a billionaire endorsement means something.*

You should be back today. Text me when you have service so I know you're alive?

Happiness streamed through him that he'd been able to help her in some small way. He'd tried to offer her money in the past, and she'd shot him down quickly. She'd gotten her small business loan, but as far as Luke knew, she hadn't done anything with it. He needed to talk to her about her plans for Deep Purple, and what month she wanted to get married, and if he had any chance at being in her life for a long, long time.

We just got back to the land of the living WiFi, he texted her. *We're going to go home and shower, and then Blaze wanted to have dinner with me and Jem to go over rodeo stuff for next week.*

Sounds good, she said.

So I'll see you tomorrow?

Yeah, she said. *Tomorrow.*

Luke did what he said, and while Corrine played in the tub, he unloaded all of their camping gear, checked it, and put it away. Once inside, he locked all the doors, told Corrine to stay in her room or on the living room couch, and then he stepped into the shower. He didn't mind the dirty water as it swirled around his toes and went down the drain. That, to him, signaled a good day's work. In this case, play, but Luke would take it nonetheless.

He got dressed, and he took Corrine over to Blaze's house. Jem was already there, with Sunny and both of his kids, and Corrine skipped off happily to play with Rosie, Cole, and Cash in Blaze's basement.

"How was camping?" Jem asked as Luke sank onto a barstool. Faith stirred something on the stovetop, but Blaze had already laid out the food—and he'd catered it.

"Good," Luke said with a smile. "I love the Tetons."

"See any wildlife?" Blaze asked.

"Just birds," Luke said. "Nothing too exciting, but we weren't in the backwoods or anything."

"You got out of the backyard," Sunny said. "That's more than we do." She smiled at Jem, who blinked back at her.

"You want to go camping, Sunshine?"

"Not even a little bit," she said with a laugh. "But your kids might."

"I'm lucky the kids are here at all," he said. "Trust me, just living in Wyoming is like camping compared to Las Vegas."

"He's not wrong," Blaze said.

Luke loved the buzz of life in his brother's house. He liked the way the conversation flowed from one thing to the next, and nothing was too heavy or too hard. He liked that they didn't ask him about Sterling, but kept the discussion on family, children, summertime, or food.

"Let's eat," Blaze said, and Luke got up to get the kids. With them all clamoring up the steps, he held the door for them. Grinning, he followed them all into the kitchen.

"All right," Blaze said. "Who's going to say grace?" He surveyed the kids like it would be an honor to be chosen. "Cole?"

"Yes, sir." Cole folded his arms and squinched his eyes shut. "Dear God, we're so glad we have a family to belong to. We're glad we get to see our cousins all the time, and that Uncle Blaze feeds us such good food. Bless Daddy that we can get a dog. Amen."

"Bless the food, bud," Jem said, turning his laugh into a cough.

Luke didn't even try to cover his laugh. "A dog?" he asked as Jem shook his head at his son.

"We're still working on how to pray," he said as he pulled his boy in for a hug. "Right, buddy?"

"I thought he did okay," Blaze said nonchalantly. "You should get a dog, Jem."

"Blaze Young," Sunny admonished. "I thought I could count on you to tell him that no, we're already drowning and we don't need a dog."

"Drowning?" Blaze asked as he piled sliced brisket onto a bun. "The man doesn't even have a job. He can handle a dog."

Jem raised his eyebrows at Sunny, who shook her head. Luke wasn't getting in the middle of that. Jem had healed and grown considerably in the past couple of years, that was true. But he happened to agree with Sunny—he still had a lot going on, and Jem tended to get overwhelmed easily.

"Blaze, don't tell him to get a dog if his wife doesn't want him to get a dog." Faith smiled at him. "And come try this barbecue sauce before I say it's worthy of eating."

He moved over to do that, and Luke could admit he stared openly. He loved watching Blaze and Faith, because they had such love for one another. If anyone had ever been as dark, grumpy, and angry as Luke, it was Blaze. And yet, there he stood, tasting his wife's barbecue sauce while she laughed and wiped a drop of it out of his beard.

Their baby sat in a play seat in the living room, and Faith was already pregnant again. On the surface, their life looked perfect, and even if it wasn't on a deeper level, Luke still wanted it.

He made sure Corrine got her food, and he helped Rosie get a bottle of soda pop from the fridge before he loaded his plate and took it to the table.

"All right, boys," Blaze said. "Let's talk rodeo."

Luke took a big bite of his brisket sandwich and looked at Blaze. He didn't really have anything to do with the rodeo, but Blaze and Jem had been volunteering in schools this year, and they'd judged some of the junior PRCA events around the area this summer.

They'd been asked to call the rodeo this year, and they'd start on Monday and go all the way through Friday, to the finals. That night, as part of their after-program, Blaze had suggested Country Quad do a short set of five songs, and Morris had jumped all over that.

Luke suspected he was bored, as Morris loved to be busy the same way he did.

So they'd be playing, but then Blaze and Jem had come up with the idea of having Luke there the whole time, on the drum set, for big moments before a score was revealed, or to provide a couple of beats after a badly told Dad-joke.

He'd agreed, but as he thought about why, he wasn't sure. He really just wanted to stay out of the spotlight for a while, because then Sterling wouldn't have a reason to doubt him.

You can't stay out of the spotlight forever, he told himself. Morris expected to hear from King Country by the first week of August, and they all expected to be back in the recording studio once school began. Then they could potentially tour next summer, depending on how things went.

Blaze outlined things for them—again—and Luke nodded along in all the right places. "Will I have access to a mic?" he asked.

Jem blinked at him. "Why would you need access to a mic?" He tossed a look over to Blaze. Sunny and Faith likewise watched him, and it almost felt like scrutiny.

"Uh, I don't know. Maybe I'll want to say something?" Luke didn't mean to phrase it like a question, and he hadn't fooled anyone anyway.

Blaze scoffed. "What do you want to say, Luke?"

He wanted to stuff his mouth with brisket and stalk out of the house. Out of all of them, he didn't express himself the most often or the best. But these were his brothers, and he loved them. They loved him dearly. He could tell them.

"I don't know," he mumbled, clearly not brave enough to say it outright. "Maybe something about how I love Sterling, and maybe she could come up to the box, and I could ask her to marry me."

Faith choked and started coughing. Sunny sucked in a breath, which seemed to make her eyes bug out of her head.

"Daddy loves Sterling," Corrine said. "He's gonna propose, but it's a secret."

Luke managed to chuckle, and his daughter beamed at him. He loved her too, and he really should involve Corrine in the proposal.

Blaze grinned and grinned and grinned, but Jem considered Luke for an extra moment past comfortable.

"Do you really want to do that?" Jem asked.

"No," Luke said instantly. "It's a very bad idea, though she will be there. She'd hate the public proposal."

"I'll say," Faith said after she'd swallowed half of her peach soda. "But you love her, Luke? That's so sweet." She smiled at him and covered his hand with hers for only a beat of time.

"I need help with the proposal," Luke said. "So would you stop grinning like a madman and give me some ideas I can use?"

Blaze burst out laughing then, and Jem took over the maniacal smiling.

"Is she going to say yes?" Blaze asked.

"I...." Luke hung his head. "I'm not entirely sure," he admitted. "I haven't told her that I love her." He looked up and around the table. "I'm going out of order, aren't I?"

"Maybe start with an 'I love you,' at the rodeo," Sunny said. "Privately. And then, I don't know. Propose later?" She glanced over to Jem. "Jem waited forever, so I wouldn't go to him for advice."

"Forever?" he demanded.

"You weren't fast," she threw back at him, and Luke started laughing.

"We're married already," he said. "So it obviously wasn't *forever*."

Faith smiled at Luke and said, "Luke, I know she loves you too. But I agree with Sunny. Maybe have a conversation with her first, and then see where your heart takes you."

"What if my heart is wrong again?"

"No, brother," Blaze said firmly. "You didn't even use your heart last time."

"This time, you will," Jem added. "But not on Friday. *Promise* me you won't propose on Friday."

"Don't worry," Blaze said as he leaned over his sandwich again. "We won't give him a mic."

38

Sterling had not seen Luke at church that day. She knew he and Corrine had made it out of the mountains safely, as he'd texted her yesterday once he'd returned. She'd expected to see him, perhaps even sit by him as she had in the past.

Even if Luke didn't come to church, he sent his daughter with his parents, but she hadn't seen Corrine at all.

Disappointment cut through her as she walked through the parking lot to get to her car. Wyoming almost always had some type of wind whipping across it, and today's seemed to want to tear down trees. Georgia had told her once that she liked to go watch the cows graze in their fields after church on Sundays, so she could really mull over what had been said.

Sterling liked the slower pace of the day too. Heck, she liked the slow pace of small-town living and country life, and she decided to take a scenic drive around the valley before heading home for her solitary lunch. She'd probably pull something out of the freezer and heat it up, and she could afford a little while to drive and appreciate the world around her.

So she drove up the apple highway, smiling at the orchards that lined both sides of the road in some spots. She'd come apple-picking in years past, but she hadn't been in a while. Perhaps she could take Luke and Corrine, and they could make an afternoon out of it.

She turned on the road that ran east between Dog Valley and Coral Canyon, passing a couple of out-of-the-way barbecue stands that had plenty of cars at them this fine Sunday near lunchtime. She went by the police dog academy that was now a therapy dog training facility, and she came down the road that led in front of Abby and Tex's farm.

They lived next door to Abby's brother and his wife, and they also had a farm. There weren't any trucks in their driveways, which meant they probably hadn't made it home from their Sabbath meetings yet. The Youngs seemed to get together in some fashion every Sunday, whether that meant all of them or just smaller factions. Sterling had eaten with Jem and Blaze one week, then Morris and Gabe another, and then the whole family on still other occasions.

Everyone had been nothing but kind and accepting, and sure, Sterling had seen them watching her and Luke, almost like they expected something to happen, but no one knew what.

She found herself weeping as she got closer to town, and she didn't even know why.

You are not alone.

The pastor's words from his sermon that day shouted loudly in her ears, and Sterling eased up on the gas pedal and moved to the side of the road. She couldn't see through all the tears, and she knew why she was crying.

She wasn't alone, and she hadn't felt alone since starting her romantic relationship with Luke. He'd healed that broken, cracked part of her that felt unlovable and undesirable. He'd given her a family, something she'd been longing for without even realizing it.

"I have to make things right with him," she said miserably. "I love him, and I love his family." She looked up into the rearview mirror, appalled at the mess she found looking back at her.

"Can he ever love me?" she whispered.

An incredible calm enveloped her, and Sterling once again closed her eyes and cried. It felt like a loving, kind father wrapping her in an embrace—something she hadn't had in her life, ever.

But she had a *Heavenly* Father, and right now, He held her and told her how very much He loved her. How very much He cared for her. How He had never truly left her alone.

Her phone rang, and she tried to pull everything back into place. She sniffled as she got it out of her purse and saw Luke's name there. She couldn't answer, not right now. Her voice would be tinny and pinched, and he'd know instantly that she'd been bawling on the side of the road.

She let the call go to voicemail, but Luke only followed that up with a text. *Where are you? Tex said you were at church today, and it ended over a half-hour ago. I thought you'd be home by now.*

He was at her house.

Sterling sat up straight and looked at herself in the mirror again. Her hair—always a lost cause—looked a little like a rodent's nest. No amount of finger-combing would fix it, and Sterling bypassed the idea and reached for the glove box, where she hopefully had some napkins.

She did, and she cleaned up her eye makeup and wiped her nose. Her skin felt a bit stretched and parched, but there wasn't much she could do about that. She had another ten-minute drive before she'd arrive at her house, and hopefully, the redness in her eyes would be gone by then.

I went for a drive around town, she said. *I'm almost home now.*

We're here. Me and Corrine. Can we wait for you?

Sure, she said. *I didn't know you were coming, or I wouldn't have gone for a drive.*

It was going to be a surprise.

"Great," she muttered as she put her phone down and started driving. Now she'd ruined the surprise. Why did everything about today feel so...weird?

The moment she turned the corner on her street, Sterling slowed again. The house on the corner had a sign staked in the lawn near the street, and she'd never seen that before.

It had her name on it.

The next house down had a sign too, and it looked very much like an almost-eight-year-old girl had colored it. It had the word "We" on it.

"Missed" read the next sign.

"You," sat on the last one.

Her house was the fifth one down, and Luke and Corrine sat on her front steps. They both looked up as she eased on by, and as she turned into her driveway, they'd both gotten up and had already started to come toward her.

Coming home to them was so much better than anything Sterling could've dreamed, and she barely had the car in park before she got out of it.

Sterling, we missed you.

No one had ever missed her before. Not for a good, long while, at least.

"You're here," Corrine said as she skipped ahead of her daddy. "We brought you lunch. Daddy went right inside your house, but we came right back out."

"It's okay." Sterling lifted the girl into her arms, though she was getting big. "I think you grew while you were camping this week." She grinned at Corrine. "I missed you so much."

Corrine hugged her tightly, with both her arms and her legs, and Sterling pressed her eyes closed as such strong emotions moved through her. She did want kids—but only if they were Luke's too.

She put Corrine on her feet, and Luke said, "Jelly belly, go get lunch out, would you?"

"Yes, Daddy." She skipped off toward the front door again, where Sterling had hung her red, white, and blue Fourth of July wreath earlier this month. She had a special birthday wreath she planned to hang on her birthday, and then Corrine's.

But right now, her eyes met the dark, stormy depths of Luke's, and she wanted to rush into his arms. She sensed he needed a minute, though, so she stood back.

"You missed me, huh?"

"So much," he said, his voice sounding like gravel in his throat. "It was good for me to get out into the mountains, though." He looked up toward them, both of his hands safely tucked away in his pockets. He wasn't exactly guarded, but he wasn't exactly open to her either.

"I got a lot of clarity there."

"Did you?" Sterling took one step closer to him. "About what?"

"Us," he said, bringing his eyes back to hers. "Me and you. Me, you, and Corrine."

Sterling drew in a slow breath, waiting. She'd kissed the cowboy first, but she wasn't going to start blurting out anything before he had a chance to speak. He'd clearly come here to do just that, and she wanted to hear what he had to say.

He pulled his hands out of his pockets and threw them up into the air. Clearly frustrated, he said, "And I can't help it." He looked a little defeated as he added, "I'm in love with you." He started nodding. "Yeah. There it is. I love you."

Sterling's smile started slowly, but grew swiftly and intensely. "You don't sound happy about it."

He ducked his head, and she watched those powerful shoulders lift as he breathed. "I'm worried it's too fast," he admitted. He lifted his head slightly, but she could only see his nose and mouth. No eyes, which so wasn't fair. "And I don't want to pressure you, because you're having some doubts about us right now, and I don't know. I just can't deny it anymore."

"You don't need to deny it," she whispered. She flew to him and gripped his shoulders. He looked right at her. "I love you, too."

His eyes widened, and she giggled and then laughed. "You—do?"

"Come on," she whispered as she edged ever closer to him. She knew she stood in her driveway, but she decided she didn't care. "You have to know how I feel about you. I haven't hidden it, and we've talked about marriage, and family, and kids."

"Once, Sterling," he whispered, but he did put his hands on her hips.

"I love you," she said again. "I want to marry you, and have kids with you, and I'll give up my studio. I don't care. I've been so hesitant about using the small business loan, and I couldn't figure out why. I've been dreaming and sketching out these plans for over a year."

Luke brought them chest-to-chest and pressed his cheek to hers, but he said nothing.

"And it's because now that I have you and Corrine, I don't want Deep Purple."

"Yes, you do," he whispered.

"Maybe, but not in the same capacity." She pulled away so she could see his face. "I want you. I want a family. I want to be a mother to your little girl."

His jaw twitched, and his chin shook, and he said, "I want all of that too. I want you to be so happy, Sterling. If that's expanding Deep Purple to be everything you've sketched out, I will make it happen for you."

"I know you will." She smiled and trailed her fingers down the side of his face. "I'm sorry I was a little hesitant there for a few days. I just—it's hard to be building toward one thing and then meet a fork in the road you weren't anticipating."

"Yeah." He cleared his throat. "And the publicity? The women who are going to take pictures with me?"

"Luke, baby." She shook her head, feeling so silly. "I know where your heart is."

"You own my heart," he whispered.

Supreme satisfaction bolted through her. "Mm, yes, I do." She leaned toward him, her eyes drifting closed. "Are you going to kiss me now, or what?"

"Right out in the open?"

"I didn't see any paparazzi on the way here," she whispered, and she waited for his lips to touch hers. When they did, an inferno roared to life, because Sterling had never been kissed by a man who loved her.

She'd never had something so sweet, so tender, so good.

"Daddy," Corrine called, causing Sterling to break the kiss. "Sterling. Lunch is ready. Why are you bein' so slow?"

"Yeah," Luke whispered. "Why are you bein' so slow?" He grinned at her, took her hand, and led her toward her own front door. "Now, we got a few things, because we couldn't agree on what to have, and when that happens, we get everything we each want."

"Oh-ho," Sterling said. "Is that how you do things? I wouldn't have guessed that of you, cowboy."

"Well, she wears me down sometimes." Luke kicked a grin at

Sterling as she went by him, and sure enough, in her kitchen she found her entire peninsula covered with food.

"I wanted spaghetti and meatballs," Corrine said. "With the garlic breadsticks. Yum, yummy."

"And I didn't want pasta," Luke said. "I got a Philly cheesesteak from this little shop down the street from Maggiano's."

Sterling grinned at him. "Of course you did." There was a big bowl of salad too, and strangely enough, fortune cookies.

"We didn't know what you wanted," Corrine said, looking at her with wide, unassuming eyes. "Daddy said you like pasta, but I said you said you wanted to try that new Chinese place."

"So we got you some Chinese," Luke said. "With the idea that if you didn't like it, you could have some spaghetti or—"

"Daddy said he'd share his cheesesteak."

Sterling looked at Corrine, then across all the food—where she did see beef with broccoli and what looked like a chicken and cashew and green bean dish that made her mouth water—to Luke.

"You said you'd share your sandwich?"

"Love does crazy things to a man," he said, slinging his arm around her waist. "Should we eat?"

"Yes!" Corrine cheered, and Sterling went around the counter to the kitchen to get down plates. Luke got out silverware, and it sure felt good to be in the same space together.

Later that night, Luke had taken Corrine to Jem's house and come back to Sterling's. They lay on her couch together, the sun slowly sinking into darkness. He'd brought back brownies and ice cream, and Sterling twined her fingers lazily through his.

"Baby?" he murmured, his lips skating along the tender skin against her collarbone.

"Hmm?"

"When do you want to get married?"

Sterling smiled at the ceiling, wondering when this had

become her life. This man, this relationship, this conversation, hadn't been anywhere on her radar seven months ago. "I grew up in Wyoming," she said. "I'm not afraid of the winter."

"I think you'd look amazing with a fur stole or jacket," he murmured. "I'm just—I don't really care when we get married, but Country Quad might tour next summer. I'd like us to be settled before then, if that's the case." He lifted his head and looked at her, waiting.

"January, then," she said. "The holidays are over. We're not into your birthday month yet. We won't be touching Valentine's Day." She lifted her eyebrows. "What do you think?"

"I think we better go ring shopping if we're going to be married in five months."

Sterling tilted her head, pressing it further into the pillow beneath her. "What do you mean? I can put something together in five months. Can I ask your momma to help me?"

Luke blinked a couple of times, and then he sat up. He ran his hands through all that gorgeous hair and sighed. "Sterling, yeah, sure, you can ask my momma for help. But...I'm Luke Young."

All the pieces sliced together. "Ah, I see. You think the wedding needs to be fancy and big."

"No," he said. "I'm saying people on social media will expect that."

Sterling threaded her fingers through his. "So are we going to live our lives according to what they expect?" She leaned forward and peered at him as he ducked his head. "You have no cowboy hat to hide behind, Luke." She smiled as he raised his head.

He did not. "No, we aren't going to live our lives like that."

"If you weren't a billionaire and a country music sensation, where and how would you get married?"

"First, I'm not a *sensation*." He rolled his eyes, though an inkling of a smile touched his mouth. "I'd get married on a farm somewhere, with my family and yours, and then I'd feed everyone steak afterward."

Sterling loved him so. "Well, in January, I think an outdoor wedding is impossible." She'd never planned a wedding before, but she knew a lot of people in town. "But the steak I can do."

She leaned over and kissed his cheek. "If you'll pay for it, I will arrange the perfect wedding for both of us."

"Done," he said. "Corrine will want to be involved. She was crying when I dropped her off at Jem's."

"She will be at my side every step of the way," Sterling promised, her smile shining through her whole soul. "And to think, I was pulled over on the side of the road, sobbing, when you called today."

"You—what?"

Sterling lay back down and sighed. "Nothing. Can you just kiss me again?"

He snuggled into her side, his head against her heartbeat. She wove her fingers through his hair, another sigh pulling through her, this one much less frustrated.

"You're going to tell me about this," Luke whispered. "Okay? I don't want you crying on the side of the road and me not knowing about it."

She nodded. "Okay, but not tonight, okay? I just want...this, tonight." She wanted him for always, and she could scarcely believe that her dreams had all come true, that she had the love of this cowboy—her beastly prince with a heart of gold.

"I can't believe this," Sterling said as her phone started going off. She stabbed at the notices from her online web booking service to clear them, then she tapped to call Luke.

"Heya, baby," he said. "What's up?"

"I just got three appointments for tomorrow," Sterling said, her chest starting to collapse.

"Three?"

"The whole morning is booked!" She wanted to throw her phone out. "I swear I blocked off tomorrow."

"Hey, it's fine," he said. "Do the appointments. Are they new customers?"

"I don't know." Sterling paced away from her ready studio to the back sliding door. She loved standing here, and she drew a hint of peace just from the position. She and Luke had been talking a lot the past week and a half. Her house was too small to keep her studio and house Corrine.

If she moved in with Luke, the house would be full. He wanted to look for something they could buy together, where they could stay long-term and raise their family, somewhere with a separate entrance for her massage studio. She'd agreed, and they'd start looking once Corrine started school again in a couple of weeks.

Meanwhile, he'd taken her to the jewelers in town, and she'd pointed out things she liked and didn't like. The process had taken a while, because Sterling had literally never looked at diamond rings with the intent of wearing one before. Never, ever.

"It's my birthday," she whined. "We were going to take Corrine for breakfast and then go horseback riding." Not that she spent a lot of time on the back of a horse. But Luke said he'd get everything saddled, and they'd be on Bryce's property, and it would be fine. Fun, even.

"It's fine," he said. "We can move it to lunch, and then go in the afternoon. I'll call Bryce right now."

"Are you sure?"

"Sure I'm sure."

The last of the fight left Sterling. "All right. I'll text you when my last appointment ends."

The following morning, Sterling ran through her clients the way she normally did. She'd never heard of these people before, but they'd all said they knew Luke, so she'd ask them about him once each appointment began. She got out bottles of water. She sipped coffee. She stood at the back door.

And when it was almost time for her first appointment, she made sure the front door was unlocked. She'd only taken one step away from it when it opened again, and she turned to greet a woman named Louise Luck.

But a woman didn't step into her house.

Luke did.

"Hey," she said, pure surprise running through her. "What are you doing here?" She looked behind him, anticipating the arrival of her client.

He didn't answer, but looked past her too. She turned again at the sound of more footsteps entering her house. "Hit it, boys." Tex started playing the guitar, his smile so, so big.

Trace joined him, as did Otis. With Luke, the whole band of Country Quad had come, and she watched as Corrine came inside and slipped her hand into her daddy's.

She recognized the tune, because it was one she heard every year on this day.

"Happy birthday to you." Luke sang by himself, the guitars getting quieter so he could be heard above them. Sterling held back tears while he sang, and she lost the battle when Corrine sang the last couple of lines with him.

She dropped to her knees and hugged the girl, then stood up and took Luke's face in her hands. She kissed him while his brothers whooped, and Sterling didn't even feel bad that she'd kissed him first.

He laughed and pulled away. "Happy birthday, baby," he said. "Corrine?"

She turned and went right back out onto the front porch. His brothers had stayed in the kitchen, and they started playing again, this time a soft, slow ballad she recognized as one of theirs.

Corrine entered the house with a huge bouquet of pink roses, and she gave them to her father. Luke looked at them for a moment before he focused on Sterling. "I love you," he said clearly. "I booked your whole morning, so I could change our plans for the day."

"You did *what*?"

He grinned, though Sterling couldn't believe he'd done that. She'd been so upset too.

"I have a couple of gifts for you." He nodded to Corrine again, and she held up an envelope.

Sterling took it from her, not sure if she should smile or not. She gave Luke a look as she lifted the unsealed flap on the envelope. She pulled out a hand-drawn note that said COUPLES MASSAGE across the top.

Her eyes darted right back to Luke's.

"It's in an hour," he said. "It's with Martina and an actual woman named Louise. I was told by all the wives that they don't work at Red Carpet, and that you like them, and that I would too."

Sterling's whole heart melted. "You got me a massage?"

"Yes, I did. And selfishly, I'm getting one too." He grinned at her and looked at his daughter again. Corrine held up a greeting card this time, sans envelope, and the front read *you're invited*.

She took it, noting that this was one of those fancy rolled paper cards from the drugstore. It had a red truck on the front, with a couple of suitcases in the bed. She loved it, and she loved the invitation inside even more.

"You're inviting me to go on tour with you?"

"I waited too long last time," he said. "I figured I better get a headstart this time."

She laughed and shook her head. "I'll have to check my schedule." She cocked her eyebrows at him as the song his brothers played changed.

They both looked at Corrine, and she held up a black ring box. Sterling's breath caught in her chest, and her pulse accelerated.

Luke got down on his knees, took the ring box from his daughter, and pulled her to his side. They both looked up at her, him with those pink roses in one hand and the ring in the other, Corrine encircled by both.

"*We* love you," he said. "We want you in our lives. We want to be a family with you." He opened the box to reveal a beautiful diamond ring in exactly the cut she liked—princess.

Her prince looked at his daughter and nodded. Corrine looked up at her. "Will you marry my daddy?"

"Yes," Sterling said in a whoosh of air, realizing in that moment that Tex, Trace, and Otis were playing the wedding march behind her. "Yes, I'll marry him."

Luke beamed with all the power of a star as he slid the ring onto her finger. Then he handed the roses to Corrine, who moved past her to take them into the kitchen, and got to his feet.

"I've wanted you for a long time," he whispered.

"I've wanted *you* for a long time." She stepped into his arms, feeling like she fit just right.

"I love you," they said together, and then Luke kissed her. Sterling had thought her life had changed on New Year's Eve with that first kiss she'd shared with Luke—and it had.

She'd thought she'd never experience a better kiss than the one he'd given her after he'd told her he loved her. At the time, it was the best thing she'd ever experienced.

But now, as she kissed her fiancé—this lovely man she was going to marry—a new winning kiss emerged.

She broke it when she realized the guitar playing had stopped. "Did they leave?"

"Yes, they did," he said, his mouth against her ear. "You're mine for the rest of the day."

"Mm, I like the sound of that." She stepped back and smiled at him. "You give good gifts, Luke Young."

"Georgia helped," he said. "She's the best gift-giver in the family."

"I'll have to thank her then."

"She helped me find something we can do together, and of course, I had to get all of the wives' opinions on the ring." He half-rolled his eyes. "Abby was quite upset I didn't go with her choice."

Sterling gazed down at her hand. "I love this one."

"I love *you*." He kissed her again, and Sterling didn't have an audience anymore, so she didn't have to stop kissing her fiancé.

39

T race Young had been praying for the right thing to say, the right thing to do, the right thing to be, for months. As he collected his carryon bag and moved down the aisle of the airplane ahead of his son, he trusted Morris would be right behind Harry.

The three of them had just landed in Nashville, and since Harry's senior year of high school didn't start for another week, they'd come a day before the meeting with Cadence Records. That would take place at nine o'clock, bright and early for the summertime in the South, and then Morris had arranged a meeting with the execs at King Country too.

Might as well keep your options open, he'd told Harry and Trace.

Trace honestly wasn't sure what options he wanted for his son. Harry seemed set on moving into country music right out of high school, and the boy had talent in spades. He'd joined a social media site on his seventeenth birthday, after waiting months for

Trace to give his permission, and he posted his songs and talent there.

Georgia had given him the best clip-on mic for his guitar for the videos, almost like she knew he'd go viral if he could just play and be heard. Millions had seen his videos, liked them, and told him he should be on the stages and in the stadiums around the country, entertaining fans.

A heaviness accompanied Trace as he disembarked, because he wanted what was best for his son. His own contracts with Country Quad and King Country weren't over yet, and he had an eleven-month-old baby and a wife back in Wyoming. He couldn't drop everything and manage Harry, nor travel with him.

Bryce moved to Nashville when he was nineteen, he told himself, just as he'd been doing for the past several months.

Bryce had also already lived on his own, had a couple of jobs, and just seemed so much...older than Harry. His son wouldn't be eighteen until February, at which point, it didn't really matter what permission Trace gave him. He'd be a legal adult, and Harry could do what he wanted.

He was such a good boy that he wanted to do what Trace approved of. Their conversations these past several months since he'd turned in that demo tape had been tense, sure. But still loving and good—Trace hoped. The last thing he wanted was to alienate his boy.

"This way," he said once they'd entered the airport. "Got everything?"

Harry had carried on one guitar—after paying the hefty fee for an oversized item—and checked another. So they had to go to baggage claim, as he didn't have anything to wear besides what was on his back.

"Got it all, Dad," he said as Morris came up beside him. Harry had grown and matured a lot in the past couple of years, and he stood only an inch shorter than Trace now. He walked with the stride of a man, and the realization almost made Trace trip over his own feet.

My boy is a man, he thought, his emotions wildly out of control —and he wasn't even the one experiencing the first few weeks of pregnancy hormones. Yes, Ev was pregnant again, just the way she wanted to be. Trace wasn't upset about it either, because he enjoyed a lifestyle where he could be home to help with the kids, and he could bring his family on tour with him.

He could not imagine doing the County Quad tour next summer without Harry in his trailer, at his side, there with him every step of the way. Pure selfishness drove through him, and Trace tried to set it aside.

"Maybe you'll be able to tour with us in the summer," Trace said, the idea popping into his head mere moments before he said it out loud.

"You're assuming King Country is going to set summer tour dates for us," Morris said.

Trace scoffed, but he didn't say anything else. None of the members of Country Quad would tour any other time of year, so if not this upcoming summer, then the next. Trace was secretly hoping for the one almost two years from now, because Ev was due at the end of April, and taking a one-month-old baby on tour wouldn't be easy.

He'd make his opinion known when he had to, and right now, he didn't have to. Morris had a separate meeting with King Country on this trip, and Trace did not envy him for the negotiations he had to endure. The paperwork. Dealing with all the country music execs and their big personalities, and then having to turn around and do it all again, but with his brothers.

"Like Bryce did," Harry said, his eyes filled with hope. "I could play a few shows. Maybe do a solo song or whatever."

"Yeah," Trace said. He fully expected to have a set list for the album in Morris's hand when they left Nashville. Then the band would be back in the white barn-slash-recording studio, perfecting their music. Recording. Practicing for the next and final tour.

"Let's see what they'll say tomorrow," Morris said. Both Cadence and King Country had been tight-lipped about why they wanted to meet, but Trace wasn't new to the entertainment industry. They didn't set up meetings to tell people no. They set up meetings to get them to sign contracts.

At baggage claim, Trace paced, the words he wanted to say brewing inside him. He wasn't sure he could, because he didn't want to slash through Harry's hopes. "I'm gonna go use the bathroom," he grumbled when their bags still hadn't started arriving.

He marched off, hurrying into a stall once he'd gained the restroom. Instead of using the toilet, he turned and leaned his head against the closed door. "Lord," he whispered, not caring if someone heard him praying in the Nashville International Airport. "I want to do what's right. I am my son's father, and I want to act as such. I want to be his biggest fan too; his loudest cheerleader. Please, please help me to know what to do and say this week."

Be honest with him.

Trace's eyes snapped open, the words still reverberating through his soul loudly enough for him to think they echoed in the bathroom too.

God hadn't given him words to use. He hadn't told him exactly what to say or what to do, but He'd also never guided Trace incorrectly. He left the bathroom to find the bags had started arriving, and Harry had his small suitcase with his clothes and toiletries.

"Just waitin' on the guitar," he said as he glanced over to Trace.

Trace didn't have the perfectly honest words ready to deliver to his son. Instead, he simply took him into a hug and said, "I love you, Harry."

Harry hugged him back, as he'd always been so good to do. "I love you too, Dad." He pulled back, his dark eyes so bright. "I really appreciate you coming with me. I know you didn't really want to, and—"

"It's not that I didn't want to," Trace said, turning to face the carousel again. "It's just hard for me to accept that you're old enough to do this. I don't want you to leave, though at the same time, I really want you to leave and go make your own way in the world."

It was a very strange place for a father to be, and Trace glanced over to his son. Like him, Harry never really said more than he needed to, and right now, he simply watched the bags go by.

"I have a whole year of high school left," he finally said.

"Yep." And it would go so fast, Trace knew. He'd been trying to hold onto Harry the way he would a handful of smoke, and no matter what he did, he couldn't do it. Something settled inside him, because he realized standing there after a long day of driving and flying that he wasn't meant to hold onto Harry.

He'd been raising him the best way he knew how, and it was almost time to let him go. His throat narrowed to the point that Trace had trouble swallowing, and even if he'd had something to say, he wouldn't have been able to say it.

"There it is," Harry said, and he moved forward to get his other guitar. He'd packed it in a hard case, and it didn't look like it had been damaged. With everything secure, the three of them made their way outside to ground transportation. Just like he did when the band toured, Morris had arranged everything, and the three of them piled into a big SUV, which took them toward the hotel.

They had two rooms, and it was almost dinnertime. Trace let

Morris be the boss, and he took the keycard he was given, just like he would on tour. Once he and Harry were in their room, with Morris just down the hall, Trace finally felt some of the tension bleed out of his shoulders.

He sank onto the bed, and Harry got to work going over his guitars to make sure they were still in tune and ready for tomorrow.

"Did they say you'd play?" he asked.

"They told Morris to have me be ready to play at Cadence." Harry looked up from the instrument. "Dad, I just want you to know I'm not going to sign anything tomorrow."

Trace's eyebrows went up. "No? What if they offer you an amazing deal?"

Harry smiled, and he was such a handsome kid. His mother was a supermodel, and Trace had been told a time or two that he was good-looking too. Harry definitely benefitted from both sides of the gene pool.

"I've prayed about it," Harry said as his fingers moved over the strings effortlessly. "And I know I'm not supposed to sign the first thing that comes along."

"Maybe they'll both offer, and you can sign the second one." Why Trace was even suggesting such a thing, he didn't know. He cursed himself and told his tongue to stay silent.

Harry shook his head and showed Trace the top of his cowboy hat. "I don't know, Dad. I just know...I feel like this is a good trip. I need to be here, but mostly it's so I can see the options. Really know what they are, instead of how I've imagined them to be."

He met Trace's eye again. "I know you and the uncles struggled for years. I mean, I know it, but I don't at the same time. To me, you've always been big rockstars."

Trace smiled and shook his head. "For a long time, we weren't. We played at every small-town fair we could. On corners in the city. Heck, Otis even wrote a jingle for a western wear company, and we sold that. We thought we'd hit it big." He chuckled, because he had been through more than he sometimes gave himself credit for.

"I can't even imagine what my momma must've thought of us," he murmured. "Luke joined right out of high school, and she threatened me and Tex within an inch of our lives. Said if anything happened to him, she'd hold us responsible."

"For Luke?" Harry laughed. "Uncle Luke is a great guy, but he does what he wants. I imagine he always has."

"Always." Trace stood, another groan-sigh coming from his mouth. "Let's get to dinner, son."

Harry set aside his guitar, and Trace once again paused in front of him. "The difference here, Harry, is you'll be doing this alone. Who am I going to threaten to hold responsible if something happens to you?" He could not stand the thought of something happening to his son. He absolutely could not, and tears burned in his eyes.

Harry saw them, and he gaped at Trace. "Daddy." He stepped into him. "Nothing's going to happen."

"You don't know that," Trace said.

"What is it you're always telling Ev?" He pulled back. "Give it to God, and He'll take care of it. Do you believe that, Dad? Or not?" He genuinely seemed to want to know, and Trace suddenly wanted to hide from his son's scrutiny. From his own lack of faith. From the question placed before him.

"Yes," he finally said. "I believe it. Putting it into action is hard."

"Well, another thing you always tell me is that I can do hard things." Harry grinned at him. "Can we go to that hot chicken place Uncle Mav is always raving about? I want to see if it lives up to the hype."

"Let's check with the manager," Trace said as he followed Harry out of the room. He had told his son that he could do hard things. He'd told Ev to give things to God and let Him handle them, after all she could do.

Now he just had to live both of those things, and he thought about Luke and how he'd said he'd started acting this year as if he had more faith, and he'd constantly asked himself: *What would you do if you had more faith?*

Trace wouldn't feel like throwing up right now. He wouldn't be worried about the meetings tomorrow. He wouldn't feel like he was losing his son just when he'd gotten to know him.

He'd trust in God, give Him the troubles, and step forward in faith—starting with hot chicken, because no, Morris didn't have a plan for dinner.

OTIS YOUNG SAT BESIDE HIS VERY PREGNANT WIFE, THE waiting room too small for his broad shoulders and her big belly to sit side-by-side. At least that was how he felt. A flurry of texts started to come in, and he couldn't read fast enough.

"Oh, boy," he said as his eyes blitzed from one message to another. "They loved Harry's demo at Cadence." He looked up, grinning at Georgia. "They want him to do a solo album." He didn't wait for her reaction before he went back to his phone, his thumbs flying.

So will you help me write more songs, Uncle Otis? Harry had finally ended with. There'd been no news from Trace on the brothers' or family text strings—Otis had gotten all of these messages privately from Harry.

Absolutely, Otis said, because there was nothing he loved more than songwriting. When it was going well, he could produce something in ten or fifteen minutes, and he knew just the style Harry would want.

Old school, like Garth Brooks or Trace Adkins. Travis Tritt, Alan Jackson, and George Strait.

Country Quad was really a rock band with cowboy hats, though Otis made sure he put in lines about pickup trucks and country lanes and small towns too. But Harry would want something more...country, as his voice and his guitar-playing definitely leant itself to that.

I'm not signing anything today, Harry said. *Morris is getting the contracts for us to go over, and of course, I can't start until next year. Plus, Dad says I should try for a couple of other labels too, now that we know there's interest.*

Your daddy's smart, Otis said. *So is Morris. They won't lead you astray.*

Beside him, Georgia groaned, and Otis abandoned his texting. "Hey," he said. "Talk to me."

"The baby is just pushing at me," she complained. She had not felt well for the past month, at least, and Otis had started coming to all of her appointments with her. Deep down, he knew something wasn't right, and he was going to push for another ultrasound today.

Originally, they'd believed that Georgia couldn't get pregnant. She had a mess of endometriosis inside her, and the doctors had told her there was nowhere for a placenta to latch on and feed a baby for nine months. They'd done three scans since she'd discovered her pregnancy in January, and yes, the placenta was small. There was a chance she'd have to be delivered early, especially as the baby grew and needed more and more from her—things she might not be able to get through the placenta.

"Georgia," a nurse called, and Otis leapt to his feet. He helped Georgia up, and she looked whiter than normal.

"Honey," he said, but she shook her head and lumbered toward the door. The nurse's smile slipped when she saw her, but she turned and led them back to a patient room.

"You look...you don't look so good, Georgia," she said.

"I was fine," she said as she braced herself against the wall. She didn't even move to sit down, and Otis couldn't take his hand off her elbow. "Then the baby started moving, and I don't know. I feel...nauseous and a little light-headed."

"Come on and sit," Otis encouraged. He was a strong man, but he wasn't sure he could catch his pregnant wife should she lose consciousness. He got her into a chair, and the nurse took her temperature and blood pressure.

Georgia had a thin sheen of sweat on her forehead, and the nurse said, "I'll be right back with Doctor Letham."

The door had barely closed when Otis said, "I think we should go to the hospital."

"We're literally at the doctor's office, Otis."

"I know, and you look one breath away from passing out." He leaned closer, wishing she could see herself the way he did. She was gorgeous, and strong, and everything he wanted. "I don't want to lose you, Georgia. You know I could."

"No." She shook her head.

"A small placenta can rupture in the last month of pregnancy," he said. "It can tear away from the uterine wall, because the pressure on it is too much. Then what? You bleed out in the doctor's office, because I can't get you to the hospital?" He didn't like what he was saying any more than she did, but the truth was, this pregnancy had risks. A lot of them, and big ones, and Otis's desperation grew alongside Georgia's silence.

Before he could get up and demand she go to the hospital, Doctor Letham entered the room. She looked alarmed already, and she took one look at Georgia and said, "Yes, you need to get over to the hospital."

"I do?" Georgia asked.

"Let's go," Otis said.

Doctor Latham hurried to Georgia and dropped into a crouch in front of her. She took both of her hands. "You have five weeks left, Georgia. Do you want to lose the baby?" She looked over to Otis for two seconds and then focused on Georgia again. "Or leave Otis to raise her alone?"

Georgia's eyes filled with tears. She let them slip down her face without hesitation. "No."

"Then you're going to go to the hospital right now. You're going to have this baby this afternoon. I'm going to be ten minutes behind you. At least at the hospital, they can do something if you start to—if something happens."

Otis stood up. "Thank you, Doctor. Georgia?"

The doctor moved out of the way, and Georgia looked up at him. Then she put her hand in his, and he helped her stand. It seemed to take ages to get from the medical complex where the doctor's office was to the hospital, though they were literally across the street from one another.

He got Georgia in a wheelchair, because she could barely walk, and he wanted to rage at the elevator as it seemed to ascend to the fourth floor with extreme slowness.

"We were told to come in," he told the woman at the check-in desk. "Doctor Latham is right behind us. We were at her office when she sent us here."

Georgia remained awake, though her eyes stayed closed and a wave of pain rolled across her face.

"Please hurry," Otis said. "She has a high-risk pregnancy, and they think there's something going on with the placenta tearing away."

"Bring her back," the woman said, and she took over control of the wheelchair once he did. Another nurse descended on him, asking questions about her name, date of birth, due date, and what complications she had. Otis answered everything the best he could while he stayed right at Georgia's side, helping her out of her clothes and into a gown.

"She's bleeding," a nurse said. "In bed. Get her in bed."

Things *moved* then, and Otis had never felt so helpless. He'd been present for Joey's birth, but that was almost fourteen years ago now, and it hadn't been high-risk or rushed. This felt like a life-or-death situation, and Otis couldn't focus on any one thought.

"Please," he prayed. "That's my wife, Lord, and I need her."

More nurses entered, and Georgia got hooked up to tubes and machines. Otis stayed right at her shoulder, one hand there and the other gripping her fingers.

"She's bleeding?" Doctor Latham asked as she entered the room. She now wore a surgical apron and coat in blue, different than what she'd had on in the office. She came right over to Georgia and Otis and looked at both of them, seemingly at the same time. "Georgia, I'm going to move this to a C-section. We need to get that baby out now."

"Yes." Georgia made quick, little nods with her head, and Otis nodded too.

"Get me an OR," Doctor Latham said. "We need this baby out in the next ten minutes."

Nurses swarmed, and Otis could barely keep up. Bottom line, they were going to put Georgia to sleep, because they didn't have time to do a local anesthetic—the epidural—that would allow her to stay awake during the procedure.

"It's okay," he told her time and again as this person came over to talk to her, and then another one brought over the medicine that would put her out. "I'm here. I'll be here for her and you. It's okay."

Maybe if he said it enough, it would be true. He kept saying it as her eyes drifted closed, and he didn't have her with him anymore.

She got wheeled out of the room, Otis practically running to keep up. His heart raced, and his only thought was to *stay with Georgia! Don't leave her!*

A nurse helped him into a set of sterile clothes, and she made him wash his hands and put gloves on. He kept his eyes on Georgia in the room the whole time, watching as they put up a drape along her waist, hiding the top half of her body.

She then led him to Georgia's shoulder and said, "If you move from this spot, I will escort you out of the room."

"Yes, ma'am," he croaked, and then Doctor Latham entered. The procedure started, and Otis had never seen anything like it.

Only minutes later, his daughter emerged from Georgia's midsection, and she wailed and wailed as an angry red infant who'd been ripped from her warm, comfortable womb.

Otis wept then, because that was his baby girl. A couple of nurses whisked her away to get her clean and dry and warm, and while Otis wanted to go to her, he didn't dare leave his wife.

He watched as they put everything back where it was supposed to go, sewed her up, and covered her. He couldn't believe the sacrifice Georgia had just been through to bring a baby into the world—for him. For her. For their family.

He loved her more than ever, and he leaned down and stroked her hair as he whispered. "I love you, baby. You did so good. She's here, and she's beautiful."

"Here she is."

Otis looked up at the nurse approaching him. "How long until she wakes up?"

"Probably an hour, Otis," Doctor Latham said. "Sorry, that was so rushed. Her placenta had partially torn away from the uterine wall. We were right, and we caught it fast." She smiled, and Otis hugged her.

"Thank you," he said, his gratitude for good doctors suddenly blooming and growing and filling the whole earth.

"Take your daughter," she said. "Hold her tight until Georgia wakes up." Doctor Latham smiled. "I don't think she'll let anyone hold her then."

Otis wiped his eyes and smiled. "Probably not." He took the baby girl from the nurse, surprised at how tiny she was. "She's little."

"Only five pounds and eight ounces," the nurse said. "She's five weeks early, but really healthy and strong." She stroked two fingers down the infant's face. "She's perfect."

Otis leaned over and kissed his baby, such love filling him. They started wheeling Georgia out of the operating room, and Otis took his baby and went with her. They put her in a recovery room, covered her with warm blankets, and told him to call if anything seemed off.

Then it was just her sleeping in the bed, the baby sleeping in his arms, and Otis wondering if he was worthy of all the blessings that he'd just been given that day.

"Sir?" someone asked sometime later. "Did you have a name for her?"

Otis opened his eyes and looked over to Georgia. She hadn't moved, and he had no idea how much time had passed. "I don't dare name her without her momma's approval," he whispered.

The nurse smiled and nodded. "Let me know when you have a name for her, and I'll get all of her name tags made."

He and Georgia hadn't really agreed on names much, not for this baby anyway. She liked Andi, but he felt like it was too common. They'd talked about something religious too, for this baby was such a huge blessing to them. Something unexpected but desperately wanted.

"What should we name you?" he asked the baby. "What would Momma like?"

"Anaya," Georgia said, her voice almost slurred.

Otis jerked his attention to her, but her eyes hadn't opened. She didn't move or speak again. "Georgia, honey?" he asked.

Still nothing.

He looked at his daughter, with her peach fuzz of light brown hair—a mix of him and Georgia. She had the strong Young nose, and she'd probably hate that at some point in her life. Otis loved it, as he enjoyed the way her chin practically disappeared into her neck. She had barely any legs, and a big barrel body and head, and oh, how he loved her.

"Anaya," he said, as it was a name he and Georgia had discussed. It meant "God answers" in the Hebrew origins, which was why Georgia had loved it. She'd said they could call the girl Ana or Andi with that name, and it would still mean something.

Otis wanted his children's names to *mean* something, and no, he didn't want to see them show up on a list for what to name a dog.

"Anaya," he whispered again, the name absolutely right. The nurse came in and checked on Georgia, and he said, "Excuse me."

"Hmm?" She came around to his side of the bed.

"I know what her name is."

"Oh, great." She pulled out a device and tapped a couple of times. "I'm ready."

"Anaya," he said. "A-N-A-Y-A. Lindsey, with an E. Anaya Lindsey Young."

The nurse typed it all in, smiled, and left. Otis scooted closer to Georgia. "After your sister, baby," he said. "I know she's here, and I know she protected you today." Tears flooded his eyes again as he looked at his blessing of a baby who now bore a name that represented God and Georgia's deceased sister.

She was absolutely perfect, and he'd never been more thankful.

40

L eigh Young bustled around the new event center at Whiskey Mountain Lodge, adjusting that flower and tucking this ribbon back into place. Michelle Hinz, who was marrying her brother today, didn't have any family in town, and Leigh had been helping her put together the perfect wedding.

Perfect for the two of them, at least.

She'd rented the banquet hall here at the lodge, which Graham Whittaker and his brothers had just built and opened this past summer. It was quite the drive up the canyon, but Michelle and Denzel just had local family coming to their nuptials.

She'd chosen sage and dusky rose as her colors, and with the white roses and ribbons and rows of chairs, everything looked clean and crisp and coordinated.

Leigh carried her two-year-old on her hip, but Rachelle needed to go to one of her aunts or her grandmother. Leigh hurried over to where her sisters milled about with their husbands and kids.

"Mama," she said, and her mother opened the circle for her to join them. "Can you take her? I'm supposed to be helping Michelle with her dress."

"Sure."

Leigh slid the toddler into her mother's arms, then smiled and nodded at Sheri and Walker—who'd been married for a couple of years now—and then Miranda and Noah, who seemed to be wrestling with their three kids all the time. Leigh knew the feeling, which was why she and Morris had decided not to hurry into having another child.

She didn't care if anyone else did, as both Faith and Everly were pregnant with their second child and their first babies had barely turned a year old. She supposed both Blaze and Trace were quite a bit older than her and Morris, who wouldn't turn thirty until next month.

In the bridal suite, she found Michelle standing in front of the mirror, the back of her dress gaping open. "I'm so sorry," Leigh said as she quickly closed the door behind her.

Their eyes met in the mirror, and Michelle smiled in the soft way she had. "You're fine. I just wanted to see what it looked like with the earrings."

"It's stunning with or without anything." Leigh stepped behind her and started zipping. "They make these clothing zippers the hardest—things—in—the—world—to zip up." She got it and the teeth moved together easily near the top.

It scooped down to the middle of her back, and Leigh adjusted the sleeves along Michelle's biceps. She peered around her and took in the big, loopy lacy design on the front of the dress. "You're so beautiful."

Michelle pressed her cheek to Leigh's, though she was a few inches taller. "Thank you for your help, Leigh."

"I'm just thrilled for you and Den," she said.

"He's okay?" Michelle turned away from the mirror and tucked one of the longer pieces of her hair. "Have you seen him?"

"My daddy and Morris are with him," Leigh said. "I haven't seen him."

Michelle wore a worried look for a moment, and Leigh linked her elbow through hers. "Are you okay?"

"I'm just nervous." She ran her hands down her stomach and took a big breath. "This is normal, right? Were you nervous when you married Morris?"

"The first time or the second time?" Leigh gave her wry look. "Both times, actually." They moved over to a couple of chairs and sat down. "The first time, it was because we were so young. But I loved him so much."

Leigh could see all of the experiences and years she and Morris had shared in that moment, and she smiled. "The second time, I was just hoping he would show up." She gave a light laugh. "I don't think you need to worry about that with Denzel. I've never seen him like this—except when he talks about cars."

Michelle giggled too. "The man loves his cars."

"He did," Leigh said. Denzel had been living on disability and his insurance settlements for the past several years while he recovered from his devastating car accident that had left him enduring a dozen surgeries, lots of broken bones, and years of healing.

He worked with a therapy dog now, and Scout would actually escort Michelle down the aisle. Her daddy had passed a few years ago, and her mother had remarried and moved out of the country. She hadn't been able to get a visa to return to the US, and thus, Michelle was here at the wedding alone.

But with the Youngs, no one was ever alone.

Morris had offered to walk her down the aisle, as had Leigh's father. Michelle had declined them all, saying Scout could do the job. For a while there, she'd said that if she could handle running a coffee shop, she could get herself down the aisle.

Michelle was one of the strongest women Leigh knew, and she attended as many of the wives' events as she could. Due to her job, she didn't come around as often as the rest of them, and Leigh had organized a coffee date for everyone simply so Michelle could come out and join them for a half-hour.

"He's talking about getting back to the shop," Michelle said, studying her hands.

"Yeah, he's said that," Leigh said slowly. She didn't really want Denzel to return to the life he'd had before. He was a talented mechanic, with a mind that could see how all the parts of everything went together. Leigh didn't understand it at all, though she could put together flour, sugar, and chocolate and make something delicious.

But his work on cars led to his obsession with cars, and that had led him to the racecar that had changed his whole course of life.

Someone knocked on the door, and Leigh looked up as Abby poked her head in. "Five minutes," she said. Scout nosed his way into the room too. "I have Scout."

"Come on in," Michelle said, and she got to her feet. "I should get my shoes on."

Abby closed the door behind her and brought the German shepherd closer to them. Leigh helped Michelle with the strap on her heel, marveling at how materials existed to make something look completely clear.

"You look like you're floating," Leigh said. She got to her feet too and smoothed down her rose-colored dress. "You're so beautiful." She kissed Michelle's cheek and took Scout's leash from Abby. It was pure black, with fake diamonds studded into it near the top where Michelle gripped it.

"I'll stay with you until you have to go, and then I'll slip in the side door," Leigh said. The event center here at the lodge had been built with care, and that meant the door right across from the bridal suite led to the front row of the banquet hall.

Michelle had to walk down the hall to the back of the room, and Leigh didn't want her to do any of it alone.

Leigh's emotions quivered right on the edge of her composure, and she let the tears fill her eyes. She would not let them ruin her makeup, though, and instead, she leaned in and hugged Michelle. "Thank you for loving him."

"Thank you for sharing him with me," Michelle whispered back.

Leigh could admit she was overly protective of Denzel. She'd been at his side for the bulk of his recovery over the past handful of years, and they'd both wondered if he'd ever lead a normal life.

Getting a dog had helped him. Having Eric and Rachelle in his life had too. Leigh and Morris dragged him along to nearly every Young family event, dinner, and activity, and he'd come. He'd become part of them.

And now Michelle was too.

Leigh looked at Michelle, and they nodded at one another. "It's thirty seconds," she said. "And then you'll be in the doorway, and Den will be looking at you, and Scout will know just what to do."

Michelle nodded, and Leigh finally stepped away from her. She took Abby's hand, and without her, she wasn't sure she'd be able to leave the room. But she did, and she and Abby slipped across the hall and into the banquet area.

After the ceremony, Michelle and Denzel were serving a coffee bar, complete with a whole host of flavorings, creams, and varieties. They even had iced coffee ready.

Since the wedding was basically Leigh's family and then the

Youngs, they'd decided to offer to provide the dinner. Denzel and Michelle had graciously accepted, and Morris had taken care of the wedding dinner.

The man loved good food, and he'd ordered from one of the more upscale restaurants in town. They were serving chicken, beef, and salmon, and Leigh moved quickly to Denzel, who stood at the altar, all dressed up and ready for this.

"You are amazing," Leigh said as she hugged him. "She's coming."

Denzel looked like he might bolt, but he stayed very still, his cane nowhere in sight. Leigh hadn't been in the room when he'd entered, so she wasn't sure if he'd used it or not. She did know he'd been practicing the walk without it, and she'd been praying with every ounce of faith she had that her brother could have the wedding he wanted to provide for Michelle.

Then, Leigh slipped next to her husband and leaned into his strength. "Hey," he said. "How'd it go? She's ready?"

"She should be arriving in the doorway at any moment." Harry and Bryce were playing the prelude music with their guitars, and Tex stood at the back wall, watching for Michelle. Then he'd signal the boys, grab his guitar from the stand, and then Country Quad was playing *You Are the Reason* as Michelle walked down the aisle.

Once they all took their seats, the ceremony would begin.

Leigh kept her eyes trained on the doorway, and she sucked in a breath as Michelle filled it. "Oh." She couldn't say anything else, but she and Morris got to their feet, and that caused a ripple effect as everyone else did too.

The light chatter stopped, and the music changed, both in the matter of a single second. Michelle's smile shone like the sun, and she held Scout right at her side as Tex softly sang the first line of the song.

"There goes my heart beating," he said, and Michelle took the first step.

You are the reason I'm still breathing.

Leigh was going to lose the battle against her tears. Denzel had been through so much, and he'd once begged Leigh to abandon him. Just cut him loose. Let him drift wherever he went. She couldn't do it, and they'd anchored themselves to each other to stay safe.

Everyone needed an anchor like that, and Leigh had several of them in her life. Morris, who brought her closer and held her tight right when she needed him to. Hilde, who she'd become close with in the past couple of years. Abby, of course.

Cecily Young anchored them all, and Leigh loved her so much, because her own mama lived too far away to depend on too much.

I'd climb every mountain
And swim every ocean
Just to be with you

Leigh swayed with Morris, because while Denzel had a hard time walking, he loved Michelle so much, he would climb mountains and swim through oceans to be with her. And she loved him the same.

She reached him, and he took the leash from her and held it out for their father to take. Daddy did, and Denzel took Michelle's arm on his left side, so she could shore him up, support him, and anchor him on his weak side.

"They're perfect together," Leigh whispered as she sat down.

"Like us," Morris murmured, and Leigh couldn't argue with that. She basked in the gratitude and love streaming through her, and she cheered louder than anyone as Denzel kissed Michelle, his new wife.

41

Tex pulled into the parking lot at the Whiskey Mountain Lodge, noting how much snow they had. "It's at least twice as much," he said to Abby and Bryce, who both rode in the truck with him. His other two children did too, but neither Melissa nor Carver had argued with him on the snow levels on the east side of town compared to the west.

But there was so much more snow on the west side.

"We're up in the mountains," Abby said, her way of conceding to him without telling him he was right. He didn't need to be told anyway. He had eyes and could see the piles and piles of snow they had here; he *knew* he was right.

"Yours is almost melted," Bryce said. "I don't even have this much at the farm." He was further north and west than Tex's place, but Bryce's land sat at the base of the foothills.

"I love this lodge," Abby said with a sigh as Tex drove right in front of the brightly lit stone and log building. The Whittakers had owned it for maybe fifteen years, right around the time Graham's

413

daddy had died and he'd returned to Coral Canyon to run the family energy company.

At that time, they'd started a new family tradition of doing a tree lighting ceremony every year, and they'd gone all-in on the ritual since making the lodge more commercial in the past couple of years.

Christmas lights in all colors dripped from every eave, gutter, and windowsill. Cheery yellow light spilled from all the windows, and when Tex found a parking spot and got out to help with the kids, he could hear holiday music playing through the night, though he'd had to park at least halfway back in the lot.

"Come on, Mel." He unbuckled his daughter and grinned at her. "Now, what's the one rule for tonight?"

"There are two rules," Abby said from the front passenger seat where she'd leaned back in to get her purse. Bryce had already unbuckled Carver and held him in his arms across the seat from Tex.

He blinked, and time froze. This could've been a scene from two years ago, if Bryce had kept his baby boy and raised him himself. He hadn't done that, and Otis and Georgia had named OJ, loved him, and had been raising him for the past three years.

They'd already had one small celebration for the three-year-old today, wherein only Tex's family and Otis's had gotten together for a birthday breakfast. Georgia had made pancakes, and OJ had blown out three candles among buttermilk batter and maple syrup.

Sometimes Tex's grandfather heart still ached, but thankfully the pinch and the longing and the moment with Bryce holding a dark-haired boy that looked so much like him didn't last long.

Time rushed forward again, and he looked at his daughter. "Rule one," he prompted.

"Stay with people I know," she recited back to him.

"There will be a lot of people here," he said. The Whittakers had built a new event center on the property, and that was where they'd all gathered for Denzel's and Michelle's wedding. But the tree lighting took place in the lodge, where each of the Whittaker brothers had lived at one point.

It was tradition.

"Rule two," Abby said as she crowded into the open doorway where Tex stood. He hadn't even let Melissa get out yet. She was a vivacious child, with plenty of energy and curiosity, and he and Abby had learned to set rules for her *before* they did something. That way, there was actually a chance that Melissa would obey them.

"Don't eat anything without asking," the little girl said.

"Who?" Abby asked. "Who do you ask? Do you get to ask Grandma?"

"No," Melissa said soberly. "You or Daddy."

"Not even Bryce," Abby said. "Or Aunt Georgia, or Uncle Blaze." She looked at Tex. "That man will give her anything."

Tex couldn't deny it, but he could laugh. He did that, and his spirits lifted. Christmas had been tough on him for the past few years, and he wanted to shake all of that away and start feeling the true spirit of the holiday again.

"Come on, baby." He helped the little girl out of the truck, and Abby smoothed down her pretty red dress. They each took one of her hands, and they started toward the lodge. "It really is beautiful," Tex said.

"I love Christmas," Abby said.

The cold air stung Tex's lungs as Bryce caught up to them and joined them. "Things going okay on the farm this winter?"

"I've never been so cold," Bryce said, but he smiled about it. He and Kassie Goodman had been living on the horse farm they'd bought together for about seven months now. He'd moved in the spring, and summer and fall had brought a lot of challenges. Bryce worked himself from dusk until dawn, though, and Tex had never been prouder of his son.

He knew he barely had time to breathe, though, and he prayed for a measure of peace and rest for Bryce this Christmas.

"Harry and I are going to practice for Luke's wedding tomorrow," Bryce said. "If that's okay."

"We're doing presents in the morning," Abby said. "You and Kassie are welcome to come, and then Grandma is hosting breakfast at The Forty-Niner."

"In the afternoon should work then," he mused. "I'll have to check on the med schedule for Tootie."

Bryce had gotten three new horses this year, all bought with grant funding. He paid for medicine with the same thing, and after he rehabilitated the horses, he tried to get them back out onto farms and ranches where they could live, work, and continue to thrive.

"What are you guys playing for the wedding?" Tex asked as the lodge loomed closer. The moment they went inside, all would be lost, he knew. He could practically see the door throbbing as it tried to hold back the energy contained inside.

"Sterling gave us free license," he said. "Which is probably a big mistake." He chuckled, but Tex didn't think so.

"Well, Harry has a good sense of things," he said. "I think he and Trace are going to Nashville again in the New Year."

"After the wedding, though," Abby said.

"I don't know how they're going to do it between that and Ev's due date," Tex said. He'd do what he had to do to help Trace, Ev, and Harry, and if that meant Ev and Keri came to stay on the farm with him and Abby while the men were out of town, so be it.

"I can't believe he's that old," Bryce said. "It still kind of blows my mind."

"Wait until you see this tree," Tex said as he reached for the door handle. "It'll blow your mind."

"Daddy, will there be a stocking for me?" Melissa looked at him, pure Christmas innocence in her eyes.

"Yeah, baby," he said. "There will be a stocking for everyone." He had no idea how the Whittakers did it, but everyone who came to the tree lighting—planned or unplanned—had a stocking on the wall. Part of the tradition was going around to find the stocking labeled with his name and see what someone else had left for him inside it.

Flipping the switch to light the tree was a big deal, and the person who did it never knew until moments before. The Whittakers gave speeches and made announcements at their tree lighting, and they invited anyone who wanted to come, including all of their guests.

Tex opened the door, bracing himself, and sure enough, the light, the laughter, the energy, the music—it all hit him squarely in the face.

And he loved it.

Bryce entered first, and Tex released Melissa's hand to let her and Abby go in next. He followed them, closed the door, and took in the scene before him. The pine tree standing sentinel in the room butted up against the far wall and the second-story loft above it.

A staircase sat just inside the door and went up to that loft, and the living room spread to his left for a while. A big fireplace sat across from the tree, and chairs had been brought in for everyone.

The Christmas tree had already been decorated, and the Whittakers did that earlier in the day. Then, they'd light it tonight, and it stayed up through New Year's. Tex only knew that, because Leigh had once worked at the lodge, and she knew all the ins and outs of their holiday traditions.

Tonight, Tex had brought his family, and he spotted Otis pretty easily. Otis and Georgia put in a lot of effort to do things with Graham and Laney, because OJ was their grandson too. Bryce hugged his uncle, and Tex watched as the crowd moved for Graham to come through it.

He took Bryce into a hug too, his face filled with happiness and light. That made Tex's heart happier, and he decided he couldn't be a wet blanket on tonight's festivities. Abby greeted Graham and then Laney before Tex even moved away from the door, and they all looked at him.

"Sorry," he said as he hurried to join his wife and daughter. "I just had to take it all in there for a second." He liked the perspective standing back had given him. He'd learned in the past couple of years that he didn't have to be in the center of everything to enjoy it.

He shook Graham's hand and hugged Laney, then hugged both Otis and Georgia. "Let me have that baby," he said, taking the little girl from his sister-in-law. Anaya was almost five months old now, and she was a smiley, happy little girl who still didn't weigh more than eleven or twelve pounds.

She'd been born early, and everyone who met her could see the light from heaven still in her eyes. Even now, she looked at Tex, and his whole soul lit up. "Heya, baby Ana."

She squealed and flapped her arms, and that made everyone in the vicinity laugh. Tex heard another familiar laugh, and sure enough, Blaze stood to his left. Todd Christopherson and Jem lingered with him, and then Tex's eye met Blaze's.

He nodded to Todd, who had his wife—a country music star herself—and one of his daughters with him.

Tex's heart started to pound, pound, and pound harder. Apparently, Mary Christopherson had told her mother that she was interested in Bryce, but she had no reason to be in his social sphere. They hadn't met at church or around town, and she didn't have his number nor a way to get it for some reason.

Naturally, Vi had told Todd, and Todd had mentioned it to Blaze. Tex saw and spoke with all of his brothers regularly, and he'd told Blaze perhaps Bryce and Mary could meet tonight. But now, he didn't want to orchestrate that.

Bryce hadn't come right out and said anything, but he hadn't dated since he'd been back in Coral Canyon. Not even one date, with one woman. He didn't have time or energy, he'd said, and Tex gave a quick shake of his head.

But Blaze was coming this way. "Hey, everyone," he said as he eased into their group. The man wore a dark pair of jeans and a bright red and dull green and white checkered shirt. Very Christmas cowboy.

"How's Faith?" Abby asked, as she lingered with the Christophersons.

"Ready to have the baby," Blaze said, shooting Abby a look. "But surviving. Come join the fun."

Tex wanted to shake his brother. Could he not read cues? Blaze could, Tex knew. He'd been exceptionally good at doing just that to succeed in the rodeo. It was all he did, so that meant he was ignoring Tex.

He went with his brother, and introductions got made. "And my sons," he said, indicating Bryce and Carver. "Bryce and Carver."

"He is so stinking cute," Mary cooed as she smiled at Carver. "Can I hold him?" She made eye contact with Bryce, who easily gave her the eight-month-old. He barely smiled, and he didn't even really seem to see the brunette in front of him, now holding his sibling.

So, that was that.

Secretly relieved, Tex found seats for his family, and they'd barely taken them before Graham got up and said, "Find a spot, everyone. We're ready to do the tree lighting." He beamed out at everyone from behind a mic, and kept going while people scrambled to find seats.

"First, welcome to Whiskey Mountain Lodge." He spread his arms wide and grinned at his wife. The crowd clapped and cheered, and Tex let himself get swept up in it.

"We have a full house tonight, and after the official lighting, you can head out the back door and to your left to the event center. That's where the refreshments, dancing, and stockings will be."

"Daddy," Melissa whispered, and Tex pulled her onto his lap.

"Yes, the stocking," he told her. "If you say one more thing about it, I'm not going to help you find yours."

She blinked at him and then folded her arms and faced the front again.

"Every year, we have someone special light the tree here at the lodge. It started with family members who we hadn't seen in a while or wanted to honor. We've had one of our treasured employees do it from time to time, and even a guest last year—someone who stays with us every year."

"Yeehaw!" someone yelled in the crowd, and Tex located the man because he was waving his cowboy hat.

"Yep, there's Ben." Graham chuckled. "We've had people snowed in here before." He coughed and said, "Colton Hammond," to which more people laughed.

Tex hadn't seen the Hammonds yet, but he knew all five of them and could catch up over Christmas cookies and wassail in a bigger room. They all lived in Coral Canyon except for Gray, who came every summer and sat with the Youngs at their fireworks picnics.

"This year, we have someone with us that we don't get to see very often," Graham said. "Well, we do, but it's...." He looked over to his wife, who edged closer to him. "Complicated." When he looked out over the crowd this time, he wore a bit of confusion in his eyes, along with plenty of trepidation, both of which were tempered with love.

"This year, out of all the years, I wanted to ask this person to light the tree in advance, because I absolutely don't want to cause more problems or put anyone on the spot."

Tex's heartbeat began to thrash in his chest. He looked over to Bryce, who stared straight ahead, his cowboy hat perched just-so on his head. If Graham asked him to light the tree, how would he handle it?

Please, Lord, he prayed. *Don't let anything happen that will drive my son further from us. We just got him back. Please, please, please.*

Graham's eyes continued to roam the crowd, never settling on just one person, and certainly not Bryce. "And technically, we need to ask this person's parents." He cleared his throat. "But Laney and I would love to have our biological grandson, Otis Judson, press the switches and light the tree."

A murmur ran through the crowd, and Tex actually got to his feet to see where Otis and Georgia had gotten to. He would handle this if he saw even an iota of discomfort on either of their faces.

"Daddy," Bryce said quietly, but Tex did not look at him.

"They were here," Graham said. "Tex, do you see Otis or Georgia?"

He did not, and he shook his head.

Bryce stood up, and somehow, he now held OJ. "They had to step out with their baby." He started to make his way toward the front of the room. "But I can help OJ."

"Bryce," Tex said.

Abby slipped her hand into his and said, "Baby, he's okay. Please sit down."

He didn't want to sit down. He never would've come if he thought this might happen. Bryce had been working tirelessly to get to a good place regarding the adoption, his biological son, and his repentance process. Tex would not allow someone else to set him back, not even one step.

Bryce joined Graham up front, and he turned his face away from the man. Graham leaned in to listen while he covered the mic, and he nodded a couple of times. When he faced the crowd again, even with the distance between them, Tex could see tears in his eyes.

"Turns out we're going to do it with him."

Laney took OJ from Bryce, her face full of adoration and joy, and together, she and Graham moved over to the wall where the bank of switches sat. "I did this the very first year of this tradition," Graham yelled out to everyone. "Merry Christmas, everyone!"

Laney used OJ's fingers to flip a couple of switches while Graham did the rest. The twenty-five-foot tree lit up, eliciting *oohs* and *ahhs* from everyone there.

Tex wasn't sure where to look. The magnificent tree would distract him. He couldn't see Bryce as others started to stand and block his view. He hadn't sat back down, and he stood still now too, feeling utterly helpless.

Abby joined him and said, "They're by the door." She pointed toward the front entrance, and Tex headed that way, despite Melissa's protests that they go out the back door to get to the stockings.

Otis now held his baby Ana, and Georgia had her arm linked through Bryce's.

"I couldn't stop it," Tex said.

"Nothing to stop," Otis said with a smile, without looking away from the far wall and Graham and Laney. "Look how much they love him."

"It's fine, Tex," Georgia said as she looked up at him. "We know we have to share OJ, and there are no better people to share him with than Graham and Laney."

Tex faced them too, but he couldn't relax. Of course they loved OJ, probably a lot the way Tex did.

"Daddy," Bryce said, his voice so quiet. "It's okay." He put his arm around Tex, and while Tex was usually the one to comfort his son, tonight, this Christmas Eve, he took that love and support from his dear, dear boy.

He continued to watch Graham and Laney holding OJ and chatting with people as they went by them. The Lord sure did work in mysterious ways, because Tex didn't understand any of how he felt, but he somehow knew that he was supposed to be standing here, watching this, and that the scene in front of him— the brightly lit Christmas tree, the little boy in Laney's arms, the way he got to see it all from a distance....

...healed him somehow.

"Merry Christmas, everyone," he said.

"Merry Christmas," they all chorused back to him.

42

S terling woke up one day in January, her eyes popping open and panic parading through her chest that she'd forgotten to set an alarm. Now, she was late for her wedding.

She sat straight up and reached for her phone to check the time. Why, she wasn't sure, as not a stitch of light came in her window. So she definitely wasn't late at all. She and Luke had set the time for their wedding to be just before lunch, and they'd chosen a Saturday so no one would have to miss school to be there.

In the middle of January, Wyoming got only a handful of hours of light, and Luke had booked them a honeymoon to the Caribbean for a week. Sterling couldn't wait, as she hadn't done much traveling with anyone, and certainly not with the man she loved.

Her phone read five-fourteen, and she flopped back onto her pillow, the light of it burning her eyes. Then she realized that someone had texted. Squinting, she lifted her phone again, trying to take in the light in stages before committing to burning her retinas again.

Luke had already texted, about ten minutes ago. *It's our wedding day! I just woke up like a little boy on Christmas morning, and I had to text you. I love you. No matter what happens today, we'll be married, and that's all that matters.* <3

She sighed as she let her phone fall to her chest. Maybe Sterling had been a bit of a nut these past couple of weeks, trying to put together the most amazing wedding. Not only for herself, but for Luke too. She didn't think for one second that there wouldn't be pictures online, because somehow, the influencers and reporters of the world had infiltrated Coral Canyon.

She'd seen pictures of her and Luke entering a restaurant together, her and Luke driving in his truck, and her and Luke walking down the sidewalk in front of his parents' condo.

There would definitely be pictures of the wedding leaked out there, and Luke himself had admitted he wanted to post some. Maybe not today, but in the future, when they'd returned home from their honeymoon.

I want the world to know you're mine, he'd told her. *And that I'm taken.*

Sterling still couldn't quite believe that she'd somehow attracted his attention, but she sat up and swung her legs over the side of the bed. After she'd snapped on the lamp, she didn't have to worry about eye damage, and she tapped out a response for him.

I've been kind of crazy the past couple of weeks, haven't I? You're right—all that matters is that we get married today. I love you, and I'll see you soon.

She lay back down and swiped over to her task list. She'd hired an amazing wedding photographer to get the pictures she and Luke wanted. The venue should be ready, and as Sterling had toured it yesterday, nearly every piece sat in place.

She was counting on Bryce to come through with the horses, and he'd confirmed they'd be in position, waiting and ready.

Leigh had texted her pictures of the cake last night. It was still in pieces, but she should be up soon to get it out of the freezer and get it all put together.

Luke had given Sterling a white diamond credit card, and she'd discovered it had no limit on it. She'd marched into The Branding Iron to find out if they did catering and how much it would cost to serve steak, steak, and more steak to over two hundred people at a wedding.

Turned out, a lot. But Luke's card had gone right through. He hadn't even asked her about any of the charges. He knew they were having a served steak dinner for their wedding luncheon, though she'd also done a chicken dish and a kid's option for the meal.

He knew they were getting married at The Oaken Barrel, but he didn't know what he'd find when he walked through the doors. Sterling's excitement had her swiping faster on her phone.

They'd planned to have the ceremony, then lunch, and then a few minutes of chatting before a sparkler send-off. No reception. No party. No dancing, either after the wedding or later that night.

Neither of them wanted things to take too long, as they had to get to the airport and fly south that day too. Sterling had no idea what shape she'd be in by evening, but given how early she'd awakened, she guessed not a great one.

She didn't have a father to do a daddy-daughter dance with, and she'd seen no reason to pay for more food for a reception when they'd just had lunch.

Luke had paid for her wedding dress, which she'd shopped for with Hilde, Ev, and Abby, and then they'd met all the wives for lunch. Sterling had shown picture after picture, and she'd sat across from Sunny, just like another lunch where the two of them hadn't been Youngs yet.

Sterling technically still wasn't a Young, and she exhaled and closed her eyes. "I feel like I've been waiting for this for a long time, Lord," she whispered. "I know it's a lot. There are a lot of pieces, from flowers, to clothes, to kids, dogs, and horses. But if at all possible, please let everything line up perfectly today."

But if not....

Sterling would still marry Luke, and she'd still be blissfully happy. She and Luke had talked more and more about their faith, and Sterling felt like she took a new leap every other day. This was just one of them. She wanted things a certain way, and she'd just prayed for as much.

But if it didn't come to pass, that didn't mean God didn't love her. It didn't mean He wasn't in charge or didn't know what He was doing. All it meant was that Sterling couldn't let her faith get shaken when God gave her a chance to grow in divine ways.

Smiling, she left her phone plugged in and went to shower. Her hair was pretty hopeless when left down, but the best part about how thick and jagged and crazy-kinky it grew was the fact that she could achieve some amazingly beautiful up-dos.

She'd booked the whole salon for her and the wives that morning, and she wanted to make the most of the appointment. She'd be doing her own makeup, and they got to enter the venue at ten o'clock that morning.

Leigh would want to be there early to get the cake set up. Sterling had entrusted Abby and Georgia to do a final walk-through of the venue ahead of her and Luke's arrival. All of the brothers had been given special instructions and had agreed to carry them out.

Excitement built beneath Sterling's breastbone, and she got ready as much as she could at home, packed her car, and left for the salon.

$\approx$

LUKE PACED IN JEM'S HOUSE, BECAUSE HE'D ALREADY brought in Corrine's suitcase and helped her spread her sleeping bag out on Rosie's bed. She'd be staying here with Jem, Sunny, and the kids while Luke and Sterling went on their honeymoon, and he just wanted to get through all the ceremonial stuff so his life could begin again.

Begin again.

"I can't believe I'm doing this," he said right out loud. Jem, the only other person in the room with him right now, didn't even respond. He and Luke had already been through this. Of course he was going to marry Sterling today. He loved her; she loved him; this was nothing like his first marriage.

"Jem," Sunny said, and Luke wasn't so far inside his own head that he didn't notice the quiver in her voice. He turned toward her to find her weeping, and alarm tugged through him. Her husband abandoned his breakfast and headed for the hall that led back into the bedrooms, his lower voice not quite reaching Luke's ears in a way where he could make out words.

Great. Now Luke was alone, and something was wrong with Sunny, and he just wanted this circus to be over.

"Are we going?" Blaze asked as he came through the front door with his very pregnant wife. He would not leave Faith's side for longer than it took him to shower, and even then, he carried a walkie talkie in with him. Luke thought they were actually pretty cute about it, and he couldn't wait to dote on Sterling during any pregnancies she might have.

He loved being a father, and that had taken him a long time to learn and realize. He loved being an uncle too, and Blaze whistled for the kids at the same time Luke said, "I just want this to be done."

"Oh, so we're grumpy on our wedding day," Blaze said good-naturedly. "Sounds like fun."

"You were too," Luke said.

"I was not," Blaze fired back. "I was nervous."

"Maybe I'm nervous." There was no *maybe* about it, but Luke wouldn't admit more than he had. "I have to be there in twenty minutes."

"I know what time you have to be there," Blaze said as he settled onto the couch. "Sterling has told me five hundred times."

"Then we should be going," Luke said, ignoring his jab at Sterling. "She just wants the wedding to be perfect. *I* want it to be what she wants."

"Luke." Faith put her hand on his arm, and he dang near jumped out of his own skin. "It's going to be amazing."

Luke looked at her, and he saw so much compassion and love. "Thank you, Faith," he murmured.

"Kids," she called, as his whistle clearly hadn't done anything to get them to come out. "We're leaving in five minutes, and you better have everything you need or Uncle Blaze is coming back there!"

One of the girls actually screamed, but Blaze only chuckled.

"Where are Jem and Sunny?" he asked.

"I don't know," Luke said as he reached for Corrine's bag. He wasn't even sure why he'd brought it in. It held her dress for the wedding, and he should've left it in the truck. "She was crying. I'm going to take this back out to the truck, and then I'll come get the kids."

"Crying?" Blaze asked, but Luke was on a mission. He accomplished it, and when he returned to the house, Blaze had vacated the couch.

"Corrine," Luke called, as he didn't see her anywhere. "Time to go." He moved into Rosie's room, and found his daughter pulling on her shoes.

"Comin', Daddy."

He reached for her. "We can't be late today, jelly bean. It's Wedding Day."

"Wedding Day!" She grinned and took his hand.

He helped her stand and then looked over to Rosie. "Ready, baby?"

"Yep." She was a skinny little thing with plenty of attitude, and she zipped her backpack closed.

Luke raised his eyebrows. "Your dress is in that?"

"No," Sunny said as she entered the bedroom. "Rosie, you're not bringing that backpack."

"But Daddy said—"

"He did not," Sunny said firmly. "You better think real hard before you speak, Little Miss. A lie is a lie."

Luke didn't want to be involved here, and he took Corrine's hand and led her out of the room. "We'll see you over there."

"Okay," Sunny called, and she certainly didn't seem like she'd been crying.

Faith waited in the living room, one hand on her belly and both eyes closed. "Blaze needs you," she said to Luke.

"Where is he?"

"Out in the driveway," she said. "His truck won't start."

Luke did not have time or patience for this. Oh, no, he did not. "Tell him to take Jem's truck. Y'all are riding together anyway."

"He won't," Faith said. "If I go into labor, he can't be 'hunting down Jem for the keys'." She opened her eyes and looked at Luke warily. "His words, not mine."

Luke looked toward the front door and blew out his breath. "Fine." He nodded toward Faith. "Corrine, go wait by Auntie Faith."

She did what he said, and Luke pulled on his coat as he went out the front door. He ran hot-blooded, but the first week of January in Wyoming was not to be trifled with.

"What's goin' on?" he asked as he approached the hood and his very non-mechanic brother.

"Like I know," Blaze grumbled. They started fiddling around, and the next thing Luke knew, he was moving Corrine's bag into Jem's truck, and everyone except for him and Blaze left.

"They took Faith," Luke said crossly. "I'm ten minutes late. Just get in my truck." He walked away from Blaze's hopeless vehicle. "You'll have to deal with whatever if Faith goes into labor."

"Fine." Blaze slammed the hood on his vehicle and stomped after Luke. The pair of them in a black mood wasn't good, and Luke didn't want to feel like this on his wedding day. So he tried to imagine himself as a window, where anything could pass through and it didn't affect him.

The Oaken Barrel sat on the north side of town, out in the middle of nowhere, and it boasted sprawling gardens in the spring, summer, and autumn, a couple of restaurants, apple orchards, and several banquet halls, cabins, and spa amenities. They booked anything from a couples' weekend getaway to large, corporate parties. Family reunions. Anything, all set against the gorgeous backdrop of the Grand Teton Mountains.

Luke looked up to those mountains as he finally pulled into the parking lot. His brothers' trucks took up a lot of the spaces, and he spied Sterling's SUV too. Relief spread through him, because she was here.

"What was that sigh for?" Blaze asked.

"I'm just—I'm a little surprised Sterling is here," he said. "Not surprised. Grateful?" He glanced over to Blaze, who he'd never really had to hide anything from. "This all feels a little surreal, to be honest. It's like I'm living in someone else's body."

Blaze smiled and nodded. "I know the feeling, but brother, try to tune in as much as possible today, okay? She's worked really hard on this wedding."

"I know," Luke said as he nodded. "Yeah, you're right. I will." He parked and went inside, only to learn that Sterling had booked the Ponderosa Building, which was a drive down past a few other buildings.

So he and Blaze loaded back up, and his brother kept texting furiously on his phone. For some reason, that set Luke's teeth on edge, as a new tension filled the truck. "Why was everyone parked out there then?" he asked as he drove past a building clearly marked as the Aspen Building.

"I don't know," Blaze said in a monotone.

"Did Faith and Jem and them find it?"

"She says they did."

Luke glanced over to his brother, but his head was bent so far over his phone, Luke couldn't see his face. He kept driving until he found the building, and he pulled up to it. The only truck he could see looked like it belonged to Bryce, and Luke seriously doubted that Sterling had dragged all of her necessary items from the parking lot in the front where he'd seen her car to the building in front of him.

But the door opened, and Tex stood there, fully dressed and ready to go. That reminded Luke that he didn't have time to sit out in the cold and question anything. He put the truck in park, turned it off, and reached into the back for his bag.

He'd chosen to get married in a tuxedo. He was a billionaire with a robust social media following, and he figured a tux was the bare minimum. He'd shaved and cut his hair, shined his shoes, and made sure every detail of their honeymoon was ready.

Sterling had done everything else, and he practically ran to his brother. "You made it," Tex said as he pounded Luke on the back.

"He's lucky he's alive," Luke muttered as he ducked past Tex. "Which way?" The interior of the building didn't seem as bright as he'd expected it to be, and it smelled faintly of horses.

"To the right," Tex said. "You've got time, Luke."

He found the groom's room easily, because Trace stood outside of it. All of his brothers were there, and once Blaze and Tex entered behind Luke, the door got closed, and the men in the room descended on Luke.

He knew how to put all the pieces of himself together, but he let Mav hand him a new cowboy hat, and he let Otis fiddle with the cufflinks at his wrists. He allowed Gabe to adjust his tie and Morris to tie his shoes.

Once he was dressed and polished, he looked around at his family. Every brother was there. Harry and Bryce, Cash and Cole and Boston. The other kids had to be somewhere else, probably with Momma or the wives.

His best friends.

"Where's Corrine?" he asked as his emotions surged, because the two of them would be standing at the altar as Daddy walked Sterling down the aisle.

"She's with Sterling," Daddy said. "Don't worry. Momma said she'd bring her over when it was time."

Luke didn't wear a watch, but it had to be getting close to time right now. His chest felt so tight, and he took a breath to try to release some of the pressure there. He faced his father and said, "Daddy, will you pray before we have to go?"

"Yep." Daddy wasn't one to say more than he had to, and he gestured for the boys to circle up around him. Blaze finished tucking in his shirt and settling his hat on his head, only to have to sweep it off as he realized what was happening.

Luke did the same, and he dropped his eyes to the floor, every cell in his body vibrating in an almost painful way.

"Dear God in Heaven," Daddy started, and Luke started to calm with just those words. His faith would sustain him over the course of the next couple of hours, and then he and

Sterling would be alone. Out of the spotlight. No more show.

"We are so grateful to come before Thee as Thy sons."

Luke felt someone move closer to him, and then someone took his hand on the right. He fumbled for the man on his left, and clasped hands with Mav. The brother who'd managed the band for so long, and done so well. It had been Mav who'd brought them all together over the years. Mav who'd made the move back to Coral Canyon first and brought everyone else with him.

"We ask a special blessing on Luke and Sterling today, as they enter into the holy covenant of marriage."

Warmth filled Luke, and asking for a prayer had been precisely the right thing to do.

"Bless any here in this company who needs something that they can have it, according to Thy will. Amen."

Short and sweet and just right. Luke squeezed Mav's hand, and then Blaze's, and they looked around at one another.

"I love you guys," Luke blurted out. They tightened into a huddle, arms going around each other until they were all smiling and affirming their affections for one another.

"Guys," Tex said, and they all started separating. "It's time." They all seemed to know what to do, but Luke was a bit lost.

"I need Corrine," he said.

"I'm texting Momma right now," Daddy said. "I have to get over to Sterling." He barely took a moment to glance up. "Just stay here, Luke." With that, he left along with everyone else, and Luke stood in the room, completely dumbfounded.

"Stay here?" Surely he wasn't supposed to just *stay here*. He had to be at the altar *before* Sterling walked down the aisle. No, this didn't make sense.

Before he could reach the door to leave the room, it opened again. He paused mid-stride as Sterling herself slipped inside. She was radiant from head to toe, what with her hair all swirled and braided seemingly into the back of her head.

The back of her wedding dress scooped almost to her waist, leaving Luke's mouth dry as she turned toward him. The dress had no straps over her shoulders and swelled in all the best places for a woman.

She smiled her pink-painted lips at him, and oh, Luke could not be in this room with her. "What are you doing?" he hissed. "I'm not supposed to—I'm pretty sure you're not supposed to be here."

If Momma found out, she'd blame Luke for sure.

"I changed things a little," she said, reaching for his hand. "Come with me." He didn't really have another option, so he let her take his hand, turn toward the door, and open it.

43

Sterling walked down the service hall at the back of the building, taking slow, careful steps as if she needed to in her heels. She did, but she didn't. She just wanted to give everyone a chance to get in place.

The guests were all in position. The brothers had streamed out of the room a few minutes ago, and Tex had told her, "He's ready. Doesn't know anything," as he'd gone by her.

Up ahead, her destination awaited, and since she'd already been inside, she could hear the music filtering out into the hallway. Faint, but definitely there.

"Sterling," Luke said, and she looked over to him. "This dress... is incredible. You're incredible."

Sterling grinned and squeezed his hand. "Thank you, Luke. You look rather dashing yourself."

He wore a tuxedo, because he wanted to be proper and dashing—and he was. In spades, what with the matching cowboy hat and the hint of a blue handkerchief peeking out of his breast pocket.

Sterling couldn't believe this man was hers. Love filled her over and over, and she brushed at his lapel and straightened his bowtie just to give herself a few more seconds before she had to open the door.

"So handsome," she whispered. She could already see the likes and comments on social media about him, and she wondered what his fans would say about her wedding dress. She pushed away the thoughts. It didn't matter what anyone else thought. Sterling loved her dress, and Luke had seemed to as well.

The moment arrived, and she put her hand on the door handle that led into the banquet hall where they'd be married. Her heart pounded through every fiber of her being. "Now, this is a little unconventional, but I hope it's exactly what we both want."

"I just want to get married," he murmured, his lips skating along the side of her neck. "Mm, yeah, I want to get married, and I want to get out of here."

"Behave," she whispered at him, though she craved the moment they could be alone too. "You're about to take me out in front of a lot of people. We can't have *my* makeup on *your* face."

"No, we can't." He didn't kiss her, but Sterling wouldn't have stopped him if he'd tried. He looked at her with such male desire that she heated from the inside out.

She took a deep breath, let it out, and opened the door. Light spilled out into the darker hallway, and she nudged Luke so he'd go first. "I know you wanted to get married outside," she said as they moved from regular hallway to Grand Teton Wonderland.

Luke sucked in a breath so hard it sounded like a shout. "Sterling," he said right out loud. She gazed around too, though she knew what she'd find. She wondered what he saw as he surveyed the huge space in front of them.

Since the Youngs knew a lot of people in town, and since Luke was the last of them to get married, and since he didn't mind all the publicity, the guest list wasn't small.

"Here you go, Sterling," Bryce said, and he held the reins of a pretty tawny horse on her left.

"Thank you." She waited while he positioned a stool, and she let go of Luke's hand while she got in the saddle, taking care to gather her skirts up. Bryce helped her spread out the skirt so it hung down over her legs and the back of the horse in perfect, lacy layers.

Meanwhile, another horse had arrived, this one brought in by Kassie, and once Sterling had herself situated, she found Luke atop his horse too.

His eyes shone with joy, and he reached for her hand again. "We're riding horses," he said. "This whole place looks like summertime in the Tetons."

"Do you like it?" she asked tentatively. She did like the real trees growing right here in the building. The Ponderosa Building had a retractable roof, and the trees, bushes, and grass could be exposed to the spring, summer, and autumn air and sunshine. In the winter, it turned into a greenhouse, and everything in the building was real, alive, and flourishing.

"I absolutely love it."

"What do you see?" she asked. "Like, when you look at it, what do you see?"

"The walls are blue like the sky," he said, looking up. "I love the sky here. The Tetons are in the distance, and there are fields and a stream over there." If he knew they'd started moving, he didn't comment on it.

"It's all real," Sterling said. "I sat down with the building manager, and we sketched it all out."

"You used a diagram?" he teased, his eyes the brightest Sterling had ever seen.

She grinned and nodded. "Finally, that skill is good for something."

Up ahead and around a corner, the guests would come into view. She almost held her breath as Luke said, "I love the evergreens. The dirt on the ground. It really feels like we're outside."

"I even have them blowing fans to simulate wind."

Luke shook his head, his wonder and awe palpable on his face. Sterling had been equally as impressed with the wedding venue, and she'd wanted to give him his outdoor wedding so badly.

"I just can't believe it," he said as he reached out and trailed his fingers along the trunk of an aspen. "This is so amazing. How did you do this?"

"Money," she said. "So technically, *you* did this."

He laughed, the dark cloud that had been hanging over his head completely gone now. "Sterling, I would've never done this. It's...indescribable. I don't even know what to say. Thank you."

"I want what you want," she said. "And today, we're getting married outside...but just inside."

The horses made the turn, and somehow they both stopped, the sound of hooves on dirt also ceasing. The guests caught sight of them, and they all stood and faced Sterling and Luke. She wanted to squirm right out of the saddle and hide, but she couldn't. Not with Luke at her side. Not with the wedding she'd planned.

Because of the horses, she couldn't have Luke and Corrine walk down the aisle first and then have all of the brothers and wives in a traditional wedding procession. So Sterling had arranged for them to stand a bit apart before they reached the main rows of seats, which did have an extra-wide aisle down the middle to accommodate the horses.

They stood in age-order and side-by-side. Tex reached up and handed Sterling a red rose while Abby gave Luke a white one.

The horses plodded past Trace and Everly next, and both Sterling and Luke got another rose. Blaze gave her a white one instead of a red one, but that didn't matter. Luke looked over to her with his eyebrows raised after he'd received the red one from Faith, and she just shook her head.

They went past Otis and Georgia, Mav and Dani, Jem and Sunny, Morris and Leigh, and Gabe and Hilde.

Luke's parents came next, and his mother shone with silver and gold and happiness as she stretched up and Luke leaned down to kiss her cheek. She gave him a pink rose, and Sterling got a yellow one that almost matched her hair.

The next group of people were all of the kids, and Sterling's eyes filled with tears at the sight of them. Beside her, Luke sniffled. Actually, sniffled.

Bryce and Harry played the guitar together, creating a beautiful harmony and melody that was somehow perfect for this faux outdoor wedding. She'd given them almost no direction, and the music definitely fit the wedding but also mimicked a campfire song.

Sterling's heart had never been so full, because all of these people had come here to support Luke. To support her. To be with them as they celebrated their love and this new start to their combined lives.

Bryce stood in the middle of all the kids, the oldest and tallest. He handed his guitar to Cash and picked up Corrine. They grinned at one another before he slipped her into the saddle in front of Luke while all the kids cheered, jumped up and down, and waved.

Luke laughed right out loud, and he waved back to all of his nieces and nephews. Sterling did too, because she loved them as much as he did.

Then the horses moved down the aisle, and she'd told the family members to hustle up and get to their seats in the front rows. They'd followed her every direction flawlessly, right down to stalling Luke so he was the last to arrive, and by the time she'd dismounted and faced her groom again, everyone was in place.

Corrine grinned at her, and Sterling bent down and brought the little girl into her arms. "I love you, baby," she whispered to the little girl.

"I love you too, Sterling." Corrine wore a pretty blue dress the color of the Wyoming sky that Luke loved so much, and she retreated to her daddy, who hugged her and whispered something to her.

Then she moved to his left side and joined her hand to his for a moment before moving to sit with her grandparents.

"I love you," Luke said before the pastor could say a word. "That was everything I didn't even know I wanted." He gazed down at her, and this time, he didn't hold back. He took her into his arms and kissed her, which caused an uproar in the crowd.

Sterling smiled against his lips and laughed into his mouth. He pulled back, grinning, and said, "Oops. Wrong order." Only then did he face the pastor, who also smiled like Luke hadn't done anything wrong.

She took his roses and combined them with hers, a symbolic joining of his life with hers. She smiled shyly up at him, hearing the *click, click, click* of the camera in the now-quiet space. Reverence hung over the crowd, and Sterling wished her brother and mother could've been there.

Travel in the winter was hard, and Sterling hadn't given them much lead-time. That way, she wasn't as hurt when they couldn't make it. She'd send them some pictures and invite them to other things, but for now, all she needed was Luke and Corrine—and all the Youngs.

The wedding procession may have taken a little longer than most, but the ceremony didn't. Luke hadn't wanted to write vows and read them, because everything he said came out in his eyes or his touch.

So the pastor gave a few words of advice and encouragement, and then he said, "Do you, Sterling Claire Boyd, give yourself to Lucas Holden Young, to be his lawfully wedded wife?"

"Yes," she said in a voice that echoed throughout the building as if she did stand out in the mountains.

Pastor Richards smiled at her and then turned slightly to Luke. "Do you, Lucas Holden Young, take Sterling Claire Boyd unto yourself, and pledge to be her lawfully wedded husband?"

"Yes," he said, his voice choked in the best way possible. Sterling gazed at him, so many happy things prancing through her.

"Then by the power vested in me by the state of Wyoming, I pronounce you man and wife. Luke, you may kiss your bride."

As the whole world seemed to erupt into cheers and whistles and yeehaws, Sterling looked at Luke, and Luke looked at Sterling.

"I love you," they said together—just like they'd live the rest of their lives.

Together.

Then he kissed her, and Sterling enjoyed the quick taste of him so, so much—because she'd just gotten everything she'd never known she wanted.

Luke. Corrine. A family.

Read on for a sneak peek at **BRYCE**, the next book in the Young Brothers series. Can he make something happen between him and Codi Hudson five years in the future?

Preorder BRYCE here:

If you'd like to get 2 chapters per week about what's going on in the Young family during these next 5 years before BRYCE begins, BECOME A CORAL CANYON RESIDENT by scanning the QR code below with your phone.

Sneak Peek! BRYCE Chapter One:

"Come on, you old man." Bryce Young smiled at his golden retriever as Lucky moved only his eyes. The rest of his body stayed perfectly still on the end of Bryce's bed. "I'm gonna eat breakfast myself then."

Lucky lifted his head at the mention of food, and he did heave himself up and off the bed. After a big doggy stretch, he trotted past Bryce, who pulled his bedroom door closed.

He'd lived in the big farmhouse on his enormous horse rescue ranch now for five years. He loved everything about his life—except how lonely it was to come home to an empty house at night and wake up alone in bed—sans the dog—every morning.

He'd attempted a few dates here and there over the past several years, but getting his ranch in operational condition, caring for the horses, applying for the grants he needed, traveling around to various farms and ranches and picking up new animals, and dealing with his big-and-still-growing family had taken all of his time.

He hardly thought of Bailey McAllister anymore, and he

didn't know what to do with that as he made coffee, squirted some salmon oil in a bowl for Lucky, then added dry dog food, a couple of spoonfuls of green beans, a tablespoon or two of warm water, and then a whole container of wet dog food.

Yes, Lucky was spoiled. Bryce would like to have someone make him a meaty, delicious breakfast every morning, but he usually made toast and grabbed a protein shake on his way out the door. The toast would be eaten by the time he entered the first barn, and he drank the protein throughout the morning as he fed, watered, rotated, and cleaned up after twenty-seven horses.

Yes, he had twenty-seven horses now, and he smiled to himself as he mixed everything together for Lucky and set it on the floor next to his bowl of dry dog food. "There you go, my friend."

He poured himself a cup of coffee and doctored it up with sugar and cream before he sat down at the dining room table. It held six people just fine, and if he put the leaf in it, he could host Kassie and his family with an extra seat to spare.

His dad had three little kids—Melissa, who was ten now, Carver, who was six, and Pippa, a bright, if not a bit rambunctious, four-year-old. When the five of them came to the farm, it was all hands on deck, and they loved him as much as they loved Kassie, who always took the kids out onto the farm and let them do almost anything they wanted.

Bryce definitely felt like an outlier in his family, but at the same time, he fit perfectly. He couldn't quite describe the feelings he sometimes had, and he usually put his head down, got down on his knees, and worked through the problem with God.

The Lord had a special way of unbraiding the parts of Bryce that didn't make sense. Then he could see them, examine them, and make a plan for what to do with them. That was what Bryce always wanted to do—make a plan. Go over the plan. Execute the plan.

He'd taken this almost desolate piece of land and made it flourish again. He'd helped over one hundred fifty horses get back on their feet and back out into the world, onto ranches and farms and small family plots of land where they could feel the measure of their creation.

He and Kassie nursed sick, abused, and abandoned horses back to health, and they both loved it with their whole hearts. Kassie had started dating Stockton Whittaker, but that hadn't worked out. She'd tried with another cowboy in town, but he'd left Coral Canyon after a few months, and Bryce couldn't remember where he'd moved to.

His thoughts meandered to the blonde woman who'd given Lucky a bath and a trim once-upon-a-time. Codi Hudson. He'd never asked her out, because she'd been one-hundred-percent right. He'd been completely overwhelmed by his move here, all the tasks that needed to be completed, and everything with the horses.

He gave Lucky his baths now, usually with the hose and then a wrestling match with a towel and brush. Bryce had looked up Codi's mobile grooming bus, but he hadn't been able to find it.

She'd moved on too. Left Coral Canyon for something else, and he hoped, something better.

"Thank you, Lord," he murmured as he finished his coffee and went to make his toast. He stood in front of the appliance as it warmed and toasted the bread, his head bent and his eyes closed.

"Thank You for this new day. Bless me to make the best of it, to be a servant for Thee if possible, and to stay safe out on the farm. I'm real grateful for Thy guiding hand in my life, for the miracles I've seen today and throughout my life, and for my daddy."

He paused for a moment. "And Abby. For Kassie, and all she does around here to make my life easier and better." He took a breath, expecting the toast to pop up at any moment. That always signaled the end of his prayer, and Bryce reasoned that he spent far more time on his knees at night. This morning prayer could be short, as long as it was meaningful.

"Thank You for my family, and for creating horses, and for the gift of repentance. Bless me to fix any wrongs I've done and help me to know where I stand with Thee."

The toast popped up; Bryce's eyes popped open. "Amen," he said, and he reached for the toast to butter it.

He did know where he stood with God, and it was right beside him. God had told him that plenty of times, and Bryce didn't doubt it this morning as he slid open the back door and let Lucky exit first. The dog turned right around and sat, his happy face begging for a bite of toast.

As per their routine, Bryce gave him a bite, and Lucky took off for the edge of the deck. It needed to be re-stained and resealed, and it was on Bryce's list of things to do. Taking care of a home, a yard, a deck, the dozens of buildings here, the land, the animals....

Bryce had learned early on to make lists and schedule things if at all possible. He'd learned to humble himself and ask for help. He'd learned to find grants and volunteers that would come help with big clean-up projects. He'd learned to listen to his body, take care of himself mentally, and be sure to feed himself spiritually.

As he faced a new day, with plenty to do and lots of challenges, he turned his face into the almost-summer sunshine and smiled.

"Maybe I'm ready for something romantically," he said out loud. The sky did not answer back—but a horse nickered from somewhere on the farm, probably upset Bryce hadn't arrived to feed him yet.

$\sim$

LATER THAT AFTERNOON, BRYCE LAUGHED AS GOLDEN BOY, the horse he was currently working with, tossed his head and sent the water in the pond rippling away from him. The equine loved to swim, which made Bryce's job of trying to get him strong enough to go back out on a farm all the easier.

Lucky barked as he ran toward the pond too, and Bryce didn't bother to try to stop the dog. That would be impossible, as Lucky loved to swim too. Plus, the sun had been beating down all day on the farm, the dry ground, and the state of Wyoming, and Bryce actually thought *he* might get in the pond to cool off for a few minutes.

Truly, he wouldn't, because he wore jeans, and no one ever wanted to be wearing wet denim for long. He had to get everyone back to the barns and house, and it was at least a forty-five-minute ride.

So no, he would not be getting in the pond. Lucky and Golden Boy seemed to be having a race from one side of the pond to the other, but there was no way for the canine to win. He barely seemed to be moving as the horse went by him.

Bryce grinned and grinned at them, and while he knew he couldn't let his animals play in the water for very long, he gave them a couple of minutes to enjoy themselves.

"Come on," he yelled when they needed to go. "Let's get on back now."

Lucky got out of the water first, while Golden Boy tossed his head and nickered again.

"Yeah, you're swimmin'," Bryce said, as if the horse understood his human English. "But we have to go. Come on. Let's get." The horses did know those last two words, and Bryce bent to pick up Golden Boy's lead.

He wasn't strong enough to wear a saddle or be ridden. He'd been neglected and underfed for years. He'd had wounds on his

449

legs that hadn't been attended to, and when Kassie had found him, he'd backed himself into a dark corner of a barn and wouldn't come out.

He did for her, though, as she possessed one of the calmer equine spirits in the world. He went right with her, no lead needed, and he got on the trailer with bleeding legs and plenty of ribs showing.

Bryce had to work hard to tamp down his anger and frustration at people and commercial operations who kept horses they couldn't care for. Or didn't know how to care for. Or were too stubborn or lazy to care for.

He knew how much work it took to keep a horse healthy and happy, and getting one who wasn't in those categories to a state of existence that didn't include suffering? It took even longer. Months and months. Years.

He owned twelve horses that lived on the farm permanently. He and Kassie had done their best, but they were either too skittish or too old or still too unwell to go back to a farm or ranch.

The other fifteen existed in various states of readiness, and as Golden Boy lifted his beautifully golden body out of the pond and shook himself dry, Bryce had the very real feeling he'd be saying good-bye to this amazing horse very soon.

"Good boy," he said to the horse as Golden Boy plodded toward him. He was a Tennessee Walking Horse—a show breed who'd never shown or learned to show—in a palomino color—light brown or gold, with a white mane and tail.

He was like a king to Bryce, and he stroked both hands down the sides of Golden Boy's head as he lowered it to press against Bryce's shoulder. "You don't muscle me," he told the horse, holding his ground. "I'm in charge here."

Horses were like big babies, and they did need to be told and shown who was boss. If they could get away with something, they did, and Bryce had quite a few mischief-makers right now. Golden Boy sometimes went along with the herd if he could, but most of the time, he let his gentle spirit show through.

Golden Boy never tried to push Kassie around, but he did try to get his way with Bryce. So he looped the lead around his neck and said, "You walk with me."

The horse did what Bryce wanted him to, and he looked around for but didn't see Lucky. He whistled, and the dog barked from somewhere to his left.

Bryce's heart fell to the bottoms of his cowboy boots. Left—north—led to the unplanted fields, and unplanted fields were full of dirt.

"Let's go," he said to Golden Boy, and he picked up the pace to try to head off the muddy mess that was going to be his golden retriever. He pushed through the vegetation that grew around the pond and arrived on the edge of the field only a minute later, but it was sixty seconds that Lucky had enjoyed rolling in the dark, rich earth.

Bryce could only blink at his dog, and he wanted to laugh but couldn't when Lucky stood up, his trademarked golden retriever smile on his face, and shook himself.

Hardly anything came off, because the dirt had suctioned to the water in his heavy coat, creating clumps instantly.

Bryce changed his plans just as instantly. "Let's get you to Kassie's," he said. Her house sat deeper on the farm, but she had a dirt lane that led right to the highway, and there were even a few pizza joints and restaurants that would deliver to her house. And right now, her garden hose was about three times closer than Bryce's.

By the time they arrived, the outer mud on Lucky's body had started to dry, and he was barely walking. Bryce had no idea if Kassie would be home or not, and he came here all the time even when she wasn't. He threw Golden Boy's line around the tethering post at the edge of her backyard and said, "Come on, you silly dog," as he headed for the hose connected to side of the house.

Lucky whined but came with him, and Bryce heard an engine out in front of the house. Perhaps Kassie was arriving home right now. He'd get Lucky at least a little cleaned off before he went to see, and as he reached the hose, the dog lifted his head.

He barked and ran past Bryce and around the corner of the house. "Lucky, no," Bryce said, because while Kassie loved dogs—she had three of her own—he still had chores to do that day, and he'd already detoured from his plans by allowing the equine-canine swim party in the pond at all.

Sighing, he followed his dog. Before he rounded the corner of the house, he heard a woman say, "Holy baked potatoes, what happened to you?"

Bryce turned the corner, only half-expecting to see Kassie. That wasn't her voice, though.... It took him two more steps to realize the blonde woman staring in horror at his dog was none other than Codi Hudson.

Her white school bus with dozens of painted dogs on it sat in Kassie's driveway, and she lifted her eyes to Bryce's just as Lucky barked and jumped up on her.

"Lucky, no," Bryce said again, this time just as fruitless as the last time. Time froze, he froze, everything froze—except for Codi as she stumbled backward and fell with a muddy Lucky on top of her.

Sneak Peek! BRYCE Chapter Two:

C odi Hudson had been bowled over by plenty of dogs. Tugged, pulled, licked, even partially buried once, as she'd taken her dog to the beach, and Gator hadn't been able to stop digging for more than five seconds.

She missed that dog sometimes, but for the most part, she didn't think of her life in Boise all that much anymore. Idaho was ingrained in her though, as evidenced by her use of *baked potatoes* as form of cursing.

"Lucky!" Bryce Young called as he ran toward her. Yes, she knew it was him. No, she hadn't forgotten about him—or his golden retriever—though they'd only met once, what? Five years ago. Maybe six or seven now.

So much of Codi's life had been blended together, shaken up, poured out, and then re-blended. She had milestones she could cling to, but all the bits and pieces in between were blurred, and she wasn't really sure where they existed on the timeline.

"Lucky, get off her." Bryce pulled his dog back, but the canine got one more lick in.

Codi sat up, wiped her now muddy and salivated-on face, and started to laugh.

"Sit down," Bryce said. "Lay down. Lay. Down." He pointed at the ground, and Lucky reluctantly slid forward on his forearms to a lay. His tongue lulled out of his mouth, and he squinted his eyes at Bryce in a very cat-like move of, *If I don't see you, you can't be mad at me.*

"Stay," he commanded, his eyes coming to Codi. She wasn't sure if he meant his dog or her, but she did see the concern and embarrassment in his face. She schooled her laughter as he knelt in front of her.

Oh, that wasn't fair. Him coming to her level only made him more attractive, and the simmering buzz of attraction that told her a good-looking man was in the vicinity started to vibrate through her whole body.

"You okay?" He reached out hesitantly, then pulled his hand back. "He doesn't usually jump at people. I'm sorry."

"It's not the first time a dog has knocked me over." She started to get up, and Bryce offered his hand to help her. She looked at it— seeing so much more than last time she'd met him. He'd grown up, though he'd definitely been a man before.

He seemed...older now, and not just in years. Wiser. More mature. She could see the years of work in his hands somehow, and she slid her palm along his and then gripped. Pure fire licked through her now, and as soon as she stood on her feet, she pulled her hand back to brush off her clothes. "Thanks," she said.

"What are you doing here?"

"I came to get my new dog." She indicated the house. "The woman who lives here sold me one of hers."

His mouth dropped open, but Codi didn't get it. With horror at all of the attraction still humming through her, she realized what she obviously already knew—she wasn't at Bryce's house right now.

Or was she?

"Let me guess," she said, her heart drooping behind her ribs. Praise heaven the Lord had put that organ in a place no one could see what it did. "Your wife sold your dog and didn't tell you?"

"Which one?" he asked, not answering her question. He looked up to the house as displeasure rolled off him. Great. So he was married. Of course he would be. The way Codi's luck with men went, he'd have to be either married or willing to cheat on her with someone who was.

Because of her last boyfriend—fiancé—she hadn't dated in almost seven years. She knew that milestone, and it would be seven years in June. Next month.

"Which dog?" she asked. "You have more than one?"

Those gorgeous eyes came back to hers. "I only have one. Kassie has three, and I told her if she wanted to get rid of Penta-gram to tell me. *I* want him."

Codi had no interest in getting involved in a small-town canine ownership spat. She hadn't technically paid for the beagle yet, but the cash sat in the glove box of her bus. Before she could decide if she should offer to let Bryce buy him or tell him "tough luck," a woman's voice called his name. She sounded like she was outside too, probably in the backyard.

"I can't believe this," he muttered. "Stay here, okay? I want to talk to you before you leave." He didn't wait for her to agree to stay, and irritation fired through her at his arrogance as he took the steps to the front porch two at a time and walked right into the red brick house.

Yep, he lived here—or had at some point—and his wife had just tried to sell his dog out from under him.

She looked at Lucky, and Lucky panted back at her. "Come on, you," she said to the dog. "Let's get you cleaned up." Codi took the dog around the corner of the house where Bryce had come from, where she found a hose and spigot. She heard Bryce and Kassie talking in the backyard, and then their voices went quiet, presumably as they entered the house.

Codi turned on the water and marveled that Lucky held so still for the cold spray she turned on him. She'd only got to groom him that one time, and he'd been good then too.

She'd only been in Coral Canyon for a year—barely long enough to start having steady clients and a steady income—before her mother had fallen ill. Codi had packed her whole life in less than twelve hours, put everything she could in the bus or a small trailer she'd towed behind the bus, and left Wyoming.

Another milestone, and she'd thanked the Lord her mother's cancer diagnosis had come in August—a very moveable month for Wyoming. She's been living in California for the past four years, at which point her mother had finally succumbed to the awful disease that had plagued her for so long.

Her daddy still lived on the potato farm where she'd been raised outside of Boise, but Codi couldn't go back there. At least not for longer than it took to visit, to tell her daddy she loved him, and to see her brother—who now ran the potato farm with his wife and two sons.

Codi had drifted though Utah, Arizona, and Colorado for the past year, living on her momma's inheritance and the grooming jobs she could pick up in random cities through social media.

When she'd finally come out of the haze her mother's death had cast over her, she'd sat down and asked herself, "Where do you want to be?"

Coral Canyon had been at the top of the list, and she'd returned only two weeks ago. She hadn't even started taking on grooming clients yet. She'd lived out of her bus until she found a place to rent that wasn't infested with spiders—and that was harder than she'd anticipated.

She'd only been in the place for four nights now, and she wanted a dog of her own. She loved rescuing dogs, but the shelter in town only had big dogs, and well, her basement rental unit only allowed dogs up to thirty pounds. She had a yard for him to play in and everything, and she'd started looking in the classifieds for dog owners trying to rehome their pets.

And she'd found Kassie and Pentagram, who was apparently a lovable, high-energy beagle who needed a stricter owner. Kassie said he was so smart, but she just didn't have the time to train him, and they'd agreed on a price of five hundred dollars.

The dried mud slipped from Lucky's fur with the water and Codi's strokes, and she rinsed him the best she could. "Maybe your daddy can be my first customer here in town," she said to the dog—only moments before he shook, drenching her in less than five seconds.

Codi simply stood there and took it, her eyes squeezing shut lest there be any errant mud, weeds, or who-knew-what-else in the water droplets.

"Codi?" Bryce called, and she told herself not to get excited that he'd remembered her name. Still, it had been a long time, and she certainly didn't remember everyone she'd met one time in the past six years.

She did remember Bryce, though, and she said, "Right here," as Lucky turned and trotted toward the corner. She followed him and found Bryce standing on the front lawn with a blonde woman with more honey in her hair than Codi had in hers. Hers seemed to drink up the sunlight and turn white instead, and Codi told herself to be nice.

Be nice, be nice, be nice.

"Kassie says you were gonna pay her five hundred for Penta."

Codi nodded and held up both hands. "Yeah, but I don't want to get in the middle of you guys." She looked between Kassie and Bryce, dying to look at their left hands just to confirm that they were indeed married. "I'll just go. I rinsed your dog with the hose, so he's not super clean or anything."

Bryce looked down at Lucky as if just realizing he was there. "Wow, thanks, Codi." He grinned at her, and Kassie elbowed him. He jolted away from her and said, "Hey."

Kassie smiled at Codi, and she just wanted to leave. "Can I have a few days to talk to Bryce about Pentagram?" She glared at him in the nicest way possible. "He knows he can't take care of another dog, but he needs some extra convincing."

"You can't take care of him either," Bryce shot at her.

"That's why I put him up for sale." Kassie rolled her eyes. "I hope we're not keeping you from anything." She did seem like a nice person, but Codi knew looks could be deceiving. Even the way a person behaved could be totally contrary to who they really were, what they really thought and believed, what they were willing to do or not do.

"No," Codi said. "Let me know if I can have him. If not, I'll keep looking." She nodded to Kassie, who smiled and nodded almost like a doll. Then she turned her back on Codi completely and practically smashed herself into Bryce's shoulder, clearly saying something to him.

He ducked his head, using that sexy cowboy hat to conceal his face and all of Kassie's head. Codi really didn't want to be here now, and she started to give the pair of them a wide berth on her way back to her bus.

Kassie left, and Bryce said, "Codi, can I talk to you for a minute?" before she could escape the situation. She paused only a few strides from her bus and looked up into the clear blue almost-summer sky.

"Sure," she said. "Why not?"

Bryce had turned in the same spot on the grass, and he pocketed his hands as he looked at her. "Uh, do you have the same phone number?"

"Yes," she said. "I can book you for Lucky right now if you'd like."

"Yeah, okay, sure," he said. "But I was, uh, wondering if you—ahem—might—if *I* might be able to use your number to find out what your *personal* schedule is like." His face turned a ruddy shade of red that made Codi's blood heat too.

"Your dinner schedule," he said with more confidence.

Codi had started to take out her phone to book his grooming appointment, but now her motion stalled. "You're asking me out?"

"Yeah."

Fire seethed inside her now, and not the pleasant kind. "In front of your house? Or I guess you don't live here anymore. But she's your ex, right?" Codi didn't dare look away from those bright brown eyes, because she didn't want to miss anything. "This whole thing is weird. No, you can't use my number to ask me to dinner."

"I have never lived here," he said, his eyebrows puckering down. "She's not my ex."

"She's—what?" Codi had all the wrong dots, and the picture sure wasn't coming into focus. "But you know her."

"Yeah, I know her," Bryce said, taking a step forward. "Let me explain it all to you. Tonight. At dinner." He fixed a smile on his face, and oh, the cowboy knew that was a game-changer. A deal-sealer. That smile had gotten him what he wanted many times in the past, Codi was sure of it.

She wasn't sure why she didn't trust him, and if she didn't, why she wanted to say yes to dinner. As she stood there staring at him, trying to formulate a response, he pulled out his phone.

"You know what? Shoot all the stars down. I can't tonight." He looked up. "I forgot I'm having dinner with my aunt and uncle."

"Are you an orphan?" she asked, because while she'd remembered his name, and knew she hadn't come here to bathe Lucky before, she actually knew very little about Bryce Young.

He chuckled and shook his head. "No, but I'm pretty close with all my aunts and uncles. Otis and Georgia particularly. They're raising my biological son as their own."

Codi's eyebrows went up, and she had no idea what to say.

"I have a lot of complicated stories," Bryce said, finally showing another round of nerves as his feet scuffed the grass and he dropped his gaze to watch them do so.

"I'll say," she said.

"So...dinner?" he asked. "I'm free tomorrow night." He looked up just enough to be able to see her from under the brim of that maddening hat.

Codi reached out and plucked it off of his head, which, oh, he did not like. She quickly handed it back to him as she said, "I don't like not being able to see who I'm talking to." The eyes said so much, and Codi had to make sure he wasn't a wolf in sheepskin.

He held his hat at his side, his expression open and unassuming. "I'll tell you all the stories—at least the interesting parts."

"You're going to try to convince me that you should get Pentagram."

He grinned, and this one held twice as much wattage as the last one. It had probably won him a lot in the past too. "Not at all," he said, stepping closer. "But see, I need your help with Kassie. She just bet me I wouldn't be brave enough to ask you out, and I have to win this one."

"You have asked me out," Codi said, having to look up at him now, because he stood so close. "So you win."

"But I actually want to go out with you," he said. "I'm crazy-busy, but I'm not as overwhelmed as I was before, and I think we'd have a good time." He laughed lightly. "Of course, I thought that about Kassie, and our first date was like being out with my sister."

"So she is your ex."

"Nah," he said. "We never even started anything. She's my best friend though. We own this farm together." He seemed... happy about it. Not prideful, and that made a thread move from Codi to Bryce, where it attached itself, bonding her to him whether she liked it or not.

"So?" he asked. "What do you say?"

Codi didn't know what to say, and she couldn't read anything nefarious or off in Bryce's expression. This whole afternoon *had* been weird, though, and Codi honestly wasn't sure if she should say yes or no.

So she stood there, considering her options, as the seconds ticked by—and Bryce wasn't going anywhere.

Preorder BRYCE now!

If you'd like to get 2 chapters per week about what's going on in the Young family during these next 5 years before BRYCE begins, BECOME A CORAL CANYON RESIDENT by scanning the QR code below with your phone.

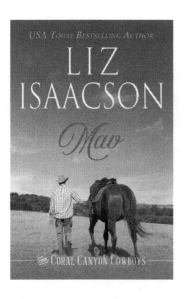

Mav (Book 0): Meet Maverik Young, the cowboy country music star ready to hang up his guitar strings in favor of being a father.

Oh, and he'd like a good woman to settle down with in Coral Canyon too, please. :)

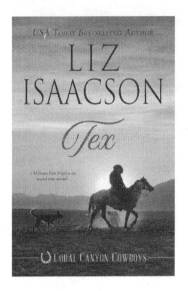

Tex (Book 1): He's back in town after a successful country music career. She owns a bordering farm to the family land he wants to buy...and she outbids him at the auction. Can Tex and Abigail rekindle their old flame, or will the issue of land ownership come between them?

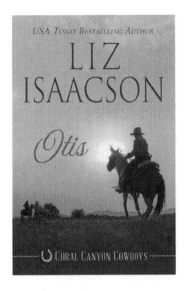

Otis (Book 2): He's finished with his last album and looking for a soft place to fall after a devastating break-up. She runs the small town bookshop in Coral Canyon and needs a new boyfriend to get her old one out of her life for good. Can Georgia convince Otis to take another shot at real love when their first kiss was fake?

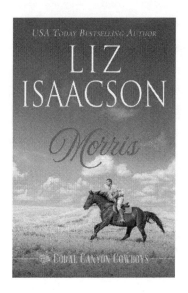

Morris (Book 3): Morris Young is just settling into his new life as the manager of Country Quad when he attends a wedding. He sees his ex-wife there—apparently Leighann is back in Coral Canyon —along with a little boy who can't be more or less than five years old... Could he be Morris's? And why is his heart hoping for that, and for a reconciliation with the woman who left him because he traveled too much?

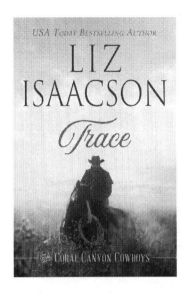

Trace (Book 4): He's been accused of only dating celebrities. She's a simple line dance instructor in small town Coral Canyon, with a soft spot for kids...and cowboys. Trace could use some dance lessons to go along with his love lessons... Can he and Everly fall in love with the beat, or will she dance her way right out of his arms?

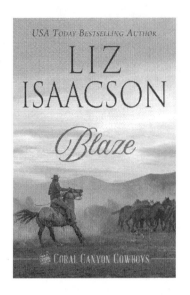

Blaze (Book 5): He's dark as night, a single dad, and a retired bull riding champion. With all his money, his rugged good looks, and his ability to say all the right things, Faith has no chance against Blaze Young's charms. But she's his complete opposite, and she just doesn't see how they can be together...

...so she ends things with him.

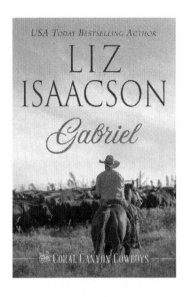

Gabe (Book 6): He's a father's rights advocate lawyer with a sweet little girl. She's fighting for her own daughter. Can Gabe and Hilde find happily-ever-after when they're at such odds with one another?

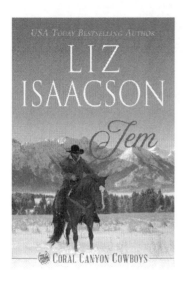

Jem (Book 7): He's still healing from his vices, and Jem has dedicated everything he has to his two kids. At least he's not mourning his divorce anymore, and in fact, he might be ready to move on. She's his former best friend, and once he breaks his wrist, his nurse. Can Sunny somehow rope this cowboy's heart?

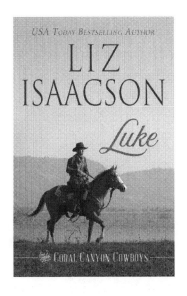

Luke (Book 8): He swore off women when his ex told him he might not be their daughter's father. But a paternity test confirmed he is, and Luke Young has dedicated his life to his little girl and his brothers' band. There hasn't been time for a girlfriend anyway. He's tried here and there, and the women in small-town Coral Canyon are certainly interested in him.

But he's been thinking about his massage therapist for a while now. Can he ask Sterling out when all they've ever been is professional? Oh, and there's the fact that she's seen practically every inch of his body... Awkward, right?

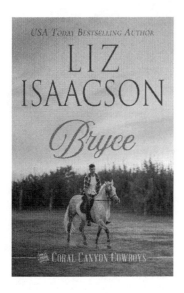

Bryce (Book 9): Bryce Young has been broken and drifting for years. After giving up his son for adoption, he left Coral Canyon and hasn't returned...until now.

Books in the Christmas at Whiskey Mountain Lodge Romance series

Her Cowboy Billionaire Birthday Wish (Book 1): All the maid at Whiskey Mountain Lodge wants for her birthday is a handsome cowboy billionaire. And Colton can make that wish come true—if only he hadn't escaped to Coral Canyon after being left at the altar...

Her Cowboy Billionaire Butler (Book 2): She broke up with him to date another man...who broke her heart. He's a former CEO with nothing to do who can't get her out of his head. Can Wes and Bree find a way toward happily-ever-after at Whiskey Mountain Lodge?

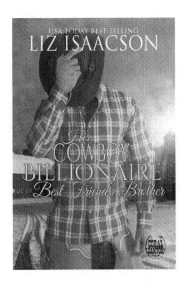

Her Cowboy Billionaire Best Friend's Brother (Book 3): She's best friends with the single dad cowboy's brother and has watched two friends find love with the sexy new cowboys in town. When Gray Hammond comes to Whiskey Mountain Lodge with his son, will Elise finally get her own happily-ever-after with one of the Hammond brothers?

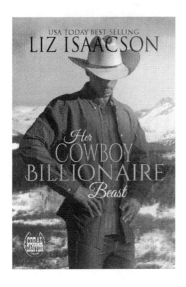

Her Cowboy Billionaire Beast (Book 4): A cowboy billionaire beast, his new manager, and the Christmas traditions that soften his heart and bring them together.

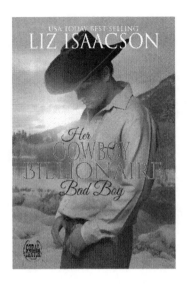

Her Cowboy Billionaire Bad Boy (Book 5): A cowboy billionaire cop who's a stickler for rules, the woman he pulls over when he's not even on duty, and the personal mandates he has to break to keep her in his life...

Books in the Christmas in Coral Canyon Romance series

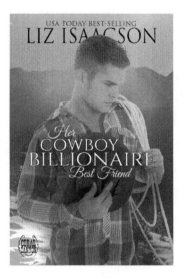

Her Cowboy Billionaire Best Friend (Book 1): Graham Whittaker returns to Coral Canyon a few days after Christmas—after the death of his father. He takes over the energy company his dad built from the ground up and buys a high-end lodge to live in—only a mile from the home of his once-best friend, Laney McAllister. They were best friends once, but Laney's always entertained feelings for him, and spending so much time with him while they make Christmas memories puts her heart in danger of getting broken again...

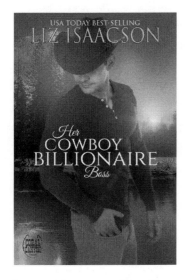

Her Cowboy Billionaire Boss (Book 2): Since the death of his wife a few years ago, Eli Whittaker has been running from one job to another, unable to find somewhere for him and his son to settle. Meg Palmer is Stockton's nanny, and she comes with her boss, Eli, to the lodge, her long-time crush on the man no different in Wyoming than it was on the beach. When she confesses her feelings for him and gets nothing in return, she's crushed, embarrassed, and unsure if she can stay in Coral Canyon for Christmas. Then Eli starts to show some feelings for her too...

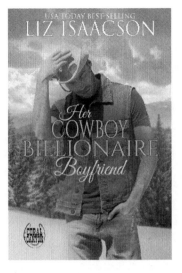

Her Cowboy Billionaire Boyfriend (Book 3): Andrew Whittaker is the public face for the Whittaker Brothers' family energy company, and with his older brother's robot about to be announced, he needs a press secretary to help him get everything ready and tour the state to make the announcements. When he's hit by a protest sign being carried by the company's biggest opponent, Rebecca Collings, he learns with a few clicks that she has the background they need. He offers her the job of press secretary when she thought she was going to be arrested, and not only because the spark between them in so hot Andrew can't see straight.

Can Becca and Andrew work together and keep their relationship a secret? Or will hearts break in this classic romance retelling reminiscent of *Two Weeks Notice*?

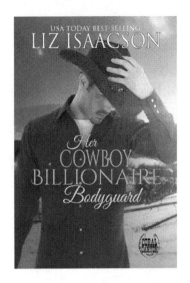

Her Cowboy Billionaire Bodyguard (Book 4): Beau Whittaker has watched his brothers find love one by one, but every attempt he's made has ended in disaster. Lily Everett has been in the spotlight since childhood and has half a dozen platinum records with her two sisters. She's taking a break from the brutal music industry and hiding out in Wyoming while her ex-husband continues to cause trouble for her. When she hears of Beau Whittaker and what he offers his clients, she wants to meet him. Beau is instantly attracted to Lily, but he tried a relationship with his last client that left a scar that still hasn't healed...

Can Lily use the spirit of Christmas to discover what matters most? Will Beau open his heart to the possibility of love with someone so different from him?

Her Cowboy Billionaire Bull Rider (Book 5): Todd Christopherson has just retired from the professional rodeo circuit and returned to his hometown of Coral Canyon. Problem is, he's got no family there anymore, no land, and no job. Not that he needs a job--he's got plenty of money from his illustrious career riding bulls.

Then Todd gets thrown during a routine horseback ride up the canyon, and his only support as he recovers physically is the beautiful Violet Everett. She's no nurse, but she does the best she can for the handsome cowboy. **Will she lose her heart to the billionaire bull rider? Can Todd trust that God led him to Coral Canyon...and Vi?**

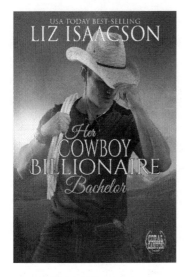

Her Cowboy Billionaire Bachelor (Book 6): Rose Everett isn't sure what to do with her life now that her country music career is on hold. After all, with both of her sisters in Coral Canyon, and one about to have a baby, they're not making albums anymore.

Liam Murphy has been working for Doctors Without Borders, but he's back in the US now, and looking to start a new clinic in Coral Canyon, where he spent his summers.

When Rose wins a date with Liam in a bachelor auction, their relationship blooms and grows quickly. **Can Liam and Rose find a solution to their problems that doesn't involve one of them leaving Coral Canyon with a broken heart?**

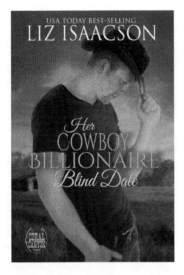

Her Cowboy Billionaire Blind Date (Book 7): Her sons want her to be happy, but she's too old to be set up on a blind date...isn't she?

Amanda Whittaker has been looking for a second chance at love since the death of her husband several years ago. Finley Barber is a cowboy in every sense of the word. Born and raised on a racehorse farm in Kentucky, he's since moved to Dog Valley and started his own breeding stable for champion horses. He hasn't dated in years, and everything about Amanda makes him nervous.

Will Amanda take the leap of faith required to be with Finn? Or will he become just another boyfriend who doesn't make the cut?

Her Cowboy Billionaire Best Man (Book 8): When Celia Abbott-Armstrong runs into a gorgeous cowboy at her best friend's wedding, she decides she's ready to start dating again.

But the cowboy is Zach Zuckerman, and the Zuckermans and Abbotts have been at war for generations.

Can Zach and Celia find a way to reconcile their family's differences so they can have a future together?

About Liz

Liz Isaacson writes inspirational romance, usually set in Texas, or Wyoming, or anywhere else horses and cowboys exist. She lives in Utah, where she writes full-time, takes her two dogs to the park everyday, and eats a lot of veggies while writing. Find her on her website at www.feelgoodfictionbooks.com.

Made in the USA
Columbia, SC
30 August 2023

22305654R00293